TRIAL & TRIBULATIONS

TRIAL & TRIBULATIONS

A Windy Ridge Legal Thriller

RACHEL DYLAN

Trial & Tribulations
Copyright © 2015 by Rachel Dylan

NYLA Publishing
350 7th Avenue, Suite 2003, NY 10001, New York.
http://www.nyliterary.com

ISBN-13: 9781517703912

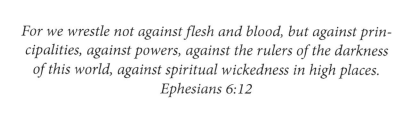

For we wrestle not against flesh and blood, but against principalities, against powers, against the rulers of the darkness of this world, against spiritual wickedness in high places.
Ephesians 6:12

ACKNOWLEDGEMENTS

Many thanks to my amazing agent, Sarah E. Younger, who continues to be my fierce advocate. Sarah embraced this story whole-heartedly and knows how much it means to me. I'd also like to thank everyone at the Nancy Yost Literary Agency for supporting my work.

Thanks to Susan for being so excited about this story from the very first time I told her about it. Her enthusiasm has been a constant source of encouragement. She's been by my side each step of the way.

Writing this specific book wouldn't have been possible without my parents who provided me with a strong foundation of faith that has weathered the storms of life. I love you, Mama. I miss you, Daddy.

CHAPTER ONE

When managing partner Chet Carter called, you answered—and you answered promptly. Just yesterday Olivia Murray had been summoned to Chet's corner office and told to pack her bags for a new case that would take her from Washington, DC to the Windy Ridge suburb of Chicago.

But this wasn't just any case. She would be defending a New Age tech company called Astral Tech in a lawsuit filed by its biggest competitor.

As she stepped out of her red Jeep rental, the summer breeze blew gently against her face. She stared up at the mid sized office building with a prominent sparkling blue moon on the outside, and she had to admit she was a bit intimidated. It wasn't the litigation aspect that bothered her, though. It was the subject matter.

She threw her laptop bag over her shoulder, adjusted her black suit jacket, and walked toward the door. Ready for anything. Or at least she hoped she was.

The strong smell of incense hit her as her first heeled foot stepped through the door. She thought it was a bit cliché for a New Age company to be burning incense in the reception area, but maybe it was to be expected. It reinforced her thoughts that this was all a money making operation—not a group of actual believers in this stuff.

The perky young blonde behind the minimalist glass desk looked up at her. "How can I help you?"

"Hi, I'm Olivia Murray from the law firm of Brown, Carter, and Reed."

The young woman's brown eyes widened. "Oh, yes, Ms. Murray. I'm Melanie." She stood and shook Olivia's hand. "Let me know if you need anything while you're here. The team is expecting you. I'll take you to the main conference room now."

"Thank you." Everything was already proceeding as normal. She couldn't let this whole New Age thing mess with her head. And besides that, she had her faith to get her through this.

Melanie led her down the hall to a conference room and knocked loudly before opening the large door. "Ms. Murray, please go on in."

Olivia didn't really know what she expected, but what she saw was a table full of suits arguing. She let out a breath. Regular litigation. Just like she had thought.

A man stood up from the table. "You must be our lawyer from BCR?" He wore an impeccably tailored navy suit with a red tie. He had short dark hair with a little gray at the temples and piercing green eyes.

"Yes, I'm Olivia Murray."

"Great. This is the Astral Tech leadership team. Don't let our yelling worry you. That's how we best communicate." He laughed. "I'm Clive Township, the CEO of Astral Tech, and this is my trusted inner circle."

A striking woman rose and offered her hand. "I'm Nina Marie Crane, our Chief Operating Officer."

"Wonderful to meet you," Olivia said.

Clive nodded toward a tall thin man with black hair who stood and shook her hand. "And this is our financial voice of reason, Matt Tinley."

"I serve as our Chief Financial Officer," Matt said.

Everyone greeted her warmly, but she felt an undercurrent of tension in the room. It was now her job as their attorney to get this litigation under control and that also meant getting them under control. Half the battle of litigation was controlling your own client before you could even begin to take on the adversary.

"Have a seat and we'll get you up to speed," Clive said.

She sat down in a comfortable dark blue chair at the oblong oak table and pulled out her laptop to take any relevant notes. She opened up her computer, but mainly she wanted to get the lay of the land.

"So the more I can learn about your company and the complaint that Optimism has filed against you the better. One of the first things I'll have to work on is the document collection and fact discovery effort. To be able to do that, I need the necessary background. I'll be happy to go over the discovery process with you, too, at some point so we're all on the same page."

"Where do you want to start?" Nina Marie asked.

"It would be helpful if you gave me a more detailed explanation of your company. I did my own research, but I'd love to hear it from you. Then we can move onto the legal claims brought against you by Optimism."

"Nina Marie is the driving force behind Astral Tech. So I'll let her explain our business," Clive said. "I'm more of the big picture guy and Matt is our number cruncher."

"Sounds good," Olivia said.

Nina Marie smiled. The thin auburn haired woman wore tortoiseshell glasses. Her hair was swept up into a loose bun, and she wore a black blazer with a rose colored blouse. "Astral Tech was my baby, but Clive has the financial backing and business acumen to make it happen."

"I'd like to hear all about it," Olivia said.

"We're a company specializing in bringing New Age theories and ideas into the tech space. We felt like we filled a void in that area. Yes, New Age has been quite popular for years now, but no company has really brought New Age into the current technology arena and made it work for the next generation. Through the Astral Tech app and other electronic means, we're making New Age relevant again. Our target audience is youth and young professionals. We don't even try to reach the baby boomers and beyond because it's a losing battle. They're too traditional, and they're not as tech savvy. We have to target our energy on the demographic that makes the most sense for our product."

"Excuse my ignorance, but you use New Age as a blanket term. I need a bit of education on what exactly you mean in the context of your business."

Nina Marie clasped her hands together in front of her. "Of course. I think a woman like you is in our key demographic. I would love to hear your thoughts on all of this. But to answer your question, New Age is a lot more than incense and meditation, although that is definitely a part of it. New Age is a way of life. A way of spiritually connecting. We care about the whole body—the environment, mysticism, spirituality. And we do that in an innovative way through the Astral Tech app that starts you on your path of self exploration from day one. You have to download it and try it for yourself. It will definitely help you understand our issues in the litigation better."

"Yes, the litigation. I read the complaint on the plane. Optimism's central claim is that Astral Tech actually stole the app from them."

Clive jumped in and leaned forward resting his arms on the table. "It's a totally bogus lawsuit. That's why we're hiring a firm like yours to nip this in the bud. We don't want any copycat litigation. This app was developed totally in house by Astral Tech employees. To say that there is any theft is absolutely false. We certainly didn't steal it. It's just a trumped up charge."

"What about the other claim regarding defamation?"

Clive nodded. "The defamation claim is actually a bit more concerning to me because it's subjective. We won't have a technical expert that can testify about that like we have on the actual theft claim."

She sat up in her seat. "What was said by Astral Tech that they are claiming is defamatory?"

"A few off handed comments about Optimism and their lack of integrity. They claim they're part of the New Age movement, but some of their actions indicate otherwise."

"Could you be more specific?"

"I can elaborate," Nina Marie said. "Optimism isn't really centered on New Age techniques in the same way we are. Their original founder, Earl Ward, was a connoisseur of many New Age techniques, but when he passed away Optimism's purpose shifted a bit under Layton Alito's rule, solidifying their allegiance to the dark arts. Layton is a ruthless leader who doesn't tolerate any type of dissent amongst his ranks."

Olivia felt her eyes widen, but she tried to hide her surprise. "Are you serious?"

"Yes, very," Nina Marie said.

"And Astral Tech isn't like that?" She couldn't help herself. She had to ask. It was better to know.

"We're a big tent. We don't want to alienate anyone who is seeking a spiritual journey," Clive said.

Well, that wasn't exactly a denial. What had she stepped into here? "And why New Age?"

Clive smiled. "Think about this as a lawyer. A businessperson. The world is becoming more and more open minded about spirituality. Which is obviously a good thing. Let everyone do what they want. We're moving away from strict codes of morality to something that fits with the modern person in this country. It's in. It's now. That's why we do it. We're using principles that have been popular for the past few decades and bringing them into the tech arena."

"For some of us, it's more than just about what makes money and make sense," Nina Marie said. "I'm proud to say that I'm a believer. A strong spiritual being. Those things have value. What we're doing matters. We have the ability to revolutionize the way people think about New Age principles."

Olivia could feel Nina Marie's dark eyes on her trying to evaluate whether she was truly friend or foe. A strange uneasiness settled over her. There was more to all of this than Nina Marie was saying. This was much larger than a lawsuit. Spiritual forces were at work here.

Focusing on the task at hand, she stared at her laptop and the page of notes she'd typed while hearing her clients talk. "I'll need to make sure you have a proper litigation hold in place to collect all relevant documents. I'll also want to talk to your IT person on staff right away about preserving all documents. The last thing we want to do is play cute and get sanctioned by the court. If Astral Tech has nothing to hide, then there's no reason to be evasive."

"But that's the thing," Matt said. "We believe we haven't broken any laws, but we also believe in our privacy and that of our customers."

Olivia nodded. "We should be able to petition the court for a protective order for any sensitive information that is turned over in the litigation, including customer lists. That's something we can handle."

Nina Marie stood up from her chair. "Let me take you to the office space we have set up for you while you're working here on this case."

"Thank you." While she was eager to get to work, she wasn't so excited about being alone with Nina Marie. But she followed the woman out of the conference room and down the hall, reminding herself that Nina Marie was still the client.

Nina Marie stopped abruptly about half way down the corridor. "I know this will sound a bit strange, but I'm getting a really interesting vibe from you."

"Vibe?"

"Yes. Do you have any interest in learning more about New Age spirituality? Anything like that?"

"No. That's not really my thing." She held back her direct answer which would've been totally unprofessional. She didn't feel comfortable in this environment, but she was also torn between her job and her faith. Could she really do both? Would defending a company like Astral Tech really be possible?

Conflicted feelings shot through her. No, she didn't believe in aliens or monsters, but she definitely believed in good and evil. Angels and demons. And this entire situation seemed like a recipe for disaster.

"I'm not giving up on you." Nina Marie reached out and patted her shoulder.

Nina Marie was quite a few inches taller than her, but that wasn't saying much considering she was only five foot three in heels.

"Once you learn more about our product offerings, I think you'll be excited to hear more about what we can do for a strong and smart professional woman like you."

"I appreciate your interest, Nina Marie, but my chief concern and responsibility is the lawsuit. So I think it'd be best if we could concentrate on that."

Nina Marie quirked an eyebrow but didn't immediately respond. Olivia followed her into another conference room, but this one was set up with multiple computer workstations around the large table. The rest of the décor matched the previous room they were in.

"This will be the legal work room for you. You should have plenty of space for everything you need in here."

"This is a great workspace." She looked around the room and was pleased by the size and technical accommodations. "I'm sure I'm going to run into a lot of factual questions as we start preparing for this first phase of litigation. Who is the person at Astral Tech I should go to with questions?"

"That would be me for pretty much anything that is detail oriented about the company or the app. Clive is good on the general business and philosophy but not so much on details. He's also not in the office everyday like I am. Matt can also serve as a resource both on the financial aspects and the spiritual ones."

"Got it." She'd never worked on such a strange case in her seven plus years of practicing law. Thankfully, she was steadfast in her beliefs. She just hoped that nothing in this litigation would require her to do things that went against her faith. Because she'd have to draw that line somewhere. And if it was a choice between her career or her faith, she'd always choose her faith.

***

Grant Baxter reviewed the document requests he had drafted one last time. He enjoyed being on the plaintiff's side of the table—even if it was for an odd client. Some wacky New Age group had retained his small but reputable law firm to sue Astral Tech—an equally wacky company in his opinion.

He didn't have any time for religion whether it be traditional or New Age or whatever. To him it was all just a convenient fiction made up to help people deal with their fears and insecurities. But if this case would help his firm take the next steps to success and keep paying the bills, then he was all for it.

He'd built his law firm, The Baxter Group, from the ground up—something he was very proud of, given all his long hours and sacrifices. Not a thing in his life had been given to him. He'd earned it all the hard way.

He couldn't help but chuckle as he read over the document requests that he had prepared. All the talk of witches and spirituality and the Astral Tech app. He'd never drafted anything like that before. His law school classes and nine years of practice had equipped him with many skills, but working on a case like this was totally foreign to him.

It wasn't like there were witches in a coven out to get him. People were entirely irrational when it came to religion. Luckily for him, he wasn't one of those people. He might be the only sane person in the entire litigation, and he planned to stay that way. One thing he was certain about. A jury was going to eat this stuff up.

"Hey, boss man." Ryan Wilde stood at Grant's door.

"What's going on?" Grant asked.

"I asked around town trying to find info on Astral Tech, but most of my contacts had never heard of them, and the few that had didn't really have anything useful to say except that they're trying to become players in the tech space."

Ryan was only about two years younger than Grant. They'd both worked in a law firm together for years, and Grant was glad that Ryan had joined him at the firm. If all progressed as planned, Grant was going to add Ryan as his partner in the firm.

"If you do hear anything, just let me know."

"Anything else you need from me?"

"Not on this. How are your other cases going?"

"I'm meeting with potential clients this afternoon on a products liability class action. It would be a good case to have."

"Keep me posted."

Ryan nodded. "You got it." Ryan walked out the door and then turned around and laughed. "I have to say, I'm glad that you're working this case and not me. I don't think I'd know how to approach it."

"Just like anything else. It'll be fine."

"If you say so. I hope you don't end up with a hex put on you or something like that."

Grant laughed. "Don't even tell me that you would consider believing in any of this."

Ryan shook his head. "Nah. I'm just messing with you."

Ryan walked out and Grant was anxious to start the discovery process and put pressure on the other side. It was one of those things he loved about being a plaintiff's lawyer. He was in the driver's seat and planned to take an aggressive stance in this case to really turn the heat up on the other side. Going through these steps reminded him how glad he was that he went out and started his own firm. He truly loved his work.

His office phone rang, jerking him back to reality.

"This is Grant Baxter," he said.

"Hello. My name is Olivia Murray from the law firm of Brown, Carter, and Reed. I just wanted to call to introduce myself. We're representing Astral Tech in the suit filed by your client. So I'll be your point of contact for anything related to the case."

Well, well he thought. Astral Tech had gone and hired a high powered law firm based in Washington, DC to defend them. "Perfect timing. I was just getting ready to send out discovery requests for documents. BCR doesn't have a Chicago office, right?"

"No, but I'm actually in town. I'm working at the client's office in Windy Ridge. So you can send any hard copies of anything to the Astral Tech office, and I would appreciate getting everything by email also." She rattled off her email address.

"Of course. And I have the feeling we'll be talking a lot. This litigation is going to be fast tracked if my client has anything to say about it. We're not going to just wait around for years letting things pass us by."

She laughed. "Yes, I know how it is. I'll look forward to your email."

He hung up and leaned back in his chair. Know thy enemy, right? He immediately looked her up on the Internet finding her BCR firm profile. A brunette with big brown eyes smiled back at him. He read her bio. Impressive, double Georgetown girl.

Seventh year associate at BCR where she'd spent her entire legal career. That would make her about two years younger than him—but definitely still a seasoned attorney and worthy opponent.

Astral Tech wasn't messing around. That let him know that they took this litigation seriously. They didn't see this as a nuisance suit. Game on.

***

"Do you think Olivia's ready for this fight?" Micah asked Ben looking directly into his dark eyes.

"It doesn't matter if she's really ready, Micah. It's a battle she has to fight and the time is now. We have no one else. She's the one God has chosen who has to stand up and take this on. She has some idea that she's meant to be here. But it might take her a little time to figure out exactly what she's going to be involved with."

The angels stood behind Olivia watching over her in the conference room. But she hadn't sensed their presence as she continued to type away on her laptop and hum a tune.

"She isn't fully appreciative of how strong she is, but she'll get there," Micah said. He stood tall, his blond hair barely touching his shoulders. The angel warrior was strong but kind—and fiercely protective of Olivia.

Ben nodded. "At least she has the foundation to build upon. A strong faith that has been growing ever since she was a little girl." Ben paused. "Unlike our friend Grant."

"I'm much more worried about him. He has no idea what he's going to be facing, and he doesn't have the skills to defend himself. Nina Marie and her followers are building up strength by the day, and she'll surely want to go after him. We can only do so much to protect Olivia and Grant against the forces of evil running rampant on this earth."

"But we'll do everything we can."

Micah looked at him. "You and me—quite an angel army."

"The best kind."

"Let's pray for her now."

The two laid their hands on her shoulders to help prepare her for the fight to come. A fight unlike anything they'd ever known before.

CHAPTER TWO

Optimism CEO Layton Alito believed in the magical powers that he espoused. But what he believed even more was that this lawsuit against Astral Tech was critical to disabling the ever growing threat to his company and his group of believers.

Some would say he ruled harshly, but that was required to keep the group unified. He couldn't have everyone doing their own thing—that would result in a fractured and less powerful group like Astral Tech. No, Optimism members were free to dabble in whichever dark arts they preferred, but ultimately he was in charge.

Nina Marie was a formidable opponent. That's why he never should've gotten involved with her in the first place. But he did and now he was paying the price. It wasn't like him to let a woman be in control. He was usually the one running the show and calling all the shots. But he'd found out much too late that Nina Marie wasn't a regular woman.

Luckily for him, he had an entire group of believers ready to do battle. And the perfect thing was that there were no forces of good involved. This was purely a battle of evil versus evil. Strangely, that excited him.

Once he prevailed in this litigation, Astral Tech would be put out of business. Then he would be able to sweep in and court the membership. As part of the Optimism system he'd created, members had to buy in. He was the recipient of money and gifts.

It was a system that was not only brilliant but very lucrative. In exchange, he made the members feel valuable. Those that actually had spiritual talents, he used and deployed in the best ways possible. Sending them out in the Windy Ridge community to recruit more members. And to wreak havoc on the Christian thorns in his side. Especially the churches.

And for those members that failed in the spiritual arena, he found other tasks for them. His power base was growing, his coffers were being filled, and nothing could stop him. All he needed to do was to stay strong in the lawsuit and then the dominos would start to fall.

He was proud of the progress that had already been made in the community. More people seeking the darkness, turning their backs on the church, and living a lifestyle that was pleasing to them. But this was only the start of the bigger plans he had for Windy Ridge.

He needed to check in with his legal counsel. He'd instructed his lawyer, Grant Baxter, to be as aggressive as the law would allow—and then some. Now wasn't the time to play it safe.

Grant wasn't a follower of his or the evil one or anything as far as he could tell. Which was fine with him. An atheist like Grant could be a powerful ally. He had a love of money, and he wanted to win. And Layton didn't need Grant to be a member of Optimism. All he needed from him was to win the lawsuit. Everyone had a role to play.

Picking up the phone, Layton dialed Grant's number.

"Grant Baxter," he answered.

"Grant, it's Layton. I just wanted to check in with you."

"You were on my list of phone calls to make today. I've sent out the first wave of discovery requests. I also talked to the opposing counsel. Get this, Astral Tech has hired the law firm of Brown, Carter, and Reed based out of Washington, DC. It's a well known firm specializing in high stakes litigation. We're talking like a top twenty law firm in the nation here."

"Really?" Layton's heartbeat sped up.

"Yes, that means they are taking this lawsuit very seriously. They wouldn't be dropping that kind of money otherwise. BCR isn't cheap."

"Who is leading the effort?"

"A senior attorney named Olivia Murray is running things. She's here in Windy Ridge working out of the Astral Tech office."

He took a breath and reminded himself to calm down. It would all be okay. "Should I be concerned?"

Grant laughed. "I've got this well under control."

While Grant might be laughing, Layton certainly wasn't at that point. He needed some clear affirmation. This wasn't just a random lawsuit. This was everything. "I can't say enough how important this case is for Optimism and for me personally. This isn't the time to go soft or be accommodating. I want you to go as far as you can and then some."

"You came to the right place when you hired my firm. We understand how the system works. You won't have to worry about me letting up on the pressure. This is what I do every single day. You saw my trial track record when you were initially interviewing me for this job."

Layton let out a breath. This was exactly what he wanted and needed to hear. "I'm glad I can depend on you. Having your work stolen from you is a slap in the face."

"Right. Astral Tech shouldn't be profiting from your hard work. I'll keep you updated as we progress."

"No letting up under any circumstances. You hear me?"

"You got it."

Grant hung up and Layton smiled. His first order of business was to track down Olivia Murray and find out everything he could about his legal adversary. And lucky for him that one of his senior Optimism members was Judge Louise Martinique. If anyone could get the scoop on Olivia and her firm, it would be Louise.

It was all going to work out. He could feel it. Nina Marie wouldn't expect his full onslaught. Between the legal assault and the spiritual one, he would prevail.

***

Olivia knew that Grant Baxter was going to be a problem. She read over the ridiculous document requests he'd sent her on behalf of Optimism. Talk about a fishing expedition.

Although what made her the most uncomfortable were all of the references to things like witchcraft and magic. She knew she was a strong person. Independent, hard working, and steadfast in her faith. But she'd never been tested in her career this way before.

She pondered whether she should call up the managing partner and tell him that she couldn't do this. But that would probably cost her the job that she desperately needed to keep.

God, if you need me to quit this case and go back to DC, please let me know. I'm not a quitter, but if it's Your will for me to say no to this, then I'll figure out how to handle the consequences.

She kept her eyes closed and took a few moments of silence to gather herself.

Then it occurred to her that God might have put her there for a reason. What if the Lord wanted her in Windy Ridge?

Could she defend this company but do it in a purely legal and professional way? She'd do her best. That's all anyone could ask of her. Not only her best in defending this case, but in living her life in a way that demonstrated her Christian beliefs.

But Olivia couldn't shake a wave of unease that had settled over her every single time she walked into the Astral Tech offices. A feeling of dread—threatening to bring her down. When she was in her hotel room at night, she didn't experience those types of dark thoughts. But when she stepped foot into the Astral Tech building, it started to hit her. By the end of the day it was like she had gone multiple rounds in a boxing ring. Her energy being sucked out of her body.

She found herself praying more and more as it was the only thing that kept her going. Olivia had grown up in a Christian home. There was a time in college when she'd taken a step back from regular church going because it wasn't the cool thing to do. It wasn't until the death of her parents in a tragic auto accident while she was in law school that she really became reconnected to God in a fierce way.

She knew there was a lot more to being a Christian than going to church, but her church community provided her with strength and encouragement. Pastor Paul, her pastor in Washington, DC, was a trusted friend. But even he didn't know all of her secrets. And now here she was in Windy Ridge, Illinois all alone.

The hair on her arms stood up. Turning quickly she saw that she was completely alone in the conference room. Closing her eyes she steadied herself.

Don't be afraid, a voice said in her head as clear as day. She shook it off, attributing it to lack of sleep. But she couldn't deny that she was feeling something stronger and more poignant. Something she hadn't felt in decades.

If she was being honest with herself, one of the reasons this litigation scared her so much was because of her past. It was opening herself up to things she'd experienced years before. A past that only she and her father knew about. Experiences that were so real and powerful that her entire body shook just thinking about them.

But right now she needed to concentrate on her meeting with opposing counsel Grant Baxter. She'd invited him over to her turf on purpose. She didn't want to be in his law office for their first meeting. She'd suggested the in person meeting to try to hash out some of the immediate problems she had with his document requests. Surprisingly, he'd accepted her offer immediately. She didn't trust him though. He was out to take down her client. That was his mission. And as Astral Tech's lawyer, her job was to protect them. Even if she disagreed with their beliefs.

When she went to law school, she knew there would be situations like this. Criminal defense attorneys defended guilty people all the time. And in this case, it wasn't like her client was necessarily guilty. This was more of a conflict of belief systems. It was her ethical duty as a lawyer to do her best job.

Melanie walked into the conference room. Her curly blonde hair was pulled back in a severe bun today, and she wore the highest heeled navy stilettos that Olivia had ever seen. "Grant Baxter is here to see you. Should I bring him back here to the conference room?"

"Yes, please. That would be great."

Melanie nodded and hurried out. Olivia stood and buttoned her suit jacket. She'd worn one of her favorite power suits today. The black pantsuit fit her petite frame perfectly. She'd spent good money to have it tailored, but it was worth it. It was one of the only things she actually spent money on—all the rest of it went to paying off her Georgetown student loans. Under the jacket she wore a royal blue blouse. Unlike Melanie, she didn't wear stilettos but low black heels.

And that was her first mistake because when the door opened revealing Grant Baxter she saw that she could've used those extra inches—and then some. This man had to be six foot two. But she wasn't going to back down now. She'd faced down plenty of high powered male lawyers before. And in most cases, she'd prevailed in the actual litigation. Mind games were just a part of being a lawyer.

She walked over to him, gave him a bright smile, and outstretched her hand.

He took her much smaller hand in his, but she gave him a hearty shake. She wanted this guy to know she might be a small woman, but she was no delicate flower when it came to her legal career.

Grant wore a dark suit and checkered navy tie that accented his aqua blue eyes. His dark hair was short and styled neatly. Thankfully he wasn't one of those lawyers that went crazy using the hair gel or cologne.

"Olivia, I'm Grant Baxter. It's nice to meet you." He let go of her hand.

She stood up straight facing him. "Thank you for coming over."

"No problem."

Melanie stepped forward. "Can I get either of you coffee or anything else to drink?"

"Coffee for me," Grant said.

"Coffee would be great, Melanie, thank you," Olivia said.

"I'll be right back."

"Thanks again for agreeing to meet here. Please have a seat." She motioned for him to sit down at the conference room table.

He sat down at the table and unbuttoned his suit jacket. "I'm hoping this will be the first of many productive discussions."

She smiled. "A lot of that depends on you, Grant. You're the plaintiff here."

He laughed. "And what's that supposed to mean?"

"Let's not engage in these games. You're going to push for the most outrageous document requests. Unreasonable timing for production. Costly and burdensome inquiries just to put pressure on my client and make their lives miserable. And by extension you're going to do everything possible to make my life miserable. But I've been there and done that. Multiple times."

He held up his hand. "And you're going to use every stall tactic out there. Complaining about the IT staff, excuses about all the data and how much it will cost to search it. You'll say you'll turn over a certain category of documents, but then it won't be everything I'm asking for. Days will pass by, and I still won't have what I need from you. Just emails and phone calls making empty promises that you know you can never keep. Deadlines that continuously get pushed back. Sound about right, counselor?"

She had to give it to this guy. He had her nailed in the same way that she had him. They'd played this game enough times to know the drill. "So how do you propose that we proceed? Because you know there's no way I'm giving you all of the documents that you asked for."

"Negotiation." He leaned back in his chair. "I'm going to play it straight with you, Olivia, because I did enough recon on you to know you're a worthy opponent at a top law firm. My client is in this litigation no holds barred."

"Really?" She raised her eyebrow at him.

"Yes. It's nothing personal. I like you. You seem like a nice person. Heck, we might even be friends. But in this litigation, I'm not going to go easy on you."

She scoffed. "And I wouldn't expect you to. Why don't we get back to the issue at hand?" She spread the printed pages out on the desk. "These document requests are crazy. You know it. I know it. A judge will know it. This is our good faith meet and confer. So let's get to it."

Two hours later, and normally after something like that she would be wanting a bottle of medicine for a pounding headache. But instead she felt energized. Better than she had felt in a while. Grant had proven to be a stellar adversary. But he mixed the back and forth with a healthy dose of humor and a disarming quality. There was no doubt in her mind that a jury would absolutely love him, and that was something she and her client would have to seriously consider when weighing whether to take this to trial.

She could picture him in front of the jury with that smile and those bright blue eyes right now. Defending the company that supposedly was the victim of theft. It wouldn't be an ideal outcome for her client. Maybe there would be a chance of settlement along the way. Each side normally realized that the certainty of settlement was in their best interest as opposed to allowing a jury to decide their future.

He looked down at his watch. "It's getting late." He smiled. "Why don't you let me take you to dinner, and we can finish up discussing any loose ends."

She sat back in her chair. "Are you asking me out?" Besides it being totally inappropriate to go out with her opposing counsel, Olivia didn't consider herself that attractive.

"Of course not. This is purely business. Think of it as career networking, too. I can throw some business your way that doesn't fit my firm's profile. I get a lot of phone calls for things I don't handle on the plaintiff's side."

She wondered what this guy's angle was. He surely wasn't asking her to dinner out of the goodness of his heart. Was he trying to soften her up? That wasn't going to happen. But on the flip side, networking was a really important part of being a lawyer. And once again she felt positive when she was around him. This was the best she'd felt since she'd walked into the Astral Tech office.

"So you up for dinner?" he asked.

"Sure. But since you asked, you're paying."

He laughed. "I do have some manners."

***

Why Grant had asked Olivia to dinner, he wasn't quite sure. It just seemed like the right thing to do. And he had wanted a nice juicy steak. He'd been eating frozen meals for the past few weeks. Now over dessert and coffee, he knew he'd made the right decision.

Truthfully, he was probably a little tired of eating dinner alone. He and Ryan usually tried to get together once a week, but they'd both been so busy lately trying to bring in new large cases.

"Tell me how you got involved in this litigation?" he asked her.

"Easy. The managing partner told me I was going to take it on and I did. I know you work for yourself, but in a big firm I'm not the one calling the shots. I get my orders from someone else and then execute on it."

"What do you think of the whole New Age angle?" He looked into her dark brown eyes and found himself truly interested in her thoughts. Based on the time he'd spent with her today, he would have a hard time believing that she would actually buy into the New Age nonsense. She seemed far too level headed for that.

"That's a good question. This is the first real exposure I've had to anything New Age. I mean, I'd obviously heard the term New Age before, but that was about the extent of it. I'd seen New Age sections in bookstores. Beyond that, this is all a different world. What about you?"

"Same thing. Honestly, religion of any type isn't something I'm very familiar with. I'm fine just the way I am. And that's not being tied to a fanciful religious belief system."

When she raised an eyebrow, it let him know that she didn't feel the same way.

"Why is that?" she asked.

"Good question, counselor." Did he really want to talk about this with her right now? But here he was about to spill his guts. She was easy to talk to like that. The kindness was evident in her eyes. This woman wasn't cutthroat. That may come back to hurt her later in her career. It had been his experience that the most successful lawyers were the ones with the killer instincts. This woman had a heart.

"It's okay if you don't want to answer," she said. "I didn't mean to get overly personal. It's just that we were discussing the New Age stuff so I was interested to hear your thoughts on religion in general."

"No, it's all right. I started the conversation anyway. So I grew up in a foster home. Or I should say multiple foster homes. Bouncing around from one to another. I never really knew anything about a supposed God beyond what I saw in the movies and on TV until I hit college. I was initially intrigued by the general concept of there being a God, but not sufficiently so to become any type of believer. I find it hard to believe that a God would allow all the atrocities in this world to exist. And if so, I don't think that's a God I would want." He paused. "What about you?"

She gave him a gentle smile that made him question his sanity. Women normally didn't affect him at all. And this petite brunette comes in and starts trying to change all of that without any real effort on her part whatsoever. He needed to put his guard up quickly.

"My father was a preacher."

"Was?"

"He passed away some years ago. Both of my parents actually."

"I'm sorry." And he meant it. He could see the pain in her eyes. She'd obviously had a strong connection to them.

"Thank you."

"Was it some sort of accident?"

"Yes. They were run off the road by another driver. The driver sped off and didn't look back. They never found the person who did it."

"Wow, that must've been rough. How old were you when it happened?"

"I was in law school. It had a big impact on my life." She took a breath. "Anyway, I was raised in the church. It was all I knew. I sang and played the piano. I really didn't realize there were people who had totally different beliefs until I went to college at Georgetown. There I met people of all different faiths, including those who believed nothing."

"That must've been eye opening."

She nodded. "It was. And I even took a break from regular church going for a few years. But when my parents were killed, I was really drawn back to God."

Interesting, he thought. Her sincerity echoed through her words. This woman truly believed in her God. "But how can a God allow something that awful to happen though? That's the part I don't understand. You hear people talking about how good God is, and then I listen stories like yours, or I think about my childhood and it's difficult for me to fathom the existence of a good God."

"That's a valid line of questioning. This life on earth isn't the main event, Grant. It's only temporary. Ephemeral. Fleeting. This earth is filled with sin, and the devil is the king of this earth."

He couldn't help but laugh. "And this is supposed to encourage me that there is a God?" He considered his words carefully. "Hearing you say something like that is one of the reasons why I reject religious notions. To tell you the truth, I have a hard time believing in anything. The abstract concepts of heaven and hell seem so unreal to me. I've never had an inkling of a religious experience. So it's difficult for me to believe that something like that exists."

"I think that's understandable, given the rough childhood you had growing up in foster homes. But you can start a journey to faith at any point."

"And you think you'll be the one to lead me there?"

She leaned back in her chair as if she was sizing him up. "You never know, Grant."

"I'll give you that." He raised his glass to hers. "To new friendships."

She raised her coffee cup to his. "Your case has no merit, by the way."

"Now you want to get into the trenches." He shook his head. "No, we've had an enjoyable dinner. I won't let you ruin it with defense litigation tactics."

"Fair enough."

"So who all did you leave behind in DC?" he asked.

"My best friend Lizzie Asher. She's a lawyer at Price Carlock. We've known each other since college. She keeps me sane." She laughed. "And she totally gets the big law firm lifestyle and struggles. I'm a really private person. I have Lizzie and a couple of other close friends. But I'm not really the type to hang out with big groups of people. I work all the time so I'm the worst with making plans and being able to keep them. After a while, friends just stop inviting you when you always are a no show or cancel at the last minute."

"So then I'm guessing you aren't married?'

"No. I've got to focus on my career first. That's all there's room for at this point. What about you? Are all your friends lawyers?"

He laughed. "Almost. You know how it is in the legal community. I've got someone working at the firm now who I used to work with at my prior firm. He's a great guy and a top notch lawyer. Also my other buddy Ty is deployed right now. He's definitely not a lawyer."

"That must be tough for you with him overseas."

"It is, but like you, work is my top priority. It can be all-consuming."

"Can I ask you something else?"

"Sure," he said.

"I know you're skeptical about God, but you aren't actually taken in by the New Age stuff are you?"

He saw her shoulders visibly tense up. She was actually worried that he might be interested in New Age propaganda. "No way. If I was going to do the whole religion thing, it wouldn't be some freaky incense witch holistic thing."

She started laughing hard.

"You okay?" he asked.

"Yes, sorry about that. You're a funny guy." She took another sip of coffee. "Although I don't think your client would like to be thought of that way by his own attorney."

"You won't tell on me. I can see it in your eyes. You think it's all a farce too. A highly profitable farce for both of our clients, but still..."

She shook her head. "Actually, I think it's all too real but not in a good way." She reached out and put her hand on top of his. "Grant, this stuff is nothing to experiment with. Regardless of whether you want to believe it or not, there is good and evil out there. And here on earth, the evil has a strength that you wouldn't believe. I don't want you to get sucked into that." She gave his hand a squeeze and then pulled back.

And he suddenly felt cold. He couldn't help but be impacted by her passionate words. How could he not respect that? Even if he had a totally different opinion. "Don't worry about me, Olivia. I promise that you don't have to be concerned about me being drawn to any of this stuff."

"I just had to say something. It's easier to get lured into it than you think. Especially when you're going to be so involved in aspects of the business because of the litigation."

It was time to shift topics. "I'm glad we've had this dinner. Just because we're legal adversaries doesn't mean that we can't also be friendly colleagues."

"You know, I'm surprised but I actually enjoyed this. I was feeling kind of down and then you came over and things brightened up a bit. Even though we argued like cats and dogs over the discovery requests."

He looked at her. "And don't think that since you and I had this nice dinner it means I'm going to let up on my document requests. I have a job to do."

She raised an eyebrow. "And I wouldn't expect anything less from you."

"You ready to get out of here?" he asked.

"Yes. Thanks for offering to drive."

"No problem." He'd insisted on dropping her car off at her hotel and driving them to dinner in the city.

"I can take a cab back to the hotel." She stood up from the table.

"Nonsense. I'll take you back." He wasn't going to just shove her into a cab.

"Thank you."

Her smile warmed his cold heart. He needed to get his head checked. If she hadn't professed her faith in God, he'd wondered if she wasn't a witch casting a spell on him. But he knew better. She was a Christian through and through. He'd actually never really talked with someone so in depth about religious things before. He knew that Ty was a Christian, but the two of them didn't get into any deep religious discussion. But Olivia had a way of getting him to talk. He figured she'd be pretty good in the courtroom too when she questioned witnesses.

They arrived at her hotel, and he pulled his SUV into one of the parking spots in the front by the lobby and placed the car in park.

"I'll walk you up." Windy Ridge was a pretty safe community, but he had a protective side when it came to women. Even if they were the enemy on the other side of the case.

"You know I'm a big girl, right?"

"Of course, but it would just make me feel better."

They walked to her room in silence.

"I'm right up here," she said.

They got to her hotel room door and she shrieked. Instinctively, he pulled her back away from the door and close to him. That's when he looked up and saw what she had seen. A bright red pentagram covered her door.

***

Olivia took a few deep breaths and gathered herself as she thought about what just transpired. Grant was still there and had refused to leave her side. Hotel management insisted that she'd been the victim of unfortunate random vandalism. Full of apologies and excuses, they'd immediately switched her to a new room—a much nicer executive suite to make up for the inconvenience.

She couldn't stop shaking because deep in her heart, she didn't think this was random. No, this was specific. She was targeted because of who she was and what she was doing. It had to do with Astral Tech. Why were they coming after her? She was representing them.

Then it hit her like a freight train. Optimism had to be behind this. How in the world had she gotten involved in this madness?

The only silver lining to an awful situation was Grant Baxter. He'd been amazing. She couldn't stop her visceral response to the door. It was like the dark forces that she had hoped to never face again had attacked her. Someone was clearly sending her a message, and it wasn't one she wanted.

But Grant had jumped into fix it mode and had literally been a God sent. That thought jarred her. Had God sent this man into her life?

She watched as he discussed matters with the last remaining hotel staff member before seeing them out.

"You should be all good in this suite," he said.

She reached out and touched his arm. "Thank you, Grant. You really went above and beyond here tonight."

He shook his head. "Hey, I was there too. I saw that nasty scene at your door. No one should be subjected to that."

"About that."

"Yeah?" He raised an eyebrow.

"Do you think your people could be involved?'

"My people?"

"You client. Optimism."

He took a step back. "Why do you say that?"

"We're representing these companies, Grant. These aren't your regular run of the mill businesses."

He put up his hands. "I understand that, but what you're saying is a huge accusation."

She took a deep breath. "This can't be a random coincidence."

His eyes widened. "How can you be sure about that?"

"While the pentagram can mean different things, it is a widely known demonic symbol. Someone was trying to intimidate me." She took a deep breath. Trying to draw the necessary strength to explain to this man how powerful the forces of darkness were. A man who didn't even believe in any spiritual realm. Maybe she should take the first flight back to DC.

"What are you thinking?" he asked.

"Whether I need to tell the firm that I can't deal with this and need to go back to DC."

He shook his head. "No, Olivia. You aren't going to run away. We're attorneys. We don't just cut and run from our clients. You know that. I'm sure there's a logical explanation. Just like the police said. It's vandalism. Unfortunate for you but still. You're reading way too much into this. I think all your examination of the Astral Tech app must be impacting your judgment."

"Yeah, like a pentagram just naturally appears on hotel room doors."

"We'll figure it out."

She sighed. "I'll never forget the kindness you've shown me tonight. But remember, we're on opposite sides of the fence here."

He didn't say a word.

"Exactly," she said.

"I'm sorry. You're really taking me out of my element here."

"It's your client!"

"You don't know that. How would they have found you?"

"Good question. Did you tell them about me?"

He blew out a breath. "Yes, but that doesn't mean they tracked down your hotel room."

"This is the closest hotel to the Astral Tech office. It would be the most reasonable place for me to say, and they could've found out my room number if they tried hard enough."

He shook his head.

"Give me a more logical explanation then." She stood hands on her hips daring him to defy her.

He ran his hand through his dark hair. Then he made direct eye contact with her. "Honestly, Olivia, I'm out of my depth right now. The moment you started talking to the cops about all of this…"

"I'm sorry," she said. "But it is what it is. That symbol has meaning."

"What are you going to do?"

"Honestly, I'm going to pray on it. Ask the Lord what He wants me to do."

"And you think he's going to answer you?"

"I don't think, I know."

He shook his head. "I'm in awe by the absolute confidence you have in your faith."

"It comes with time. If it's something you're interested in, I'd be happy to talk to you about it."

"Thanks. But believe me, I'll be just fine on my own without any God." He paused. "But I do care about your safety. Are you sure you're okay here alone tonight?"

"Yes. I'll be fine."

"I have a rental condo that's currently vacant. If you need a place, the offer is open."

She laughed trying to lighten the mood. "I guess it pays to be a plaintiff's lawyer, right? You've got the big house in the Chicago suburbs and a rental condo."

He grinned. "Will you give me a call tomorrow and let me know how things are going?"

"Sure. And I'm sorry that our nice night ended on such an awful note."

"No need to apologize. I have to admit I've never dealt with anything like this in my whole thirty six years on this earth. You're exposing me to a lot of new things, Olivia. But I think it's time for me to go if you're sure you're okay for the night."

"Definitely. Thank you for everything today."

"No problem. And please call me tomorrow and let me know how it's going. And we can try to decide where to go on our document requests."

"Good night, Grant."

He walked out of her hotel room leaving her all alone. And even though she should feel afraid, a strong sense of determination washed over her. If this was how it was going to be, she would be ready the next time. This was a fight she was ready to take on.

CHAPTER THREE

Nina Marie's head pounded, and she wasn't sure why. But she had a sneaking suspicion that Layton was starting to play games with her. She didn't like it one bit. *Would he really go after me personally?* Of course he would. She'd stolen his precious technology and then broken off their sexual relationship. She tried to make him think that his efforts didn't work on her, but that wasn't true. He was very strong and while she was too, she wasn't immune to his powers.

Layton was so used to always getting his way—with his movie star good looks, strong jaw, blonde hair, perfect blue eyes, and stellar physique. But he'd never dealt with anyone quite like her before. She wasn't one of his yes women like those he surrounded himself with.

In a different place and time, she probably could have fallen for a man like him. But she'd committed herself to another. A greater and darker force than Layton could ever be.

Of course she hadn't been forthright with Olivia about Astral Tech's full purpose. Yes, the business itself was based on straight forward New Age principles, but Astral Tech was much more than a company. Behind the company stood a group of believers who were united in their passion for New Age spirituality.

Under Clive they'd been welcoming of those who were on what she would call the soft side of New Age. They'd formed sub groups or teams based on their interests. The most powerful team, the one she was on, served the evil one and took whatever he was willing to give.

Clive didn't want to run Astral Tech like the dictatorship that Layton ran at Optimism. He'd always said that it was better to have more members with diverse interests. Although if it was up to her, everyone would be united in their allegiance to the evil one. Unlike the fractured Astral Tech, the membership of Optimism was cohesive. She wanted that cohesion for Astral Tech.

The lawsuit threatened her and for that reason she was intent on managing it. And the lawyer Olivia Murray. At first Nina Marie just got a strong and vibrant energy from her. But then it hit her—the stench of Christianity. This woman wasn't just a Sunday Christian. No, there was something different about her.

Although after further reflection, Nina Marie saw it more as a challenge than anything. She'd converted others. She could use Olivia's drive and legal ambition to her advantage. If she could deploy Olivia's gifts, then she could be unstoppable.

Nina Marie couldn't help but be jealous of someone like Olivia, who had such raw, natural talents. It bothered her that Olivia chose to use her gifts for the church. She had felt firsthand what supposedly godly Christians could do. That was a part of her life that she never wanted to revisit.

A light knock on her office door had her wanting to scream at whoever was daring to bother her, but when she saw Olivia standing there with a deep frown pulling down her lips, she knew something was up.

"Olivia, come on in."

Olivia walked in and took a seat across from her at the desk. "I need to tell you something."

"What's wrong?" She could already tell this litigation was going to be a huge challenge for her to manage.

Olivia looked down and didn't say anything just yet.

"You can tell me. Whatever it is, we'll deal with it." Normally she wouldn't be so accommodating, but this felt different to her.

Olivia's dark eyes met hers. "When I got back to my hotel room last night, my door had been vandalized."

Nina Marie sucked in a breath. "Oh, Olivia. I'm so sorry. Was anything stolen from your room?"

Olivia shook her head. "No, I don't think anyone actually went into my room, but that's not the main point. In my opinion, this wasn't just a random act of vandalism."

"What do you mean?"

"Someone had drawn a pentagram on my door."

Nina Marie's stomach dropped. Layton wouldn't dare send his people to harass Olivia would he? "Olivia, I'm so sorry. I don't even know what to say."

"I think it has to do with this litigation. Since I'm working for you and Astral Tech, I assumed that no one associated with this organization would want to make my life miserable."

"Absolutely not."

Olivia leaned forward. "But what about Optimism?"

Her voice didn't waver. This was an accusation. Nina Marie tucked her hair behind her ear. How much did she want to share with Olivia? What would benefit her the most? "Unfortunately, Layton Alito has no qualms about playing dirty."

"That's exactly what I was afraid of."

Nina Marie stood up and walked around to the other side of the table where Olivia sat. "I don't want you to worry another second about this. Your job is the lawsuit. Let me handle Layton. I can protect you from him."

Olivia's dark eyes widened. "Nina Marie, you're the client, and I'm working as hard as I can on this lawsuit. But I do not want you taking any action to protect me that involves anything spiritually related."

Nina Marie laughed. "I can assure you that I know what I'm doing. You have nothing to fear from me."

"I'm sorry. I'm just not comfortable with that."

Nina Marie decided it was better not to push Olivia right now. If she did, Olivia might go running back to DC. Nina Marie plastered a smile on her face. "I would never want to make you uncomfortable." Lie. "But if there's something you would like me to do to help you, please let me know."

"I just wanted to inform you of the situation. If they're coming after me, they may be targeting other Astral Tech people as well."

Nina Marie nodded. "Very good point. I'll also get some extra building security."

"Thank you. I'm going to get to work." Olivia stood up and walked out of the office.

Nina Marie immediately picked up the phone. "Clive, get down here. We have a problem."

Less than five minutes later, Clive walked into her office, his green eyes full of questions. "What is it?"

"Layton is attacking us."

"How so?"

"He went after Olivia last night. Or he sent his members to do it."

Clive raised an eyebrow as he stood leaning up against the wall. "I need details. What happened?"

"Olivia's hotel room door was covered in a pentagram."

"Isn't that a warm and tacky welcome for her." He huffed. "This is not good."

"You're telling me. We need to fight back immediately."

Clive took a seat and rubbed his chin. "This was his plan all along. A two pronged attack. Legal and spiritual. Get us to put our energy into the legal problems to take our minds off of our real battle. I used to think that the two groups could co-exist. But

I underestimated Layton's desire for power. He won't rest until he destroys us and poaches our members."

She knew what they had to do. "We will fight back."

"Obviously. Let's gather everyone at my place Sunday night. We will make him pay."

***

Grant waited for his phone to ring to get word that Olivia was doing all right. Maybe he really needed to be worried about himself. Not only had he taken on the role of Olivia's defender, something he had no right or business doing, his entire worldview was being warped by the recent events.

Last night when he'd gotten home, he'd fallen asleep from exhaustion. But he felt like he hadn't slept at all. While he couldn't remember exactly what happened in his dreams, he felt like he'd been in the middle of some huge fight. All that talk of New Age stuff and pentagrams had gone straight to his head.

He prided himself on his reliance on logic and science. Thirty six years of believing what he believed—simply that there was no God or devil or demons or anything. That was what science told him, and that's what he chose to believe. He wasn't about to fall down this rabbit hole. No way, no how.

As he had told Olivia, he was in an unknown area right now. The lawsuit—that he could handle. But he started to have second thoughts about his client. Grant didn't believe for one second that any actual spirits or demons were involved in what happened to Olivia's hotel room door. But humans? Definitely a possibility. What if Layton wanted to welcome the opposing counsel to town by trying to shake her off her game from the start? It might seem like a good strategic move, but it was illegal. Grant refused to support something like that. His reputation was at stake.

Maybe a phone call to Layton would put his mind at ease. There had to be a perfectly reasonable explanation for everything—like the police said. He certainly wasn't going to jump into the spiritual explanation because to him that just seemed impossible. Even in the face of Olivia's ardent speeches about everything.

He picked up his office phone and dialed Layton's number and his secretary transferred him.

"Layton Alito," he answered.

"Layton, it's Grant."

"Ah, how are things going? I want to hear all about it."

"Everything with the lawsuit is still fine. I had a meet and confer yesterday with opposing counsel, and of course I'm following your direction to stand firm on our requests."

"A meet and confer?"

"That's a fancy lawyer term for us meeting and talking about the discovery requests. The court requires that you talk to the other side and try to resolve as many disputes about documents as you can before you bring anything to the court."

"Okay, that makes sense to me."

"But that isn't exactly why I called. There's something else I want to talk about."

"What is it?"

"Olivia Murray, my opposing counsel, remember me telling you about her yesterday?"

"Of course. I did some recon on her and the firm for my benefit. Quite a large law firm. I think you were right. It shows that Astral Tech is worried about this lawsuit if they're spending that type of money on an elite firm."

"I agree. But this is about Olivia. Last night her hotel room door was vandalized. And while this isn't my area of expertise, they're talking about it being related to some type of demonic activity or something."

"That's unfortunate," Layton said flatly.

"Layton, I've got the legal aspects of this case covered."

"And that's what we're paying you for."

"But if there is something going on that is beyond that…" How in the world did he ask this question?

"I don't know what you're talking about."

"Is it possible that any employee of Optimism could've been responsible for what happened to Olivia."

Layton laughed. "Of course not. That's absurd."

"Because tactics like that would not go over well in front of a judge. Especially given the nature of the work of the companies. We want the judge to take your technology seriously and the fastest way to lose credibility is to start pulling stunts."

"You can calm down, Grant. I give you my word that I have no idea who was responsible for the vandalism, but I can tell you it wasn't one of my employees."

"Good, good." He felt better hearing the specific words come out of Layton's mouth. "I'm your lawyer. I always need you to be forthright with me so I can best protect your interests." He paused. "I'll keep you posted on case developments."

"And, Grant, I want you in court on this as soon as possible. The more we can disrupt their business the better."

"Understood."

Then he hung up. Now he had a good reason to check in with Olivia and to ease her mind about his client's involvement. He couldn't even begin to imagine her going to a judge and claiming that his client was harassing her, especially with such crazy tactics. He needed to squash this now before it got out of hand, so he dialed her cell and waited.

She picked up after a few rings.

"Hey," he said. "It's Grant."

"Hi, sorry I haven't called you. It's been a whirlwind around here today."

"First off, are you doing all right?" He hoped her answer was going to be yes.

"Yes. Just a busy day but nothing like last night obviously."

"That's one of the reasons I called. I spoke to Layton Alito. He assured me that no one at Optimism was involved."

She sighed loudly. "Grant, I appreciate you asking him. I really do. But you can't believe that he'd actually admit to you that he was doing something like that."

"Why not? I'm his lawyer."

"Yes, and that means you deal with his legal issues. The rest of his type of work is up to him and his people at Optimism."

"I think we all just need to take a big step back from this and try to be rational."

"I know what I know. I'm sorry if that doesn't fit with your view of the facts. I guess it's to be expected that we'd disagree about this just like we disagree on everything else."

"I wasn't trying to upset you." He could hear the tension dripping from her voice. "I'll send you over a letter today outlining my view of the meet and confer from yesterday."

"Look forward to it."

She ended the call before he could say anything else.

***

Olivia turned around in the conference room after feeling a light tap on her shoulder. But there was no one there. A chill shot down her arm as she surveyed the room and was clearly the only person in there. Was she imagining things?

She looked over at the clock and saw it was nine a.m. on Sunday morning. She'd been there two hours, having come in early to get some uninterrupted work done, since no one else would likely be there. But now she knew what she needed to do.

She wanted to step away and find a church service to attend. She did a quick search for churches near the office and found one that was only a couple of miles away. Before heading out, she wanted to touch base with Lizzie. She knew Lizzie wouldn't be going to church for another hour so she gave her a call.

"Olivia, I'm so glad you called," Lizzie said.

She immediately knew something was wrong. "What happened?"

"Pastor Paul had a heart attack."

She gasped. "Oh no. Is he okay?"

"Thankfully, yes. But he's taking an extended leave of absence. And since the associate pastor is also out with a back injury, they're looking for a temporary visiting pastor. I think they're going to be emailing out something to the congregation today after the service, but I'm glad I was able to tell you."

"Wow. I just can't believe it. Paul is in such great shape."

"I know. Puts everything into perspective doesn't it?"

"That's actually another reason why I called you. I really need your prayers right now. Things are getting a bit crazy here."

"Anything you want to talk about?"

"Someone drew a pentagram on my hotel room door."

"Are you serious?"

"Unfortunately so."

"Did you call the police?"

"Yes, they are saying it's an act of random vandalism, but I think it has to be connected to the work I'm doing here."

"Olivia, I think you need to come home. This is getting dangerous."

"I know, but I feel like I can't leave. I've been praying on it a lot, Lizzie, but I need your continued prayers."

"Are you going to try to find a church there?"

"Yes, actually I just looked one up that is close to the office. I'm going to leave right after we get off the phone."

"If you need anything, please call me. And keep me posted on what is going on."

"I will."

She closed up her computer and headed out. She arrived at Windy Ridge Community Church a few minutes later and let out a deep breath. It was like going home.

When she walked through the church door, she was immediately greeted by warm, smiling faces.

A man in a dark suit walked up to her. "I'm Pastor Dan Light. Feel free to just call me Dan or Pastor Dan. Welcome to Windy Ridge Community Church."

"Great to meet you. I'm Olivia Murray. I'm here in town for work, and I really wanted to find a church I can attend while staying here."

"You're welcome here for sure. Come on in, we start in less than five minutes."

She looked up into Dan's light blue eyes. His dark hair was cut short and had only the slightest thread of gray at the temple. She figured he was in his forties.

The church wasn't too large or extravagant, but it was nice. Brightly colored stained glass adorned the chapel and rows of dark oak pews filled the room. And what Olivia noticed most was that it was over half full. Knowing church attendance was in decline these days, she saw the turnout as a positive sign.

She took a seat in the middle of the church on the right side and readied herself for worship. Pleasantly surprised at the blend of traditional and contemporary worship music, she sang her heart out, finding strength in the words of the songs.

At some point, a man had taken a seat beside her. His eyes were dark brown and his blond hair hung loose touching his shoulders. There was something almost magnetic about him, pulling her toward him—but not in a romantic way. And she couldn't shake the feeling that she'd seen him before, but she couldn't place him.

Pastor Dan stood up and delivered a sermon about forgiveness that resonated with her. She was glad she'd attended Windy Ridge Community Church today. After Pastor Dan concluded the service in prayer, she looked over ready to say hello to the mystery man beside her. But he was gone. How could she have missed him getting up?

What she really needed to do was to talk to Pastor Dan. And she hoped he'd be able to talk now after the service. She walked down to the exit door where he was greeting people, but she hung back until the last person had shaken his hand.

He looked over at her. "I hoped you enjoyed the service, Olivia."

"I did. Thank you." She paused. Hopefully, he wouldn't think she was completely crazy. "I know this is bad timing, but is there any way you can meet with me now? I have some things I really need some guidance on and they're very important."

"Right now actually works great." He broke eye contact. "My wife and I used to do lunch with some of the congregation after service, but she actually passed away a few months ago so I'm still not quite sure what to do with myself."

"I'm so sorry." Her heart broke for this man.

"It's all right. She's with the Lord now. Would you like to talk over lunch?"

"Honestly, I think it might be better if we talk here so we can have privacy."

He raised an eyebrow. "Are you in some type of trouble?"

She shifted her weight from foot to foot. "Maybe, but not the kind you think."

He nodded. "Let's go into my office, and you can explain it all to me."

She was led into his spacious office that was attached to the general church office. A beige couch was positioned on one side and a big dark wood desk with multiple chairs on the other. He motioned for her to take a seat in the large maroon chair, and he sat down at his desk across from her.

"So what is troubling you?"

She took a deep breath and prayed she was doing the right thing by coming here and laying this on Pastor Dan. "I'm a lawyer. I work for a large law firm in Washington, DC. But one of our clients got sued. My client's office and the office of the company that is suing them is here in Windy Ridge. So that's why I'm here now."

"All right. I'm with you so far."

"I'm a senior associate at my firm, so I've had a lot of experience in complex high stakes litigation. I was given this case by the managing partner at the law firm. I have a lot of school debt, and I want to succeed in anything I've been given. So I did as I was instructed, and got on a plane here to start the defense of the case. I've been working out of the client's office and preparing for this first phase of the litigation."

He gently nodded encouraging her to go on.

She looked down and then back up at him. "The problem is that my client is a company named Astral Tech, and they are being sued by another company called Optimism."

Recognition flashed through his eyes. "I am very aware of those businesses."

"Then you can probably imagine where I'm going with this."

"You're struggling with how you can represent a company who engages in practices which are against your beliefs while still retaining your career and your ability to pay the bills."

"Well, there's definitely that, but if that was all it was, I probably wouldn't be keeping you from eating your lunch."

"What happened?"

"Please hear me out before you jump to any conclusions."

"I'm listening."

"And I'm sorry to put this on you. I just found out this morning that my pastor back in DC had a heart attack. So I can't take this to him right now."

"I'm sorry. Is he doing all right now?"

"The prognosis looks good, but he'll be out for a while."

"I'm here to help however I can."

"When I returned to my hotel room two nights ago, someone had drawn a pentagram on my door."

He leaned forward. She had his full attention now.

"The police said it was likely random vandalism, but I don't believe that for a second." She paused steadying herself. "I think someone associated with Optimism did that to me, and I fear it's just beginning."

"I'm so sorry, Olivia. I'm afraid that what I will tell you will only add to your concerns."

"I'd like to hear whatever you know."

"The church community here strongly believes that both businesses are tied up with the occult and demonic practices. Since the inception of Astral Tech and Optimism, the occult activity in our neighborhood has greatly increased. It comes in waves and often in a variety of different forms. We have a couple of members who are formerly associated with both organizations. And from what I can gather from my own research and discussions with those people is that these groups are very intensely involved in witchcraft and other types of dark arts. Optimism has been around for a long time in different forms. I'm more familiar with them and how dangerous they can be, but I know that Astral Tech is also an emerging threat."

"And I take it from your grim expression, that you believe in all of this. That there is this extreme evil out in the world that has the power to hurt us all."

"Absolutely. I know not all Christians believe the exact same thing when it comes to the spiritual realm, but I believe the devil is strong and uses these people to further his mission."

"A couple of times, I've almost packed up and gone back home—ready to face the consequences from management at the law firm. But I can't explain to you how much I feel something pulling me back. Wanting me to stay. And right now even though I feel like I'm in a constant state of prayer, I don't know what is best for me."

"Your faith is solid?"

"Yes. That I am certain of."

"Then the Lord may have put you here as part of His plan, Olivia."

"Every time I go into that Astral Tech office I feel the life being sucked out of me."

"The power of evil has a strong hold on that place. You're going to be up against a lot there."

"I told Nina Marie, basically the woman running the show at Astral Tech, about what happened to me. I think she's going to go after the guy Layton Alito at Optimism. There could be a dispute raging between the two groups that goes beyond this litigation."

"You can use that to your advantage. They'll be focused more on each other than on you." He ran a hand through his hair. "And I have to say this too. It's possible that you're here because you need to help someone else. Someone who otherwise might get sucked into the ways of darkness, or to save someone who already is. You need to keep your eyes and ears open at all times."

She nodded. "Will you pray for me now?"

"Of course." He walked over and they stood together. "Dear Father, please arm Olivia in this spiritual battle that she has stepped into. Lord, You brought her here. She's a strong believer, but she'll be tested and needs You now more than ever. And give her guidance to know how best to handle the situations that she will encounter. And give me strength, Lord, to provide her with any assistance that I can. In Your name, Amen."

"Thank you. And I'm sorry to dump this on you."

"Like I said before, this was already our problem as a community."

"Before I go, there's one more thing. Who was the man sitting beside me during your sermon today? He had long blond hair, dark eyes, and facial hair."

He looked at her with narrowed eyes. "What?"

"Yeah, I just really felt drawn to him and was hoping I'd be able to talk to him a bit but by the time the final prayer was over, he'd just up and gone."

"Wow," he said. "Olivia, I looked over at you multiple times during the sermon. There was never a man sitting beside you."

"Are you certain?"

"Absolutely."

Her heartbeat sped up, "Dear Lord."

"Thank you, Lord, is more like it. The angels are around you, Olivia. They're readying for battle too."

Her eyes filled with tears overwhelmed by it all. "I don't even know what to say."

He grabbed her hand. "*The Lord is my light and my salvation; whom shall I fear?*"

***

Nina Marie watched as Clive organized everyone in the large basement of his house. Before they got down to work, he needed to debrief the group on what had happened.

Clive stood to address everyone. Tonight represented a full compilation of believers in the Astral Tech way. Those that practiced witchcraft, those who just sought some type of holistic spiritual way, and then the powerful but smaller group who focused more on worshipping the evil one.

The entire Astral Tech staff was present. But there were plenty of people who were a part of the group who weren't on staff. Teachers, doctors, judges, customer service workers. It was a diverse group, many of whom, because of their professions operated under a cloak of secrecy. Others in the community didn't know of their affiliation with Astral Tech.

"Let's get started," Clive said. "I wanted to gather everyone here today to explain certain facts that have come to our attention that are very disconcerting."

To the outside observer who had preconceived notions about the occult, it may have seemed like a strange scene. There were no black cloaks or sacrifices. No burning of incense or fanciful candles tonight.

No, the Astral Tech way was different. More advanced and technological, but no less powerful. If anything, the type of army that Astral Tech was assembling would be unbeatable. Even against Optimism. This gathering looked like a group of professionals chatting after a dinner party.

"What's going on?" Matt Tinley asked. His brown eyes were filled with suspicion.

Nina Marie had thought it better for Clive to tell all the employees at once so she hadn't filled Matt in. He would most likely be upset for being left out since he was a member of the executive leadership team. Matt knew he was clearly number three in the pecking order and it bothered him.

"We believe that we are under a direct attack from Optimism." Clive's loud voice boomed through the basement.

"We all know that. They've filed a lawsuit," Matt said. A few other mumbles filled the room.

Clive shook his head. "No, Matt. It's much more than that. For the benefit of everyone in the room, I'll give a little background. We've hired the law firm of Brown, Carter, and Reed out of Washington, DC to defend us in the lawsuit filed by Optimism. The firm has sent out a senior attorney named Olivia Murray to work out of our offices and lead our defense in this stage of the litigation."

"Is she one of us?" Marta Lynch, one of the elder Astral Tech members asked.

"No, she's not. But she's a great attorney. Although now the game appears to have changed." He took a few steps closer to the group. "Olivia returned to her hotel room the other night to find a pentagram drawn on her door."

A few surprised sounds echoed throughout the room as people started talking amongst themselves. "Quiet, everyone. We need to focus here."

"You think Optimism is going after our lawyer?" Matt asked.

"To put it simply, yes. An attack on two fronts, legal and spiritual. And what better way to weaken us than to spook our attorney. The vandalism itself was a bit cliché but clearly contemplated with the purpose of trying to send a signal. If she quits the case, that puts us at a strategic disadvantage. Then another lawyer would have to get up to speed which would cost us precious time and energy in the vigorous defense our of case."

"More than that, though," Marta said. "They're trying to send us a strong message that they're out for blood. They won't rest until we're annihilated, or they've taken away members of Astral Tech and converted them into their group. They've always hated our approach. They see us as too progressive and inclusive. This lawsuit is just another mechanism for them to attack us."

"That's true," Clive said. "Nina Marie and I have started strategizing, and we believe that the best approach is a highly aggressive one using all tools at our disposal." He motioned throughout the room. "Tonight is the first night of a long battle. But one we have to win."

"Clive's right." Nina Marie stood from her spot in the corner of the room and addressed the crowd. Clive had laid out the initial thoughts, but now the operational details were up to her. "Everyone will be responsible for playing a role in this. We also need to keep our numbers strong. If there was ever a time you thought you could successfully bring another member in, now is the time to do it. The evil one is with us, but he's a fickle master.

We must keep pleasing him to keep his favor. The dark forces are surrounding us, but we have to be more aggressive in calling on them to help us. Our primary target is Layton Alito. He is Optimism. If he falls, then their house crumbles."

"Right," Clive added. "And even though he'll have a strong cloak of protection, with a concerted effort we can break through it."

"What are we going to do about this lawyer girl?" Marta asked. "I'm getting a very uneasy feeling about her just based on your description. How do we know we can trust an outsider who doesn't believe like we do?"

"She cares too much about her job and her professional reputation to cause any problems," Nina Marie said. "I've got her under control so everyone else can concentrate on their tasks. She isn't the one who is a threat to us right now. Believe me, I'd know if she were. For our strategic purposes, she's a member of our team."

"We can't afford to take our eyes off Layton," Matt said. "This really is a battle of old versus new. That's why he could never make the app as successful as we have been able to. We have technical capabilities that they don't. They rely purely on past methods of warfare. That's where we have the strategic advantage."

"For those who want to join, let's have a group prayer," Clive said. "Then we can break off into our respective teams and plan our strategy."

Nina Marie listened as Clive reached out to the evil one. It was true that not every member of Astral Tech actively participated in this type of worship. Some chose to see themselves as gods. But the end result was the same. A group of powerful people who were drawn to forces of darkness. She allowed herself to let go and be submersed by the evil that surrounded her. By the end of this thing, Optimism would be defeated…and she would be in charge of Astral Tech.

***

Pastor Dan sat in the church conference room surrounded by his leadership team. He felt like he needed to tell them what he had learned from Olivia. He was still grieving from the death of his beloved wife, but right now he had to turn his attention to this newly cemented threat.

"Thanks for staying after Sunday night service. There's something I wanted to make everyone aware of related to our long standing problems with the occult in our community."

After he filled them in on what he knew, he got ready for questions. He knew there would be some after what he had just laid out for the group.

"What's your read on the attorney?" Chris Tanner, the associate pastor, asked.

"I think she's afraid, but very steadfast in her faith. I also think she has a very strong spiritual connection. Especially after she saw the angel this morning in church."

"Let's not get ahead of ourselves," Sofia Garcia said. She pulled her dark hair up into a makeshift bun. "All we know is that she thought she saw someone sitting beside her, and that you didn't see the person. But you were focused on preaching. We can't just assume she saw an angel. For all we know, this woman made it up. This was her first time walking into our church. I don't think we should automatically think everything she says is truthful."

"I know you're skeptical about this," Chris said, "and that is completely understandable, but we can't dismiss her, Sofia. There's a reason why she's here even if we're not fully sure of her intentions or her story." The former Army Ranger was always on guard.

"Chris is right," Beverly Jenkins added. "I know I'm just an accountant by trade and not a theologian, but I've been going to this church since I was born. I believe we have a strong spiritual body here. The Lord wants to take care of us, but we have a responsibility to this community."

"Where does that leave us then?" Sofia asked.

"I want everyone to start praying for Olivia because I think she's going to need it. And if there is some evil battle brewing between Astral Tech and Optimism we need to be ready for an uptick in demonic activity within our community. I haven't decided whether we should bring this to the entire church body yet or wait until we see how it starts playing out. We can vote on that now or later if you prefer."

"I think we wait to tell the church body anything," Sofia said. "But I guess my view is obvious." She paused. "Also, if these two groups are set on annihilating each other, why wouldn't we just step back and let them do it? Less trouble for us. Wouldn't it be better to have only one group left instead of two?"

Dan shook his head. "Because they've already started targeting true believers, and they're not going to stop. They gain their strength from spreading their evil. I see this as a consolidation of power, but not anything less dangerous."

"Dan is absolutely right," Chris said. "They're a cancer in our community, and they take every opportunity to bring us down by spreading their beliefs. And now that they have that app for phones and computers they can reach every person in Windy Ridge and beyond. Especially the younger demographic that are always on their phones and computers."

"That's a good point," Dan said. "We need to make sure our youth groups are protected. Sofia, since you're in charge of the youth ministry, I'll leave that up to you as how best to proceed."

Sofia nodded. "We actually haven't talked to them about the Astral Tech app since it first came out. So I need to make sure that they're aware of all of the dangers of it."

"And to do that, we as a church need to ensure that we understand it as well. I think our core leadership group is comfortable enough with technology to figure it out, but everyone needs to take a look at the features on it and be prepared to take action against what they might use it for."

"Why should we buy it though?" Beverly asked. "Isn't that just adding money to their coffers?"

Dan nodded. "Good point, Bev. I'll purchase a copy and do a deep dive on it then report back to the group on everything."

"Are you sure you should be spending your time doing that?" Sofia asked.

"I told you, Sofia. I have a feeling about this. The Lord brought Olivia into this church. And I think we have a role in this fight. A critical role."

"So where are we on telling the congregation?" Chris asked.

"I think we should next Sunday," Beverly said. "That will give Dan enough time to review the app more closely."

"All in favor of that?" Dan asked.

Every hand went up—even Sofia's.

"Great," Dan said. "We can't let the forces of darkness take over Windy Ridge. We must get ready for battle."

CHAPTER FOUR

The weeks flew by with each side in the lawsuit feverishly working on reviewing documents. Olivia readied herself for the scheduling conference in front of the judge based on an aggressive motion that Grant had filed citing her stalling tactics. But he was the one being unreasonable. Yeah, she'd given the standard excuses for why it was taking her some time to produce the documents, but they were legitimate.

Grant was also seeking to push for a very quick timetable for trial once the discovery period was finished. So this hearing was really important and would set the pace of the case.

With each passing day, she felt more beaten down. No matter how much sleep she tried to get. And sleep was a problem too. Her dreams were becoming more and more troublesome.

So as she walked into the courthouse wearing a classic navy pantsuit and sensible heels, she tried to think about the positive. And that was that this judge was probably going to be much more annoyed at Grant for filing this frivolous motion for a scheduling conference and motion to compel at this stage in the litigation.

She walked into the courtroom and saw that Grant was already sitting in the back row. They had a ten a.m. calendar call, but another judge was currently hearing other cases.

Taking a seat on the bench right beside him, he looked at her and smiled. They both knew better than to talk in the courtroom so they sat quietly waiting their turn.

When their case was called, they approached their respective counsel tables. Their assigned judge had an emergency, and the court clerk let them know that for the purposes of this hearing today, the on call judge was presiding.

"I'm Judge Louise Martinique," the older woman with her long gray hair pulled into a tight bun said. "I'll be hearing your arguments regarding the scheduling order and motion to compel today while Judge Wingfield is out of town due to a personal issue."

Olivia made eye contact with the judge and the hair on her arms started to rise. Suddenly a wave of coolness flooded over her. She hadn't had a case of bad nerves in front of a judge since her first courtroom appearance many years ago. And this wasn't going to be a difficult hearing.

But after Grant argued his motion and it was her turn, she stood behind the podium. Silence rang throughout the courtroom. A serious case of nerves seized her. She could barely speak. It was as if someone was gripping onto her neck, and she couldn't get the necessary air. Fear filled her heart and a bead of sweat formed on her brow. Her body flashed from cold to hot.

"Do you need a few more minutes, Ms. Murray?" Judge Martinique asked.

"No, Your Honor."

The judge nodded for her to proceed. And finally she could actually breathe again. She'd never had a panic attack before, but she wondered if what she experienced was how it felt.

An hour later, they were walking out of the courtroom, and she couldn't believe what had happened. The judge had sided with Grant. It seemed impossible given the facts, but it was like the judge wasn't even hearing a word she said. Once she was finally able to get the words out, and that part was still bothering her.

Judge Martinique had also set a three month discovery period to commence immediately with a trial to come shortly after although that date was still to be determined.

"Tough day, huh?" Grant asked.

"You can wipe the smug grin from your face." She walked quickly, anxious to get away from him. "If I didn't know any better, I would think you had bribed the judge."

He laughed. "That's a pretty serious charge, Olivia. Maybe it had more to do with the fact I was right and that you could barely present your weak case."

She felt her cheeks flush. "I don't know what happened at the beginning. I have never experienced any issues speaking in court."

"Happens to everyone. Like I said, maybe it was because you knew your arguments were weak."

"Weak?" A strong gust of wind had her tucking her hair behind her ear. "Don't you mean entirely reasonable? What judge grants a motion to compel document production this soon? These things take time. You know how it works. She was relying on a very literal interpretation of the discovery rules."

He grinned. "Let me buy you lunch. It's the least I can do."

"Why would you think I'd want to spend more time with you after how that hearing just went?"

"Because you enjoy spending time with me when I'm not in scorched earth mode. I'm funny, charming and witty."

"You are so full of yourself, Grant."

"Of course I am, but I'm also good company when I want to be. Don't be a spoilsport." He tugged on her arm. "Come on. I'm paying."

She relented mainly because she was starving and not necessarily because she wanted to spend more time with Grant Baxter.

At the restaurant, she almost salivated when the server placed the huge gourmet cheeseburger and steak cut French fries in front of her. And she planned on enjoying every bite. Once she had ordered the burger, he did the same.

"So have you had any more issues?" he asked.

"Nothing like what happened before." She questioned how much she should share with him. Their relationship was strange in that he was her opposing counsel, but there was also a lot of other stuff going on that made things much more complicated than normal.

"I'm sensing a but here?" He popped a French fry in his mouth after he slathered it with ketchup.

"I can't pinpoint one thing, but I just know that things are off with me. Especially while I'm in the office, but it's not just there. It's getting to be all the time."

He raised an eyebrow. "Next thing you're going to say is that your loss today was because of these spiritual forces."

She shook her head. "It's not nice to mock me. You were there that night at the hotel. You saw exactly what I saw."

He immediately frowned and put down his burger. "You're right. I shouldn't make light of what happened at the hotel." He paused. "But is it possible that you've let it get into your head? Sometimes after a traumatic event, that can happen."

She took a bite of her burger and carefully considered his statement. "Honestly, Grant, I would prefer this to be my mind playing tricks on me, but I know deep down that's not it."

"How do you know?"

She took a deep breath. "It's just a feeling, but one so strong that I can't just deny its existence."

"Once again, you're jumping way out of my realm here. But I admit I'm really intrigued by hearing your thoughts. I see you as a very professional, smart, and rational person."

"Uh, that sounds like a compliment but not really?"

"It's just a bit inconsistent to me. What I'm trying to say is because you are so level headed, it's strange to me that you'd have this emotional and spiritual side that would be so strong."

She nodded. "I've always had it, though, for as long as I can remember. When I was growing up, I felt so connected to my faith. And the flip side of that is being afraid of very real threats to my faith."

"You're talking about demons or ghosts or something?"

"Demons, yes. Probably not in the sense that you're thinking, though. Not red tailed beings with pitchforks sitting on our shoulder trying to get us to sin."

"Then what is it?"

"I believe there are angels and demons. Forces of the Lord that are supremely good. And then those forces of evil that come from the evil one—the devil himself."

"Are you talking about tangible beings that you can see with your own eyes?"

"Most often they are invisible, but there are instances where people have actually seen them."

"Where are you getting these ideas from?"

"The Bible. There's a key verse in Ephesians. It says: *For we wrestle not against flesh and blood, but against principalities, against powers, against the rulers of the darkness of this world, against spiritual wickedness in high places.*"

He leaned back in his chair. "That sounds quite ominous. Rulers of the darkness? Like a horror or sci-fi movie?"

"It is ominous, but it's not like the movies. The bottom line is that there are invisible forces at work here on this earth—both good and evil. They're all around us. Even now."

"How can you tell which is which? Especially if you're saying they are invisible most of the time."

"That's a very discerning question for you to ask. It's not always so cut and dry because evil forces can attempt to masquerade as good ones. But the most basic answer to your question is a very strong foundation of faith that allows one to tell the difference. And like I said, for me, the evil forces sap the life out of me. Fill me with depressing and dark thoughts. The devil comes at people in many different forms, but the outcome is the same."

"That's an awful way to live. Like you're trying to fight off forces of evil? And you live like this every single day?"

"No, it isn't really like that. When I was very young, I had some issues with all of this. But then it basically faded away. Of course, everyone faces struggles in their lives, but this is different. I haven't felt this type of aggressive spiritual opposition against me since I was a young girl."

"And you think it's all connected to the work we're doing here?"

She nodded. "I absolutely do. And I know that you don't believe your client is involved, and that's just a point on which we'll have to disagree."

"I'm sorry you feel badly, but at least nothing else threatening has happened to you. I'd take that as a positive."

"For now it is."

"So, enough about all of that. Was being a big firm lawyer always your plan?" he asked.

She laughed. "It was my plan based on necessity from student loans. I enjoy the work, but I don't feel passionate about it like I do other areas of the law."

"Like what?"

"I participated in a domestic violence clinic in law school for a semester. It really changed my life. Once I can pay off my student loans, I would love to shift from the big corporate law firm practice to using my legal skills to help those who have been victims of domestic violence. I'd even love to start my own clinic."

He leaned forward. "That's sounds like a very difficult path."

"It may be, but it's one I feel strongly about. And what about you? Are you going to stay in plaintiff's work for the long haul?"

He nodded. "That's my intention. My firm is starting to flourish, and it's an amazing thing to see something I worked so hard for come to fruition."

"You should be proud of that. It's quite an accomplishment."

"Thank you." He smiled.

They finished up lunch and, as promised, he picked up the check.

"I guess I owe you documents now, given the judge's order." She sighed. "But she gave me seven days to comply, and it will take me the full seven."

"I'm sure it will." He grinned.

***

While Layton had developed the New Age app that Nina Marie had stolen, in his dark heart he still believed the best way to bring people to the evil one was through old-fashioned means of power and persuasion.

And right now he had his sights set on the young strawberry haired woman who had visited the Indigo bookstore each week for the past month. She obviously had an interest in the books that Indigo carried—everything from New Age to more substantial books on witchcraft and demonic worship. His best subjects were those that were drawn to the New Age philosophy. New Age was like a gateway drug—and a beautiful and effective one at that.

He didn't really believe in the more traditional New Age crap that was out there about cleansing the body and mind. No, he believed in the darker arts. Those were the ones that gave him power and prestige—both within his group and outside. And those were the powers that it took to get rid of his predecessor once and for all and to gain the top position at Optimism.

It was time to make his move on this unsuspecting woman engrossed in the stacks. He walked further into the bookstore and smiled at Morena. She worked part time at Indigo and also just happened to be one of his best members. Her long curly blonde hair fell softly over her shoulders. To anyone else she looked dainty and pretty. But he knew better. Morena could be lethal if it was required.

It helped to have people everywhere. It also helped that he could use his good looks and charms on naïve women. He'd pegged his target correctly as he fixed his eyes on her. She stood reading a book in the New Age metaphysical section. As he drew closer to her, he guessed that she might actually be college age as opposed to high school. For his purposes, that was even better.

"Reading anything good there?" he asked.

Startled, she looked up at him with big blue eyes. A dusting of freckles covered her small turned up nose. He immediately flashed his best smile to disarm her. He was also counting on some help from Morena who was nearby. She had great powers of persuasion and really connected with other young women.

"I could spend all day in here," he said. Then he waited to see if he would get a response.

When her eyes softened and she smiled, he knew it was game over. Too bad because he enjoyed a little challenge.

"Yeah, after I found this place, I just keep coming back," she said. She gripped onto a book tightly. "So many things to read and so little time. Especially with my course load."

"You're in college?"

"Yeah. Windy Ridge Community College. How about you?"

Wow, could he really pass for a college student? Doubtful. And he shouldn't start the lies just yet. Especially about something like this. "No, I actually have my own business."

Her eyes lit up. "I'm majoring in business."

This was far too easy and as Morena winked at him, he took another deep breath. Knowing Morena, she had been practicing her witchcraft on this woman, probably for weeks, now to soften her up. "If you're interested in the New Age subject matter, then you would probably be quite intrigued with my company. It's called Optimism, and we provide a variety of New Age services including the latest technologies."

"Really?"

"Sure. Would you be interested in an internship?"

Her breath caught. "You can't be serious."

"Why not? You're obviously motivated. We could use more people like you in the company." And that was the truth. He could see the fire brewing in her eyes.

"I'm Stacey Malone." She outstretched her hand, and he took it carefully into his own.

"Layton Alito. I'm CEO of Optimism. Nice to meet you." He pulled a card out of his jacket pocket. "Call this number to set up coming into the office. We can work around your class schedule."

"Thank you, Mr. Alito. I won't let you down."

"I'll hold you to that, Stacey. And please, just call me Layton."

He turned around and walked out of Indigo. His plans were falling into place. His cell rang, and he saw it was Louise calling.

"How did it go today?" he asked.

She laughed. "It was priceless actually seeing her reaction to me. She is strong, no doubt. But I caught her off guard, and she had no conception of what was happening to her. I gave her a negative ruling, too, so that should add fuel to her stresses regarding the lawsuit."

"A defensible ruling I hope?"

"Of course. You don't have to tell me how to do my job."

"Good. I can't afford to lose you and what you bring to the table."

"I trust other preparations are going well?"

"Yes. And I think it's time to start testing Olivia more. We need to know just how capable she is."

"Do you need any help with that?"

"No. I've got it under control. I'll keep you posted." He ended the call. Louise was a great ally.

It was time to put Olivia Murray to the test.

***

Olivia walked out of Astral Tech and sucked in a breath of fresh air. That place was continuing to take it out of her. But the good news was that she had the first wave of documents identified to hand over to Grant based on the court's unexpected order.

Although two could play at this game. She wasn't going to turn them over until the deadline, and she'd drafted up her own very aggressive requests. He wasn't the only one who could litigate hardball style.

The Chicago summer breeze hit her cheeks as she walked toward the car. She hummed to herself and was thankful to be out of the office for the day.

As she took another step, a tremendous pain hit her. Engulfing her body and causing her to moan. Like a punch to the gut. She stopped and crouched down to the ground in the parking lot as searing pain shot through her from the top of her head to the bottom of her feat. She tried to scream but no words came out.

It was like at the courthouse but so much worse. Being held in a chokehold that she couldn't get out of. An ever tightening grip around her neck. Her world became dark with the fog of evil threatening her life. Awful wailing flooded her ears, and the pain enveloped her entire body. Her pulse thumped strongly.

She was under attack. It hadn't been since she was eleven years old that she felt something this evil coming after her. The difference was that this felt much stronger than when she'd been attacked as a child. But she'd fought this battle before, and she had no doubts that she was on the winning side. She couldn't let the forces of evil overtake her.

Pushing herself up to her feet, she prepared for this fight. Pain emanated throughout her body, and she knew what she needed to do. Standing firm, she rebuked the powers of darkness in the name of Jesus.

A loud shriek sounded in her head. But then she was able to breathe again and was no longer in pain. The wind whipped up, blowing her hair as she looked all around her, searching for anyone. But nobody was in sight. No, she was fighting an invisible enemy.

Quickly, she walked the rest of the way to her Jeep and got in. Steadying herself she took a few deep breaths. Then she jumped when she saw the man sitting in her passenger seat. But it wasn't just any man. It was the long blond haired man with the beard from church.

"Don't be afraid," he said. His deep voice calming, and his dark eyes filled with compassion. "I'm Micah."

"I'm not afraid of you." She knew with all of her heart that she had nothing to fear from this man. This angel.

"I'm sorry about what happened out there. But they're going to test you. You need to know that you can handle it. You can fight back. Just like you did this time."

"I've fought before. Years ago."

He smiled and the kindness touched his eyes. "I know. I was with you then, too."

"Really?" Thoughts flashed through her mind. Memories of seeing this man decades ago in her dreams. That's why he seemed familiar to her.

"Yes."

"But why me? Why now? I have so many questions. Do I need to go back to DC and get away from all of this?"

"No. You are not to leave Windy Ridge."

"Really? Why not?"

"God has chosen you, Olivia, for a very important fight. A spiritual battle that threatens this entire community and beyond. If the forces of evil are not defeated here, they pose a threat greater than we've seen in years."

So the Lord had put her there for a reason. "What can you tell me about what I'm up against?"

"Both groups are very strong. Astral Tech is utilizing cutting edge methods, but Optimism is relying on the oldest lies and tactics out there."

"Nina Marie is very involved isn't she?"

"Yes. Her, Clive, and Matt, though she is the strongest and most focused on the task. Plus a group of others that follow them. But at this point, they aren't coming after you. That will change, and even if they end up helping you, don't ever mistake the fact that they are the enemy."

"I understand."

"But the immediate battle is the one against Layton Alito and Optimism."

"Then why do I feel so awful in the Astral Tech offices if they aren't targeting me?"

"Demons and evil forces thrive there. And those forces are doing everything they can to try to sway you to the darkness. Each day, trying to break you down. But so far they haven't even been able to touch you. Although they're very persistent and will keep on trying. Their goal is to try to bring you over to the their side to help in the fight against Optimism."

"Am I strong enough for this?"

"You won't be fighting alone. I'll be with you along with other angels. Also go to Pastor Dan. Let him know everything we've discussed."

She nodded. "Of course."

"There's one more thing that's very important."

"What?"

"Grant Baxter is also vital to this mission."

"Grant? He's not a believer in anything."

Micah smiled. "Not yet. But that's where you come in. You have to find a way to break through to him without pushing him away. Because we really need him for this fight."

"But how?" She looked down and back up. Micah was gone.

She drove straight to Windy Ridge Community Church and prayed that Pastor Dan was there.

***

Nina Marie stood staring out the window of her office at Astral Tech trying to get a handle on the events that had just transpired. She'd almost run outside, thinking that Olivia was having a heart attack or something. But then she'd gotten a whiff of Layton and knew that he was responsible for this attack.

She'd watched with interest as Olivia had a long conversation by herself in her car. It was strange, and Nina Marie thought she might have been on her phone hands free. But it also occurred to her that Olivia might have been praying.

What intrigued her even more, though, was how Olivia fought back against the evil onslaught. Nina Marie had vastly underestimated Olivia's strength. She'd recognized Olivia's Christian devotion, but hadn't realized that she was so spiritually gifted. In the short term, that would be a tremendous benefit. As long as Olivia didn't decide to turn against her own client, everything would be okay.

It was time to level the playing field. If Layton thought he could attack the Astral Tech lawyer at will, he was sorely mistaken.

She had to fill Clive in on this latest troubling development. Not wasting any time, she drove over to his house since he wasn't in the office.

After he ushered her in, she watched as Clive took a big sip of his dark-colored drink. Who knows what concoction he had put together and how many different types of liquor he had in there. He'd begun to drink a lot lately, and Nina Marie worried that he might not have his head in the game to go against Layton and the others. Although the minute that Clive really faltered, she would step up and fill the void. So if he wanted to drink himself to death, what could she really do?

Right now though she wanted his attention. Because as long as he was technically in charge, he needed to be fighting this thing with all of his energy. They sat in his formal study which was one of her favorite rooms in Clive's expansive house in Windy Ridge. Definitely one of the nicest in the neighborhood. The dark oak desk was accented by tall ornate bookcases. The maroon rug on the floor was an import—one of kind. And the other furniture was just as expensive and unique. Only the best for Clive. Including the fancy antique chair she sat in that had been reupholstered to match the rug.

"What was so urgent that you came running over here and interrupting my evening relaxation time?" he asked.

"It's about our lawyer."

"What about her? I think she's been doing a great job so far. I was assured by Chet that she was their superstar attorney." He downed more of his drink.

"That's not the issue. I told you that she was being targeted by Optimism."

He swirled his drink. "Yes, and there's more?"

She leaned forward to prop her arms up on his oak desk. "I actually just witnessed her being spiritually assaulted right outside of our office."

"What? Are you sure?"

"Absolutely. But it isn't the attack that freaked me out, Clive. It was her response."

"How so?"

"I knew there was something a bit off with her, but now I'm convinced I know why she's made me uncomfortable. She fought him off a like a battle hardened warrior. I've never seen anything quite like that."

He laughed. "Now isn't that ironic. We have ourselves a Christian attorney do we?"

Nina Marie shook her head. "Not just a Christian who pops into church on holidays." Nina Marie stood up and clenched her fists. How was she going to get through to Clive?

"What are you trying to tell me, Nina Marie?"

"This girl is very powerful. If she was strong enough to ward off a direct attack orchestrated by Layton—and I'm sure that's who was behind this—then who knows what else she could do?"

"If she's that strong in her faith, she's not going to work with us—even if it is against Optimism."

"No, she's not. I'm worried about her turning on us."

Clive laughed. He stood up and walked over to her and wrapped his arm around her shoulder. "My dear, Nina Marie. I think all the stress from the lawsuit is getting to you. There's no way one woman can take us down. Most certainly not both of our organizations. We've got hundreds of members between the two groups. Years of experience. It will take a lot more than one short little lawyer to bring down our empires."

She took a step back from his grasp. "I don't think you're taking this seriously enough. I know what I know."

"As do I. I'm not saying we just let her run rampant. We should protect ourselves, but as long as she's focused on winning the lawsuit and is doing her job, that is my top priority. It's our jobs to concentrate on the spiritual aspect of the battle against Optimism."

"You're not listening to me."

"I am. I'm telling you that you're wrong. Olivia Murray is not the enemy. Not now and probably not ever. Now get out of here before you totally ruin the rest of my night. Your target is Layton Alito. Execute on that directive and everything will be fine."

"You should know that I'm planning on engaging in some pay back against their attorney tonight."

"That's more like it. How do you think that will go?"

"He'll have no idea what's happening. I almost feel sorry for the guy." She laughed thinking about how much fun it would be. "Unlike Olivia, he has no spiritual foundation at all. A total blank slate. A non threat as far as I'm concerned. Although he could be a fun diversion."

"Good enough. Why don't you tend to him, and I'll see in you in the office tomorrow." He turned around and went back to sit in his chair behind the desk.

She wasn't a woman to sit back and take orders. She'd bide her time, but there was no way she was going to assume that Olivia wasn't a threat. Because she knew deep in her gut that she was the biggest threat they would face. Maybe not tomorrow. But eventually they'd be at war with their own attorney.

CHAPTER FIVE

Grant walked into his house and was ready for a big dinner and a night of relaxing in front of the TV. Maybe he'd order Chinese food with some fat noodles and greasy egg rolls. He'd been hitting the gym every morning, so in his mind he deserved something totally unhealthy.

Throwing his keys on the table, he stopped short as he entered the living room. A shadow caught his eye. Was someone in his house? That couldn't be possible. He'd armed his security system today and had just turned it off.

Instinctively, he rushed to the kitchen and grabbed the biggest knife he could find. He had a gun for personal protection, but it was locked up in his bedroom. There's no way he could get to it now.

Taking slow and deliberate steps, he moved toward the living room where he had seen the shadow. He started to sweat as the temperature in the room became inexplicably hot.

Scanning the room, he didn't see anyone. He took in a few deep breaths, realizing that his mind was probably playing serious tricks on him. Maybe he was coming down with the flu.

Then he felt something grab onto his wrist so tightly that he dropped the knife. It hit the dark hardwood living room floor with a resounding thud.

"What in the world?" he said out loud. A wave of nausea washed over him as flashes of light filled his vision making him entirely disoriented. "Leave me alone."

He didn't even know who or what he was talking to. But something was in that house with him. "I said, leave me alone," he shouted as loud as he could.

Then he could've sworn that he heard a woman's laughter right in his ear.

Suddenly the room temperature dropped back to normal and the sickness lifted off of him.

To say he was freaked out was an understatement. Confused, he picked up the knife off the floor and walked back toward the kitchen.

He took a seat at the table now not so hungry for Chinese food. Pulling out his cell, he dialed Olivia. Yeah, she would think he was crazy, but he had this nagging desire to talk to her. Maybe she could tell him he was imagining things. Or something.

He just knew that he had to talk to her.

"Hello," she answered.

"Olivia, it's Grant." His voice was ragged as he tried to keep his breathing in check. He wiped a bead of sweat off his brow.

"Are you okay?" she asked.

"No. I'm not. I'm not feeling well."

"Where are you? What happened?"

"I'm at home, and I have no idea what happened. You're going to think I've been doing drugs or something. But I can't even explain it."

"What's your address? I'm coming over there."

"Right now?"

"Yes."

He rattled off his address.

"We're on our way right now."

"We?"

"Yes, I have Pastor Dan with me."

"I don't know if that's a great idea."

"Yes, it is. Just hold tight."

He hung up and the pressure built at his temples. He couldn't even begin to process what had happened. Clearly, he was ill. He had to be. Sitting in a daze, he was broken out of it when the doorbell rang.

Jumping up, he went over to the door. Olivia walked in with a man at her side. He was probably in his late thirties or early forties with dark hair that was slightly graying.

"Grant, this is Pastor Dan Light from Windy Ridge Community Church."

Dan outstretched his hand, and Grant shook it. "Please come in."

He directed them to the kitchen because he didn't want to go back into the living room right now.

They took a seat around his large kitchen table.

"What happened?" Olivia asked with eyes wide.

"It's going to sound completely psychotic."

Dan shook his head. "Don't even worry about that. Just explain what happened as best you can as you experienced it."

Trying to pull himself together, he went to the refrigerator and pulled out sodas for the three of them. Then he sat back down after popping the soda top and taking a huge gulp. *Here goes nothing.*

"I got home from work ready to order dinner. I put my keys down and walked into the living room. A movement caught my eye. Like a shadow. I didn't think anyone could actually be inside the house because of my alarm system. But out of an abundance of caution, I came into the kitchen and grabbed a large steak knife. I made my way back to the living room." He stopped and took another a sip of soda. He wasn't even thirsty, just nervous.

"You're doing fine," Olivia said.

"Anyway, I was standing there, and I started sweating. It felt like an oven. And that came out of nowhere. I always keep it really cool in here. Then the craziest thing of all happened. Something grabbed onto my wrist. So hard. Strong enough to make me drop the knife. At this point, I was about to lose it. I yelled out to leave me alone. I don't even know who or what I was yelling at. Then I heard a woman laugh. It was so clear right in my ear. And just like that it all ended. The room cooled down quickly. I picked up the knife and came into the kitchen and called you. What in the world happened here?"

"Grant," she said. "We're under attack."

"What do you mean?" he asked.

"Olivia also had an experience when she left the Astral Tech office today," Dan said.

"Are you all right?"

"Yes, but something came at me pretty hard. Like a punch to the gut. Debilitating pain. A chokehold. I fought back."

Grant shook his head. "I'm lost. There has to be a rational explanation for what is happening to us. Like some sort of virus we both have that is making us delusional. Maybe we should go to the hospital and get checked out."

"Grant, unfortunately a hospital isn't going to help you. You're in the middle of a spiritual warfare situation here," Dan said. "We believe that each company is going after the other's lawyers. That makes you a target of Astral Tech and Olivia a target of Optimism."

"That just seems like a big stretch. Even if I were to consider the hypothetical that a spiritual realm existed. These are legitimate corporations. Isn't that a bit unbelievable?" Grant asked.

"Unfortunately, it's all too real," Dan said. "Olivia let me know your background, and I can imagine that you're very disturbed by all of this and in a state of disbelief."

"You better believe it. You want me to think that I'm being attacked by an evil sprit. I don't know how to comprehend something like that. It's completely outside my mental capability at the moment. I think it's more likely that I was suffering from a fever or something." He touched his own forehead. "See, I'm still sweating."

"I know you're a skeptic when it comes to faith, Grant. But right now, you need to start to reconsider," Olivia said.

"I've never been more confused in my life. Like any minute, I'm going to wake up from a long deluded dream and say, man, that was crazy. But I'm still not ready to take any type of leap to the supernatural. It makes me think it was some physical ailment. That is the most logical explanation. A virus and a fever."

She reached out and grabbed his hand. "I'm sorry, Grant, but this isn't a bad dream. It's real life. We're in the middle of this dispute between our clients and now it's turning ugly. You have the ability to step away from this though. You're your own boss. You could withdraw from the litigation. It would be the safest thing for you to do. It would provide you with ultimate protection. There'd be no reason for anyone to come after you if you aren't involved with the case as Optimism's lawyer."

"I've never withdrawn from a case in all the years I've been practicing law."

"But you've never dealt with anything like this either," Dan said. "You have a way out now if you want to take it. If you don't though, you're going to need to start thinking about how to fend off these attacks."

"Let's play out your hypothetical just for the sake of argument. Even if I were to believe your position here, then why can't we reason with them? Tell them to cut it out, start acting like professionals or we're both out of here," Grant said.

"You're assuming that the business is the most important thing to them," she said. "And it's not. They have a much larger and sinister plan."

Yeah, in a moment of weakness he had called Olivia, but now he was thinking it hadn't been the best idea. He would just have to man up and deal with this on his own in a way that made sense to him. "Thank you both for coming over. I really appreciate it. But now that I've calmed down, I think I just need to be alone to try to wrap my head around everything."

She nodded. "Would you be okay with us praying for you before we go."

At this point, he didn't believe in prayer, but it was easier to agree than argue with them. "All right."

"Pastor Dan, why don't you lead us in prayer?" she asked.

Grant kept his eyes open even though they closed theirs.

"Dear Lord, first thank You for keeping Olivia and Grant safe today through some pretty scary situations. They're going to need You to be by their side each step of the way. We know that we are in a battle against the devil and those who do his bidding, but You are stronger than all of that. I pray a special prayer of protection and guidance for Grant, Lord. That You may open his heart to Your Word and Your everlasting love. And for Olivia, continue to give her the wisdom to do Your work. The fight is long from over and we all need You. In Your name we pray, amen."

Grant watched as Olivia opened up her eyes and looked back at him. She was unlike any woman he'd ever met. And the way she was facing down this situation right now made him respect her even more. Even though he didn't really believe in all that she did. The way she stood by her beliefs was admirable.

"We'll be going, but if you need anything just call me," she said.

"And here's my card with my cell number." Dan handed him the card. "Don't ever hesitate to contact me day or night. This is more than a job for me, it's my calling. So I'm here for you. Even if you're unsure right now, that is perfectly normal. You're not used to being exposed to these forces. They are powerful though, Grant. I just want you to be on guard."

Grant was fascinated by Dan. Like Olivia, he was steadfast in his Christian faith. Grant led them out the front door and locked it behind them. But there was a tiny voice in his head telling him that no locks or alarm system would keep him safe from the forces that had come after him today.

Grant took a deep breath. He really wasn't ready for this whole religion thing. Or the battle of good and evil. And whatever all of that entailed. But regardless, it seemed to be the path he was being forced to take.

When his computer chimed a little later, he had never been happier to see Ty who was calling him via Skype. Because of Ty's role as a Navy SEAL, they didn't have much contact, so Grant always tried to answer when Ty reached out. Even if it was a night like the one he was having.

"Man, I'm happy to see you," Grant said.

Ty smiled. Even though he looked tired, his brown eyes were still full of life. It was a relief to know he was safe.

"What's been going on?" Ty asked.

"Some pretty crazy stuff, but nothing like what you're dealing with over there."

Ty nodded. "Well, since I can't talk about anything I'm doing, why don't you entertain me with your craziness for a few minutes."

When Grant got done telling the story from that night, Ty sat in silence.

"You think I'm losing my mind, man?" Grant asked.

Ty rubbed his chin. "I know we don't talk about religion. Mainly because I know you're not into it, and I try to be respectful. But you know that I'm a believer. And what you're telling me really freaks me out. I think you need to listen to this pastor and the opposing lawyer. They know what they're doing and you don't. I can't have you getting yourself hurt."

"Ty, we've known each other since high school. You're really telling me that you believe what I'm telling you could actually be true?"

Ty nodded. "I do. And because I do, I'm going to be worried about you."

"Absolutely not, Ty. I can take care of myself. I can't have you being distracted while you're out in the field protecting this country. I promise I will have this totally under control after I wrap my head around it."

"I know you're a tough man, Grant. Growing up in foster homes and everything you went through made you the man you are today. But it's okay to ask for help. Even guys like me need help sometimes."

Grant laughed. "Yeah, like you've ever asked for my help."

"That's not true. Remember advanced calculus in college?"

Grant was so fortunate to have a friend like Ty. "Yeah. Okay that was one time over twenty years."

A deep voice sounded in the background, and Ty looked over his shoulder. "Sorry, bud. I've got to get out of here. But promise me that you won't do anything stupid."

"You got it."

Ty's picture disappeared from the screen. It was great to see him. But Ty's perspective didn't exactly make Grant feel much better. If anything just the opposite. Could all of this be real?

***

Pastor Dan and Olivia rode in silence for a few minutes after leaving Grant's house.

She was the first one to start talking. "I don't know if he can really handle this right now. I'm worried for his safety. What if they actually hurt him? They're capable of it. I'm sure of it."

Dan nodded but kept his eyes on the road. "He isn't strong enough now, but that's also a benefit in disguise. They won't think he's much of a threat. They won't go all out against him. This is mostly just fun and games for them as far as he is concerned."

She shuddered. "I'm sure Grant doesn't feel that way."

"No. But he trusts you. I can see it in his eyes."

"I need to tell you something else."

"What?" Dan asked.

"When I saw Micah today in my car after I was attacked, he told me that Grant was vital to this mission."

"Really? Why didn't you tell me that?"

"I got sidetracked with the details of the attack."

"Well, who am I to say any different? If Micah thinks we need Grant, then we need Grant. And I can tell you that Grant needs you. You're going to be the one to lead him down his faith journey. Not me."

"You sound so confident about that, Pastor Dan."

"I can see it. While the two of you may be adversaries in the lawsuit, the fast friendship and bond you've formed is evident. The Lord has a purpose in all of this."

"I'm not doubting that."

He pulled up to her hotel. "I'm going to walk you up."

"Good because there's one additional thing I want to talk to you about."

They walked into the hotel and took the elevator up to her room. She let out a breath as the door came into her sight. "No pentagram on the door tonight."

"You were worried there might be?"

"Frankly, yes. After all that's happened today it was on my mind. But come on in."

Since the vandalism incident, she'd been upgraded to a spacious suite. She led him into the living room. "Please have a seat."

He sat in one of the big plush black chairs, and she settled down on the large beige sofa across from him.

"What's on your mind, Olivia? Besides the obvious."

"What happened to me today triggered a lot of memories that I had somehow suppressed, or at least hadn't consciously thought about in many years."

He leaned forward, intent on her words. "How so?"

"When I was about eleven years old, I came under serious spiritual attack. Having grown up in the church, I knew something was wrong with how I was feeling. My dad was a preacher so I went to him and told him what was going on. He was the only one I felt I could go to who wouldn't think I was crazy or just a child with an overactive imagination getting frightened from watching too much TV."

"And how did he respond?"

"He was receptive but also very afraid. Thankfully, he believed what I was telling him. I could see it in his eyes. Even though I was young, I had a very solid foundation in faith. My father basically taught me how to use prayer to fight off the evil one and all the demonic spirits that came at me. It was a lot for an eleven year old to take it in, but it built on the principles I had heard in church since I was old enough to understand parts of the sermons. We talked about putting on the whole armor of God. We talked about rebuking the devil."

"You were so young to face those tribulations."

"Yes, but he put it all in terms I could understand. He also instilled in me the importance of learning the Word and being able to use it. There were certain verses we would say together each day until I had them committed to heart. One of the ones I remember the most is *greater is He that is in you, than he that is in the world.*"

"First John, four-four."

"My struggles continued for about six months, and the battle was continuous. Always at night. I'd go to sleep, but then be awakened by awful and terrifying feelings. Sometimes dread, sometimes pain, sometimes hatred. But always the feeling that a spiritual presence was in the room. Then one day it just stopped."

"And you have nothing to attribute that to?"

"No. Besides the fact that I was getting stronger through it all. And even more committed to my faith. I really felt so close to God."

"And so today outside Astral Tech when you were attacked, it brought this all back."

"Yes, very vivid memories have been pounding through my head since then. I don't know what this all means, but I wanted to share it with you. I thought it was important that you understood my history with all of this."

"We're all special to God, but, Olivia, I think you've been called for a specific purpose. Everything you've told me about your upbringing and your childhood encounters with evil up until now when you face those threats again in this highly unusual situation. God has brought you here. He needs you in this."

"How can I do my job as a professional and defend this company at the same time?"

"You can do your legal job and your spiritual one."

"And if the two conflict at some point?"

"You already know the answer to that."

She nodded. "Yes, I definitely do."

"Sometimes God puts us in certain situations that at first blush would seem like we shouldn't be there. But he has us there for a reason. I believe for you that this is one of those times."

"I do too," she said softly. "It's not everyday that you are visited by an angel. So I can't turn my back on that."

"I've gotten the church's leadership committee up to speed but will need to let them know about the latest events from today. We're stronger as a body in Christ than we are as individuals. I want to start prayer groups for you and Grant ASAP."

"How will the church feel about all of this? I know not all churchgoers really believe in the literal spiritual realm, especially to the extent we're talking here."

"You're right that there are definitely some skeptics amongst the group. But they're also faithful and will pray for those who ask for prayer."

"Has there been any past history of overt spiritual warfare in the Windy Ridge community?"

"Yes, right after I arrived here about eleven years ago. We had some problems with demonic worship and some ritualistic animal sacrifices. At that time, Layton's predecessor was still in charge around here, but Layton was definitely up and coming. About a year later, Layton took over and then started Optimism—the company and group."

"What happened to Layton's predecessor?"

"He supposedly died of natural causes, but I think Layton killed him. I may have mentioned it to you before that Optimism is the old guard. Very heavy into traditional witchcraft and they have a majority female membership. I think Layton is threatened by other men."

"Interesting. And Astral Tech?"

"Younger, and more focused on this app and reaching people through social media and new means. I'm not as familiar with Clive or his second in command, Nina Marie, as I am with Layton. I'm actually spending tomorrow analyzing the app. If you have any insight from the work you've done that you can share, please let me know. But I don't want to put you in any awkward position because of your legal obligations."

"Don't worry about that. I have a clear understanding of attorney-client privilege, and I won't violate that. But there is nothing wrong with me sharing my factual observations about the app with anyone, including you. Honestly, I haven't had as much time to analyze it yet as I wanted to, with all the legal matters and document review and analysis that has had to be completed. Optimism is taking a highly aggressive stance in the litigation. So much so that they forced an early scheduling conference on me. And to make matters worse, the judge who was filling in for our regular judge sided with Optimism. It was the craziest thing. I had a panic attack in front of her.

And then her decision made no sense. She clearly favored Optimism."

"Which judge was it?"

"Louise Martinique."

Dan blew out a big breath. "Isn't that convenient."

"How so?"

"Louise is old friends with Layton. I don't have direct evidence tying her to Optimism, but it wouldn't surprise me."

She snapped her fingers. "Wait a minute! That would explain why I had that mini panic attack today in court. Maybe she was the cause of it."

"Certainly possible. But like I said, I have no proof of her association. Only a hunch."

"I feel like I'm the proof." She let out a breath.

"Don't let that get you down. You still did your job to the best of your ability. You're a very strong woman, Olivia. The Lord wouldn't set you on a path that would have you bear more than what you were able to. He's got a plan. One that seems like it has been in the works since you were young. I'm glad you let me know about that. It really puts it all in perspective."

"You never know how some people are going to react. Even preachers. But at this point, I need your help and those in the church. I can't do it on my own."

He reached out and patted her shoulder. "We'll be there for you."

"I'm counting on it." She paused. "And how are you doing? I know you are still facing a very difficult time of your own. I feel badly that I'm adding to that burden."

"You're right that dealing with my grief is a daily battle. But in a way, having something else to focus on, even if it is this situation, is a good thing. My wife wouldn't have wanted me to stop helping others. That wasn't her way."

"If you ever want to talk about her or anything, I'm here for you too."

"Thanks, Olivia."

$$***$$

The next day, Dan sat in his office at the church. He'd spent the last few hours playing around with the Astral Tech app. On its face it seemed fairly harmless, but he knew better than to believe that. The gateway portions of the app talked in general terms about New Age theories. There was a lot of information about meditation and a healthy diet. He didn't have any problem with that per se. It's when you were meditating on evil that you got problems.

With each task he checked off in the app, though, he was able to unlock more and more layers. It was about hour three that his eyes widened. That's when he saw the section on spells and witchcraft. The app made it seem like it was fun and games. The graphics were very vibrant and the interactive nature of the app was impressive. It would especially be enticing to young people.

He kept tapping his tablet going through the motions. *Lord, help me find a way to shut this thing down*, he prayed.

"Pastor Dan."

He looked up and saw Olivia at his office door.

"Come on in. Glad you could make it. I've been working with the app for hours."

"What are your thoughts?"

"At first, mostly cosmetic stuff. Very high level, trendy New Age items. But after you get further into it, then you can see a lot more dangerous things. Look here." He slid the tablet in front of her.

"Witches and spells," she said. "Level one. I wonder how many levels there are?"

"That's what I'm trying to find out. The app makes you complete certain tasks before you can move on. That's why this is a bit time consuming, but well worth it in the end."

"I agree with you."

"I hope you don't mind, but I asked the church leadership to swing by and meet you. They should be here any minute."

"Of course I don't mind."

It wasn't long before associate pastor Chris Tanner walked through the door. He must've come from a workout given his t-shirt and gym shorts. He still kept his blond hair in a buzz cut even though he was no longer in the army.

"I'm Chris Tanner, the associate pastor here at Windy Ridge Community Church. We haven't met yet because I've been filling in preaching at another church in town while their pastor is on a mission trip." He stretched out his hand and Olivia took it.

"Olivia Murray, nice to meet you."

Chris smiled showing a dimple on his right cheek. "I hear you've had quite a stay so far in Windy Ridge."

She nodded. "That's for sure. But I've never represented a New Age company before, so I really didn't know what to expect."

"I've been going over the app," Dan said. "It's taken me the better part of a day, and I still have a long way to go before I fully understand all it can do."

"Let me know if there's anything I can do to help," Chris said. Then Chris turned and looked at Olivia, his hazel eyes serious. "Are you really doing okay?"

"Surprisingly, yes. I feel like this is all part of God's plan. I'm ready to do whatever is necessary to fight this battle."

"I filled Chris in on what happened to Grant," Dan said.

"Yeah, I spoke to Grant and he's trying to talk himself out of thinking he really experienced anything."

Chris took a seat in one of the chairs. "That's totally natural. If you have no experience with any of this, then I would think it would be better to believe it was just in your head."

"I think he's really in denial," she said. "I'm not sure what will pull him out."

Dan leaned forward, resting his elbows on the desk. "If they keep coming after him, then I assume he'll start feeling something. Like I told you, Olivia, I'm just not sure if they think that Grant is their top priority right now."

"Are we interrupting?" Sofia and Beverly walked into the office.

"Not at all." Dan was eager for Olivia to meet these two strong women of faith. "Olivia, I'd like to introduce you to our youth director Sofia Garcia and our financial administrator Beverly Jenkins."

Sofia was closer to Olivia's age, but Beverly seemed to be much more welcoming to Olivia. Sofia remained skeptical of the entire situation.

"It's very nice to meet you." Olivia shook hands with both women.

"What did we miss?" Beverly asked.

"I've been going through the Astral Tech app today," Dan said. "Sofia, were you able to touch base with any of the youth about it?"

"Yes. In our group meeting, they claim they haven't heard much about it, but I can also see some hesitation amongst them in wanting to come forward. These kids are young and impressionable. I get the sense an app like this could be very interesting to them. So I wasn't surprised when I got an email from one of the girls saying she wanted to talk to me about it in private. I'm scheduled to meet with her tomorrow."

"Good," Dan said. "Let us know right away what you find out."

Olivia nodded her head. "Really when you think about it, it's a brilliant recruitment strategy. The app will draw in young people much quicker than any face to face type meetings ever would."

"How's the lawsuit going?" Chris asked.

"Optimism is taking a highly aggressive stance in the litigation. I have a feeling that the case is going to move much faster than normal. As you can imagine, I am limited on what all I can discuss with you because of my legal relationship with the client."

"We understand that," Dan said. The last thing he wanted was to put Olivia in a compromising position and hurt her legal career. "As far as the legal battle goes, you represent Astral Tech and that's your job."

"Right. It's all this extra stuff that makes things messy." She paused. "For what it's worth, I think the two organizations are really targeting each other right now—and the lawyers. I don't think they've turned their attention back to the Windy Ridge community or this church."

"Right," Dan said. "I told Olivia about some of the issues we had with Optimism when I became pastor here a decade ago. We had some rough times, but since then it's been a bit more covert. Each year there may be an incident or two but nothing major."

"Is it possible that Layton has been using this time to build up his group?" Beverly asked.

"Anything is possible with that guy," Dan said.

"Also, just because you're not seeing what you think of as traditional manifestations of the devil's work around the community doesn't mean that Optimism has stopped working," Olivia said. "From everything I've learned about Layton, he is cutthroat and highly ambitious. Maybe he's biding his time for a bigger plan."

"A plan that got disrupted when his technology was stolen by Astral Tech," Sofia said.

"I obviously can't comment on the alleged theft," Olivia said. "But I just wanted to point out that you may have a sleeping giant on your hands. If Optimism and Astral Tech are going after each other, then who knows what will come out on the other side."

"It could get ugly and innocent people could get hurt," Beverly said. "I'm going to say it because no one else has come out and put it on the table." She paused and looked out the office window. "Just because they are going after each other, doesn't mean that their end goal is any different. To spread the evil one's message and to bring people into their dark realm. To get Christians to turn away from God, and to inflict as much harm as possible on believers. We as a church need to be ready for this. We can't just sit back and think that they'll destroy each other and we'll go about our merry business. I'm older than anyone in this room. I've lived through a lot in my life. So while the battle takes different forms, it's still a battle."

"Maybe we need to do some self-reflection as well," Dan said. "Yes, we've had quite a respite over the past few years, but could it be that's because these groups didn't see us as a threat? If so, that means we need to do more."

"Why would you purposely try to provoke them at this time?" Sofia asked. She stood with her arms crossed. As always, she was the most critical one of the group.

"It isn't about provocation," Chris said. "Dan is right and so is Beverly. Maybe we've been too lax. Our attendance numbers are respectable, but they continue to decline with each year. If we're going to get Optimism and Astral Tech out of our backyards, we need to take action to prepare."

He knew what they needed to do. "We'll start by having a special prayer meeting Sunday night. It's time we prepare everyone for what is going on here. We don't want anyone to be caught off guard."

"Let's bring it in for a prayer now," Chris said. "Dan, you lead us."

Dan stood hand in hand with his leadership team and Olivia. It was at that moment that he realized the importance of what they doing. The Lord had chosen them, and they wouldn't let Him down.

CHAPTER SIX

O livia couldn't believe the three-month discovery period that Judge Martinique had ordered was winding down. All the relevant players had been deposed and much to Grant's dismay, Olivia had filed key briefs with the court. She was proud of all the work she'd put in—and most of all the favorable results.

Once they had gotten back in front of their assigned judge and out of the grasp of Judge Martinique, she had won a big legal battle by getting parts of the case dismissed. The only claim that was left was the allegation that Astral Tech stole the app.

Olivia knew that was the claim to be the most afraid of, but everyone back at BCR was touting her victories. And since she literally had done all the work herself, no one else could claim the credit. Chet had called her multiple times praising her for her stellar performance. But it was far too soon to celebrate. They still had to get through the rest of the case.

There had been an odd, almost unsettling calm between the companies, at least on the spiritual side. Both groups seemed very preoccupied with the lawsuit. And Olivia wondered if her standing up against the evil forces had knocked some of the wind out of Optimism's resolve. At least for a while.

Whatever the reason, she'd taken the mini truce and ran with it. Pouring all of her energy at work into the lawsuit and trying to set herself up for a victory in the end. But she wasn't so naïve as to believe that the spiritual battle was over. It was only a matter of time before things heated up again. And she was going to be ready when they did.

She and Grant had seen each other a lot, but only on matters limited to the litigation. There were less lunches and dinners and more depositions and in her opinion, frivolous motions filed by Grant that had kept her super busy.

Ever since he'd had that spiritual experience at his house, he'd pulled back from her. She thought it was probably easier for him to process that way. And she didn't think it was her place to push it. At least not then. But on the other hand, she'd been told that Grant was important so there was a lot more she needed to do as far she was concerned. She was trying her best to be patient. And when the Lord spoke, she would listen.

Windy Ridge Community Church was working to build up prayer teams. Pastor Dan hadn't wanted to let up because everyone knew in the end there would still be a fierce battle and the church had to be ready. Because if it wasn't, then nothing would stand in the way of the forces of evil taking over Windy Ridge.

Having the respite from the direct attacks had allowed her to put her spiritual energy into getting herself ready for what was to come. Her prayer life in general was getting stronger, and she knew that she wasn't alone in the fight.

She'd also been spending her time on litigation strategy. Her latest endeavor was something that she needed Grant to be on board with. So she'd asked him to meet her to discuss something related to the case. She smiled to herself because she knew he wasn't going to like it.

***

"I came here because you asked," Grant said. He'd agreed to meet Olivia, but that was just out of professional courtesy. "But there's no way my client is going to agree to a mediation." He looked into

Olivia's big brown eyes as she sat across from him at the Windy Ridge Coffee Shop.

She picked up the large pink mug and took a sip. "I think it would be beneficial to get the parties in the same room." She looked down and back up. "And I actually don't know whether my client would agree either."

He laughed. "So this is all your great idea, huh? You just drop it on me before you even talk about it with your client."

"Well, what do you think?"

"I think," he leaned in closer to her, "that you wanted an excuse to meet me face to face and check on what I was up to. Wanting to see if I had any tricks planned for the final days of the discovery period."

She smiled warmly at him. He was going to have to be careful with her. Between all the craziness, their clients, and her kind heart, he could see himself being attracted to Olivia Murray. And that wasn't a road he should even get close to going down. For about a million different reasons—only one being that they were on the opposite sides in a lawsuit. In fact, he'd been trying his best to keep his distance from her over the past three months. This was actually the first time they'd met outside of a specific litigation task.

"It's both actually," she said. "I do think we should schedule a mediation. Just to get everything out on the table. But you're also right that I wanted to check on you. Not about your litigation tactics, but about how you are doing. The past few months have been intense, and you always avoid talking about what happened at your house three months ago. Each discussion we've had, you've skillfully redirected. You experienced something you'd never had before. That was bound to be pretty difficult for you."

He nodded. "Yes, but with the passage of time, I've put it all in perspective. Nothing else has happened. I wasn't feeling well. Maybe I was so tired and stressed out."

She narrowed her eyes at him. "C'mon, Grant. You're not that tired or stressed. In our line of work being tired and stressed is just another day at the office. What you experienced was real. So real that you called me immediately after it happened and gave an account of what you felt. It also happened to coincide with the attack on me that afternoon. We have a situation here."

She was getting riled up, and it was kind of amusing to watch. "Is that what you're calling it?"

"Yes. I realize we're on opposite sides, and we have to do our professional duty. But we also have to protect ourselves. We're in the middle of this spiritual battle between two very powerful and strong evil groups, and I don't want you to get hurt."

"What about you?"

She took another sip of coffee. "I'm better equipped to deal with it than you are."

"That's an understatement."

"Which is another reason I wanted to meet with you. I wanted to invite you to a church service at Windy Ridge Community Church."

No way was he going to church with her right now. Even if someone had attempted to do some crazy witch voodoo on him. "No. I just don't think church is for me at this point."

She reached out and grabbed his hand. "After what you experienced in your own home, are you really sure that you want to go at this thing alone? Because I'm here to tell you as someone who has experience with this that it will only get worse, not better."

He shook his head. "No. My mind was just playing tricks on me. If you don't let yourself think it can happen, then it won't happen. I just have to be more aware of things, that's all. And do I need to remind you that things have been quiet? Unless you haven't told me, things have been calm for you on that front too."

She leaned back and crossed her arms. "You're trying to talk yourself out of what you know in your heart actually happened."

He waved his right hand. "Nah. Like I said, too much work, too little food and a lack of sleep. There are no such things as spiritual forces, Olivia. There just aren't. I know you believe differently but science and just plain old logic would say otherwise."

"If you're going to keep this up, I'm going to get a croissant or scone. Do you want something?"

"Sure." His stomach growled at the thought of it. "Whatever looks good."

"Be right back." Olivia walked away from the corner table and up to the front of the store.

He wasn't fooling himself. He had to be right about what happened because honestly the alternative was far too much for him to consider. Olivia already bought all of this and was so fully immersed that he couldn't count on her to be rational. And no, he wasn't saying that the vandalism against her didn't happen. But he wasn't ready to say that any spiritual force was at work. The mind was a delicate thing. And the powers of persuasion were great. He knew that first hand as a trial lawyer.

What he needed to do was put back on his rational thinking cap and not buy into any of this spiritual mumbo jumbo. That was going to be his best defense.

Olivia walked back a moment later with an assortment of pastries.

"I figured you could take whatever you don't finish back to the office."

He grinned and picked up a big blueberry scone. "Is this how you treat all your opposing counsels in your cases?"

"You'll never know," she said. "But back to the issue at hand. You up for Wednesday night church service?"

He shook his head. "I'll pass." He could see the frustration building in her as she smoothed down the napkin in front of her. "It's not personal."

"I'm not going to push you. But I have to warn you that this is far from over. For either of us. Don't let this respite fool you, Grant."

"You've mentioned that."

"All right." She set down her croissant. "What are your thoughts on mediation then? The court will probably order it at some point. Why not get it out of the way now?"

"Because I can guarantee you that our clients won't be sharing pastries and chatting across the table from each other."

"All the more reason to do it. Let them get out some of their frustrations face to face."

"To hear you tell it, though, we should be concerned about some type of magical confrontation."

"Don't mock this." Her tone was no longer light.

He put up his hand. "I'm not mocking any of it. I'm just trying to figure out what your end goal is here. We both know there is zero chance of settlement. So why mediate?"

"Like I said. It will be a useful exercise for them to be able to get things off their chests."

"That's if they would even agree to be in the same room as each other. You've done enough mediations to know that it's a distinct possibility that they would want separate sessions with no interaction."

She leaned back in her chair. "That wouldn't be good."

"But that is the most likely scenario."

"The poor mediator."

"Exactly."

"Just float the idea and I'll do the same. I still think it could do some good. And if we pushed a joint session, with the mediator's help maybe we'd get it."

"You're optimistic." He laughed. "No pun intended."

She gave a weak smile. "I've got to run. Enjoy the scones."

***

Layton was thrilled to have Stacey Malone sitting across from him in his office. Her strawberry blonde hair was down today cascading past her small shoulders. He was attracted to her, no doubt about that. Even if he did have about twenty five years on her.

But he needed to stick with the mission at hand. There was no time for dalliances right now.

"Stacey, I hear you had a great meeting the other day getting settled into your internship."

"Yes." She smiled. "I'm really excited about it."

"What draws you to the New Age way of life?"

Her bright blue eyes sparkled with excitement. "I can't really describe it, but I feel so strong and powerful when I'm practicing New Age techniques."

"What techniques have you been using?"

"A lot of meditation. Some cleansing. I've been doing a bit of reading on the topic too. That's why I spend so much time in Indigo. I really enjoy their selection of reading materials."

He nodded. "That's all a great start, but I think you have a lot of untapped potential. I can feel your aura, the energy that you have which is very strong. I would love to introduce you to some of the practicing spiritualists here at Optimism." He used the word spiritualist because he wasn't exactly sure how she would react to the word witch.

Her eyes widened. "Yes, I would love that. I have to admit I've dabbled a bit in spells but I wasn't very successful."

"It's an art. Here we will be able to teach you all about it."

She leaned forward in the chair. "How soon can I start?"

"No time like the present. You'll remember Morena from the bookstore. I'll have her work with you. Let's go to her office now."

"Great." Stacey stood up and walked toward the door.

He was right beside her placing his hand on her back guiding her to Morena's office down the hall.

"Morena," he said.

Morena looked up at him and smiled. "Layton, Stacey, so great to see you today."

"In addition to being our intern, Stacey is your newest pupil. She's ready to start right away."

Morena's brown eyes focused on Stacey. "That's great news."

Layton put his arm around Stacey. "She's special, Morena. So make sure you take great care of her. She's going to be one of our most gifted members. I can feel it."

Stacey blushed. "I hope I can live up to your expectations. I'm willing to work really hard."

"That's all anyone can ask of you," Morena said. "I've got this from here, Layton. I'll keep you posted on her progress."

"Wonderful." Layton walked out leaving the two women together. He couldn't wait to see what Morena could do with a young energetic powerhouse like Stacey. The girl didn't realize how much untapped potential she had. But luckily he did.

***

"You want to do what?" Layton's big blue eyes practically bulged out of his head.

"Mediation," Grant replied. He wasn't going to back down. Layton needed some tough love. He'd brought Layton into his office and now Layton was sitting with his mouth dropped open on the other side of his desk.

"Why in the world would we want to mediate? I want to destroy them. Take this case to trial and embarrass them. Get back what is mine," Layton yelled. "No way."

"Listen to me. You hired me for a reason."

Layton threw up his hands. "And it sure doesn't sound like you're doing your job to me if you're suggesting mediation."

"If you'd give me a minute to explain, I think I can clear up any misgivings you may have."

Layton crossed his arms around his chest. "Misgivings is putting it lightly."

"We wouldn't be going to mediation to settle the case."

"Then why would we go?"

"To rattle Astral Tech. We'd do a joint session at the beginning where both sides' lawyers present their case. It would be sure to get a reaction from Clive and Nina Marie. It's a tactical move."

"To get inside their heads?"

"Two fold—definitely to get inside their heads, but also to hear what their initial take of their defense will be. It will provide us strategic insight as we move forward into the next phase of litigation headed to trial."

Layton rubbed his chin. "Maybe you have a point."

"I told you. This is what I do for a living." When Olivia had mentioned mediation, he didn't like the idea. But then he realized he could totally work this to his advantage.

"You said the lawyers will make a statement. What about us? Can I talk directly to Clive and Nina Marie?"

"It would all depend on the mediator. Each mediator has a different philosophy. Generally though, they're trying to resolve the conflict. So they don't want to do anything to fan the flames."

Layton huffed. "But I want to agitate them."

"Right. So the selection of a mediator would be important. And both sides have to agree."

He laughed. "How do you expect us to be able to agree to anything?"

"Leave that to me. If you give the mediation the go ahead, I'll make sure it happens."

Layton smiled. "You really think you have that Olivia Murray wrapped around your finger, don't you?"

"I wouldn't go that far, but I'm confident in my ability to do my job."

Layton's smile disappeared. "Don't underestimate that woman. I don't trust her, and I think she's a more formidable opponent than you would think."

Wasn't that an interesting way to put it? "Don't worry." But then he felt compelled to say something else. "Remember what I told you about making sure we're on the up and up as far as the litigation goes."

Layton frowned. "And I told you there was nothing for you to be concerned about."

"Why do I feel like there's something that I'm missing here?" Normally he wouldn't push his client like this, but he had to be clear on this point.

"Everything is fine. We're all behaving in a professional and legal manner. Now I'm going to head back to the office. Let me know when you figure out the logistics for the mediation."

Grant shook Layton's hand and walked him to the main reception area before returning to his office.

But then he decided instead of calling Olivia, he would go see her at the Astral Tech office. Layton's visit had started off his day on a high note. Although Grant had to admit that he didn't trust Layton. Unfortunately, he didn't trust a lot of his clients. It was just the nature of the business.

Olivia might not appreciate an unannounced visit, but this was his first step in gaining back the upper hand in their professional relationship. He'd cleared his head and was ready to face this entire situation like his old self would—logically and rationally. None of this spiritual crap would influence his legal strategy.

He walked into the Astral Tech lobby and the receptionist, Melanie, gave him a big smile. It was almost like she was flirting with him, but he didn't have time for that right now. Come to think of it, he rarely had time for women these days. His life was all about growing his law practice. When he'd taken the chance and started his own firm a few years ago leaving the more established firm, it had been a risk. But it had paid off big time. He had a growing client list and a stellar trial track record.

Girlfriends weren't very understanding when you canceled on them all the time. It just wasn't worth the hassle right now. Especially since every woman he'd ever dated had really failed to keep his attention. If he did ever settle down, and that was a big if, he would want someone he was attracted to and who was smart enough to spar with him.

"Mr. Baxter, nice to see you again," Melanie said.

"Hi, Melanie. I'm here to see Olivia. I don't have an appointment though."

She grinned. "No problem. Let me give her a buzz. Have a seat."

He took a seat on the plush navy sofa and waited for a few minutes. Then he heard the sound of heels clacking on the floor.

Looking up, he saw Olivia walking toward him. She looked great today in a black suit and red blouse. Her long dark hair was down instead of being pulled up in a bun or ponytail.

"Grant, what are you doing here?" she asked.

"Can we go to a conference room and talk?"

"Sure."

She may have said sure, but her wrinkled brow let him know that she was skeptical.

She led him down the hall to the conference room that she was using as an office where they had met before.

"What's going on?" she asked right when the door closed.

"I have updates on the mediation."

Her eyes widened. "Really."

"Yes." He took a seat.

"Well, don't just sit there staring at me. Tell me."

He laughed. "You look great today, by the way."

She snorted. "Don't try to soften me up with compliments."

"All right. Even though I was just stating a fact. I'll move onto the mediation. My client has agreed to the mediation. The sooner the better."

"Really? How in the world did you pull that off?"

He leaned back in the chair. "I can't divulge my secrets. Especially not to the enemy."

"I won't push you. Thanks for taking it to your client."

"I did my part. Now it's your turn to step up and get your people to agree. Then we'll have to settle on a mediator which I'm assuming will be a contentious process."

Smiling, she looked him in the eyes. "Why would you ever think that anything related to this litigation would be contentious?"

"I love your sarcasm. Get your client on board and I'll go ahead and propose a list of mediators. Then you can shoot them all down and we can go from there."

"Agreed." She bit her bottom lip. "Is everything else going okay?"

He knew what she was getting at, even if she didn't come right out and say it. "Yes, I'm totally fine. Feeling much better. Don't even think any more about that."

"You know that if that changes, you can talk to me about it. That's totally different than the legal issues we're dealing with."

"Don't give it another thought."

The door opened and he saw an auburn haired woman walk through the door. Her dark brown eyes immediately locked in on him.

"Am I interrupting?" she asked.

"No, we were just finishing up. Nina Marie Crane, this is Grant Baxter, the attorney for Optimism."

A slow smile crept across Nina Marie's face. She walked over to him and outstretched her hand. He stood and took her hand in his. Right when they connected he immediately felt uneasy. She didn't break eye contact or the handshake.

"Very nice to meet you, Grant. Just because we're at war with Optimism in this lawsuit doesn't mean that we can't be friendly."

Talk about distrust. That's the only way he could describe it. There was something sinister about this woman. Underneath it all, he wondered what her real motives were.

Finally, she dropped his hand, and he took a deep breath. "Okay, Olivia. Let me know when you have updates on what we discussed." He clearly wasn't going to discuss the mediation in front of Nina Marie. That was Olivia's job, to take it to her client first.

"Nice to meet you, Grant. Come back and visit anytime." Nina Marie winked at him.

He couldn't get out of the Astral Tech office fast enough.

***

"Isn't he a cutie," Nina Marie said.

Olivia waved her hand. "Right now he's my opposing counsel. So I'm not concerned with whether he's attractive."

Nina Marie walked over to her. Olivia felt Nina Marie's touch on her arm. "Olivia, you're an absolutely awful liar. I think you're quite taken with the man."

Olivia took a step back straightening her suit jacket. "I think you have the wrong idea, Nina Marie. Romance is the last thing on my mind right now." And that was the truth.

Nina Marie nodded. "Maybe so. But just because you're fighting in the courtroom doesn't mean that you can't also tangle outside of it. If you know what I mean."

Olivia understood exactly what Nina Marie meant, but she didn't want to have that discussion. "About the case..."

"Yes, what did he want?"

"We've been discussing a mediation."

Nina Marie's eyes widened and she laughed. "Olivia, please don't tell me you're that naïve."

"It was my idea."

"Why? There's no way that Layton Alito is going to settle this case out of court."

"It's not about settlement. It's about strategy. We'll get to hear their arguments in the mediation. It will help me prepare our defense. It will also give you a chance to put some pressure on them. If they see we're not afraid to try this case, maybe they'll think twice."

"Hmm. You are a good lawyer, aren't you?"

"Yes, I like to think so."

"But is it really worth it?"

"There's really no downside for us. Besides taking the time out of your schedule and the emotional toll it may take on you." She was baiting Nina Marie. Once Olivia threw down the challenge, Nina Marie wouldn't be able to say no.

"What emotional toll?"

"You know. Coming face to face with Layton might be intimidating for you. Having to hear about the case. You might even want to say something to Layton or he may say something to you. Sometimes in mediation things can get rather heated. Tensions and emotions run hot."

Nina Marie flipped her hair back behind her shoulder. "No, Olivia. It's not me who has to worry about any of that. It will be Layton and his thugs that will be the ones hurting when this is over."

"So you agree to the mediation? We'll have to get Clive onboard too."

"Don't you worry about Clive. If I say we're mediating, then we're mediating."

"Good. Just confirm it with him and give me the green light. We'll get it set up as soon as possible."

Nina Marie smiled. "I'm looking forward to this."

Olivia thought it better not to ask Nina Marie if she was the one who had gone after Grant. After seeing how Nina Marie had acted toward him, it definitely made her suspicious. But on the other hand, she didn't want Nina Marie to think that she and Grant were that close. It would be better this way.

"Anything else you want to discuss?" Olivia asked.

"How are you doing? I know that you had a bit of a scare with that hotel room nonsense right after your arrival. But you haven't raised any concerns at all since. Have you had anymore issues?"

She didn't want to lie, but she also realized it was better not to reveal everything to Nina Marie. She couldn't trust her so she just didn't answer her question directly. "I'm doing fine at the hotel now. I'm focused like a laser beam on this litigation."

Nina Marie patted her shoulder. "Good, because I'm counting on you to take down Optimism."

"I'll do my best."

"I know you will." Nina Marie paused and looked her in the eyes. "You're an interesting woman, Olivia."

"I'll take that as a compliment." She controlled the chill that shot through her. She could practically feel the evil oozing out of Nina Marie. Even though she wore a smile and a warm touch, this woman was dangerous. But on the other hand, there was also something vulnerable that Nina Marie was hiding beneath her perfect smile. And Olivia intended to find out what it was.

CHAPTER SEVEN

The past week had flown by in a blur for Grant. But as he got ready to walk into the mediation, he was prepared and ready to make a big impact.

He'd briefed Layton extensively on what to expect and how to behave, but he had no realistic expectation that Layton would listen to him. The man was a loose cannon. Today he hoped to use that to his advantage. If Layton's tactics could put some fear into Astral Tech, then all the better.

They'd agreed to conduct the mediation at his law office since he had multiple conference rooms that could be used for each side to have their own private time.

"Olivia," he said. He walked over and shook her hand. Her touch always made him warm, even as he tried to shake off any undercurrent of feeling he had for her. "Let me show you to your private conference room." Then he turned to Nina Marie. "Nice to see you again, Nina Marie."

"Likewise," she said. Her mischievous brown eyes troubled him greatly.

"And I don't think we've met. I'm Clive Township."

Grant shook the distinguished looking gentleman's hand. "Nice to meet you. Right this way."

He led the three of them into the conference room designated for Astral Tech for the duration of the mediation. "We'll have the first session at ten a.m." He looked at his watch. "Just enough time to grab some coffee. The mediator is already in the room."

"We'll be right in," Olivia said.

"See you in there." He walked down the hall to the main conference room that was being used for the first general mediation session of the day.

"Layton, do you need anymore coffee before we start?" he asked.

"No. I'm ready to get this going."

Layton was all business so far today, wearing a designer black suit and purple tie that Grant wouldn't be caught dead wearing.

The mediator, Mary Beth Moore, a retired judge, walked into the room. The petite gray haired woman might look sweet, but she had a reputation for being very tough. She was the only person that he and Olivia could agree upon.

Grant walked over to Mary Beth. "Anything else you need?"

"No, I'm good. Has the other party arrived?"

"Yes, I just showed them their private room. They will be in here soon."

"Wonderful." She sat down at the head of the conference room table.

Not long after, Olivia walked into the room followed by Nina Marie and Clive. Nina Marie wore a bright red dress that wasn't entirely appropriate for a legal mediation. Clive on the other hand wore a conservative navy suit and tie.

He watched as Olivia did introductions with the mediator and her client. Olivia had her game face on and a gray power suit to match. She was giving him a cool vibe today. They both had a job to do here.

"Why don't we get started," Mary Beth said. "Optimism, you're up first since you're the plaintiff here."

"Thank you, ma'am." Grant stood up. He loved presenting his case. Being a trial lawyer was more than a job for him. It was his passion. Although today he was going to have a completely hostile audience instead of a jury.

He took a breath and looked directly at Nina Marie. "Juries don't like thieves. And at the end of the day, that's what this case will come down to. A jury will determine if they believe that Nina Marie stole the technology for the app from Layton Alito. I contend that a jury will side with Optimism once all the facts are presented. The jury will hear about how Nina Marie seduced Layton into a romantic relationship just to gain access to his technology."

He kept his eyes mostly on Nina Marie expecting her to have an outburst at any moment. But instead, she smiled at him. Was this woman truly psychotic?

Spending the next thirty minutes of his allotted time laying out the case, by the time Grant sat down he was a bit deflated. Not one single outburst from the Astral Tech side. He'd purposely been as inflammatory as possible and nothing. Not one peep.

Now it was Olivia's turn. Standing up from her chair, she made eye contact with him before she directed her attention to Layton. "There's an old saying—there's two sides to every story. And once a jury hears both sides, there will be no doubt that Astral Tech should face zero liability in this lawsuit. A lawsuit born out of jealousy and revenge. After Nina Marie ended the romantic relationship with Layton, he was mad. A man of his background wasn't used to being dumped and humiliated. He wanted revenge. So he plotted this entire lawsuit as a means to try to get back at Nina Marie for what he felt was a personal slight."

She stepped out from behind the table and moved toward the front of the room. "Optimism has the burden of proof, and they simply won't be able to provide one shred of evidence that would implicate Nina Marie in the theft of the app. The Astral Tech app was created in house at Astral Tech through the hard work and creative genius of Nina Marie and her team."

Grant noticed that Layton was placing all of his attention on Nina Marie, not on Olivia. That couldn't be a good sign. But Layton had promised him that he would stay on task and act professional.

"The evidence will show," Olivia said, "that once Nina Marie spited Layton, he went on the warpath. The jury will see email after email of the exchanges between the two, demonstrating Layton's animus for Nina Marie after she broke off the relationship. The emails will also show threats to ruin Nina Marie. What better way to do that than to try to take down the company she cares so much about?"

"Liar!" Layton rose from his seat. His face reddened with anger.

Olivia didn't even flinch at his outburst. "I think a jury will clearly be able to determine the true set of facts here. I don't really think there's anything else I need to say. Especially if Mr. Alito acts this way in the courtroom."

Nina Marie smiled and Layton made a growling sound before he literally threw himself across the small conference room table. He launched at Nina Marie, wrapping his hands around her neck.

But in a split second, Grant had his hands on Layton, pulling him off of her. What a disaster.

"I will not tolerate violence," Mary Beth yelled. "Mr. Baxter, please control your client."

He needed to get Layton out of the room ASAP. He guided him out the door and into their private conference room.

"What in the world were you thinking, man?" Grant asked him.

Layton's face was still red as he stood with clenched fists. "Olivia was spewing lies. Lies all put into that head of her by Nina Marie. Didn't you see the smirk on Nina Marie's face?"

"Remember, Layton. We were supposed to use this opportunity to get inside their heads. Not the other way around."

Grant watched as Layton took a few deep breaths and shifted his weight from one foot to the other.

"That is one evil woman. Don't you ever forget that."

Grant reached out and put his hand on Layton's shoulder. "Do you think you can handle continuing this mediation? Because if you have another outburst like that, the mediator will end it anyway. And it will allow Nina Marie and Clive a victory we don't want to give them."

"What would be the next step?"

"We can end the mediation right now. That's the beauty of mediation. Any party can just walk away."

"The alternative?"

"We would go back in there, and finish up the joint session. Once that is over, each side will meet privately with the mediator."

Layton sighed. "Do you still think there is some strategic advantage to staying?"

"Only if you can pull it together."

"Nina Marie really got inside my head. I'm usually so good at controlling my emotions."

"But Nina Marie didn't say a word."

Layton shook his head. "She doesn't need to speak to wreak havoc." Layton pushed his finger into Grant's shoulder. "You need to be careful, too. Who knows what she'll do to you."

"Layton, I think the stress of the litigation may be getting to you." How could he say this without totally offending his client. "Nina Marie can't do anything to you unless you let her."

Layton laughed. "Son, you have no idea what you're dealing with here."

Grant took a seat and motioned for Layton to do the same. "Well, explain it for me then."

Layton rested his arms on the table and leaned toward Grant. "Nina Marie consorts with the devil."

Grant had to keep from rolling his eyes. Was everyone around him crazy? "I hate to break it to you, Layton, but there is no such thing as the devil. Or God, or heaven and hell. Or whatever else it is you think you know."

Layton shook his head. "You just wait. Once Nina Marie attacks you, then you will understand that she isn't just operating on a human level. The evil one supports her and will allow her to do unimaginable damage to you. And since you have no spiritual protection because you aren't a believer, then you're in even more danger."

"Listen to yourself right now." Grant quickly pushed away any thoughts of what had happened to him months ago. No, that was him being paranoid and sick. Not a result of witchcraft. Of that he was now sure.

"I know it sounds outlandish to a skeptic, but you asked me and I told you. This is not your regular legal case. If you want out, now is the time."

"No way. I've never withdrawn from a case, and I'm not about to start now."

"Then you need to consider asking the evil one for protection."

Grant huffed. "How can I ask him for protection if he doesn't exist? And more than that, you said Nina Marie was in bed with him. Why would he protect someone if he was aligned with the other person."

Layton grinned. "You really have no conception of how this all works, do you?"

"No, I don't."

"The evil one will definitely play both sides."

Grant couldn't believe he was going to ask this, but he had to. "Then the obvious question to me is why would anyone serve him?"

"Because the power and riches he can provide on this earth are immeasurable."

"I'm fine with earning my power and riches the good old-fashioned way. Hard work."

"You're so naïve."

"I have a feeling this could be an extended philosophical discussion. Right now we have an immediate issue about what to do with the mediation."

"It's over. I'm not in the mood to tangle with Nina Marie again today."

"Are you sure? They could see us walking out as a victory."

"I'm fine with that. We'll still prevail in the end."

"All right. I'll go inform the mediator."

***

Micah looked over at Ben who stood outside the conference room wearing a deep frown.

"Are we just going to let this be a free for all for the time being?" Micah asked.

"We can only do so much when they are going after each other. Our job is to protect Olivia and Grant and give them what they need when it's time for them to do battle. This Layton and Nina Marie thing is a sideshow."

"It's all very personal for Layton."

Ben nodded. "And Grant's got a long way to go. I thought that after Nina Marie attacked him that he would start to question things, but he's only moved further away from it all with the passage of time. He's afraid of what he felt that night."

"It's going to take more than one attack." Micah took a step back. "He was able to quickly rationalize it away. He doesn't want to believe that any of this is real."

"He's only seen the dark side and the workings of Satan. Olivia needs to help him see the other side."

"She's trying, but if she pushes too hard she could lose him forever."

"Failure isn't an option. Maybe it would do some good if Nina Marie came after Grant again. That may be the only way that he'll start to get the picture."

"Or we could pay him a visit," Micah said.

"No. He really needs to come to this through his own volition. Most people will believe if an angel of the Lord appears to them and tell them to. No, for him to be the warrior that he will need to be it has to be him searching it out. Not the other way around."

"There's one more thing we need to talk about."

"All right," Ben replied.

"The young woman, Stacey. She is dangerously on the brink with Morena. I think we have to intervene or risk losing her forever."

"She wasn't forthright with Morena about her religious background."

"Why don't we go to her now?"

"All right. Let me take the lead since you did so with Olivia," Ben said.

***

Stacey sat in her small one bedroom apartment with books spread out around her. She also had a few supplies she'd gotten from Indigo. She probably shouldn't be spending her money on this stuff, but she couldn't help herself.

It was like she couldn't say no. A force was pulling her to learn and read more about witchcraft and the dark arts. She'd also found out from Morena that a lot of stuff she'd learned at Windy Ridge Community Church growing up just wasn't true. She'd had that sinking suspicion which is why she stopped going to church a year ago anyway.

She'd never felt this powerful before in her life. This much in charge of her own future. Morena had made promises to her about what she could accomplish and the thing is that she actually believed every single one of them. Especially since Layton Alito the CEO of the company had taken such an interest in her. She understood from talking to Morena that Layton didn't just take time out for everyone.

She was no fool. She could tell that he had more than a professional interest, but she didn't care. This was all just part of being a grown up and making adult decisions which would further her goals in life.

Lighting a candle, she opened the book in front of her preparing a spell. Morena had explained that there were a couple of different areas she could work on. But to her, casting spells seemed the most interesting. Morena had taught her that she had preconceived notions about the devil. He wanted his followers to have freedom. Something she would've never ever gotten in the church. No, just the opposite.

Pastor Dan and everyone at the church were always telling her what she could and couldn't do. But it appeared there was a way for her to have a lot more flexibility. It wasn't like she was sacrificing small animals to him. No, what she had in mind was much less barbaric but no less effective.

Her aspirations of finishing college and getting a top notch corporate job actually seemed feasible for the first time. All thanks to him. What he'd given her—power and confidence.

It was time to thank him.

She took a deep breath preparing herself, but then the candle blew out.

"Ugh," she said. She picked up a match and again lit the large purple candle that smelled of sweet lavender. Closing her eyes, she was about to start to chant when the light from the candle no longer illuminated under her eyes.

Opening up her eyes, she saw it was out again.

"What in the world?"

"Stacey," a deep male voice said.

He seemed so near that her heart constricted in fear. How had someone gotten into her apartment?

"Don't be afraid."

It was so dark now in her room, and she couldn't see anything. Scrambling around the floor for something to use as a weapon, she kept talking. "Who are you?"

"I'm not here to harm you, Stacey."

"Then why did you break into my apartment?"

"I didn't break in."

A light exploded so bright in front of her eyes, she had to raise her arm to shield the rays. There standing right in front of her was a man with dark hair and striking hazel eyes. A bright light emanated from him. She knew immediately that this was no regular man.

"Who are you?" she whispered.

"My name is Ben. I'm an angel of the Lord. I've come here to speak to you about the path you're starting to go down."

Her hands trembled and her entire body started to shake. "But I don't understand."

Ben took a step toward her, and she scooted back on the floor away from him. "I think you know exactly what I'm talking about. Witchcraft, demonic worship, the dark arts. You've turned away from God, Stacey, but I can guarantee that He has not turned away from you."

"Why are you doing this?"

"To give you the opportunity to stop. A way out. Layton Alito is an evil man and his witches are no less so. If you go further down this dangerous path, I fear you will be lost forever. And I don't want to see that happen."

Her heartbeat sped up and she tried to speak, but no words came out.

"It's your choice, Stacey. No one can make you pick one way or the other. It's all your decision."

"Then why are you here?"

"To plead God's case. To help you remember how much God loves you. To remind you about what joy you used to have in your heart before you turned to darkness."

She didn't even realize that tears had begun to run down her face. And just like that, the warmth she was feeling from the angel Ben faded and she became cold.

"What are you doing here?" Ben asked.

For a moment she was confused. But then she realized that the question wasn't directed at her. She looked over her shoulder and a dark figure stood looming large behind her.

"She's mine," a loud voice said. "Leave her alone."

She couldn't see his face, but the figure was clothed all in black with a large dark hood covering his head. Suddenly freezing, she wrapped her arms around herself. As if that would provide her with some warmth and protection.

"Stacey, remember I said you had a choice," Ben said. "It is up to you. Not him."

"Who are you?" she asked the dark figure.

A lavender light emanated from the man as he removed his hood. Standing before her was one of the most handsome men she'd ever seen in her life, with jet black hair and bright sparkling blue eyes. "I'm here to guide you and protect you. Don't listen to this false prophet. I'm not going to hurt you. There is no need for you to be afraid of me. It's the angel that is trying to steal your soul."

"Stacey, he's lying to you," Ben said. "Trying to deceive you by being pleasing to the eyes."

This man standing in front of her was gorgeous and smiling, but she still felt cold, despite the light that now surrounded him.

"You still didn't tell me who you are? What's your name?"

He kept smiling. "I'm your friend. My name is Othan and my mission is important. You'd begun to do such great work. Think of all you have accomplished in a short time. There is more work to be done. You could have everything you ever wanted in life and more. But you have to abandon this God that the angel speaks of."

"I don't understand." Who was this beautiful creature tempting her with everything she wanted?

"It's simple," he said. "You've begun your education in the dark arts. What I can promise you on this earth, the angel cannot. All of his promises about the future are empty ones. I offer you power, freedom, riches, independence, and pleasure now. All you have to do is follow the prince of this earth."

She stood up and took a step closer to the man who called himself Othan. But he wasn't really a man. Her gut was telling her that. Yes, he had the form of a handsome gentleman, but it was a farce. As she looked closer into his blue eyes, a chill shot down her arm.

She knew in her heart what she had to do. Right then and there.

"Rebuke the devil and he shall flee," she said quietly.

"Don't do this." The man hissed and moved toward her. "You're not thinking straight," he said. "I'll give you one more chance. Here take my hand, and I will show you unimaginable riches and power. The angels of God will bow down to you."

The long dark cloaked arm stretched out toward her. *Lord,* she prayed, *I am sorry for what I have done. But I need you now.*

On her silent prayer, the light from the angel Ben exploded.

"Tell him to go, Stacey. In the name of our Lord, cast him out away from you."

She took a deep breath. As she looked up into his eyes which were no longer blue, nothing like human eyes anymore—but yellow eyes filled with pain and rage, she tried to find the words.

It had been over a year since she'd been to church, but before that she'd gone her entire life. The words would come to her.

The stench of death and destruction poured off the hooded man. He no longer even looked like a man. She'd never been so afraid in her life. Or so certain that she'd made a horrible mistake in turning away from God. One that could've changed her entire life.

The creature moved closer toward her and she heard herself scream just as Ben stepped in between Othan and her. Seeing Ben protect her like that gave her renewed strength.

"I rebuke you in the name of Jesus Christ. Leave me."

The creature screamed in pain just before he vanished in a cloud of darkness, leaving her alone with Ben. More tears flowed down her face and she couldn't stop shaking.

Ben put his hand on her shoulder. "Are you okay?"

She shook her head, because no she wasn't okay. She'd never be okay again in her life. "What just happened?"

"That, my friend, was a demon."

Sucking in a breath, she had known the answer before he gave it, but hearing the actual words come out of his mouth just solidified her fear. "I don't even know what to say."

"Stacey, what you just saw is only the tip of the iceberg. I'm sure Morena is making this witch thing seem cool and young and hip. But there's nothing good involved in the devil's work. You can dress it up and call it all different types of names, but it's still evil. And very powerful and destructive."

She had to get a grip and stop shaking. "What have I done?"

"It's not too late, Stacey. You can walk away from this now, but you need to walk totally away. Go back to church. You're going to need support, because Layton and Morena will come after you again. This is far from over."

"And my internship?"

"You know the answer to that. I need to go now, Stacey. But never forget that the Lord is always with you."

And just like that she was all alone in her room again. But she was afraid to be alone. She did the only thing she knew to do—fell to her knees and prayed.

***

Layton sat in his office seething about the mediation. Nina Marie had gotten to him, and he didn't even know if he could blame it on witchcraft or just her being her. That fact made him even angrier.

But he had to keep his cool, because he had a much larger plan. One that included his asset on the inside of Windy Ridge Community Church. At the right time he would employ the valuable resource he had cultivated. Now was no time to lose sight of the long game.

A loud knock sounded at the door, but before he could even answer, Morena walked in.

"We've got a problem," she said. She stood with her arms crossed.

"We have a lot of problems. What is yours?"

"Stacey."

"What? I thought she was doing great. We just talked about her. Her progress has been phenomenal."

"I got a report from Othan. He was at her house last night."

"Why in the world would he ever make himself known to her right now?" He stood up. "It's far too soon for her to be consorting with demons."

"Othan claims that he had no other choice because an angel named Ben was at her apartment."

"Really?" Now wasn't that something. Angels just didn't appear to anyone. "That means that Stacey is even more talented than we thought if the angels have taken an interest in her."

"I know."

"How did Othan present himself?"

"He claims it was all going well until she rebuked him. Then the literal fangs came out."

He sighed and ran a hand through his hair. "You know sometimes I think we'd be better off without the demons. They can't control themselves and then something like this ends up happening. He should've never gone there even in one of his handsome forms. He should've given us a chance to handle it without his interference."

She nodded and pushed a strand of blonde hair out of her eyes. "Now we have a mess to clean up, and if we don't act fast we're going to lose her."

"What do you suggest?" Layton asked.

"First, I think she needs a little time to think about all of this. Then I think you should talk to her. We have to get her back to what she seemed to be really drawn to which was the New Age side of things. Like you said, she's not ready to be fully submersed."

"Talk about a way to screw up a fabulous opportunity. I will talk to her. I refuse to let her go back to church. I saw on her intake file that she used to be a churchgoer. Do you know which one?"

Morena's bright red lips turned down into a frown. "Which one do you think?"

"Are you kidding me? She went to Windy Ridge Community Church?"

"Yup."

"Of all the churches in the Chicago suburbs." He rubbed his chin. "I don't like the feeling of any of this. Too many coincidences."

"I agree. Which is all the more reason to be persistent. It's a long battle."

"Let's see if she comes back to work. Then we'll determine how best to handle it."

"Good." She paused. "How did the mediation go?"

He threw his head back. "Disastrous. I swear that Nina Marie is getting stronger by the day. We have to turn our attention to neutralizing her. We also need to make a stronger effort against that lawyer. Nina Marie may be too strong to take a hit, but Olivia Murray is another story."

CHAPTER EIGHT

O livia needed to brief the managing partner, Chet Carter, on the litigation and provide a mediation update. She'd been dreading this phone call, but it was one she needed to make.

After getting his secretary, Darlene, and waiting for a minute, his voice came on the line. "Olivia, tell me how it's going out near the Windy City."

"Strange, sir. Very strange."

"How so?"

"This is unlike any litigation I've ever been involved in." She hadn't told him about the incident that happened to her hotel room, but she couldn't leave him totally in the dark. After all, there was a good possibility he would still want to swoop in and be first chair in the trial.

"Each litigation is a bit different," Chet said. "They all have their own unique quirks."

"This is a lot more than that. Not only is there extreme interpersonal animosity between two of the key players on each side because of a romance gone wrong, there are some things that come along with representing a New Age company that I wanted to make sure you were aware of."

"Like what?"

"It's not unusual for there to be talk of witches and spiritual forces in our meetings. These people believe they are not only in a battle in this lawsuit, but in some type of turf war over the New

Age kingdom." How else could she say it without him thinking she was completely delusional?

"Are you buying into any of this, Olivia?"

This was such an awkward conversation to have, but it was best to divert the question away from a direct answer. "I'm very focused on the litigation, but I wanted to prepare you for all of the external elements at play here. No one likes to be blindsided."

"How did the mediation go?"

"Layton Alito flipped his lid. I don't know what set him off. My presentation was no more inflammatory than Grant Baxter's."

"What did he do?"

"He jumped across the table and tried to choke Nina Marie."

"You can't be serious."

She sighed. "Unfortunately so."

"Maybe we should discuss sending additional staff just to make sure you have more people around you. I don't know if I like the feeling of you being alone to deal with all of this mess."

"There's plenty of legal work that I have people doing back in DC. But as far as it helping with all the drama, I don't think additional bodies will change that."

"What about private security?"

"I don't think that's necessary at this point." Private security wasn't going to be able to do anything against the forces of darkness. "I think Layton's anger is directed at Nina Marie specifically. But honestly she doesn't really seem that threatened by him. It's almost like she enjoyed seeing him come after her."

He laughed. "Sounds like they're an interesting bunch. In good news though, we just received full payment on the first three invoices. Between all the hours you've been working and the rest of the group here in the office, it was a hefty bill."

"Well, there's always that." Chet was all about the bottom line. Since she wasn't a partner yet, the finances were much less of a concern for her. And oh yeah, the fact that she was smack dab in the middle of a battle between two evil enterprises.

"Keep me posted. If you have any concern whatsoever for your physical safety, Olivia, you need to let me know immediately. I know I talk a lot about the money, but I need to know my lawyers are safe."

"Thank you, Chet. I really appreciate that."

"Talk to you later."

The line went dead, and she got ready to make her next phone call on her list.

"Lizzie," she said.

"Olivia, how in the world are you?"

"Just plodding forward with the litigation."

"I'm sorry I've been so delinquent on answering your calls. This current trial has totally kicked my butt. I've been an awful friend."

"Don't even think about apologizing. I know exactly how it is."

"How are you holding up spiritually?"

"It's tough. But I'm trying to keep my prayer life strong and remember that God has a plan."

"I have a piece of good news. Pastor Paul is going to be back preaching next month."

"That is wonderful. I'm glad he took the time off and listened to his doctors."

"Yeah. I hear he wasn't so happy about the diet changes, but who is?"

"I hope you aren't too run down from the trial."

"I'll be okay. And even though I'm in the middle of the trial, if you need me, I'll make it happen, Olivia."

"You've always had my back, Lizzie. I'm so appreciative of having you as my best friend."

"Awww. Now you're going to make a girl cry."

Olivia's heart warmed. "I know you have work to get back to. Keep me posted."

"Same to you."

She ended the call and reflected on her friendship with Lizzie. She was grateful for having someone she could always count on.

But now it was time to make the final call on her list.

This time to Grant and back to the issue at hand. Even though he wasn't the one that assaulted her client, she had to make clear to him that Layton needed to be kept on a tight leash. She might even go to the court and file a restraining order, but she should run that idea by Nina Marie first.

She stood up out of her comfortable conference room chair and walked down to Nina Marie's office.

When she got to the door, she saw that Nina Marie was sitting behind the desk tapping away on her computer.

"Nina Marie," Olivia said. "Do you have a minute?"

"Sure." She motioned for her to come on in. "For my star lawyer, I have more than a minute. What do you need?"

"Do you want to file a restraining order against Layton?"

Nina Marie laughed. "Layton is the one that needs protecting from me. Not the other way around."

Olivia smiled. "I thought you might say that. But we would be filing this more as a strategic move. Not necessarily to actually prevent him from doing harm to you."

"What's the strategy? Your mediation one worked out so well, I can't wait to hear this one."

"We've got the upper hand after the mediation. I say we should strike now. At the very least, this will be more paperwork for them and a distraction. I'm sure it will elicit an emotional response from Layton."

Nina Marie took off her glasses and placed them in front of her. "You really do have the mind of a strategist. Are you sure you wouldn't have any interest in coming to work for us after all this is over?"

"I can best serve clients at the law firm. But before I went and threatened Grant with the restraining order, I wanted to make sure it wasn't an empty threat and that you would be on board."

"Absolutely."

"Great. I'll make that call to Grant and then get the paperwork ready to file with the court."

"Good job, Olivia. First the mediation and now this. I'm glad to have you as our lawyer."

"You're welcome." Olivia shut the door behind her, and then she walked back to the conference room.

Honestly, she didn't know how to deal with the praise from Nina Marie. Of course she wanted to do her job to the best of her ability and uphold the ethical standards that were required of her as a lawyer. But she couldn't help but feel a little awkward to receive those words of encouragement from someone she knew was evil and had the ability to hurt so many people. There was a piece of her that wondered if there was any chance for Nina Marie to ever turn away from the darkness.

Lord, I'm just doing the best I can here. I hope it's enough, and I hope that I can continue to do Your will.

Instead of giving Grant a call, she decided to pay him a visit. He'd popped in on her unannounced before. It was time to turn the tables.

When she arrived at his office, she smoothed down her navy suit jacket and walked into the reception area.

"I'm here to see Grant Baxter."

"Is he expecting you?" The older woman asked with a raised eyebrow.

"Just tell him that Olivia Murray is here." The woman working today wasn't the same one who was at the desk during the mediation.

A few minutes later Grant walked out into the lobby. He looked striking today in a dark suit and hunter green tie that offset his blue eyes.

He smiled at her as he showed her to his office. "So what do I owe this lovely surprise visit?" He paused and lifted up as his hand. "Wait, are you here to gloat about the mediation?"

"Not exactly."

"Please take a seat then."

She sat across from him as he took a seat behind his desk in a huge chair. "I'm not here to gloat, but I am here to talk about the events that transpired at the mediation."

"Uh oh. I don't like the sound of this."

"As a professional courtesy, I wanted to let you know that we'll be filing a restraining order against Layton Alito. He physically attacked my client in the mediation in front of all of us including the meditator. I feel confident a judge will grant our petition."

Grant leaned back in his chair and crossed his hands above his head. "Well played, Olivia. I must say. I was almost starting to feel sorry for you, but you've shown you're more than capable of taking care of yourself. To think for a minute I was wondering if I was going crazy. But it was all for show. To gain advantage in the litigation. So again, well played."

She shook her head. "You're mistaken. Yes, I'm litigating this case as hard as I can and doing the best I can. But in no way did I mislead you about the other things that have been going on ever since I arrived in Windy Ridge almost four months ago." Her frustration started to build and she took a deep breath. "You felt it too, Grant. Don't forget that."

"If you're right, then maybe I should be the one filing the restraining order against your client." He threw down the gauntlet.

"If you take a minute and think about all of this, you'll see that I've always been straight forward with you about everything."

He waved his hand in the air. "Including the witches and demons part." His voice dripped with sarcasm.

"What has gotten into you?"

"I'm tired of everyone talking all of this nonsense and acting as if it's a rational approach."

"I hate to break it to you, Grant, but you took on a New Age company as a client. That's what they do."

He looked at her with his big blue eyes wide. "I expected incense and meditation and holistic medicine or something. I'm not even sure exactly what I expected, but I can surely tell you it wasn't all of this."

"All I can say to you is that nothing I've done or said has been untruthful or misleading. I'm doing my job the best I can, but I've never had a case like this before either."

"And yet you're here trying to push the envelope and no doubt try to get a reaction from my client."

"Wouldn't you do the same thing if you were in my position?"

He didn't answer, and she knew she had him on that one.

"Grant, is everything all right otherwise?"

"Yes. I feel fine. The mediation wasn't ideal obviously, but none of that will matter when it comes time for trial."

"Good. That's all I needed. I didn't want to just drop the filing for a restraining order on you without any notice. I'll be filing it with the court by the end of the day today."

"Great." His sarcasm was still in full effect.

"You used to like me, you know. I'm not the enemy here."

He frowned. "Unfortunately, at the rate this is going, if you aren't the enemy, you will be very soon. And I'm sure you'll start to feel the same way about me. It was probably foolish to think we could have a friendship while a case as stressful as this was ongoing."

"It doesn't have to be like that."

He nodded. "Actually, I think it does. From here on out, if you have business to attend to, please make an appointment." All the warmth had left him as he spoke devoid of emotion.

"I understand. And I'm sorry." She stood up and walked toward his door.

"Olivia, wait."

She turned around.

He looked at her but didn't say a word.

"Yes?"

"It's nothing. I'll talk to you later."

She walked out feeling like she'd just lost a battle even when she should feel victorious over the restraining order.

***

Pastor Dan took a sip of coffee as he put the finishing touches on his Sunday morning sermon. While he enjoyed preaching, this message he was preparing was particularly resonating with him.

"Pastor Dan," a female voice said.

He took off his reading glasses and looked up at his office door. "Stacey! I haven't seen you in such a long time."

"Can I come in?"

"Of course. Please have a seat."

"Sorry I didn't schedule a time to talk or anything." She sat down across from him.

Something was off with her. The smiling and vivacious young woman he knew looked anything but. She fiddled nervously with the hem of oversized shirt.

"Whatever it is, Stacey, the church will be here for you. Just tell me what's going on."

She placed her head in her hands, and he thought she was about to start crying. But instead she looked up at him. "I'm ashamed for what I've done."

"The fact that you're sitting here in my office right now is a big first step. I'm sure whatever it is we can work through it together with the Lord's help." His mind raced wondering what had happened to Stacey. As a college student she was faced with a lot of issues.

"It's not going to be what you think." She sighed. "I guess I have to just spit this out. Lately, I've become involved with a New Age business called Optimism."

He eyes widened. He could only thank God, though, that Stacey was safe, sitting in front of him right now. "I'm familiar with them."

She nodded. "Then you know how bad this is going to be. I met Layton Alito in the Indigo bookstore. He introduced himself and offered me an internship. I've been working with Morena. I don't know if you know her."

"I don't think I do."

"Anyway, needless to say, I've been headed down a dark path." She shook her head. "Honestly, I didn't realize all I was exposing myself to. I was intrigued by a lot of the New Age philosophies I read, and I was admittedly drawn into some of the aspects of witchcraft."

"Why the change of heart?"

"If I tell you, then you may want to take me to the hospital and have me psychologically evaluated."

She looked perfectly in control as she spoke, so he felt comfortable continuing this conversation. "Try me."

Not making direct eye contact for a moment, she took a deep breath. Then she focused her attention back on him. "I was visited by an angel last night."

"There's nothing crazy or wrong with that, Stacey. I believe you."

"That's not the only visitor I had. The angel said his name was Ben. He was talking to me about the dangers of what I was doing experimenting with Optimism."

He nodded. "Then what happened?"

"Another man appeared in the room. He was gorgeous. Or at least at first he was. He said his name was Othan." Her voice started to shake.

"It's okay, Stacey. Take your time."

"I was so cold when he was there. Even though on the outside he was smiling and handsome, I knew something was terribly wrong. I rebuked him and his eyes turned this awful yellow color. Not human."

"Did he leave?"

"Yes. Then Ben told me that Othan was a demon." She put her head back in her hands. "He just said it. Just like he was telling me about the weather or football game or something. But like, oh yeah, that was a demon. As you can imagine, I pretty much freaked out. Pastor Dan, I've never seen a spiritual being in my entire life. I know we talked about spiritual warfare in church, but I really didn't think it could be like this. And now I've gotten myself in trouble with Optimism. I'm sure they're going to question me about leaving."

"Let's just take this all one step at a time. The first thing I'd like to do before we go any further is to pray for you."

"Right now?" she asked.

"Yes." He walked over to where she sat and placed his hand gently on her shoulder. "Dear Lord, thank You for protecting Stacey and for bringing her to church today. Lord, I know that Stacey has been experimenting with some dangerous things, but now she's here looking for Your forgiveness and Your guidance as she starts to break away from that path and all things related to Optimism. She'll need Your protection and help, Lord, on this journey. Give me and the other church members the strength and wisdom to help her. And keep her safe from the dark forces that will come against her. In Your name, Amen."

He stepped back around to his desk and looked at Stacey's tear-stained cheeks.

"I'm so sorry, Pastor Dan."

"You don't need to apologize to me, Stacey. God's forgiveness is all that you need. And it was brave of you to take action against that demon."

"I don't know how I let myself believe that this was all right. More than all right. That this was what I wanted and that it wouldn't hurt me but help me."

His heart broke for her. "That's the allure of the devil. He has many tools at his disposal to make following him seem like the most logical choice. But you shouldn't dwell on all of that. You're here now and I think you're ready to completely disavow him, right?"

"Yes. I'm not going to lie. Standing in the presence of that angel really changed everything for me." She looked down and then back up at him. "Although maybe even more so than the angel was feeling the presence of Othan. I've never been that full of fear in my life. The transformation that happened right before my eyes really threw me for a loop."

"I can imagine that it would. But you're safe now, here in the Lord's house."

"Have you ever seen angels and demons before, Pastor Dan?"

"Not like what you're describing. I've definitely felt the presence of both, but never seen them with my eyes like what you are describing."

"You still believe me though?"

"Of course. Just because I haven't seen something doesn't mean I won't believe it. That's what faith is all about, remember?"

"What do I do now?"

"I'm going to call the church leadership and see who is available to come over here now. I'd like us to come up with a plan for how you combat these forces of evil. Just try to relax and take a few deep breaths." He picked up his cell and started making calls.

"Pastor Dan, can you talk?"

He looked up seeing Olivia rushing into his office. Her cheeks flushed.

"Oh, I'm sorry. I shouldn't have just barged in here like this." She took a step back into the doorway.

"No, actually it's perfect timing that you are here. I'd like you to meet someone."

She took a hesitant step into the office and looked over at Stacey.

"Olivia Murray, this is Stacey Malone. She's had quite an experience. I've invited the church leadership over for a meeting to discuss this. But the very short version of the story is that she's been working at Optimism. And she's had a spiritual encounter with both sides."

Olivia smiled and walked over to Stacey. She outstretched her hand. "It's nice to meet you, Stacey. And I'm glad to see you here at church."

He watched as the ladies shook hands and then Stacey studied Olivia with a high level of skepticism.

"Olivia is actually representing Astral Tech in the litigation between the two companies," he said.

"Really? I heard about that when I was in the Optimism office. I don't understand, though." She paused and looked to him and then back to Olivia. "Why are you here in church if you represent them?"

"I work for a law firm and was given this assignment. So instead of saying I couldn't take it on, I felt compelled to stay."

"We believe Olivia has also been targeted by Layton to try to throw her off her game in the litigation. She's had some similar experiences to yours. Including seeing angels."

"Really?" Stacey's eyes widened as she turned her attention back toward Olivia.

Olivia knelt down beside Stacey. "Believe me, I know it's scary. And at first it seems like maybe you think you're going crazy. But deep in your gut you know that it's real. Once you accept that, then you can move on."

He heard voices coming down the hall. "Sounds like the rest of the group is arriving. Let's huddle up in the conference room where we'll have more room." He hoped that this meeting was a good idea.

***

Two hours later, Olivia was exhausted. The leadership team was there minus Beverly, who had other church obligations. Stacey had told her story to everyone in great detail, which led to a serious debate. One that was still ongoing as to how best handle the situation.

"I think we need to at least consider the possibility of sending her back in," Sofia said.

She was the only supporter of this suggestion, as everyone else had shot her down.

"No way," Dan said. "It's far too dangerous. Stacey can't walk the line between good and evil."

"Dan's right," Chris said. "This isn't the CIA. Spiritual warfare is a totally different arena."

"Do I get a say so in this?" Stacey asked quietly. She'd barely said a word since she told her story.

"Of course," Dan said.

"What if I want to do it? What if I can help? To make up for the wrong I've done?"

"You don't have to do certain acts to atone for what happened, Stacey. The Lord has already forgiven you."

Olivia finally felt compelled to speak. "I agree with Pastor Dan. I've experienced firsthand how strong the evil is that Optimism is a part of. I would never want someone to be exposed to that who isn't one hundred percent ready. And given all that Stacey's been through, I feel it would be a disastrous decision. One that could end up with Stacey being hurt—both physically and emotionally." She turned her attention to Stacey. "I know you want to make this right. But the best thing you can do now is to help out in other ways. Going back in is a risk so big that you may not make it back out. Even if you go in with the best intentions."

Stacey shook her head. "I know I can do it. My eyes have been opened."

"And they could be quickly shut again if you immerse yourself in evil," Chris said.

"But at the end of the day, it's my life and my decision." Stacey lifted up her head in defiance.

Olivia felt uncomfortable with the direction this was going.

"Why don't we all just step back and take a deep breath. There's no need to make a final determination right this second. Stacey, I know you're probably exhausted and would like sometime to yourself to think."

She nodded.

"Are you going to be all right at your apartment alone?"

"I'll be fine." She said the words but they weren't exactly filled with confidence.

"She can always stay at my place if she wants," Sofia added. "As you all know, it's just me and a few empty rooms."

"Thank you for offering. I think once I get back and get some rest, I'll feel a lot better. I didn't sleep much last night after all of this happened."

"I'll walk you out to your car," Chris said.

"I'll tag along." Sofia stood up.

The three of them left the room, leaving Olivia alone with Dan. He looked tired as he rubbed his temples. Probably from the headache that she was starting to feel herself.

"Are you okay?" she asked him.

"Yeah. Have to say, wasn't expecting this today." He leaned back in his chair. "What did you think of her?"

"I think she's scared and confused, but doesn't want to show her weakness. I think it would be an absolutely awful idea for her to go back to Optimism. I'd be very afraid for her."

"She practically grew up in this church, but then stopped coming about a year ago. I understand the need to grow and experiment, but she stumbled into the dark stuff and it looks like Layton found her."

"And if Layton is really interested in her, he isn't going to let her go easily. To purposely try to go back into that lifestyle as some sort of spy is outrageous to me. What would we stand to gain?"

"Learning about their operational plan, I guess." His blue eyes met hers. "But I totally agree with you. We need to stick close and help her get through this. I'll talk to Sofia in private and make sure that she isn't going to push this idea any further."

"Why would she suggest it to begin with?"

"Sofia is our resident skeptic. Yes, she's a believer in the Lord, but I don't think that she believes Stacey actually saw any spiritual forces. So to her, she probably doesn't think the risk is as great."

"You and I both know that isn't the case."

"We've got to be vigilant." He let out a breath. "What did you need? You showed up and then everything was about Stacey."

"It's Grant. He's totally shutting me out. First, he accused me of concocting all of this spiritual warfare to gain a strategic advantage in the litigation. Then, he basically just said that he couldn't be my friend right now. He's really going through an internal struggle."

"There is one piece of good news in that."

She raised her eyebrow. "And that would be?"

"At least he's not being won over by Layton either. We still have a great chance with him. It's just going to take time and patience."

"I never said I was giving up. Just that I feel like we've suffered a big setback."

"Don't let him lock you out. Be creative. I'm sure you can come up with something."

"Even if it's more litigation related, at least I will have reasons to make him face me."

"Exactly." He reached out and touched her arm. "You're strong, Olivia. And you're also the leader in this battle, whether you want to be or not."

She took a deep breath. "I'll do my best." She paused. "I need to pray for guidance because I'm feeling a bit lost right now."

"The Lord will guide you, Olivia. I am sure of that."

"How are you holding up?"

"Why do you ask that?"

"You look a bit tired, and I imagine that you're feeling the weight of all of this on your shoulders."

He crossed his arms. "I am. But that's a responsibility I've chosen to take on. I can't imagine it any other way."

"Even the strongest people get worn down sometimes."

"True. And having Stacey show up today and talk about angels and demons by name, was more than a bit disconcerting."

"But you believed her?"

"Yes. She seemed so certain in her retelling of events. Didn't you think?"

"Yes, I did. But like I said, I'm worried about her. If she's experiencing such strong presences, then there's a reason for that. She could be important to the larger battle. To gain so much attention from both sides, that has to mean something, right?"

"I hadn't really gotten that far in my thought process, but you make a really good point. That only makes the situation more difficult and high stakes."

"I also hate to be the one to say it, but what if her desire to go back in undercover is really just part of her wanting to go back into the darkness? Or at least have the opportunity to rethink leaving it today?"

He smiled. "Aren't you just a ray of sunshine?"

"I'm trying to be realistic here."

"I know. Was just trying to provide a little lightness to this very serious situation."

"Get some rest, Pastor Dan. You're going to need it." She stood up, worried that he was under even greater stress than he let on. "I'm going to head home to the hotel."

***

Sofia had insisted that she follow Stacey to her apartment and get her settled in. Although Stacey tried to resist, if she was being honest with herself, then she would admit that she was beyond grateful for the company.

She'd known Sofia for many years and felt comfortable with her. Even though she was a bit embarrassed about the entire scenario.

"I'm glad you came back to the church, Stace," Sofia said, using her nickname.

Stacey unlocked her apartment door and ushered Sofia inside. From the looks of it, there was nothing out of place. Absolutely no sign that she'd had a literal spiritual experience in her living room the night before.

"I'll stay here as long as you need me to. I realize that you had a traumatic experience."

"Yeah, it was pretty crazy. I honestly had no idea that things like that really happened to people, you know? I'd learned all about spiritual warfare growing up in the church, but to actually see it in front of my own eyes…"

Sofia walked over to her and grabbed her hands. "Stacey, you've been under so much stress with your school and the internship at Optimism. I just want to ask you to consider that maybe you were so exhausted that you fell asleep and dreamt all of this up?"

"You don't believe me?" It hurt that Sofia questioned her story, but at least she did it in the private and not in front of the others.

"No need to get defensive, Stace. It might be easier for you to handle this if you think of it in that way. It also might give you the strength you need to go back to Optimism."

"You think I should go back in and try to get information on the group to give back to the church?"

"That decision is completely up to you. I just want you to examine all of your options and not foreclose something just because people are talking about how you'll get caught up in all of it again."

"Why are you so skeptical? How does that work with your beliefs? I've known you long enough to know that you're a believer. You teach the youth group. You're one of the smartest people I've ever met."

"That's exactly why. Yes, I believe in the Word of God, but I also think that people get too caught up in being literal about spiritual warfare."

"Do you believe that in biblical times that people saw angels and demons?"

"That was a different time. Our world is different now."

"That's a very interesting theory."

"Wouldn't it make a lot more sense that you had a dream?"

Stacey nodded. "It sure would, but I tell you, I can't shake the feelings I have."

"Are you hungry? Do you have anything here I could fix you for dinner?" Sofia's brown eyes filled with warmth.

"You don't have to do that."

"It's the least I could do." Sofia walked into the kitchen and started opening the cabinets and refrigerator.

Luckily, she'd just gone to the store that day to take her mind off things, so there was stuff for Sofia to work with.

"How about spaghetti?"

"Sounds wonderful." And it did. She couldn't remember the last time someone cooked for her. She was a decent cook, but food was always better if someone made it for you. It also helped that Sofia was an excellent cook.

When they sat down at her small kitchen table to eat less than an hour later, Stacey felt her stomach rumbling as the tomato aromas floated through the air.

"So, what do you know about the Astral Tech app? Did you learn anything about that at Optimism? I'm working on how to talk to the youth about it in more detail than I have so far."

"I actually don't know specifics about the app itself. I just know how upset Layton was for what he thought was the theft of the app. He really believes that the app was his creation and that Nina Marie stole it." Stacey wrapped some spaghetti around her fork and took a big bite.

"Yes, the lawsuit. Everyone's favorite topic these days."

"He really hates Nina Marie. Morena gave me some of the background on everyone and told me about their history. Sounds like a really nasty breakup. From what I could gather, Layton isn't one to get attached to women. He's usually the one ending things, but with Nina Marie, it was different. If I read between the lines, it was almost like he was mildly obsessed with her."

Sofia took a sip of her iced tea and then leaned forward. "What did you think of Layton?"

She could feel the heat rush to her cheeks. "Honestly, I'm embarrassed to say that I was pretty taken with him. He seemed so smart and kind."

"And it doesn't hurt that he has celebrity good looks."

"Right." She took another bit of pasta as she considered her next words. "But I can't help but wonder now if he's just a wolf in sheep's clothing. All of the Optimism people I met were great looking and friendly on the outside. And then even that demon who visited me looked so handsome at first."

"You really believe you saw a demon, don't you?"

She nodded. "It was one of the most vivid experiences of my life. I don't blame you for being skeptical. I would've been the exact same way if I hadn't experienced it. When I was reading about the New Age mysticism and witchcraft, I saw it as more of a philosophical and fun thing."

Sofia shook her head. "And then you found out that it isn't just fun and games."

"Exactly. But it's so easy to get drawn in. The books are really intriguing and Morena is such a great teacher. She was always pushing me to read more and seriously think about my life."

"This is all great information to have, Stacey. I'm worried that they're going to start targeting more of our youth. If you found it attractive, then others will as well."

"Yeah, and Morena and Layton make things seem so normal. Plus, the internship was huge for me." She sighed. "Speaking of that, I should probably get to my school work. My college course load is pretty heavy. Just because it is community college doesn't mean it isn't challenging."

"Of course. You seem pretty settled, so I'll get out of your hair, but if you need me at any point just call me. You have my cell number." Sofia started taking the dinner dishes to the kitchen.

"I'll clean up since you cooked. So don't worry about that."

"All right. And remember, Stacey. Don't let anything get inside that head. The mind is a dangerous thing and can see things when it wants to."

"Hopefully, I'm done with any spiritual sightings, at least for a long time."

Sofia gave her a quick hug. "Get some rest. I'll check on you tomorrow."

Sofia let herself out and Stacey took a deep breath. What a day. Sofia was trying to help by attempting to convince her that she had dreamt up the episode from last night. But just as she had told Sofia, she knew that what she'd experienced was real. The question now was, what was she going to do about it?

"I can do this," she said out loud. She really wanted to go back to Optimism and try to learn what she could about them to help the church. The only person who was in favor of that idea was Sofia. Which made sense. If she didn't really believe in the physical nature of spiritual warfare then she wouldn't be as worried about the safety aspects.

But Stacey was stronger than everyone else imagined. She had taken on that demon, hadn't she? Didn't that count for something?

Yeah, she had royally messed up, but this was a way to give back to the church and start making amends for her sins.

Then it struck her. She didn't need to tell Pastor Dan and the others about her going back to Optimism. Once she did and brought back valuable information, they'd see that she was more than capable of handling herself.

So as much as seeing Layton and Morena again freaked her out, that was exactly what she was going to do.

CHAPTER NINE

Grant focused on the road but even as his eyes were glued to the street his mind wandered. He wasn't himself lately. Ever since he started working on this case, his world had been warped.

He'd never considered withdrawing from a case before no matter how tough the facts were or how high maintenance his clients had been. And he wasn't really considering it now, but it would make his life a whole lot easier.

What he needed was a strategy for handling not only his client but the opposing side, including Olivia. The first step was putting aside all of the spiritual stuff he was bombarded by on both sides. There was nothing that any of them could do to him unless he allowed the mind games to ensue.

He'd accused Olivia of playing him. He didn't really believe that, but it was awfully convenient that she got everything she wanted in the end. Not only did she get the mediation, but she now had the paperwork in motion to get a restraining order. He'd have to figure out a way to get that excluded from the jury during the trial. It would be highly prejudicial for a jury to see that restraining order. That would play right into Olivia's theory of the case that this was a romance gone wrong between Layton and Nina Marie.

It was time to buck up and deal with this like a man. It wasn't like him to be rattled by such insanity.

Looking into his rearview mirror, he slammed on the brakes and swerved off the road, letting out a curse.

As the car skidded to a stop on the side of the road, he tried to catch his breath. He got out of the car and opened the back seat door. Nothing. There was nothing there.

How was that possible? He'd seen someone in the backseat. What in the world? Had he completely lost his mind?

Realizing his breathing was uneven, he tried to calm himself. He walked around the car in circles looking for any indication of there being someone present. Seeing nothing, he leaned against the car door trying to pull himself together.

He knew what he had seen—the figure of a person in the backseat—in his backseat.

Had he gotten too close to this case that it would make him become delusional?

Get it together, he thought. It was time to drive home and try to get some serious shuteye. This was two times now when he'd been really tired and had strange experiences.

He got back into the car and started the engine. No, he wasn't going to call Olivia. She'd claim victory, and he still had an ounce of pride left.

Needing to talk to someone, he dialed Ryan's number. Talking shop would help calm him down.

"This is Ryan."

"Ryan, sorry we didn't get to talk today at the office. I wanted to check in with you on your cases." He wasn't going to let Ryan know how messed up he was, or Ryan would never want to become his partner in the law firm.

"I pitched for a new case today that's why I was out. I was so bummed that I didn't get the last products liability suit, but I have a great feeling about this one."

"What's the product?"

"Some type of health food supplement. Unfortunately, quite a few deaths have results from those who have taken it. I've met with members of those families that would make up the class action and be the class representatives. They told me today that they'd narrowed it down to our firm and one other."

"That's the best news I've heard all day, Ryan. If there's anything I can do to help swing the case our way, just let me know."

"That's good. I know one of the family members in particular wanted to talk to you since you're the head of the firm."

"Set something up and I'll make myself available."

"Are you okay?"

"Yes, why do you ask?"

"You just seem really preoccupied lately." Ryan said.

"I'll just be glad once this case goes to trial and I can move onto something else."

"I can't blame you. Let me know if you need anything."

"Thanks." He ended the call relieved to at least here that his firm might be bringing in another large case.

By the time he walked into his house, he'd talked himself down quite a bit. He was going to go straight to bed. There was no way he'd allow himself to be sucked into the madness with the rest of the people in this litigation.

***

"We need to make sure we're all on the same page," Nina Marie said. She looked at Clive as he sat on the big red sofa in his living room. He'd become so unfocused on the task. She was going to have to step in and take charge if they were going to prevail in this lawsuit and their battle against Optimism.

"I don't know why you're so worried. We have the upper hand, Nina Marie. The mediation went our way, the judge granted our petition for a restraining order against Layton. What more could you want?"

He was so naïve. "This is just the beginning of a long battle. We can't claim one victory and sit patting ourselves on the back."

He raised an eyebrow. "And what would you have us do then?"

"For one, I'm committed to this campaign against Grant Baxter. If we can spook him off the case that will obviously help our cause."

"You seem to have that well in hand. What do you want me to be doing?" he asked with a raised voice.

"We need to take this opportunity while they are down to really go on the offensive. Both of us need to go after Layton. We're much stronger as a team than working independently."

Clive blew out a breath. "Honestly, doing the devil's bidding is becoming quite tiresome for me."

"What?" she asked. "What are you talking about?"

"I didn't really want to have this talk right now. But maybe it's for the best if we do. I'm losing interest in fighting. I don't really think the rewards are worth it."

"You must not be feeling well, Clive. You're not thinking clearly."

"I'm thinking more clearly than I have in years. I'm taking some time off and going to sit on a beach somewhere away from all this darkness I've surrounded myself with for all these years."

"Wait a minute," she said. "You're not considering converting are you?"

He laughed. "Of course not. But I am considering the fact that it's about time I stopped worshiping the devil and focused on myself. I don't need him."

"You better be careful what you say. I don't need to tell you how powerful he is. You committed yourself to him. You can't just walk away. Especially not now in the middle of this lawsuit."

"I would still meet any legal obligations. It isn't like I'd be a no show for trial or anything like that. But this day to day warring between the factions is frankly getting old. I'd like to live in peace for a while."

She wanted to scream. Being in charge was what she wanted, but not with him running away from what they'd built together. "You won't find any peace. It's too late for that."

He shook his head. "I refuse to believe it."

"But I need you in this fight. I need you by my side to take out Layton once and for all."

"I'm sorry, Nina Marie. The decision has been made. It's just a matter of implementation. I'll be CEO in name only. And once this litigation is behind us, you'll become the next CEO."

"You really are foolish to think the evil one is just going to let you walk away."

"What can he do to me?"

"Hurt you! How can you even question that after all the things you've seen over the years? The evil one and his demons wield so much power on this earth. You won't be able to escape that even if you find the most remote beach on the planet."

He looked up into her eyes. "It won't matter. He can't hurt me more than what I'm already facing."

"What are you talking about?" Her mind raced.

"I'm sick, Nina Marie."

"What do you mean?"

"I have cancer. Stage four pancreatic. As you can imagine, the prognosis is pretty grim. I'm not going to sit around worshiping the devil as I prepare to die."

The breath felt like it was being sucked out of her body. "Are you sure?"

"Yes, I've seen the best doctors. They are all in agreement."

Now it all made sense. His strange behavior, him pulling back, his lack of interest. This could change everything. "You're not going to die," she said.

He smirked. "If only you had the power to heal me. But you don't."

Yes, she wanted to take over Astral Tech, but she hadn't really wanted anything to happen to Clive. Especially not like this. "I'm at a loss for words."

He nodded. "I was too for a while. Now that I've had some time to think about it though, I've come to the conclusion that I'm personally done with all of this. I still need the business to function from a purely financial perspective, but I have no interest in anything else."

"What are you saying?"

"That if you want all of the activities of Astral Tech to continue, then you'll need to be the leader. I am done with all aspects of serving the devil."

She reached out and touched his arm. "This is the sickness talking, Clive. It's not you."

"No, Nina Marie. Like I said, I finally feel like the fog has lifted off of me. And I want to live out my last days my way. That doesn't include anything having to do with demonic forces. For all I know, I'm sick because of the lifestyle I've led."

"Do you really believe that?"

"To be completely candid, I've thought about it a lot. I've wondered if I'm being punished for the evil life I've led."

"We can go to the evil one—all of us united as one and ask him to heal you."

"It won't work. I'm certain of that."

"But how can you know if we don't try?"

He looked up at her with eyes filled with sadness. "It's over. When it's the right time, I'll call a meeting where I will hand the reins of the spiritual group over to you."

"They may not want to stay if you leave though. What if we have people go to Optimism?"

He shook his head. "I hate to say this, but it's no longer my problem. I hope you can respect that. Not until you really face the prospect of death do these things really crystalize in your head."

Her body felt numb as she heard his words. "Okay." What else could she say to a dying man?

"I need you to keep this to yourself. As far as everyone else is concerned once I'm ready to announce, I'll be taking an early retirement."

"And you think our members will believe that?"

"Doesn't matter. That's all I'm going to tell them." He sighed. "And assuming I'm still alive and able, I'll be back for the trial. Since no trial date has been set yet, I can't make any promises." He looked down and then back up. "They don't really know how much time I have left, but we're talking months not years."

"I'm sorry, Clive. I know right now you want to step away from all of this, but I'm going to continue what you've started. I'll make you proud."

"Oh, Nina Marie, don't be so melodramatic. I've always known that you wanted to run the show."

"But not like this," she said quietly. Yes, she wanted victory, but only when it was fairly won. "I'll let myself out." She needed some time alone to come to grips with the revelations of the day.

***

Grant felt more rested than he had in a long time. He had woken up with a renewed purpose—to fight for this lawsuit as hard as he could. Once he put all his attention back on the legal issues and away from all the extra curricular nonsense that everyone else was obsessed about, he felt more like himself.

He'd convinced himself of the fact that he was so tired last night that he had started hallucinating. He needed to take better care of himself. Starting today he was going to make himself get sleep and not skip meals. It had occurred to him once he'd gotten home last night that he hadn't eaten all day long. No wonder he was seeing things. He couldn't run on empty any more.

He was also energized by his latest legal strategy. A strategy that Layton had just signed off on. So he whistled as he pulled up to Astral Tech's office. It was time to give Olivia a taste of her own medicine.

Smiling at Melanie as he walked in, the two of them were becoming fast friends because of his frequent visits to the enemy's office.

"I know you have to be here to see Olivia."

"That's right. How're you doing today?"

"I'm fine and yourself?"

"Great, Melanie. I'm doing great."

She gave him a weak smile and stood up from the large desk. Today she wore what he recognized to be her signature high heels and a black dress. "Come on back."

He followed her down the hallway to the room where he knew Olivia would be working. And he couldn't wait to see Olivia's reaction to the papers he intended to give her. It was about time he took control of things.

"Grant." Olivia stood up from her chair. Today her long dark hair was hanging loose down past her shoulders. She wore a gray pantsuit and a fancy looking silver necklace.

"Sorry to drop in unannounced."

She stood with her arms crossed. She wasn't stupid. "What do you have for me?"

He shouldn't really take this much pleasure in what he was about to do, but he couldn't help it. "Since you were so kind as to give me notice before you filed the restraining order, I thought I would do the same and return the favor." He set his briefcase on the table and opened the latch pulling out her copy of the legal filing. Handing it over, he waited to gauge her reaction.

Her dark eyes quickly skimmed the first page. "You've got to be kidding me. You're seeking an emergency injunction?"

"Why do you seem so surprised?"

"If the harm to Optimism from Astral Tech selling the app was so great, you would've filed the brief for the injunction with the complaint. You and I both know that."

He shook his head. "On the contrary, not until I reviewed the first set of documents that you provided in response to my document requests did we fully appreciate the extent of the harm. By your client continuing to use the stolen technology, my client is suffering with each day that passes. We're going to ask the court for an emergency hearing as soon as possible."

She flipped her hair over her shoulder and took a few steps toward him. "This is exactly the type of stunt I expect from plaintiff's lawyers. I don't know why I thought you were better than that. But you've proven me wrong."

For a moment he almost felt a shred of shame, but then he straightened his shoulders and looked her in the eyes. "I'm vigorously defending the interests of my client. You would do the same thing. Every day that Astral Tech profits from the stolen app, irreparable harm is done to my client. And the Astral Tech app dilutes the Optimism brand. A judge will see that when presented with the evidence."

"So you're going to try to get the judge to order that Astral Tech must stop selling the app."

"Selling and marketing. All of those activities must cease."

She laughed loudly. "That will never fly. The judge will never interfere with commerce in that way. Especially not on these set of facts."

"He will when he sees the evidence supporting our theft claim."

"I've seen the documents, remember? I'm the one who turned them over to you. There's nothing in there to support your theft claim."

"Maybe you should've looked more closely."

"What are you talking about?"

"You'll see all the evidence outlined in the supporting brief."

"So that's how it's going to be, huh?"

"Just business, Olivia. Nothing personal." He could tell she was trying to keep it together but a little red blotch on her neck let him know that he was clearly getting to her.

"I think you've said everything you've needed to say. You can see your way out." She turned her back on him and walked away to take a seat in front of the computer.

It was just the reaction he wanted. He had her frazzled. And the hearing on the injunction would no doubt be highly contested. This could be a turning point in the case. He couldn't help whistling as he walked back down the long corridor toward the front of the building.

He was so preoccupied he could barely come to a stop before running right into Nina Marie.

Her big brown eyes flashed in surprise, and then her mouth turned into a frown. "What are you doing here?"

"I had to talk to Olivia." He took a step back. "I was just leaving."

"You know that your client is crazy, right?" She took a step closer to him edging him back toward the wall.

"I'm sure that's going to be a topic on which we disagree."

She reached out and touched his shoulder. He flinched.

"You're a cute one, you know. Too bad you're the enemy."

He had to be professional, so he kept his mouth shut.

"I know you're not totally innocent when it comes to Layton's tactics. So I'll say this. Even though I have no reason to dislike you personally, since you're Layton's lawyer you're caught in the crossfire."

"Are you threatening me?"

She laughed. "I think you understand exactly what I'm saying. We'll use every means at our disposal to fight this lawsuit."

"I think it's time for me to go." He turned around and started walking toward the lobby, but she grabbed his arm.

"You've been warned." Her brown eyes now held no warmth but were ice cold. She let go of his arm and walked back toward her office.

He couldn't get out of there fast enough. By the time he started his car, he was ready to speed down the road. Nina Marie's threat wasn't exactly thinly veiled. But c'mon. What could that woman actually do to him? Just because she was crazy and believed in witchcraft didn't mean he did.

Although she could certainly use other more traditional means to come after him. Especially after she talked to Olivia and found out why he had been there. The filing of the injunction paperwork was likely to start a real war between the two companies. He'd known that when he came up with the idea, but it was something they needed to do.

And it wasn't like it was a waste of time. They actually had a chance of winning. When he'd read those emails between Nina Marie and Layton, it definitely changed his opinion on the strength of the case. Had Olivia missed them in her review of the documents, or did she just have a great game face to not give away that there were some smoking gun documents in the set she turned over to him?

Either way, those documents changed the landscape of the case. He knew it. And she'd know it soon.

***

Olivia stared down at the pages sitting on the large conference room table. How could she have missed these documents in her review? They were labeled for production so they were clearly in the set that was supposed to be turned over to Optimism.

But Olivia had personally read every single email that she gave Optimism. Or at least she thought she had. She didn't make mistakes like this. The end result of all of this would still be the same. She would've had to have turned over the emails to Grant because there was no reason to withhold them—like attorney client privilege. But it sure would've been nice to have not put them in the first production. To have had more time to strategize a response.

Now she had an even bigger problem. How was she going to explain this complete blindside to Nina Marie and Clive—and ultimately Chet. This would make her look really bad. Like she was being sloppy.

Taking a deep breath she read the email exchange between Nina Marie and Layton again.

Nina Marie,

You won't get away with this. You're a thief! You stole the technology for the app and I can prove it.--L

***

Layton—you're obviously upset because I broke up with you. You need to move on and stop harassing me.

***

What about the files you removed from my laptop? I know you have them on your computer. Including the designs.--L

***

I'm not an idiot. Those files are long gone. Have a nice life.--NM

Ugh. That last email was basically an admission by Nina Marie that she'd stolen files from Layton and then deleted them after the fact. Things like this would not play well in front of the jury.

And the strangest part was that it didn't even sound like something Nina Marie would say. Why would she have ever put something like that in writing? Was she just letting her emotions control her?

The only thing she could do now was talk to Nina Marie. That was the first step. She picked up the conference room phone and asked Nina Marie to come down.

Within a minute, she was walking through the door with a Cheshire cat grin on her face.

"I saw Grant on his way out. I think I got into his head a little bit."

"Well, don't get too cocky. When you hear why he came by here, you probably won't feel as good."

Nina Marie walked all the way in and took a seat beside her at the table. "What is it? You've got a very serious lawyer look going on right now."

"Grant was here letting me know that he was filing the papers for an emergency injunction with the court."

"What is that?"

"Basically, he's going to ask the court to stop Astral Tech from selling and marketing the Astral Tech app."

Nina Marie sucked in a breath. "Based upon what exactly?"

"That's the thing. I have to apologize up front."

"For what?" Nina Marie asked cutting her off.

"In the first set of documents that were produced to the other side in the litigation, there was an email that I didn't see. I believe I reviewed every document myself, but it's possible that I could've made a mistake. Anyway, here's the email exchange between you and Layton. They're going to use this as an evidentiary basis to support their argument for an injunction against Astral Tech." Olivia pushed the piece of paper in front of Nina Marie.

Nina Marie pushed her glasses up on her nose and started reading. The further she read, the deeper her frown became and her eyebrows narrowed. Then she shook her head. "I never wrote that last email. The one time stamped at five fifteen p.m."

"Are you sure?"

"I'm absolutely positive. How dumb do you think I am?"

Olivia sighed. "Before we even get any further into this, I guess the first question I should ask, even though I asked it initially, is whether there is any factual basis to Layton's claim against you."

Nina Marie leaned back in her chair and crossed her arms. "I'm offended that you would even ask me that at this point, Olivia."

"Remember, I'm your lawyer. Whatever you say doesn't go out of this room. But I need to know to be able to defend you properly. I can understand you being hesitant when you first met me to tell me everything, but we're way past that point now."

"Let's say hypothetically even if I reviewed the technical specifications for Layton's app, there is no way I would've revealed it in an email. But that's just a hypothetical. I think you realize I would never engage in theft. It's beneath me."

Olivia wanted to groan. Nina Marie was walking a fine line. But her job wasn't to make value judgments. Her job as a lawyer was to zealously defend her client. Everyone deserved a defense under the American judicial system. And she wasn't going to let this derail her efforts. "So any idea how this email appeared?"

"You said yourself you don't remember seeing this. What if they hacked into our system once they got the documents and changed this particular email? Layton and his people have very strong technical skills."

"Let's pull up the original email on your computer from the archives."

"All right." Nina Marie stood up, and Olivia followed her down the hall.

Nina Marie sat in front of her computer and started searching her mail archives for the email in question.

"Do you think Layton and his team have the ability to not only change the document but to also make it untraceable?"

Nina Marie nodded. "Unfortunately, probably so."

"Although if we hire the right expert they can probably detect any edits. Everything done on a computer is traceable in some way."

"Unless you're so good that you can erase it."

"Unless he has former NSA employees on the payroll, I highly doubt they're that good." She paused. "But I need to make sure before we go down this path that you are one hundred percent above board with me. Because if I make the representation to the court that this email is falsified and you in fact did write it, then that will result in huge problems for both of us. Do you understand that?"

Nina Marie nodded.

"No, I need more than a nod. This is my career on the line here. I need you to look me in the eyes and tell me you didn't write that email."

Nina Marie looked up. "I didn't write that email."

"Okay."

"This is a lot more aggressive side of you, Olivia. I like it."

"Thanks, I guess."

"I do have one other question though. Given my hypothetical statement earlier, how will you handle my testimony?"

Olivia blew out a breath. "We'll cross that bridge if and when we get to it."

"I told you it was better for you not to know." Nina Marie took off her glasses.

"We're in this together right now. I need to know what you know."

Nina Marie reached out and grabbed her arm. "Given your religious beliefs, I find it hard to believe that you'd want to know everything."

"What do you know about my beliefs?"

"Enough to surmise that you don't want any part of what we're actually doing here at Astral Tech."

"If it's at all relevant to the lawsuit, then I need to know it. Beyond that, you're right."

Nina Marie stood beside her. "What are you afraid of, Olivia?"

"I'm not afraid," she said quickly.

"You say that but your eyes indicate otherwise."

"I'm solid in my faith. I have nothing to fear from you."

"Your strength and dedication is admirable. Even if it is misguided. You could do and be so much more on this earth than what you are. I could help you with that."

Olivia shook her head. "It's not this earth that I'm concerned about."

Nina Marie cocked her head to the side. "You truly believe in the heaven and hell scenario, don't you?"

"I do. And given the nature of your work, I would've thought you do to."

"I think the notion of hell is greatly exaggerated."

"And yet you believe in the devil."

"Yes, the evil one. I do. But I don't adhere to many of the biblical prophesies of the future. Unlike you, I'm much more concerned about the here and now. The one life I have to live and living it the way I want."

"It doesn't have to be like that," Olivia said softly. *Dear Lord, was there any way she could reach Nina Marie? Or was it far too late?*

"Don't even think about trying to convert me." Nina Marie chuckled. "It's just not gonna happen. I love my life too much. And I've seen what people who claim to be Christians can actually be like."

Olivia knew she was taking a risk in what she was about to say. But she went ahead anyway. "Are you really that happy, Nina Marie? Or are you lonely and unsure? Using Astral Tech and its activities to cover up the deep wounds of your past."

Nina Marie took a step back. "Don't talk to me about old wounds you know nothing about."

"I know enough to tell that you were hurt badly before. You were hurt by someone who supposedly was a Christian."

Nina Marie didn't respond.

"I can tell you that Christians aren't perfect. We make mistakes like everyone else. But if someone really hurt you, Nina Marie, I can guarantee that wouldn't be something sanctioned by the God I worship."

"Enough. Let's get back to the real issue here. And that's not you psychoanalyzing me. Remember I'm the one approving your legal bills."

She'd pushed enough for now. The reaction from Nina Marie told her a lot. "All right. If you tell me that you didn't write that part of the email, then our next step is to hire an expert who can prove it."

"Do it. I know we have a tight budget, but on this issue, spare no expense. We want the best."

"I can't reiterate how important this is. If the judge grants the injunction, you won't be able to sell or market the Astral Tech app. An entire chunk of your business will be put on hold."

"We cannot allow that to happen. You cannot allow that to happen. If you need more lawyers working on this, then so be it."

"Thanks. I'm on it. I have to draft our response right away. With these type of emergency court filings, the court date could be as soon as day after tomorrow."

"We can't lose this, Olivia. I'm putting my trust in you."

Olivia nodded and wondered how in the world she was going to handle this challenge.

CHAPTER TEN

Stacey had made up her mind. As she walked into the Optimism office, she was confident in her decision. The further away she had gotten from the *event*, as she was thinking of it in her head, the less afraid she was. After the event, she'd called in sick for the rest of the week. Different church members had called, emailed, and texted her. She had assured them all that she was doing fine.

Yeah, she still believed she saw something although now she wasn't as sure that it wasn't in a dream. At any rate, she could kill two birds with one stone. By keeping her internship, she'd have that to add to her resume. She'd also be able to help out the church by reporting back anything she found out at Optimism.

Now she hadn't quite figured out the logistics of working with Morena and making her believe that she was still on board. But she could do it.

As she walked down the brightly lit hallway she came face to face with Layton. His blue eyes widened slightly before going back to normal. He broke into a big smile. "Stacey, you missed a few days. Morena told me you were out sick. Are you all better now?"

"Yes, thank you. Much better. The tea she suggested really helped my sore throat."

He cocked his head to the side measuring her statements carefully. Could this man see right through her? No. No man was that powerful.

She smiled trying to put on a happy face. "I'm excited to be back at work. Thank you again for this internship. It will really be a huge boost for my resume. Before I left, Tony had suggested I could shadow him in finance for a bit. I'd be really interested in that too."

Layton nodded. "Of course, of course. There's plenty of time for you to become acquainted with all aspects of the business. And I must tell you, Morena has spoken very highly of your natural skill when it comes to the New Age arts."

She felt her cheeks redden. "She's just being nice."

He huffed. "Morena is never just being nice. It's not her style to compliment when there is no merit to do so."

"Thank you." She took a step back, and he grabbed onto her shoulders.

"You've got a lot of potential, Stacey. I know there will be doubts, self-doubt and otherwise, that creep in, but you need to stay the course. You have an amazing future ahead of you."

Was he talking about as a businesswoman or specifically about the New Age angle? "I'm glad you have faith in me."

"Faith isn't the right word. It's more like confidence. People like you don't come along every day, and I'd hate to see you squander this opportunity because you can't handle certain aspects of the New Age lifestyle."

It was like he was staring into her soul and could see that she was a fraud. He was testing her, but she wasn't going to back down. Not now anyway. She had to give this a shot. "I'm here, aren't I?"

He smiled. "Yes, you are. I'm sure Morena will want to work with you this morning. Let's go see if she's in yet."

"Great." While she said that, that was the last thing she was feeling. Nervous was more like it. She'd spent more time with Morena than Layton, and she feared that Morena would notice something was off. That she'd tried to start praying again. She'd been very successful right after the event, but less so over the past few days. Everything seemed so jumbled up in her mind. She had turned down an invitation to a prayer service Sunday night at church.

"Morena, hello," Layton said.

Morena stood up from behind her desk. Stacey still couldn't get over how beautiful she was. Today her long curls were pulled partially back from her face. Her skin was flawless, and she wore only a touch of pink lip gloss. She was the last thing Stacey would've ever pictured if she were thinking of someone who worked with the devil. She shuddered just thinking about it, and reminded herself that looks were so often deceiving.

"Stacey, I'm so glad you're back. How are you feeling?" Morena walked around to the front side of the desk to greet her.

"Much better. The tea you suggested was really therapeutic."

"I can show you how to make it yourself instead of paying the outlandish price the store charges."

"That would be great."

"Well, I'll let you ladies get to work." He turned to her. "Stacey, if you need anything at all, or just want to talk, my door is always open to you." There was actually a warmth in his bright blue eyes. The thought occurred to her. What if she was totally wrong about them? What if she was just delusional the other night and these people were completely normal and running a flourishing business?

"I appreciate that, Layton. More than you could know. I'm taking this internship really seriously."

"Let's do lunch soon and you can pick my brain about all the aspects of the business." He walked out leaving her alone with Morena.

"I'm so glad you came back, Stacey."

"Why wouldn't I come back?" She needed to put on a great acting performance right now. She wasn't sure enough about anything to spill her guts to Morena. She needed more time to gather all the facts and figure out how she was going to handle all of this.

Morena reached out and grabbed her hand. "Like Layton said, you have a lot of potential. And when you have that potential, sometimes you're challenged more than anyone else. Does that make sense to you?"

She nodded because it did make sense. So much so that it scared her.

"You don't have to be afraid of me, Stacey. I'm here to help you and guide you, and I'm never going to push you down a path that you don't want to go down. That's not what we're about here at Optimism. You have the power and control over your own life. You just need to grow into that knowledge and accept it. Once you do, there is absolutely no limit on what you can do. You can make your own way, and do it purely the way you want. Not the way I want or Layton wants. We each have a special path."

"You really believe that?" This sounded too good to be true.

"I can tell you're skeptical, and I don't blame you for that. You're a really smart woman with a great head on her shoulders. Not just book smarts although you definitely have that. Your instincts are strong, and they're a great asset. You need to learn to trust them."

"What if they're pulling me in different directions?"

Morena squeezed her hand. "You'll know exactly what to do when the time comes."

Strangely, she felt calm even though she thought she would be afraid. "So what are we going to do today?"

"I thought we'd step back and re-evaluate your efforts and interests. You tell me what you'd like to learn more about."

Before she could even formulate her thoughts she answered. "I'm still interested in the New Age healing methods."

Morena let go of her hand. "Perfect, then we'll work on that."

Stacey felt like that was a safe area for her. It was still New Age, but didn't cross the line into overt witchcraft. Something she was still a bit afraid of dealing with even if it was just a ruse.

Although as she started to listen to Morena talk about different healing techniques, she wondered if she was lying to herself. Wasn't she actually still interested in all the New Age techniques including the spells and witchcraft? Couldn't she draw the line before making any demonic connections?

While she definitely didn't want to worship the devil, she started wondering if there was truly any harm in experimenting with witchcraft. It wasn't like she was asking the devil to do anything. The New Age witchcraft relied on her own power—not that of any other spiritual being.

She decided then and there that she would keep an open mind. No one at the church needed to know that she was having second thoughts about all of this. She could keep it all together and stay safe. She knew she could.

***

Olivia had basically worked around the clock for forty-eight hours writing the response brief to the emergency injunction motion filed by Optimism. The hearing was scheduled for today, and she needed an extra cup of coffee to get her head on straight.

She walked out of the bustling Windy Ridge coffee shop and down the street to the courthouse. Her strategy was multi-prong. First, she'd found a forensic expert who she felt could provide testimony that the smoking gun email had been digitally altered. The problem was that she just retained him last night, and there was no way he was ready to testify today. But he was going to show up at court to demonstrate to the judge that they were serious about this claim of fabrication. She planned on asking the court for a stay in the action until the forensic examination could be completed.

But because she knew how these things often worked out, she couldn't rely on that as her sole strategy. So she'd also written a detailed brief in defense of Astral Tech and refuting all claims of theft with regard to the app. Taking a hefty gulp of coffee, she let the dark roast tickle her tongue as she strategized.

She'd told Chet that she had this under control. And because she was the one on the ground and doing all the work, he'd decided to let her handle the hearing on her own. She was relieved in part because trying to prep Chet to take over the hearing would've been a bit of a nightmare.

Entering the courthouse, she walked into the lobby area for a few minutes to finish her coffee. The courthouse lobby had a few chairs and benches, so she took a seat in one of the chairs. She had plenty of time before the hearing started. Opening up her briefcase, she took out the outline that she had prepared. The judge would give each side time to make their arguments. She had never prepared full-out scripts, but instead used bullet points to trigger the points she wanted to make. It was much more effective for her that way. And it also allowed for the judge to interrupt with questions without throwing her off her game like a script would do.

"Hey there."

She looked up and knew who it was before she saw him. "Hello, Grant."

He smiled and she had to admit that he looked handsome today wearing a dark navy suit with a maroon tie.

"How are you doing today?" he asked.

"I'm wonderful." There was no way he was going to see her sweat. Yeah, when he'd initially told her about the emergency injunction he was seeking, she'd flipped out on him and let her emotions get the best of her. But now that she had time to process it, he wasn't going to rattle her. Once she'd been convinced about the alteration of the digital file, she felt much better about their chances.

He knelt down beside her chair. "What have you got up your sleeve, counselor?"

"Why would you think that?" She didn't break eye contact with him.

"Because you almost seem smug and, at the very least, a bit too confident, given the facts."

"Ah, the facts. We'll just have to see, won't we?"

He laughed. "Going up against you is a challenge, Olivia. But I have to admit, it's never dull. Man, I love my job."

She couldn't help but smile. "We'll see if you feel that way after the hearing is over."

"I admire your confidence, even if I think it's a bit misplaced given the circumstances. Any judge in the country will look at this set of facts and rule in favor of Optimism."

The thing was that Grant didn't know about her claim of document tampering. Since she'd just secured the expert last evening, she hadn't put anything about it in her brief that she'd filed by the five p.m. deadline last night. And there was nothing saying she had to tell him now. He'd find out soon enough.

She looked down at her watch. "We should probably be headed into the courtroom."

"Yes, ma'am. After you."

She stood up from her seat and threw her empty coffee cup in the trashcan before going through the security line.

About a half hour later, Judge Wingfield took his seat at the bench, and Olivia was ready to go. From the intel that her firm had gathered, Wingfield was a seasoned, no-nonsense type of judge. In his early sixties, sharp, witty, and slightly impatient. He wore glasses and had big dark eyes and gray hair.

Since Grant had filed the motion for an emergency injunction, he'd get to speak first.

"Hello, folks," the judge said. "Looks like we've got an emergency motion for an injunction. I just finished reading both side's papers that were filed with the court. But I'll hear arguments now from both of you. Mr. Baxter, you're up."

Grant stood up from the counsel's table and approached the podium. "Thank you, Your Honor. As you've read the papers, I will be brief. Simply, this is a case of theft of technology. We have clear evidence in the form of an email exchange between Layton Alito, the CEO of Optimism, and Nina Marie Crane, the Chief Operating Officer of Astral Tech. In this email, Ms. Crane all but admits stealing the app that was developed by Mr. Alito, my client. The email was attached to my motion filed with the court as Exhibit One. Does Your Honor need another copy?"

"No, Mr. Baxter. I have it right here in front of me." The judge motioned to the stack of papers. "I must say it is an interesting email. I'm sure Ms. Murray will have something in response, but please continue."

"Thank you, Your Honor. As I was saying, the email is compelling evidence that Ms. Crane stole the technology from Mr. Alito's computer. Astral Tech will try to make you believe that this is just a lover's quarrel gone wrong, but that is just background noise. Regardless of any drama between Mr. Alito and Ms. Crane, the theft issue is separate and must be addressed. Every day that Astral Tech is able to market and sell this stolen technology is a day my client is irreparably harmed. This evidence also supports that we would most likely succeed on the merits once this case goes to trial. And under any balancing test, my client is harmed more than Astral Tech. Given all the factors for an injunction weigh in our favor, we would respectfully request this court to issue an injunction to stop the marketing and selling of the Astral Tech app until this case has been fully litigated."

"Are you finished, Mr. Baxter?"

"Yes, Your Honor."

"All right, then. Ms. Murray, the floor is all yours."

"Thank you." She stood up and walked to the podium. This wasn't a normal hearing. She'd never argued an issue quite like this before, but she felt strongly about it, which always helped.

"Your Honor, you've read my response brief to the motion for injunction. And I'm happy to discuss our substantive response, but there is an issue not raised in the briefing which will be of great importance to the court."

"Well, Ms. Murray, after a preview like that, you have whetted my appetite for something interesting. Please proceed."

"After reading the motion and reviewing the exhibits presented by Optimism, of course I met with my client to discuss the allegations. It is the contention of Astral Tech that the email exchange Optimism has attached as Exhibit One to their brief has been digitally altered."

"Objection." Grant stood up from his seat. "This is the first I'm hearing of this outlandish claim, and there's no basis for such an assertion."

"Mr. Baxter, you really haven't given Ms. Murray a chance to make her argument. Now please sit back down."

Grant frowned and took his seat. She knew she had to win over the judge on this quickly. She didn't want him to think this was all a ruse or stalling tactic.

"Your Honor, Mr. Baxter hasn't heard of this because he just filed this motion two days ago. I've been working nonstop to investigate all of the allegations and prepare a response. That included meeting with my client and examining all the evidence that Mr. Baxter presented. During that examination, my client reviewed the email exchange in question and is fully certain that she never wrote the last email in the chain."

"Is she willing to testify to that under oath?" Judge Wingfield asked.

"Of course. But knowing that Mr. Baxter would just claim that she was trying to cover up what she had done, I have retained a forensic expert. An expert that can examine the raw data and determine if it has been altered."

She glanced back at Grant, and he scowled at her. Then he rose from his seat again. "Your Honor, you can't really believe this story that Ms. Murray has concocted."

"Your Honor, my expert is here in the courtroom right now. He hasn't had time to actually perform the analysis, but I asked him to come today in case you wanted to hear from him. I would ask for you to stay this motion for an injunction until my expert has had time to examine the data. Given that Mr. Baxter's case for an injunction relies almost exclusively on this email exchange, I believe we should have a chance to prove the fabrication."

"Well, well. I must say that when I read the papers I thought this would be pretty much an open and shut case, given the evidence presented. But Ms. Murray has raised a possible defense—and a serious one at that. Ms. Murray, you do know that if it turns out that the email is legitimate, you would've made a representation to this court that I would not appreciate. And if I determine that you are using this as a tactic to buy time, I would definitely consider sanctions against you and your client."

She nodded. "I am well aware of the gravity of the situation, Your Honor. But I believe, given the circumstances, my client has a right to have a chance to present evidence to disprove the authenticity of the email."

Judge Wingfield sat quietly for a minute. She took deep, even breaths trying to think about the next step.

"Your expert, where is he?"

"He's in the third row, Your Honor. Mr. Blake Sanchez."

Blake nodded and raised his hand.

"Mr. Sanchez, I have no need to swear you in as a witness quite yet. But if I'm considering Ms. Murray's proposal as an option, I'd like to hear from you as to how long it would take you to make a finding regarding the authenticity of the email."

Blake stood up. "Yes, Your Honor. Since we're only dealing with one email that is in question here as opposed to a lot a data, I believe I could make a determination within a few days."

"Very well then. Ms. Murray, I'm going to allow you to pursue this path. Mr. Baxter, I presume you will want to hire your own expert in this matter."

"You've presumed correctly, Your Honor."

"All right. We will reconvene a week from today. That should allow both parties ample time to investigate and present findings on this email."

"Thank you," she said.

"See you next week." The judge stood up and left the courtroom.

She walked back toward Blake. The forensic expert was tall and thin. He wore a nice black suit with a navy tie. His dark hair was styled neatly, and he definitely looked the part of an expert witness. "Can you meet me at the Astral Tech office later today to start working on the data?"

"Yes. I need a couple of hours to tie up something else. How about two p.m.?" Blake asked.

"That's perfect, thank you."

"See you then." He walked out of the courtroom.

Olivia went back up to the counsel's table to grab her stuff.

"We need to talk," Grant said. His tone let her know that he was angry.

"Sure," she said.

"Not here. Let's go outside." His voice was gruff, and his blue eyes flashed with annoyance.

None of this was her fault. She wasn't going to let him take his anger out on her. They walked in silence from the courthouse and out into a sunny and mild fall day in Chicago.

"The deli down the street has some outdoor seating, let's go there."

She didn't bother to argue with him. She just walked by his side, struggling to keep up with his brisk pace.

Once seated outside at the deli, she leaned back in her chair and waited for him to speak.

"Don't you have anything to say for yourself?" he asked.

"I don't know why you're acting so hostile. First, you were the one that said this was business and not personal. Two, you're the one who filed this totally unnecessary and inflammatory motion. And three, your client falsified evidence. So if anyone deserves to be angry now, it's me, Grant, definitely not you."

His eyes widened. "You can't truly believe that nonsense you were talking about in there. Digital alteration? Fabrication? Get real, Olivia. Your client has played you and you stepped right into it. Now you're probably going to get sanctioned when this is all said and done."

"Why is it so hard for you to believe my client's side of the story?"

"Because your client is a liar."

"And yours isn't?" She challenged him directly.

He blew out a breath. "I don't know why I consider you a friend when you're my rival, but for some strange reason, I do. It's not like I would've ever acted this way before with any of my other opposing counsels."

"So why me?"

He shrugged. "I have no idea. But if you would've come to me with this hair brained idea first, even if it was last night, I could've stopped you from making a huge mistake that would adversely impact your career."

"And how are you so confident?"

"Because digital alteration is a pretty crazy step to go through. We can win the lawsuit without it. Even if my client were willing to do something illegal, which I'm sure he's not, he wouldn't take that kind of risk with no need to do so. He's a smart businessman. That's why he's so successful."

She laughed. "So it's not out of knowing between right and wrong, but that it wouldn't make good business sense to do so."

"It doesn't matter the motivation. All that matters is the result. Which is why I'm sure that your fancy expert will tell you exactly what I already know. The email is one hundred percent legitimate." He paused. "And you're in a world of trouble."

"While I appreciate your concern, I think you're wrong. Think about it logically, Grant. Why would Nina Marie ever say something like that, even if it were hypothetically true? You talk about Layton's business smarts, well Nina Marie has them, too."

He shook his head. "I guess you had to do what your client told you to. But still…"

"I'm a big girl, Grant. And if something happens to me, it's not on you. We're both doing our best to represent our clients."

"Cavorting with the enemy now, Olivia?"

Olivia looked up and Nina Marie stood in front of their table smiling.

"Grant and I were just discussing the issue surrounding the evidence fabrication."

"Yes." Nina Marie looked at Grant. "I knew Layton was a snake, but this really is a bit much even for him."

Grant cleared his throat. "I don't really feel comfortable getting into this discussion right now, beyond saying that I believe the experts will confirm what I already know. That the email exchange is authentic."

Nina Marie smiled, but the smile wasn't sincere. Olivia knew her well enough to know that. "Grant, you are a worthy opponent, but I know Olivia has this under control." Nina Marie turned and looked at her. "Will I see you back at the office?"

"Yes. I'll be back as soon as we finish up here."

"Very good. And nice to see you, Grant. If you get your head on straight, I hope you realize that nothing good can come from working with Layton. It's not too late for you to step away."

And with that Nina Marie turned and walked down the street.

"I don't trust that woman, Olivia."

"Why would you trust her? You're in a lawsuit against her."

"No. I mean personally."

Olivia almost choked on her soda. "I didn't realize you had a personal relationship with her."

"Not like that. But she just keeps popping up, and I really don't like engaging with her."

"Grant, I know you don't want me bringing this up, but I have to ask you this. Do you feel like Nina Marie is doing something to you?"

He rolled his eyes. "Are we back to this again?"

"Yes, we are. I want to know if you feel like she's coming after you."

"I'm over all of that. The only thing Nina Marie can do to me is annoy me. Nothing more."

"You need to be careful."

"Are you threatening me now?"

"Absolutely not. But I'm telling you to watch your back. All of these people, Grant. Your client and mine, they are playing on a different field. The legal aspects are one thing, but you know that's not what I'm talking about."

"For me to be worried about that would presume that I believe in all that stuff."

She couldn't help it. She reached out and touched his arm. "I know you felt something that night at your house, Grant. I saw it in your eyes. Heard it in your voice. We're in the precarious position of being in the middle of this spiritual fight, and I don't want you to get hurt."

His eyes softened and he put his hand on top of hers. His touch was warm, and she felt drawn to him. The words of Micah pounded through her head. She had a responsibility to try to get Grant to see that there was another way. That there was an unseen world out there. But she didn't even know how to begin to get him to open up his heart and mind. It was like after he was confronted with it at his house, the only way he could handle it was to step into a world of denial.

"You know, Olivia, you are about the most interesting person I've ever met."

She laughed. "Maybe that's just because you think I'm crazy with my talk about the spiritual realm."

She noticed that he hadn't removed his hand from hers. And she didn't move either.

"I don't think you're crazy. I think you deeply hold the beliefs and think they are true with all of your heart. That's one of the things that I find fascinating. I don't know how anyone can have that type of faith…in anything really."

"Don't you think that's a sad way to live?"

He looked down and back up into her eyes. "It's the only way I know how to live."

"I've asked you this before, but I'll ask you again. Is there any way you'd consider attending a church service with me?'

He shook his head. "What's the point?"

"You're curious. I can tell that. Yeah, you're not ready to jump into all of this. Especially with the spiritual warfare parts of it. But you're yearning for something more in your life, Grant. I can feel it."

He squeezed her hand. "That may be true, but have you given any thought to the fact that you interest me much more than religion does?"

Her cheeks turn hot. "We're friends, Grant. And opposing counsel. You know what that means as far as conflict of interest."

"Believe me. That's the only thing that's kept me from asking you out on a date."

"Me? Really?"

"Yes, you."

"I don't know what to say."

"You're funny, smart, and beautiful. And for the life of me, I'm drawn to you. I find myself wanting to know more about you and why you believe what you believe."

"I'm more than willing to share my faith journey with you."

"I appreciate that, Olivia. But what if I want to know about more than just your faith journey?"

Finally, she pulled her hand away. "I don't really know what to say."

"You don't have to say anything." He smiled.

She looked at him. "I asked you to come to church with me. If you're really that interested in me, as you say you are, and want to know the true me, who I am as a person, then you'll go to church with me this Sunday. As friends."

He leaned back in his chair, and they sat in silence for a few minutes.

Then he reached forward and grabbed her hand again. "All right. I'll come to church with you, but just this once. This isn't a commitment or anything like that." He paused. "And it doesn't mean I'm buying into all of the other stuff."

She nodded. "Of course. I understand that." Her heart practically exploded. This was the breakthrough she'd prayed for.

"Then it's settled. Let's go to church—as friends." He grinned.

She couldn't help but smile back at him. "I'm looking forward to it. I should run now, though. I need to get back to the office."

"See you Sunday then," he said.

"Sunday it is." Olivia felt like she had just won a major victory—one that could change everything.

CHAPTER ELEVEN

What in the world had he been thinking? Grant was letting his growing feelings for Olivia mess with his judgment. Church? He had really gone off the deep end now.

There was no way they could have any type of romantic relationship while they were still working this case. And it wasn't even clear to him if she would ever think of him as more than a friend anyway.

Although, because he couldn't help but want to know more about Olivia, he'd caved and accepted her church invitation.

He kept telling himself that this would be a purely academic exercise. Like a college class on something he was totally unfamiliar with. It wasn't like he was changing his life or anything.

He'd called Olivia yesterday and asked what he should wear. Was this a suit and tie type of thing? Much to his relief, she claimed that most of the church members wore more casual dress. So he had opted for khakis and a button down with a lightweight jacket. Why was he nervous? He had no clue.

Olivia had insisted on picking him up. She probably thought he would bail otherwise, and she had good reason to think that. But once he'd committed to something, he wasn't going to make excuses. This was one church service. How big of a deal could it really be?

As he paced around his living room, he wondered what he had signed up for. When the doorbell rang, he let out a breath. That had to be Olivia.

He opened the door, and she stood on the other side smiling. Wearing a light pink dress and her hair falling softly around her shoulders, he felt his heart nearly stop. He had to get a grip.

"You ready?" she asked brightly.

"Ready as I'll ever be."

"I promise it won't be that bad. Come on." She grabbed his hand and pulled him outside. He locked the door and then walked to her car.

They arrived at the Windy Ridge Community Church just a few minutes later, and he honestly felt like he was going to be sick.

She stopped the car and looked over at him with her big brown eyes. "You look a bit pale, Grant."

"I'm okay." He could shake this off.

"There's no reason to be nervous. It's not like anyone is going to put you on the spot or make you talk or anything like that."

"Well, that makes me feel better." He laughed and unbuckled his seat belt.

They walked toward the church together, and he looked up at the building. The only time he had ever been in churches was for weddings and funerals. He truly had no idea what to expect. He'd seen pieces of sermons on TV, but never real ones, just the ones in movies. And the preachers were always over the top—at least he hoped those portrayals were exaggerated.

One thing he did know, as they stepped through the front door of the church—Olivia was in her element. She smiled warmly and joy emanated from her.

He wondered if his presence had made her this happy, or if this was just the way she always was when she went to church. He figured it was probably the latter.

Pastor Dan stood at the foyer door greeting people and his eyes also lit up when he saw them walking toward him.

"Grant, it's so great to see you again."

"Thank you." He shook Dan's hand.

Then Dan gave Olivia a warm embrace. It was clear to him that the two of them had grown close. Then an awful thought hit him. What if she was interested in the pastor? Yeah, he was a little bit older than her, but that didn't matter. Dan said something to her in her ear and she laughed. Wouldn't that just be ironic? How in the world could he compete with that man? A man of God. He took another deep breath.

"Grant, let's go in," she said. She grabbed him by the arm and walked down the church aisle.

For a moment, he was just in awe taking it all in. It seemed like a pretty large church to him. And there was amazing stained glass in bright colors adorning the chapel. A large stained glass cross was the centerpiece at the front of the chapel. He did know enough about Christianity, just from pop culture, to understand that the cross had some key significance.

They took a seat on the right side of the church in the middle and music started to fill the place. He leaned down toward Olivia. "Uh, I hope I'm not expected to sing, because I can't carry a tune to save my life."

"Don't worry. You don't have to sing if you don't want."

After a few introductions and announcements, they were all told to stand. The words of the songs were placed up on the big screen. He didn't really know what he was expecting, but it certainly wasn't anything like this. He almost felt like he was at a concert.

In his mind, a church just had a stuffy choir singing old songs. But this music felt current. Something called the worship team was in the front of the church leading the singing. It included people playing all types of musical instruments, including the drums and guitar. He couldn't help but tap his foot to the beat of a song he'd never heard before.

Of course, he made no attempt to sing, but the music portion of the program wasn't nearly as bad as he thought it would be. What surprised him even more, though, was hearing Olivia's voice. She was clearly a gifted singer whose voice rang out perfectly in tune and with a strong purpose.

When they sat down, it was time for Pastor Dan to do his thing. He tried to push away his thoughts of jealousy and think about what the man was trying to say. He was here, and he'd promised himself he would listen.

Pastor Dan walked up to the podium carrying what he presumed was a Bible and a tablet. He guessed even churches were moving into the high tech phase these days. Which of course made him think about the Astral Tech app.

"I'm glad to see all of you here," Pastor Dan said. "Today we're going to talk about temptation. We're all tempted. Even Jesus was tempted by the devil. We're going to look at the temptation of Jesus and see what lessons we can take away from that to use in our own lives."

Interesting, he thought. He wasn't aware of this story that Pastor Dan was about to tell.

"If you have your bibles, please turn with me to Matthew chapter four. We'll start with verse one."

He looked over and Olivia had her bible on her own tablet. She put it between the two of them so he could read too. He listened carefully as Dan read the verses and he followed along. The story seemed thought provoking to him. Apparently, Jesus went out into the desert for forty days and was tempted by the devil multiple times.

"So let's unpack this a bit. Jesus has been fasting in the desert for forty days and nights. He's tired and hungry. And that's when the devil appeared to Him. Now before we jump into specifics, it's important to remember that the devil can tempt you at any time. He's basically the king of temptation. He'll dangle whatever it is you most want and desire right in front of you. He'll offer to give it to you. But always for a price."

So far, Grant was sufficiently intrigued and kept listening. Interested to hear what would be next.

"Here the devil comes to Jesus and basically says, if you're really who you say you are, then why don't you turn these stones into bread. See, the devil knew that Jesus had been fasting and was hungry. And that much was true. But Jesus didn't waver. No, he relied upon scripture and told the devil that man was not supposed to live by bread alone but by God's Word." He paused. "I also want to point out something else here. Jesus is the son of God. The most powerful. He is Lord. The beginning and the end. And yet, when confronted by Satan, he relies on the Word of God. If Jesus relies on the Word in His battle with the devil, then doesn't that let us know how much we as individuals must rely on the Word of God? When we're putting on the full armor of God to take on the devil, it all starts with the Word."

Okay, Grant was with him until this last part. He would have to follow up to get clarification on that. What armor was he talking about? Was this a physical war? Confusion set in but he kept listening. He looked over at Olivia. Her eyes were glued on the pastor.

"Undeterred, the devil comes at Jesus a second time. He takes him up to a pinnacle of the temple and says, if you're really who you say you are, then cast yourself down. And pay attention to what the devil does here. He starts quoting scripture back at Jesus. He says, isn't it written that the angels will lift you up in their hands so your feet won't even touch the stones? And what does Jesus do in response? He, of course, quotes more scripture, telling the devil that he shouldn't tempt the Lord. Well, the devil gives it one more try. That's something to remember everyone. The devil doesn't just come at us once. No, he's pesky. He's persistent. He'll keep coming over and over. And let me tell you, if he starts to sense the slightest weakness or wavering in your faith or your determination, he will keep coming and coming. Banking on the fact that one day you will break."

Grant pondered the words. Wondering if there even was such thing as a devil, and if the devil would even care about a man like him. He was a nobody. A bad news foster kid who had barely managed to make something of himself. And he definitely wasn't a spiritual threat to anyone.

Pastor Dan cleared his throat and took a sip of water. "So after two failed attempts to tempt Jesus, the devil tries to go for the touchdown pass. A big move. Hoping for a victory. He takes Jesus up on top of the mountain and says look at all of this. All the kingdoms of the earth. Everything out there. If you bow down and worship me, I'll give all of this to you. Isn't that a great deal? The devil was putting it all out there. Offering Jesus the world. But the catch was that Jesus had to fall down and worship the devil. And by this time, Jesus had had enough of the devil's games. He was done. Finished. He rebuked the devil and cited scripture back to him yet again. Saying that God was the only one to be worshiped. And at that point, after Jesus rebuked him, the devil fled. At least for then."

Grant sat taking in all the words as he carefully reread the scripture from the tablet Olivia held in her hand. Pastor Dan went on in detail for a bit providing background, context, and some lessons regarding the passage he had read.

"What can we take from all of this? There are a lot of things, but I'll leave you with a few closing thoughts. One, we must know the Word, live the Word, and use the Word. Because in a battle against the devil we must be armed with the Word. If the devil knows the Word well enough to cite it, then we as Christians should most certainly be better prepared and more well read then him, am I correct?"

A few amens rung out from the congregation. Grant looked around but figured based on everyone's reaction, that the response must have not been an abnormal occurrence.

"And secondly, you will be tempted by the devil. Even Jesus was tempted. You need to know your foe. Know that he is real and be prepared for battle. He will come at you, but you can rebuke him. You can resist him. And let me remind you again, if you rebuke the devil in the name of Jesus, he will flee from you. That doesn't mean he won't come back. Like I said at the beginning, he is persistent. But for that moment, you can find peace in the Lord once you tell the devil to leave you alone in the name of Jesus."

Grant had never heard anything like he was hearing from the pastor today. It was as if an entire different worldview was being presented to him. One that he'd never even considered.

"It's that time of the service where we're going to the Lord in prayer," Dan said. "And if there are any of you here right now who have never accepted Christ as your Lord and Savior, did you know you can do it right now?"

Actually, Grant didn't know that. But he wasn't nearly in a position to be thinking about that right now. Although he had to admit that it was kind of cool, that the option was available. Who knew?

"So if you're not saved and you want to be, you can ask God to come into your heart right now. It's not about you. It's about Him. About what He did for you. How He died on the cross and arose from the grave three days later so that you would have eternal life."

Whoa, this raising from the grave thing was something. He'd heard passing references to it in his life, but it never hit him to put all these pieces together. Talk about being confused. He zoned out for the last couple of minutes while Dan spoke.

"Let us pray," Dan said.

Grant decided to close his eyes and listen to the prayer.

"Dear Lord, we come to You today and thank You for all the many blessings You've given us. I know that right now we have people in this congregation who really need You, Lord. We all have needs. Spiritual needs, physical needs, emotional needs, financial needs. Please give us strength and guidance. And let us lean on You because that's what You want us to do." He paused. "And Lord, I also know that there are those here today who haven't yet come to know You. But they're here, God. They've taken the first step. I pray that you will guide them along the path. A path that starts and ends with You. And finally, Lord, I want to say a special prayer for those here who are facing some battles. Those who are being tempted by the devil just like You were. And those who are facing down evil in their daily lives. You know who they are, Lord. You've heard their prayers. Please be with them. Grant them the power to do battle against the devil. And the peace to continue. We ask all of this in Your name, amen."

Grant opened his eyes and looked over at Olivia, who had a couple of tears flowing down her cheeks. He couldn't stop himself as he reached out and wiped a stray tear away.

"Are you all right?" he asked.

"Yes. Just a lot on my mind, that's all."

He wasn't sure where this flood of emotion was coming from that he was seeing in her, but he knew it was genuine. He followed her lead as she stood up and walked back down the aisle toward the church exit.

Pastor Dan was standing by the door shaking hands. When it was their turn, he shook Dan's hand.

"So, what did you think of the sermon, Grant?"

"It was interesting. A lot of new information and, if I'm being totally honest, some of it was a bit confusing."

"That's totally understandable. If you want to talk about any of it, or anything, for that matter, my door is always open." He paused and looked toward Olivia. "And you have a great friend here who is totally on top of all of this stuff."

She smiled at Dan and gave him another hug. "Great sermon."

The two of them walked out of the church and to her car.

"Want to grab some lunch?" she asked.

"Sure."

"I'm in the mood for pizza. Would you object to that?"

"A man never objects to pizza."

She laughed. "Pizza it is then."

"Can I ask you something?"

"Sure," she said as she started the car.

"Are you and Pastor Dan involved?"

"What?" she asked loudly. She stopped the car in one of the parking spaces and looked over at him.

"I mean, romantically."

"What in the world would ever give you that idea?"

"You just seem really close to him, and all the hugging and smiles."

"I'm sure Pastor Dan is a wonderful man, but I don't have any interest in him like that. The poor man just recently lost his wife. I'm sure he's still grieving."

"Doesn't mean he isn't interested in you."

"Pastors care about all of the congregation. What you think is romance is you not fully understanding how caring and loving a church body can be."

"Maybe. I didn't mean to offend you with the question."

She started driving. "You didn't offend me. Just surprised me. It wouldn't have even occurred to me to look at him in that way. Although, I wouldn't see anything wrong with it if I did. But I don't. Okay?"

"Got it." He'd obviously said something wrong, but it was too late to take it back now.

He gave her directions to his favorite pizza place in the neighborhood. They ordered an extra large with everything, because he'd assured her he would take the rest home.

She picked up her iced tea and took a sip. "I want to hear your unfiltered answer to what you thought about the sermon. I knew you were going to be polite and professional when Dan asked you."

He laughed. "What, did you think I was blowing smoke up his—"

"Grant!" She cut him off.

He put up his hands in defense. "Seriously, what I told him was the truth. But it's just really complicated. I came out of there a lot more confused and with more questions than I went in with."

"I'm all ears."

"That's the problem. I'm so overwhelmed, I don't even know where to start with the questions. Pretty much every single thing he said today was new to me, except the most basic of propositions."

"Such as?"

"Well, I'm obviously aware of talk of the existence of Jesus and of the devil. But beyond that, everything is murky. Especially the whole rising from the grave after three days things."

She nodded. "I think you got thrown into a pretty deep sermon. Which is good and bad. We may need to step back and start with some more core ideas to be able to build upon."

"And you want to be the one to teach me?"

"If you're interested."

"I don't really know what I want right now." He sighed and looked into her eyes. "But I'm at least searching for answers to some questions."

"That's good, because I don't want you to go down this road because of me. If you want to take this path, it needs to be for you and about what you feel."

"So talking to you is just an added bonus."

"I guess so." She smiled.

"We don't have to go there now, over pizza. Give me a little time to think about it. Then we can talk later. How does that sound?"

"Perfect."

And just in time, the pizza arrived. He needed some time with his own thoughts before he started peppering her with questions.

The only thing he knew for sure was that he was left searching for more. A lot more.

***

Olivia sat down with the forensic expert, Blake Sanchez, on Wednesday morning. He'd worked all weekend to deliver his findings. But then he had taken two more days to write his report and get everything in order. Her heartbeat sped up as she waited for him to speak.

All kinds of doubts bombarded her. What if Grant was right? What if Nina Marie had straight up played her? It wasn't exactly like Olivia thought Nina Marie was trustworthy. But the thing that she kept coming back to was the fact that Nina Marie was shrewd, careful, and calculating. Would she have ever sent an email like that?

Guess I'm about to find out, she thought.

"So, Blake, thank you again for working over the weekend and the long hours this week."

"No problem. In my business, the long and erratic hours are perfectly routine. Most people aren't calling in guys like me unless there's a high stakes problem."

And she knew that. Blake Sanchez was one of the best, working at a top litigation consulting firm that specialized in computer forensics, but he charged a hefty hourly rate.

"Talk to me, Blake." She hoped that she hadn't just ruined her career by going down this dangerous path.

"To put it simply, the file has been digitally altered."

She let out a breath and sent up a prayer. Thank the Lord that she wouldn't be sanctioned by the court. She knew the firm would freak out if that had happened.

"All right. Give me details."

"The biggest finding was that the digital alteration was done on site. Specifically at Nina Marie's computer."

"You mean from inside the Astral Tech building? From her office?"

"Yes. I assumed it was an outside network hack, but once I uncovered everything, I found out that wasn't the case. I went through this step by step in painstaking detail for the expert report I'm providing to you. And I can testify to these points as well."

She nodded. "Okay, I don't need every single detail, but give me the major high points."

He opened up his laptop. "Sure. I can email you a summary report, too. But the facts I've gathered are this: The email was digitally altered from Nina Marie's computer. I wasn't able to nail down the exact time of the alteration because the person covered those tracks. I can provide a window of a couple of days. That's the best I can do and still be able to provide solid technical support for my finding. I know you would prefer an exact time, but the person who did this had skills. Most forensic guys would've actually missed it. But the guy or girl made one mistake which left an opening for me to step through, so to speak, to get the digital footprints I needed to make this conclusion."

"All right. I need you to be one hundred percent honest with me. Your honesty and forthrightness is much more important to me than what your actual answer is."

"Believe me, Olivia, in my business I'm used to these types of highly sensitive matters. My job is never to advocate. That's the job of the lawyers. I'm here to provide my expert opinion and analysis as a computer specialist."

"Great, and I definitely appreciate your professionalism. My question is this: How certain are you of your findings? Will Grant's computer guy that he hires come in and say the exact opposite?"

Blake smiled and shook his head. "Absolutely not. This isn't a gray area, Olivia." His brown eyes were intent as he stared at his laptop. "Look at this." He pointed. "These are the digital signatures I was able to identify. This is irrefutable evidence of alteration."

"My next question is this…"

"Go for it."

"You said that you're certain that the changes were made on Nina Marie's desktop computer?"

"Yes. And I know that because this was a change made to the native file residing on her hard drive and not to the file as it sat on the shared server. Plus some other highly technical things I can go into if you need me to."

"No, that's just the starting point for my next question. Are you able to tell whether someone logged in with her password or hacked into the computer?"

Blake smiled. "I didn't know if you were going to ask me that."

She couldn't help but smile back. "Is that a good thing or bad thing?"

"I like it when lawyers think through all the technological issues. It makes my job a lot easier. And yes, I did determine that it wasn't a hack like what you would think of on the street as hacking into a computer, but someone did break the password."

"And I'm guessing if someone is sophisticated enough to pull this off to begin with and almost completely cover their tracks, that cracking a password wouldn't be difficult."

He nodded his head. "Let me put it to you like this. Cracking the password would be a complete piece of cake for this guy." He paused. "And I keep calling him a guy. That's an assumption on my part based totally on statistical probability of who would most likely do something like this. It's not something I would ever testify to as to my opinion, because I realize there are human factors not known to me, and it could be a male or female who did this for sure."

"The gender of the perpetrator isn't as important as the fact that it actually happened. That's why I wanted to be crystal clear with you on the alteration itself and whether it happened. In your opinion, is there any room for another expert to have a different theory on the fabrication?"

He chuckled. "You've been a lawyer long enough to know that an expert can be paid to say anything. But anyone who is truly a computer forensic expert couldn't deny this evidence."

"So I'm assuming they're not going to just roll over. What would you do if you were presented with this if you were on the other side?"

"Concede the alteration happened, but claim that my client didn't do it. Things like whether the person had access to the building, and are there security cameras here which could document everyone's coming and going during the couple day window I provided you?"

She was writing furiously on her legal pad. "You're so right. I didn't even think about the cameras. The issue will be whether we still have the tapes from those days, or if they've already been recycled back into the rotation."

"The person who did this had to have been in the building. So if the other side can prove they were never here, then that would be a big defense for them, in at least proving they didn't do it. It doesn't resolve the issue of the fact that the email would then be thrown out because it was altered, but it would get them off the hook for any criminal liability."

"Interesting."

"You're thinking something. I can tell it when lawyers go into lawyer mode. They get the whole furrowed brow and big frown look. And you're tapping your pen." He looked over at her hand which was tapping away on her legal pad.

"I'm just trying to think back."

"Has anyone from the other side been into the building that you know of?"

No, he wouldn't have. It couldn't have been him. "The only person I know of for sure that has been in the building is the lawyer for the other side."

"Ouch, that would be huge if the lawyer was found to basically be evidence tampering. How well do you know that guy?"

"Well enough. I can't see him doing anything like that. Mainly because I can't imagine he'd risk his career over this litigation. It's just not worth it from any angle."

"Stranger things have happened. Never underestimate a desperate lawyer. Especially if they feel backed into a corner."

"But still." She leaned forward in her chair. "There's a big difference in pushing the envelope on litigation tactics and basically breaking into the other side's computer and planting evidence."

Blake grimaced. "Yeah, when you put it like that. I just don't know. That's out of my territory. All I know is that the person who altered the email did it from Nina Marie's desktop. Beyond that, I can't help you out."

"You've already been beyond helpful. I'm very impressed with your work here, Blake. I'll definitely recommend my firm use you again."

"That would be great. We're always happy to get more of BCR's business. I've heard that you have one vendor you use in DC which is understandable. But I'd like to think that my people and I are the best. And we go anywhere you need us to go. So traveling isn't a problem."

"I will pass that along, don't worry about that. Do you need any help from me getting ready for court?"

"No, I'll finish up this report, and then you'll need to disclose it to Grant so he can provide it to his expert."

"If you come up with any more ideas on how they will try to debunk your theories, please let me know."

Blake smiled widely. "Believe me, these aren't theories. They're facts. Yes, I have opinion woven into them, but that file was digitally altered from Nina Marie's desktop. That is a fact."

"Thank you. I'll walk you out."

She led him into the lobby and then immediately went looking for Nina Marie. She would be thrilled with the news. But she was still worried about who the culprit was.

"Nina Marie." She walked into her office since the door was open.

"What do you have for me?"

"Blake's done with his analysis of your computer and all of the evidence."

Nina Marie's eyes were wide with interest. "And?"

"He's convinced that the file was digitally altered."

She threw her hands up. "And it took an overpriced expert for you to believe me."

"No, it's not that. If I didn't believe you, I wouldn't have stuck my neck out in the first place."

"Really?"

"Really. This is my job on the line. I told you that."

"So where does this leave us?" Nina Marie pushed back from her chair and walked over to where she was standing.

"That piece of information wasn't the biggest revelation that Blake uncovered. Basically, he determined that the change to the email happened on your desktop. Right here in your office."

"What?" Nina Marie asked with a raised voice. "Are you sure?"

"Unfortunately, yes. Now, the person was highly skilled. So Blake can only give us a window of time for when it happened. And I don't know if the security cams will have the footage form those dates."

"It's Layton, I tell you."

"Has he been here?"

"Yes. He came once to see me." She blew out a breath. "I was stupid and left him in my office alone for a few minutes while I was dealing with something else. What an idiot I was."

Her heart jumped a bit. She couldn't help but be relieved. She would much rather think that Layton did this than Grant. "But this is actually good. If we can show that it was him, not only would the email get thrown out, their chances of winning the injunction would almost evaporate and Layton could be brought up on criminal charges. He had to have broken your password to get into your computer."

"Or correctly guessed it."

"I don't know the law well enough on this without researching it, but I'm sure there's something we could go after him with. At the very least, it's a huge blow to the lawsuit. They will try to exclude this from the jury. We'll have to fight to get it in. Between this and the restraining order, we can paint him in a very negative light."

"So what now?"

"I need the security tapes."

"Let's go to IT, and I'll have them pull it for you now. I want this to be your top priority. Do you hear me?"

"Yes." This was the break in the case she needed. It could be a game changer.

CHAPTER TWELVE

Grant held his tablet in his hand while he finished his dinner. Much to his surprise, Olivia had gifted him an electronic copy of the Bible on Sunday after they'd gone to church together. He'd discovered there were Bible apps as well, but he'd had enough of dealing with apps because of the lawsuit. He'd spent a chunk of the day and night on Sunday fully engrossed in reading and taking notes.

He'd been a bit overwhelmed at first, but she'd also been emailing him different reading suggestions. He'd even exchanged a couple of emails with Pastor Dan. Feeling kind of stupid for questioning Olivia about her and the pastor, he was now more comfortable with all of it.

But still the questions abounded. He had so much to learn before he could even know what he wanted to question further. So each night after work and during his lunch breaks, he'd been spending time reading the Bible. Not front to back, but based on Olivia and Dan's suggestions. And then sometimes, he would just pick a part that looked interesting to him.

While it was only Wednesday evening, he felt like it had been much longer since he started down this path. His doorbell rang, and he got up from the kitchen table. He wasn't expecting any visitors.

He looked through the peephole and saw Olivia on the other side. But instead of wearing that beautiful smile, she stood with arms crossed. A deep frown on her face. Something was wrong.

He opened the door. "Are you okay?" he asked.

"Can I come in?"

"Of course." He actually took her gently by the arm and guided her in.

"Am I interrupting your dinner?"

"No. I just finished. Have a seat."

She looked down at the kitchen table where his empty Thai takeout box sat alongside his tablet.

"You're reading the Bible?"

He laughed. "Isn't that why you bought it for me."

Finally a smile. "I'd love to talk about that, but first I need to tell you something else, and I wanted to deliver this in person, not via email."

"What is it?" His pulse thumped loudly as he wondered what she was about to drop on him.

"I had a long meeting today with my computer forensic expert, Blake Sanchez. You saw him in court last week."

"Yeah? I've got my guy lined up, too, as soon as your guy turns over his findings."

"Take a seat, Grant."

"You're acting like someone died, Olivia."

She shook her head. "No, but this isn't going to be news you want to hear."

"Let me guess..." He paused and leaned toward her. "Your paid expert is going to testify that the email was fabricated. Shocking. I knew that right when you hired him. These computer guys can always come up with a theory. That's the nature of the expert game in litigation."

"It's not that simple. Yes, that is what he concluded, but it's the details that will concern you."

"I'm listening."

"Blake has determined beyond all reasonable certainty that the changes to the email took place inside the Astral Tech office, on Nina Marie's office desktop."

"No way."

"There's more. Blake couldn't give an exact time stamp, but he did provide a window that we then cross referenced with the Astral Tech security video. There were two people connected to Optimism who were in the Astral Tech offices during the window."

"And they were?"

"You and Layton Alito."

He recoiled. "Are you accusing me of something, Olivia? Because if you are, then you should just come out with your accusation. Or have you already written your brief asking for sanctions against me, or something worse? And you just wanted to what, deliver the good news personally?"

She reached out and grabbed onto his arm tightly. "Calm down and just wait a minute. I'm not accusing you of anything. I know you wouldn't have done something like this. But I am accusing your client. Layton has put you in a terrible spot, Grant. And I wanted you to know now. My expert will be emailing out his final report any time now, but I wanted to explain this to you before you got the email to hand over to your expert."

He blew out a breath. "How confident are you in your guy's assessment and his abilities?"

"Blake is one of the best. It's not my place to tell you how to handle your client. But as another member of the bar, and as a friend, I ask that you think long and hard about how you want to proceed."

"I'm not a quitter, Olivia. We've been over this before."

"Yeah, but that was before all of this happened. Layton could face criminal charges. Not to mention how this is going to play out in your lawsuit."

"Are you thinking settlement?"

"I think both sides would be well served to consider ending this. But the hatred is so strong between Layton and Nina Marie,

I don't know if there's a business solution out of this like there would be in normal corporate litigation."

"Right. There's often animosity between competitors, but this is highly personal."

"And throw in the spiritual elements and you've got big trouble." She sighed. "This is much more than a lawsuit to them. You and I both know that."

He put his head in his hands, all of a sudden developing a headache. She was right. If Layton had broken into Nina Marie's computer and altered an email and then Grant had used that email as the basis for the emergency injunction—then what a mess. "I'm going to need some time to figure this all out. Thanks for giving me the heads up. My expert will no doubt want to conduct his own assessment."

"Of course. But I'm confident he'll come to the same conclusion. I'm sorry, Grant. You don't deserve any of this."

"Neither do you."

Silence fell between them as they sat looking at each other but not speaking. Until Olivia looked away and broke the silence.

"So tell me about your Bible reading."

He never thought that he would feel more comfortable talking about the Bible than about his litigation, but then again, he'd never faced a case like this before. "I'm a bit overwhelmed but still intrigued at the same time. I have appreciated your emails pointing me to certain things I should read. Pastor Dan has also sent me some good places to go. I've started a list of questions and thoughts I have." He lifted up his legal pad that was beside the tablet.

"Can I ask you something?"

"Sure."

"What changed for you? When we first met, you wanted nothing to do with any of this. Then after what happened to you here at your house, I thought you'd had a breakthrough, but then after that you shut off again. Why now?"

Good question, he thought. "I'm not sure either. You're totally right, though. When we first met, I had my worldview, and it was something I was entirely comfortable with. I mean, I wanted to be a good person and live my life in a way I was proud of. But that was about it. There wasn't any higher power or anything that I even considered. I told you that growing up and being bounced from one foster home to another had a huge impact on me."

"It would on anyone. You shouldn't be down on yourself about your past. You did the best you could do. And look at you now. You're an amazing lawyer with your own law firm. You have a lot to be proud of."

"Thank you. It took a lot to get here. Which is why, when this case came in, I thought initially it would be fine. Maybe a bit odd, but I had no idea that people actually believed in this New Age stuff beyond a superficial level. Then I see your hotel room covered in a pentagram, and I knew something was wrong."

"Very wrong."

"But it's always been easier for me to accept the rational explanation. I don't rely on emotions."

"You've built up a wall to protect yourself as anyone in your position would have."

"Hey now. If you want to talk about walls, you have them, too. They're different than mine, but they are still there."

"Believe me, I know. You're not the only one who has had difficulties in life. After my parents were killed, my world was rocked down the core." She sat silently for a minute. "But back to you. I shouldn't be as concerned about the why as I am about how to help you move forward. I want to provide any support I can to you as you try to determine where you want to go spiritually."

"I appreciate that. Most of my friends have been hands off when it comes to my spiritual side, they know how I feel." He laughed. "I know it's not funny, but just hearing the words come out of my mouth, sometimes I wonder who am I? Am I the same man I was when this case started?"

She smiled. "Don't you see, Grant? It's a wonderful thing that you've changed. Your heart is opening up. The Lord wants to be there for you if you'll let Him."

"You really believe that?"

"Yes, God isn't going to force His way into anyone's life. He'll knock at the door, but you have to let Him in. Does that make sense?"

"Strangely enough, it does. Now if I could just get my head around the whole dying and then being raised from the dead three days later. Honestly, I am struggling with that a bit."

"That's all right. In time, all of this will fall into place, as long as you're wanting to continue to seek Him out."

"It's like you said. I've been thrust into a really unique situation without having the tools to understand it, much less to deal with it."

"You're talking about the spiritual warfare?"

He walked to the refrigerator and pulled out sodas for them both. He opened his and handed the other can to her. "Yeah, I think the first sermon I heard was a useful building block. But I'm having a hard time understanding how the New Age stuff fits into all of it."

"I guess I think it's theoretically possible to be involved in New Age type activities that don't directly correlate to anything demonic. But the problem is that once you open the door to things like witchcraft, then you're inviting that type of presence into your life. And what you're inviting in isn't a good thing. It's evil even if it looks good on the outside."

He tried to let her words sink in. "So what I think I've learned, and correct me if I'm wrong, is that the devil, the same devil that tempted Jesus, works his will through invisible forces of evil that we understand as demons?"

"Yes, that's it."

"And that if someone starts doing witchcraft or makes other attempts at trying to connect with spirits, that's like an invitation for the demons to come to you?"

"I think that's a fair way of looking at it. And for some people, I think that's how they get involved. They may have interest in the invisible realm, or witchcraft, or anything like that, and that's how it starts. But that isn't all. Then there are people who unquestionably seek out the devil."

He let out a laugh, but it wasn't filled with humor. "I'm sorry, but you're losing me on this point. Why in the world would any rational human being want to connect with the devil? Even for someone like me, who had no religious background, I know enough to know that everything about the devil is bad, right?"

She tucked her hair behind her ear. "These people aren't all the same, nor do they always have the same motivation. But oftentimes they seek power. Following the devil often means putting yourself first over others. You do the devil's bidding and you profit—that profit could be financial or in a myriad of other ways. These people aren't as concerned about what happens after we die as they are about what is happening here on this earth. They want to enjoy all the pleasures this world has to offer—even if many times those pleasures are self destructive."

He rubbed his chin as he listened intently to her words. "I don't know where all of this leaves me."

She reached out and touched his hand. "Don't let it discourage you. Just keep on with what you're doing. You're not trying to become a theologian overnight. I'm glad you're reading the Bible and thinking about these things. I have to warn you, though. If they get the sense that you're going to be a spiritual threat, then they may come after you more."

"You really think that I was attacked that night here?"

"I do believe that, and I think you do too."

"What about you? Aren't you worried about being attacked again?"

"Obviously I don't want to face that again, but I'm not afraid. The Lord said that if God is for us, then who can be against us? I carry that with me. I meditate a lot on the Word of God. I prepare myself for battle by knowing that my God is stronger than the devil will ever be. And while the devil may seem to have a bit of a free reign on this earth, that's only temporary. He can only do so much to me when I have God on my side."

"Seeing you so steadfast in your faith has been pretty amazing for me. You're really a special woman, Olivia." How he wanted to bring her into his arms and hold her close. But while this case was ongoing, he knew he couldn't. He wondered if after it was over if there could ever be a future for them. She lived in Washington, DC, and he lived in Chicago. Could it ever work? And the bigger question, would she even be interested in a man like him?

"Thanks for that. You're pretty special, too. I should be going, though, before it gets too late. Look for the report by email in a bit, and once again, I'm sorry that your client lied to you."

Ouch, that again. He'd allowed himself not to think about that for a few minutes. Now back to reality and what he had to do. "Thanks. I'll walk you out."

When he closed the door behind her, he was filled with a sense of dread. He was going to have to present this evidence to Layton, and then prepare for what were likely the lies that would follow.

***

There was a little voice inside of Stacey's head urging her on. She sat at home in her apartment with a New Age spell book in front of her. She had no reason to be looking at it now. She wasn't at work. No one was there with her. Reminding herself that she was supposed to be making amends for what she'd done, not making it worse. But then she kept coming back to the fact that she was still drawn to the spell book. Still curious.

Steadfast in the belief that she was not going to ever worship the devil, she wondered what harm could really come of dabbling in a bit of witchcraft. It was interesting to her. Learning not only the history of witchcraft, but also the current day applications.

It certainly didn't seem like Morena or Layton were worshiping the devil. No, they were both smart businesspeople. Just like what she wanted to be. She'd know if they were sacrificing animals on their lunch break. She laughed to herself at the ludicrousness of it all.

What she needed to do was to get her head on straight and stop stressing about all of this. Wasn't there a happy medium between devil worship and being a bible thumper?

Her mind went back to the experience she had in her living room, though. And a chill shot down her arm. She'd gone back and forth over whether she thought it was real or whether she'd dreamt it up. The further away it was, the more dreamlike it seemed.

Stop being irrational, she thought. It was time for her to take charge of her own life. Live it the way she wanted. Not the way her parents had wanted her to. No, she needed to make her own way, and this internship was the first step in doing that.

A light knock at the door had her jumping. She hopped up off the sofa and looked out the door seeing that it was Morena. What would she be doing coming to her apartment? She hoped that she hadn't messed up the review of orders that she'd been asked to double check today. Morena was currently splitting her time in between working at Optimism and the bookstore Indigo. When Morena had asked for help, Stacey immediately took her up on it.

Opening up the door, Morena stood on the other side and flashed her a big smile. Hopefully that meant she wasn't in trouble.

"Morena, hey."

"Sorry to just drop by. I had your address on file, and I wanted to stop by to talk to you about something."

"Sure. Come on in." She led Morena into the living room and offered her a seat.

Morena's eyes immediately went to the spell book sitting open on the couch. "Brushing up on some homework?" She laughed.

"Just some light evening reading."

"I'm glad to see you're taking this so seriously. Not everyone has the same dedication that you do. Which is part of the reason I'm here."

"Can I offer you anything to eat or drink?" She was trying to be a polite hostess, even though she didn't exactly have a lot around the house as a struggling college student.

Morena smiled. "No, dear. I'm good."

"All right. So what do you need to talk to me about?"

"Layton and I have really been watching your progress around the office. You're so dedicated to your internship, and you're really going above and beyond. You're by far the best intern we've ever had since we started taking on interns."

She felt her neck flush with the praise. "Thank you. I am trying really hard. I want to do well, and I need to be able to get a good job at a company when I graduate. Even though it's just community college, it still costs a bit of money, and I'm doing it all based on student loans. Which, as you can imagine, adds up."

Morena's blue eyes sparkled. "I'm so glad you brought that up. That was one of the reasons why I wanted to stop by. Layton wanted to come too, but he got tied up at the last minute with something related to the lawsuit against Astral Tech."

"Okay." Stacey had no idea where Morena was going with this. But from all the compliments, it definitely didn't seem like she was about to lose her job.

"Optimism would like to offer you a tuition scholarship. You continue your internship, and we will pay for the rest of your school. In exchange, you commit to working at Optimism for two years after you graduate."

"Wow," she said. She couldn't even begin to wrap her head around this. What a dream come true. If she didn't have to keep taking out tuition loans, she'd actually be able to eat something other than boxed noodles for the next two years. "This would be life changing for me, Morena. I don't even know what to say."

"I realize that a two year commitment might seem like a big deal to you, so you should take your time to think about it. But if we're investing in you, we'd like you then to put those skills you've learned in the classroom to work for us. A lot of companies have programs like this, and you would be our test case. Basically a pilot program to see how it works."

"Thank you so much. I am really at a loss for words."

"Like I said. No commitment tonight. Sleep on it and take a day or two. Then we can revisit it."

"I'm beyond thrilled to hear this news." Her eyes even started welling up with tears. "I thought you might be here to fire me."

"Oh, there's no need to cry, Stace. Of course we aren't firing you. You're a superstar. Which actually brings me to the other reason why I dropped by tonight to chat."

"I don't know if anything can top the news you already gave me."

Morena grinned. "This isn't meant to top that offer, but merely to supplement it."

"All right." What else possibly could Morena have to say? At this point, it didn't even matter. She was on cloud nine.

"Layton and I would like to personally invite you over to an Optimism meeting at Layton's house Saturday night."

"Really? What kind of meeting is it?"

"This will be more of a social gathering. Optimism business will be discussed just because it always is. But this will be a time just to get together and hang out as a group of like-minded people."

"Who all will be there?" Her mind raced with all the possibilities. Would this be an intimate gathering, or some huge party?

"The key Optimism people, plus some other friends of Layton's in the community."

"That sounds exciting."

"Oh, it is most exciting. But I just wanted to talk to you about it before it happened, to prepare you for some things that might be discussed."

"Like what?" Her curiosity was further piqued by Morena's statement.

Morena reached out and grabbed her hand. "Can I trust you, Stace?"

She'd noticed that she'd become Stace lately with Morena instead of Stacey. "Sure. I hope I haven't done anything to make you think I wasn't trustworthy. Because if I have, I'd love the opportunity to correct that."

Morena shook her head, tossing her blond curls back and forth. "No, no. It's just that what I'm about to tell you is highly sensitive. And even if you decide you're not up for it, you need to be able to keep all Optimism business to yourself. You might not even remember that when you took on the internship you signed a NDA."

"NDA?" What in the world had she signed?

"Oh, forgive me. I've been around the lawyers for this lawsuit too long. An NDA is a Non Disclosure Agreement. It basically says that whatever you see, hear, read, etcetera, about Optimism while you're employed by the company, you must keep confidential. Meaning you couldn't go out with one of your friends today and talk to them about what Optimism is working on or doing."

She nodded. "All right. I think that makes sense. I haven't been babbling about my work to anyone."

"Good, good. But this goes beyond what strictly happens in the Optimism office. The NDA also covers outside of the office events sponsored by Optimism. Like the one this weekend at Layton's house."

"Don't worry about me. My lips are sealed." After she said the words, though, it occurred to her that she wouldn't be able to tell anyone at the church about things she witnessed from here on out. Would that even be a problem? Did she even want to tell the church? No. She'd been dodging all their calls and ignoring the emails from Sofia. Right now she was thinking about this totally amazing opportunity that had just dropped right in her lap.

"Well, then, taking you on your word, I just wanted to give you a little information to prepare you for the event. As you know, Optimism is a New Age company. You've been learning all the facets of our business from finance to technology to marketing. Right?"

"Yes, I'm really enjoying it, too."

"But you also realize that as a group we also have other interests. For instance, this spell book." Morena picked up the book. "This book has a lot in it that is of interest to Optimism. And when I say Optimism, I'm not just talking about the business. You need to start thinking of Optimism in a bigger way."

"How so?"

"We're like a family. A community of people who enjoy the same things. Who believe in the same thing. Even if those beliefs aren't exact, all of our members have an interest in the New Age activities that the company then supports. Am I making sense so far?"

"I think so," she replied. Although she wasn't exactly sure where Morena was going with this. It was like she felt like Morena was trying to say something without exactly spelling it out for her.

"So while we're at this meeting, we're going to discuss things about the company and about New Age activities. Those things may include things from the spell book or other aspects of witchcraft. They could also encompass spiritual elements."

"Spiritual elements," she whispered.

"Yes. You know what I'm talking about, right?" Morena put her hand on Stacey's shoulder.

"Yes. Does everyone in Optimism believe in those spiritual elements?"

Morena laughed. "That's a tricky question. At Optimism, within our believer community, we use the New Age terminology very loosely. Much more loosely than we do on the business side. On the corporate side, we're selling a product. People have expectations for what that product will be and how it will be marketed. But on the purely spiritual side of things it's a bit different. Everyone believes in the spiritual realm yes. But we aren't exactly always all on the same page about how best to go about things. We have a part of our group which focuses almost exclusively on witchcraft. Then we have a group that is more attuned to other things, and it's that group that I wanted to make sure you weren't caught off guard by."

Her heartbeat started pounding. Her apartment started to feel even smaller than it already was. Because she knew where Morena was about to go with this conversation. And talk about being conflicted. "What group are you referring to?"

"Those that prefer less New Age type philosophies and are more traditionalist."

"Traditionalist in what?"

"Demonic activities." Morena said with a straight face. It was as if she hadn't just said something that would be outrageous to most people. But no, Morena wasn't fazed.

She didn't respond immediately.

"I can see the wheels churning in the brilliant mind of yours. Talk to me, Stace."

"Can I be honest with you?"

"Of course."

"I'm really not that into the demonic aspects of things. It just seems a bit dangerous to me. I find myself drawn much more to the witchcraft and spells and learning about that."

Morena nodded. "That is not going to be a problem. Like I said, we have a solid foundation of people who think just like that. I'm only telling you this now so you aren't surprised when activities or discussions come up that reference demonic activity."

"What about you and Layton?"

Morena smiled. "I'm open to anything, but as you could probably tell my specialty is witchcraft. Layton on the other hand has a very strong connection to the demonic forces. It's really one of the things that makes him such a successful leader of the group and the business itself."

She shrunk back on the couch a little bit.

"Stace, you have nothing to be afraid of. If the demonic part isn't your thing, you won't ever be forced into it. Layton will not think less of you at all. He is excited about you exploring your spiritual talents however you want. He has really high hopes for you."

"That's good to hear."

"I've laid enough on you for one night. Think about it all. The scholarship, working at Optimism and the social event Saturday night. I can answer any questions you think of tonight at work tomorrow. How does that sound?"

Stacey looked at Morena. The woman was beautiful, so put together, and so kind to her. It was hard to believe that any harm could ever come to her from Morena. "Thank you so much. You've given me a lot to think about. But I'm super excited about this scholarship and for potentially working at Optimism."

"As you should be." Morena stood up and walked to the door. "I'll see you in the office tomorrow afternoon. I'm working at Indigo in the morning."

Stacey closed the door behind Morena. Where did she go from here?

***

Grant had invited Layton to his office Thursday afternoon. Grant's expert had worked all night reviewing and analyzing Blake's report. He was given access to Nina Marie's computer under supervision on Thursday morning to conduct his own analysis.

And while Grant's expert had layered it through a bunch of technical language, the bottom line was evident. The email had been altered on Nina Marie's desktop in the Astral Tech office. Just like Blake had said.

Now Grant was left with a huge mess to clean up. The first thing he had to do was to confront Layton. Depending on how Layton handled things, Grant seriously considered withdrawing from the litigation. It wasn't always easy for a lawyer to withdraw, but under these circumstances he was more than justified.

What was he going to do? Is this the point where if he were a Christian that he would pray? It was all so new to him. He didn't really know, but it certainly felt like he needed some help and guidance right now.

It occurred to him in that moment that he had no idea how to pray. He had heard Olivia and Pastor Dan pray. He'd even seen people praying on TV and in movies. But the act of uttering a prayer himself seemed beyond daunting. Yeah, he was all alone in his office, but what if he messed it up?

Then he thought back to his first jury trial. He was so nervous that he got sick before he walked into the courtroom. But then once he started his opening statement and looked into the eyes of the jurors, the nerves and worries faded away. He had been prepared. He just had to execute.

Why couldn't he think of this in the same way? While he was nowhere near as prepared to pray as he was to take a case to trial, he had put in a good bit of effort in reading and thinking about things. It was time to try this.

God, I'm new at this, as you know. If You would've told me a year ago that I'd be sitting in my office praying right now, I would've told You that You were crazy. But here I am. I'm still not sure of everything, and I have a lot of questions. But I am sure that I'm still interested in learning more, and right now I need Your help. I've gotten myself into a precarious situation, and I need Your guidance to shepherd me through this client meeting. Amen.

He let out a breath. It surely wouldn't win any awards for best prayer, but it was a start, and he felt good knowing he had tired. Maybe next time would be easier.

His intercom buzzed.

"Grant, Mr. Alito is here to see you."

"Please send him back, Cindy."

He had to keep it together. This was going to be one of the most awkward and intense conversations he'd ever had with a client.

Layton walked in looking every part the suave CEO. Today sporting a black designer suit and gray striped tie.

"Grant, I could tell by your message that this was a pretty urgent meeting."

"Have a seat." Grant motioned for him to take the chair across from the desk.

"So what has you all agitated today, Grant?"

Stay calm, he reminded himself. "Both experts have reviewed the computer forensic evidence regarding the email in question."

Layton smiled. "Great, and what do they have to say?"

"It's not great at all actually. Both experts agree that the email was digitally altered, and that the alteration took place on Nina Marie's desktop computer inside the Astral Tech office."

Layton huffed. "That's impossible. There's no way they could prove such a thing."

Grant leaned forward in his chair. "Layton, it's time to get real with me. Not only can the experts show that fact, they also agree on a window of time when the alteration occurred. Only two people associated with Optimism went inside the Astral Tech office during that time. There are security cameras to show that only you and I were there. I know for a fact, I didn't do it. Which leaves you, Layton."

"That's crazy."

Grant pounded his fist on the desk. "Stop playing games."

Layton let out a loud and dramatic sigh. "I'm not playing games. This is just the way it has to be for us to continue."

"Why in the world would you do such a thing?"

"I don't know what you're talking about." Layton continued to deny his involvement. He was even more slick than Grant had given him credit for.

"We don't need to have you fabricating evidence to win. Don't you see we had a strong case, and you just blew it through your stupid move."

"You're insulting your client. That doesn't seem very professional of you."

"And it's not professional of you to lie and steal." He knew then and there what he had to do. "I'm sorry, Layton. But given these set of highly irregular facts, I'll be filing a motion to withdraw from the case. I'll hand it to the judge tomorrow at the hearing. I more than think he would understand when he finds out you fabricated evidence."

Layton leaned forward in his chair. His face now deadly serious and his blue eyes focused on Grant like laser beams. "Let's get one thing straight right now, Grant. You will not file that motion tomorrow."

"Why wouldn't I? You deliberately deceived me, made me file a motion that was based upon false evidence—evidence that you created yourself by illegal means. No sane lawyer would stay on a case like that."

Layton crossed his arms in defiance. "You don't get it."

"Then spell it out for me."

"All right. You won't withdraw from this case. You'll go on representing Optimism."

"This is starting to sound like a threat."

Layton laughed. "I haven't even started to lay out my threat yet."

"So there is one?"

"If you try to withdraw, I'll say that I had nothing to do with the fabrication and it was all you. That you wanted to win so badly, you needed the money and decided to take drastic action. You're the one who said that the only two people on that tape are you and me. This will ruin you. Ruin your entire career. You will be disbarred."

"It will be my word against yours."

"Ah, but you can't violate attorney client privilege."

"Have you ever heard of the crime-fraud exception?"

"Don't get cute with me, Grant. I didn't want to bring up this other matter, but I will if you start thinking you can just walk away."

"What other matter?"

"The fact that you not only fabricated evidence, but that you've been cavorting with the opposing counsel."

"Leave Olivia out of it."

Layton raised an eyebrow. "Ah, just as I suspected. You are smitten by her. I'm sure a judge would want to hear all the tawdry details of your affair. Talk about a conflict of interest."

"There is no affair and you know it. You're really about to cross a line, Layton."

Layton stood up. "I'm going to leave you with these thoughts. But I think you know me well enough now to understand that I'm not making empty threats. Be there at court tomorrow to conduct business as usual, or I'll have no choice."

"And just how do you expect us to get around this evidence fabrication issue?"

"They can't prove that you or I did it. It's as simple as that."

"I can't put you on the stand knowing that you're lying."

"You can and you will." He stood up and walked out of Grant's office slamming the door behind him.

Would this case be the end of his legal career?

CHAPTER THIRTEEN

Clive was dead.

Nina Marie still couldn't wrap her head around it, but she'd gotten the news and processed it the best she could. Now was no time to mourn. No. She had to act.

So she'd called the emergency meeting on Thursday night and had everyone gathered at her house.

She thought Clive would've had more time, but obviously that wasn't the case. They hadn't even had their transitional meeting with the group that they'd discussed when he first told her that he was sick.

And while she was a bit sad to lose him, now she had to concentrate on solidifying her power base. They had a succession plan for the company, so there was no question that she would be CEO.

But her bigger concern was for the community of Astral Tech itself. How would everyone react to her stepping in—especially Matt, who would no doubt want the role for himself.

The crowd talked amongst themselves as everyone took a seat in her very large dining and sitting area. A few people pulled in extra chairs from the kitchen. The news of Clive's death hadn't been disseminated. Thus far, she was the only one that knew.

"All right, everyone," Nina Marie said. She looked out into the audience of Astral Tech members. At this point she had their full attention, as they were no doubt curious about this emergency meeting.

"I'm afraid I have some sad news to share with you tonight." She took a deep breath and tried to put on a face of sympathy even though she wasn't that torn up. "Clive has passed away."

Stunned gasps went out through the group and people started talking amongst themselves. Then Matt made eye contact with her. "What in the world happened?"

"Clive was struggling with pancreatic cancer. He kept his sickness to himself until just recently when he confided in me. He didn't want Astral Tech's focus to be on him right now. So he preferred that I keep his diagnosis to myself. I didn't think he would pass away this quickly, but given the circumstances I know he was starting to suffer. So this was for the best."

"When did he die?"

"I received word this morning. I spoke to him yesterday. He had plans to take some time off and go to St. Thomas. But obviously that didn't happen."

Everyone started chattering and Nina Marie gave them all a few minutes to talk. There was definitely some sadness and tears in the room. All of the Astral Tech members generally liked and respected Clive. He was a uniter, and really a fan of the big tent theory. Nothing like Layton that was for sure. But now he was gone and she had to do her best to squelch any concerns or fears ASAP.

"Okay, everyone. I know this comes as quite a shock. But I can assure you that Clive had come to terms with his situation, and that he wants nothing more than for Astral Tech to thrive and grow. Which is why I wanted to get everyone gathered together tonight. Effective immediately, I am CEO of Astral Tech. This follows this corporate succession plan that we have had in place for years. We're going to continue to aggressively fight this lawsuit. And I become more encouraged with each passing day that we will gain a total victory."

"And what about our spiritual leader?" Marta asked with a raised eyebrow.

Nina Marie should've known that there would be multiple people vying for that spot. Now wasn't the time to show weakness or feign a democracy. She had to step in and take over.

"I will fulfill that role as well. I've basically been second in command for years. It only makes sense."

"But what if we have a different opinion?" Matt asked.

"You're free to have any opinion that you want, Matt." Even though as she said it with a smile, happiness was the last emotion she was feeling. "Let's have a reality check, people. Am I as likeable as Clive? Most certainly not. But I am the most powerful Astral Tech member here, I have the evil one's ear, and I'm not afraid to do whatever it takes to get the job done."

More grumbles sounded through the group but no one openly defied her. "I'm going to need everyone to play their part though. This lawsuit is heating up, and we'll have the opportunity to take down Optimism once and for all. Now is the time to start the full court press on your recruiting efforts. I know we can do better on that front than what we have. And while I know not everyone here is of the same mind when it comes to all of the dark arts, whatever you do practice, you need to be focused on with a renewed effort. A battle is coming, people, whether we're ready or not."

"Nina Marie's right," Matt said. "Once word gets out of Clive's death, Optimism will make a big push to dismantle us. Pick us apart piece by piece. Destroy not only our business through the lawsuit but our entire community. We cannot allow that to happen."

Nina Marie appreciated Matt's support, but there was a fine line in her mind between him being helpful and trying to usurp her power. She'd worked for years to gain the proper strategic position so that one day she'd be able to lead Astral Tech. She just hadn't planned on it happening quite like this.

"We must be vigilant," Nina Marie said. "There is no doubt that Optimism members will be coming to you and trying to either recruit you or worst case scenario—do you harm."

"Has anyone experienced any attacks lately?" Marta asked.

A murmur of no's went through the room.

"Don't get complacent." Matt stood and walked over beside Nina Marie. "Everyone should be on high alert. And I think we should continue to use our teams."

"Yes, there's no point in diverging from our teams." Nina Marie's end goal was to abolish the teams, but right now she needed them and the team leaders to be involved. "Team leaders, Matt, Marta and Eloisa. I want constant updates from you." The teams were currently divided into those who practiced witchcraft, those who were more into the holistic New Age methods, and then those like her—a combination of things, but also actively participated in demonic activities.

"You're right," Marta said. "I'll want to see all of those in my group when we break apart here for the night."

"There's no need to delay any team meetings. I don't have anything more to add at this point," Nina Marie said. She watched as Marta led her people out of the house. They would most likely be going out into the woods somewhere do their witchcraft. Eloisa huddled with her group in the back of the dining room. The New Age crew was the one she was the most worried about. Their commitment to her ultimate cause wasn't as strong. Some of them didn't even really believe in the devil. But she couldn't afford to alienate anyone right now.

And then there was the most important group of people. Led by Matt, these men and women sought the evil one and embraced all that came with it. Matt also took them out of her house. She could've followed, but she wanted Matt to feel like he still had some measure of control over something so that he wouldn't push for supreme leadership within the group.

She wanted her own private time to reflect and meditate with the evil one and his demons. She knew that they were a strong force around her, and that she had power. But these were not normal circumstances. What could she offer them that Layton couldn't? It wasn't exactly like loyalty was high on the list of top demon characteristics. No, they were fickle. They wanted to be on the side of the winner. So that's what she had to make sure happened.

Tomorrow was a big day in court. She had no doubt that Layton would bring his A game. Who knows what kind of story he would concoct to justify his fabrication of the evidence? She would go to the forces of darkness and ask for help. And if that didn't work, she'd take matters into her own hands.

***

Grant had barely slept. He'd tossed and turned thinking about what he should do. Not only what the law required, but also what his conscience required. As he walked into the courthouse on Friday morning, he was prepared to do what he needed to do.

He met a smiling Layton in front of the courtroom. You'd never known they had such a heated argument just the day before by how Layton warmly shook his hand.

"I trust you have considered what we discussed yesterday."

Grant nodded. "Most definitely. Let's go in. We don't want to be late."

They walked into the courtroom, where Olivia was already seated at counsel's table. Beside her was Nina Marie, who was operating as the company representative today. Her expert Blake Sanchez sat in the first row of seats.

Grant's stomach churned but he soldiered on. Doing the only thing he could do. He couldn't even face Olivia. He took a seat at his table and waited for the judge to enter.

As the minutes ticked by, Grant's palms got sweaty. He wiped his brow and took a few deep breaths as Judge Wingfield took the bench.

"Good morning, everyone. I'm ready to hear arguments with regard to the authenticity of the email relied upon by Plaintiff in their motion for an emergency injunction."

Grant stood. "Your Honor, may counsel approach the bench."

"Yes, you may."

Grant didn't even look over at Layton although he could feel his evil stare.

"What is it?" Judge Wingfield asked.

Grant and Olivia stood in front of the judge.

"Your Honor, I'm going to be filing a motion to withdraw from the case. As you will hear today, the evidence relied upon in the motion I filed with this court has been altered. Given those facts, I ask that you grant my motion to withdraw and stay this proceeding today until Optimism can retain new counsel."

Olivia gasped, but didn't say a word.

Judge Wingfield frowned deeply and crossed his arms. But he sat in silence for what felt like an hour, but what was probably only a minute.

"Don't bother filing a written motion, Mr. Baxter. Your request for withdrawal is duly noted, but I deny it. You got yourself into this mess, and now you're stuck with it."

"Your Honor, given the circumstances, I would ask you to reconsider."

"You should've thought this out before you put fabricated evidence before me and wasted everyone's time on an emergency injunction. You just ought to be glad I'm not outright sanctioning you right now. You know better, Mr. Baxter," he chided.

It stung. Being rebuked like that by the judge. But could Grant really blame him? He'd really gotten himself into a mess and there was no way out.

"Just so we have a clear record, I'd like to proceed with the testimony today regarding the email," the judge said. "I'm assuming you're prepared to do that, Ms. Murray, as I see your expert is here today?"

"Yes, Your Honor. I'm prepared to move forward."

"And Mr. Baxter, your expert is here as well?"

"Yes, Your Honor." Although it was probably a losing battle to even try to call his expert to the stand.

The judge nodded. "Good, then let's get to it."

Grant felt his shoulders slump as he walked back to his counsel's table. Layton leaned over and spoke in his ear. "I see that went well. Looks like you're stuck with me regardless, huh?"

Grant didn't even respond. The judge had refused to release him from the case. That meant, regardless of what he wanted, he had no basis to withdraw. Not if the judge wouldn't allow it.

Grant didn't know if he could make it through the hearing, but he put on his best professional face. He even tried his best to argue that while both experts agreed the email was altered, that there was no proof that anyone associated with his client did it. It was probably a losing battle, but that's the only play he had to make.

It was obvious from the rolling of Judge Wingfield's eyes that he had really gotten on the judge's bad side. But just as Olivia was about to start speaking, the judge stopped her.

"I'm sorry." He gripped his chest. "I'm having chest pains." He was holding onto his chest. "Can't breathe."

That sent the courtroom into a complete frenzy. The court clerk yelled to the bailiff who was radioing out asking for an ambulance ASAP for the judge. Then the bailiff ran over to the judge.

Grant stood stunned and then he looked back at Layton who had the faintest smile across his lips. Was it possible that Layton was somehow responsible for this? At this point, Grant knew the man was evil. The question was whether he actually had any spiritual powers that could've really harmed the judge.

The paramedics came in and removed Judge Wingfield on a stretcher. The clerk walked back over toward Grant.

"Counselors, obviously we're going to have to reschedule this hearing."

"Of course," Grant said.

Olivia nodded.

"I'm going to check on the judge," the clerk said. "You'll hear from my office soon with details." The clerk held back tears as it was clear she was worried about her boss's health.

Grant turned around and Layton was already walking out of the courtroom. He wasn't in the mood to talk to him.

Grant gathered up his stuff. Olivia walked over to the table.

"We should talk once I get done with Nina Marie."

He nodded, feeling totally defeated on every level.

Grant waited outside the courthouse sitting on a bench in the sun, trying to process everything that had just occurred. Maybe it was time for a second prayer attempt? Because one wasn't going to get the job done if what had just transpired was any indication of how things were going to go.

God, it's me again. Still trying to figure out this praying thing, but I realize that if You're God You saw what just happened in there. I was trying to do the right thing. The legal and ethical thing and the judge just wasn't having it. I do hope the judge is all right, though. I'd never want anything to happen to him. And, God, if Layton was responsible then I feel even worse. What can I, as one man, do against a monster like that?

He put his head in his hands and leaned over. Feeling utterly helpless and alone.

"Grant."

He recognized Olivia's voice.

She sat down beside him on the bench. "I don't even know where to start."

"Me either. Olivia, I feel like I'm in the middle of a nightmare right now. You heard the judge. I'm stuck with this for the duration. I don't know if I'll make it through a trial."

She reached over and patted his arm. "Yes, you will. The sooner the better. Then you can put this all behind you and move on."

"If what happened in there today was any indication, then we both know how this all will play out."

"Don't even think about it right now. There's nothing you can do."

"Easy for you to say," he snapped.

"I know you're upset. I'll go now. If you want to talk later you know where to find me. I hope you'll also consider going to church again on Sunday."

He didn't respond. Right now he just wanted to wallow.

She got up and left him sitting alone, and feeling more confused than ever.

CHAPTER FOURTEEN

Stacey had gone back and forth over what to wear to the social gathering at Layton's house. She'd settled on a straight forward black dress that hit right above the knee. It wasn't showy, but it was one of the nicest dresses she had. She never went to fancy dinner parties. The college parties she was used to were all low key and usually involved her wearing skinny jeans and a tank top.

She'd considered everything that Morena had said very carefully. While she didn't plan on making any final decisions until after the party, she knew which way she was leaning. There was just no way she could turn down the scholarship offer.

She wasn't an idiot and knew there were strings attached. But at this point, she figured she could live with it. How crazy could Layton's friends really be?

Well, she was about to find out. As she stood outside his front door, she took a few deep breaths before she pushed the doorbell. It really wasn't a house. It was a mansion. She'd never seen anything quite like it, and she was convinced that the inside would be even better.

She could have it all one day if she stuck to this path. So much more than her family had ever had before. The brick multi story mansion literally took her breath away. She couldn't wait to see the inside of it.

She pushed the doorbell and waited. It was only a minute before the door opened. Layton stood on the other side smiling broadly. He looked amazing tonight wearing a tailored blue suit and striped tie.

His eyes trailed down her body, and she immediately became self-conscious. Hoping that her dress was nice enough for his fancy party.

"Stacey, you look lovely. Please come into my home."

"I wasn't sure what to wear." She fiddled with the hem of her dress as she smoothed it down.

"No worries. You look ravishing."

He ushered her through the foyer and into a large living room that opened into an even larger dining area. The formal dining room was unlike anything she'd ever seen. A huge crystal chandelier dangled down sending shimmering rays of light across the room. The dark hardwood floors were pristine. The fine china that was set out on the large tables had to have cost a fortune. Everything screamed rich and extravagant.

"We're having a bit of a cocktail hour right now before dinner. Feel free to roam about the house. Most people will be on the main floor, but you're welcome to look around."

"Layton, this house is gorgeous. It's literally taking my breath away."

He smiled. "It's amazing what one can do with money and a top notch interior designer."

She took a moment to continue to take it all in. The living room was furnished with another opulent looking chandelier, and oil paintings hung on the walls. The room was filled with plush chairs and two large white sofas. She almost cringed as she watched someone drink red wine while sitting on the white sofa.

Her eyes met with Morena's who was walking her way. Morena looked absolutely like a model tonight. She wore a long red dress with a huge slit up the leg. Stacey felt totally inadequate in her simple black dress. But there was nothing she could do about it now.

Even more impressive were the jewels around Morena's neck. There had to be thousands of dollars of diamonds between the necklace and large dangling earrings.

"I'm so glad you decided to come to the party," Morena said. Morena took her arms and looked at her. "Don't you look nice this evening."

"I'm sorry. I feel a bit underdressed. But honestly this is one of the nicest dresses I have."

Morena shook her head. "You look beautiful, and you know what? I'm sure Layton would approve of a clothing budget for you. I'd love to take you shopping for a few things to wear to events like this. That is, if you're going to be taking him up on his offer."

"Thanks again for the opportunity. I'd like to give you my answer on Monday if that's okay?"

"Most definitely. Try to relax and have a good time tonight. Why don't you get a glass of wine and try to unwind?"

"I'm only twenty."

Morena laughed. "There's no one who is going to be carding you here, Stace. Come on, let's get you a drink."

Stacey wasn't a drinker. Yeah, she'd been to college parties, but drinking just wasn't her thing. The community college scene actually had a lot more parties than she'd expected, but generally she preferred to hang out in smaller groups.

But when Morena handed her the glass she took it.

"What is this?"

"A flute of champagne. I think there's going to be a lot of celebrating tonight."

"About what?"

"Just stay tuned and you'll hear all about it." Morena grabbed her hand. "I'm so glad you're here. It's an exciting time for Optimism and things are only going to get better."

Stacey tentatively sipped the champagne. She had to be careful not to drink too quickly, or she would be a goner in no time.

But after the cocktail hour and a long dinner that included wine, she was really starting to feel it. The guests gathered after dessert in the living room area with Layton standing at the front of the room commanding everyone's attention.

"I'm so glad all of you could make it tonight. What I originally had envisioned as a low key dinner party was amped up quite a bit by a few events that I'd like to share with everyone."

Stacey's mind wandered thinking about what could have changed the tenor of the gathering to one of celebration. It made her wonder if something had happened with the lawsuit that she wasn't privy to.

"I haven't had the opportunity to share the news with all of you so I'll do it now. The first piece of news is that the CEO of Astral Tech, Clive Township, has passed away. I hear that it was pancreatic cancer."

The energy in the room shifted. Stacey could feel it as people started talking amongst themselves.

"Everyone." Layton held up his hand. "I know there is a lot to discuss but let me finish the updates first."

The crowd hushed and Stacey couldn't turn away from watching Layton.

"I know this is a shock to us all who had no idea that Clive was even sick. As you can imagine, this impacts a lot of things for us. From the lawsuit to our spiritual efforts against Astral Tech. I think that all of us can agree that we have a common interest in making Optimism as strong as we can. This is an opportunity for us to shut down Astral Tech as an opposing organization once and for all."

Now she could have heard a pin drop in the room. No one said a word. Not even a single whisper.

"We have to capitalize on these events. Strike now while Astral Tech is in complete disarray. I have heard through my sources that Nina Marie has taken over. And while there's no doubt that she is strong, I do not believe she has the confidence of everyone else to be their leader. If we can pick off Matt or Marta and bring them to Optimism, that would just be the first move. It would be a crushing blow to them."

"And how do we do that?" Someone in the room asked.

"Old fashioned recruitment. We offer them things they can't get at Astral Tech, and make it clear that Astral Tech is the loser in this scenario which brings me to the next point. We had some excitement in the courtroom on Friday as our judge seemed to have suffered a heart attack. I believe we will be getting a new judge, and we can use this opportunity to start afresh in our prosecution of the lawsuit."

"What do we do now?" Another woman she hadn't met asked.

"We do what we do best," Layton said. "We use our skills to take out Astral Tech one by one—either by bringing them to Optimism or making sure they will never be a threat to us again."

"And Nina Marie?" Morena asked.

"Leave Nina Marie to me. I'll need the rest of you to work on Matt and Marta. I don't think Eloisa is worth the trouble. She doesn't have as much power or potential as Matt and Marta. But if anyone thinks they could sway her to our side, then so be it."

People started to talk again.

"One more thing before we move on," Layton said. "I'd like to introduce everyone to our newest recruit, Stacey Malone. She's been working as an intern at the office, and I'm hopeful that she's going to accept a position for full membership with us."

Her face flooded with heat as Layton pointed her out and the eyes of the entire room were on her. The people standing right beside her said hello. So far she had to admit that she was having a good time and hadn't felt uncomfortable—beyond the issue of everyone else being more fabulous and put together than her.

"All right. Now that everyone has caught up, we can continue the party. At some point, I'll be in the parlor for those who want to engage in some of our spiritual work. I hope everyone will stop by to visit me before you leave for the evening."

Interesting, she thought. What exactly was going to happen with Layton in the parlor?

Morena walked back over to her. "I'll go into the parlor with you whenever you're ready."

"What exactly should I expect?" She realized she was whispering and didn't know why.

"Don't be afraid." Morena squeezed her shoulder. "Have another glass of wine and then we'll go in."

Stacey debated it for a minute and then realized that the wine sounded like the best option. Because whatever lay behind that parlor door, Stacey knew it would have something to do with the spiritual aspects of Optimism.

And she recognized from her own experience—whether it was real or just a dream—that she was stepping into some pretty powerful stuff. Was she ready? What did she even want?

As she drank another glass of wine and sat on the sofa while Morena worked the room, Stacey tried to seriously consider her options. What did she want? Was she still a Christian? Had she abandoned her faith for a second time? Was that okay with her?

Her mind swam from the wine, and she couldn't focus. All she knew for sure was that she enjoyed being around these people. That she needed that internship and scholarship. And that she'd love to live like Layton and Morena did.

Did that mean she'd be willing to renounce her faith once and for all? She'd been on a whirlwind journey ever since meeting Layton. After the spiritual experience in her apartment, she thought she was ready to return to God and living a Christian lifestyle. But there was something so strong pulling her in toward Layton and Morena. It just felt right.

There wasn't anything wrong in doing something for herself, right? It wasn't like she was hurting anyone in the process. And these decisions could impact her future career.

Morena sashayed back over to her. "Are you ready?"

She drained the last of her wine and nodded her head. "Yes. Let's go."

Morena led her up a huge spiral staircase to the second floor. She noticed that there was another floor above that, too.

"Right this way." Morena took her arm and led her to a room where the door was shut. Morena knocked a few times and then walked in.

Stacey followed her and as she stepped foot into the parlor, her breath caught. The room was dark except for various candles lit and scattered throughout the room.

She hadn't known what to expect, but Layton stood there smiling. He looked like the same man who was downstairs except there was something a little different. She couldn't put her finger on it.

"Come on in, Stacey." Layton motioned for her to join him by the large candles in the center of the room.

"What are we doing?" she asked.

"We're going to pray to the evil one that he gives us strength and victory over Astral Tech. That we're able to vanquish them in this battle once and for all."

She didn't have to ask it because she already knew. But she wanted to make sure she was fully appreciating what he was saying. "When you say the evil one, do you mean like Satan? The devil?" Her voice was soft and timid. Her heartbeat started to race.

Layton grabbed both of her hands. "There's nothing to be afraid of, Stacey. Look at me and Morena. Do we look scary to you?"

She shook her head but didn't say anything.

"Exactly. Your fears come from years of false information about the evil one that you got from going to church. The truth is that the evil one wants us to flourish here on this earth. Just look around this house and see how he has rewarded me for my loyalty to him. You can have all of this and more." He squeezed her hands. "I know you can feel it. I can sense your spiritual abilities. They are strong. Some of the strongest I've ever been exposed to. You've seen things haven't you?"

"Yes," she whispered. "But the things I saw did scare me. A lot."

"No more fear, Stacey. Only enjoyment and pleasure." He released her hands and then ran his hand down her cheek. "Just repeat after me."

He started talking, and she closed her eyes doing as he instructed her. The supplication to the devil was straightforward. With each additional word she became more confident. Less afraid. And more sure that she was about to experience something unlike anything she'd ever felt.

As she accepted the darkness, she felt herself being overtaken by something stronger and much more dangerous than she anticipated. But there was no turning back now. She stepped into the fire and didn't look back.

***

Olivia had gotten a text message from Grant simply saying that he'd meet her at church. That had been good enough for her. The poor guy was going through so much. Not only the issues with the lawsuit, but trying to come to terms with his new interest in faith and how that impacted all aspects of his life.

She'd had one of the most quiet weekends since she came to Windy Ridge. She'd actually taken Saturday off. The first day off of her time there. After a long phone call catching Lizzie up, she'd gotten a haircut and highlights. It was a small splurge, but she figured after all the hours she had put in that she could justify a little spend. She also couldn't have her hair looking frayed if they went to trial. Jurors were human and were often especially critical of the appearance of women lawyers. It was just all part of it, and Olivia had accepted that fact a long time ago.

Olivia walked into the church. She let out a breath when she saw Grant talking to Dan at the entrance of the chapel. Not wanting to interrupt, she hung back waiting for them to finish talking.

Lord, thank You for bringing Grant back to church again. I can see You starting to work in his life and it really is something amazing. I care about him and want him to know what all You can do in his life.

She finished her prayer and saw Dan walking away from Grant to go greet other churchgoers. Then she took the opportunity to go over to Grant.

"Hey," she said.

"Hey."

"I'm glad you could make it."

He ran a hand through his hair. "I felt like I needed to come. I need all the help I can get right now."

"Don't beat yourself up, Grant. You had no control over what your client did. All you can do is the best you can do."

"I don't even want to think about it while I'm here. I'm just looking for a few moments of peace."

"You've come to the right place. Let's go find a seat."

They walked together down the church aisle and took seats near her normal spot on the right side.

"Wonder what Pastor Dan is going to preach about today?" he asked.

"I don't know. Guess we'll find out."

The funny thing was that Olivia was seeking some peace too. For different reasons but all interconnected. She and Grant were tied up with these New Age businesses. And right now she was actually eager for trial on an accelerated basis. The sooner this was done, the sooner she could stop working with Astral Tech.

But that left her wondering how this was all going to end up. When Pastor Dan asked everyone to take a few minutes to pray in silence, she did just that.

Lord, did You bring me here so that I could get to know Grant? I thought this was bigger than just him or me? But I think that's a part of it, right? And where do I go from here? What do I need to do? Wait until the trial is over and then figure it out? I'm confused and looking for guidance.

Olivia glanced over at Grant as the worship music began. He didn't sing, but she noticed the slightest tap of his foot to the drumbeat. What a long way he had come in a fairly short time. It was pretty amazing to see God's fingerprints all over Grant's faith journey.

Olivia took her seat and readied herself for the sermon. *Lord, speak to me through this message today.*

Pastor Dan stood behind the pulpit, but for the longest time he didn't speak. He finally took a deep breath and started preaching. "I thought long and hard about today's sermon, and I went back and forth about it. But when the Lord lays something on your heart, it's best to listen and not disregard what He has to say."

He walked out from behind the pulpit. "Today I want to talk to you about spiritual warfare. It's not news to many in this congregation that we have active groups in the Windy Ridge community that follow the devil. These groups operate under the façade of being legitimate companies who focus on New Age philosophy and techniques. And I think it's about time that we prepare ourselves to wage a spiritual war, because the battle is on the horizon."

He took a few steps forward. "We've been co-existing with these groups for some time. But as of late, they have been more aggressive and more powerful. Spreading their demonic message through technology in hopes to recruit a new generation of followers. We as a church can't let them rule our community. We have to fight back. But to do that, we have to ready ourselves. We can't go into a spiritual battle against the invisible forces of the devil and think that we will walk out unscathed or that the battle will end quickly."

Olivia's head started to ache. Pastor Dan was basically trying to prepare the church for what was to come. Deep in her heart, she knew it was going to be a struggle.

"I know that I've mentioned some of our issues of late that we've had with these groups, but now I need everyone to be on high alert. While it appears at the moment that there is a huge fight between the factions, we can never forget that all of those evil groups are our enemies. We have to be ready for that because if we're not, they're going to make major strides in Windy Ridge and beyond. We can't allow that to happen. Not in our community. Not in our church."

Olivia couldn't help but notice that Dan didn't call out the groups by name. Although it was clear to her exactly who and what he was talking about. Something must have spurred him to preach so passionately about this topic today. A chill shot down her arm as the recognition hit her that this battle was closer than she had thought.

"I want everyone to really think about this in your prayer time. We're going to need our prayer teams to work even harder than normal. The Lord has our backs, but we can't go into battle unprepared or be lackadaisical. Most people here are believers in the Lord Jesus Christ. And I'm here to tell you today that the forces of darkness controlled by Satan are real. We can't live complacently."

Olivia listened as he continued his message referencing scripture to be used to meditate and pray upon.

When the service was over, she looked over at Grant. He sat expressionless.

"What are you thinking?" she asked.

"Honestly, a lot. I can't even begin to describe how many different feelings are flooding through me right now. But I can tell you one thing. What he said—it affected me."

They started filing out of the church.

"How so?" she asked

"I know you've been trying to describe this whole spiritual warfare thing to me ever since that first night we were together when your hotel room door was vandalized. But not until today did it all start to click. The pieces are starting to come together. And my role in all of this. It has to mean something, right? That I would be the one representing Optimism and you with Astral Tech?"

It was time to tell him. She hadn't wanted to freak him out, but he was ready. "Grant, I didn't want to tell you this before because I didn't think you were ready. And the last thing I wanted to do was to scare you off or for you to think I was trying to push something on you."

"What is it?" He pulled her over to the corner of the church lobby.

She took a deep breath and looked into his eyes. "Grant, I've been visited by an angel."

"Are you serious?"

"Yes. And he told me that you were going to be an important part of the battle against the forces of darkness in Windy Ridge."

"Me? But look at me. I'm no one. I'm still getting my feet wet. I can't do battle against anyone." His voice cracked.

She grabbed his hands. "Listen to me, Grant. You said it yourself. You're here for a reason. I'm here for a reason. This didn't just happen by chance. You know that, don't you?"

"Yes. But I'm still not sure that I'm equipped to do anything about all of this."

"You're stronger than you think. You've already taken the biggest first steps. You're seeking out the Word. You're asking the right questions. And you feel a connection to God. I can see the changes in you. Right before my eyes. So don't count yourself out before this even starts."

"How did you know you saw an angel?"

"The first time I didn't realize it. But then it became very obvious to me."

"I thought these spiritual forces were invisible. That's what Dan keeps talking about."

"Yes, generally they are. But there are certain circumstances where people can see angels or demons. Generally, though this battle is an invisible one, but that doesn't make it any less real—or less dangerous."

"Believe me, I get that."

Pastor Dan walked over to them. "Glad you two stuck around."

"What prompted that sermon?" she asked.

"You haven't heard?" Dan asked her. "I assume you had."

"Heard what?"

"Clive Township is dead."

"What? No, no one told me. I've been in constant contact with Nina Marie, too."

"I found out that he died of pancreatic cancer. And while Clive was definitely a menace, he was much more cautious than Nina Marie will be. With Nina Marie at the helm of Astral Tech, she's going to go full out against Layton. Not only in the litigation but spiritually as well. Which means this is all going to come to a head pretty quickly."

"Wow," she said. "I can't believe she didn't tell me."

"Do you have a trial date yet?" Dan asked.

"No," they said in unison.

"But," Grant said, "Judge Wingfield had indicated we were going to be put on the fast track trial calendar because of the expedited discovery. Now that he's had a heart attack, we don't know yet whether he will be able to come back to the case or not.

More than likely they will assign us a new judge. So it will all depend on the judge and on if either side pushes for a quick trial."

Dan nodded. "I think Layton and Nina Marie will want it to happen soon. They each see this as the first step to taking down the other."

"This isn't a normal litigation," Grant said. "A defendant would not usually push for a faster trial, but I guess I can see it happening here."

"I want the two of you to be extremely cautious," Dan said. "You're literally being thrown into the lion's den, and I don't like it. I know you have a job to do, but you have to go in with your eyes fully open." He turned to Grant. "How are you doing in the midst of all of this?"

"I've had a rough few days. But I don't have a choice except to move forward and do the best I can with the lawsuit."

"What about spiritually?" Dan asked.

"I'm getting there. I feel like right when I think I have one aspect figured out, then I have more questions about another."

"I'm here for whatever you need." Dan gave him a hearty pat on the back and then walked away to talk to some other people.

"I assume you're going to call the clerk's office first thing tomorrow morning?" she asked.

"Yes. If you get to them before I do, I'm hoping you'll let me know what they have to say."

"Of course. That's just professional courtesy." She took a deep breath. "The trial is just the beginning. You realize that?"

"Yes. But once it's over, I'll be filing another motion to withdraw effective ASAP. They can find someone else to handle any post trial matters."

"Keep your head up, Grant. And keep your focus on what matters."

He gave her a weak smile. "That's exactly what I plan to do."

CHAPTER FIFTEEN

Grant decided that instead of calling the clerk's office on Monday morning that he was just going to go down to the courthouse and talk to the clerk himself. He was high strung from caffeine and the lack of sleep.

He had found himself starting to pray pretty often. It felt like it was his way of furthering his fledgling relationship with God. And once he did it, then it started to become easier.

The clerk's office had only opened about fifteen minutes before, and he was one of the first people in line. That was the thing about a courthouse. It was always busy.

He waited patiently—or as patiently as possible—while the few people in front of him were helped. When it was his turn, the clerk immediately recognized him.

"Mr. Baxter," she said.

"How is Judge Wingfield?"

"Thankfully he's doing all right. He's going to be in the hospital for a few more days, and he's going to take some time off. So your case has been reassigned. Which is the reason I assume you're here?"

"Yes, ma'am."

She nodded. "Judge Louise Martinique is going to be taking over. She handled one of your prior hearings."

"Yes, she did." That was the hearing where Olivia had totally choked. She was not going to be happy about this at all. But there was absolutely nothing he could do. This was all way out of his control.

"And I was going to send out an email and call you both this morning. The judge wants to see you in court at nine a.m. tomorrow to conduct the hearing and set a trial date."

Interesting, he thought. Why would she be so gung ho on setting a trial date? "Thank you for the information."

"You'll receive the formal notice from me via email this morning. I'll still be the clerk on the case since it was Judge Wingfield's case."

"Thank you." He walked out of the courthouse and pulled out his cell phone to let Olivia know what he had just found out.

He dialed her number and waited for her to pick up.

"Hello," she said.

"Hey, it's Grant. I'm down at the courthouse, and I just spoke with the clerk."

"What's the deal?"

"The case has been assigned to Judge Louise Martinique. You remember her, don't you?"

She groaned. "Yes. How could I forget?"

"The clerk is sending us the notice this morning, but we have a hearing tomorrow at nine a.m. She wants to hear arguments on the injunction and set a trial date."

Olivia muttered something he couldn't understand.

"What are you saying?"

"I think Layton is behind this. I have reason to believe that he and Judge Martinique are at least friendly and could be something else. Remember when I had the issues in front of her the last time."

"What? You think she's one of them? A senior judge?"

"They can be anyone, Grant. Don't let occupations fool you. Evil can appear anywhere and in multiple forms. But this is my problem not yours. Thanks for letting me know about the hearing once you found out. I've got to get back to work, but I'll see you in court tomorrow."

"See you then."

He ended the call and pondered what Olivia had said. Was she insinuating that her bad performance and anxiety were caused by Judge Martinique? This was one thing he was still really struggling with. How did all of this spiritual warfare stuff really play out?

Yeah, he'd had that experience in his house and his car that he couldn't explain. He'd tried to say it was fatigue or stress, but it had been so real. If he hadn't have had that though, he would have a really hard time even going down this road.

Having that knowledge and experience led him to believe that there was something out there. A spiritual battle waiting to be waged. He still didn't quite understand how he would be prepared to fight it. And what exactly he would be called upon to do.

What he had to do first was to get through this lawsuit with the most difficult and dangerous client he'd ever had. He'd thought more than once about whether Layton was behind Judge Wingfield's heart attack. And how convenient it was that now Judge Martinique would be the judge in the case. If Olivia was right and Judge Martinique was loyal to Layton, then that would explain a few things.

He should be happy that he was going to be getting a more favorable judge. One that didn't hate him because he'd presented fabricated evidence to the court as the basis for an emergency injunction. But he just felt sick about the whole thing.

There was no glory in winning through cheating and deception. He was a very competitive person and a highly driven lawyer, but definitely not this way. He was starting to realize that there was more to life than just making money off of lawsuits. And he had one person to thank for that—his opposing counsel. She'd helped him start this journey of faith that he could feel was literally changing him from the inside out. There was no turning back.

***

Olivia dreaded walking into the courtroom to face her nemesis—Judge Louise Martinique. But first she was meeting Nina Marie outside the building, and she had to raise issues with her. Like why hadn't she, as the company's lawyer, been notified about the passing of the CEO?

That seemed like a pretty important fact for her to be made aware of. Generally annoyed at the moment, she took a deep breath. She asked the Lord to give her patience and the ability to get through this hearing without any outside influences impacting her performance.

Nina Marie walked up to her wearing a long beige dress and pumps. She looked like a consummate professional, not a spiritual warrior.

"We need to talk," she said.

"What's wrong?"

"What's wrong? What's wrong is that I had to find out from someone not associated with Astral Tech that Clive had passed away. Why didn't you tell me that?"

Nina Marie let out an exasperated sigh. "I've basically been running the company for a while now. It didn't really seem that relevant to bother you about it."

"Bother me? We've seen each other since this has happened. Remember, on Friday at the hearing?"

"Oh yes, but things got so dramatic with the judge that I wasn't even thinking about that."

"From now on, you have to keep me in the loop on major company business like this, okay?"

"Fine," Nina Marie said.

"There's one more thing. We have a new judge, and I want to know what you know about her. Her name is Judge Louise Martinique."

Nina Marie gasped. "She's one of them."

"One of who?"

"Optimism."

"How do you know?"

Nina Marie's mood noticeably shifted. She crossed her arms around her and tapped her foot. "I know the enemy. Trust me on this one. This is a huge problem for us. If she's the trial judge, we have no shot of winning."

"It's a jury trial though. The decision is up to the jury, but I'm not going to lie. The judge's rulings on certain issues could definitely impact our case. So while the jury is the ultimate decider of the verdict, having a biased judge is not where you want to be. If we could prove her association with Layton, we could move to disqualify her as the judge."

Nina Marie shook her head. "They're super careful about these things. Members like that with such powerful connections never have a trail. The best we could do was probably show them attending some of the same social events. But I know even as a non lawyer that won't be enough."

"No, it won't." Olivia rubbed her temples trying to figure out how best to handle this. "We just have to go with it. Do the best we can, and really try to be as likeable as possible to the jury. In the end, that will matter the most."

Nina Marie grabbed onto her shoulders. "You do whatever you need to do. You have my full support."

"We should go in." Olivia had such a strange relationship with Nina Marie. She was pretty sure she'd never again defend someone like her or a company like Astral Tech. She didn't really know what God's plan was for the actual litigation. Her and Grant both had major issues they were dealing with. She just had to trust in

Him and know that even if the storms were raging, that she'd live to fight another day.

For now, she couldn't focus on Nina Marie being the adversary even if she ultimately would be. As she walked into the courtroom, her stomach clenched with nerves. What if she locked up again and couldn't talk? What if Louise Martinique really was wielding some evil powers against her?

She leaned over to Nina Marie as they took their seat at their table. "Be prepared for the possibility that Judge Martinique may come after me."

"What do you mean?"

"Last time we were in front of her, I basically had a panic attack. I've never had one before, so I think she had something to do with that."

Nina Marie raised an eyebrow. "She won't dare make a move with me beside you."

Olivia was highly uncomfortable with the idea that Nina Marie would be providing her any type of protection. She didn't need the cloak of evil to fight evil. No, the only true answer was to fight evil with the Word of God. "Nina Marie, please don't do anything. I'll be able to handle myself."

"I can't make any promises," Nina Marie muttered.

"All rise," the bailiff said.

Olivia glanced over to the other table where Grant and Layton stood at attention. There was one thing she was sure of—this was bound to be interesting.

Judge Martinique looked just as Olivia had remembered. Her long gray hair was pulled back from her face, and her dark blue eyes locked right away on Olivia.

"Good morning, everyone. I will be taking over this case, given Judge Wingfield's health issues. Today I am hearing arguments on the emergency injunction. I've read all the papers that were filed. I also understand that experts have been retained by both sides to testify to the validity of the email that was used as the basis for filing the motion. Is that correct?"

"Yes, Your Honor," Olivia and Grant said in unison.

During an hour of arguments and expert testimony, Judge Martinique scribbled notes down on her legal pad. "I've heard enough. I'm ready to rule. As to the motion for emergency injunction, the motion is denied. As to the issue regarding the validity of the email and the question of who altered the email, it is my finding that there is evidence from both experts supporting the fact that the email was altered. I'm not convinced, however, by defense counsel's argument that plaintiff or his counsel was responsible for the alteration. Therefore, I rule to exclude the email at trial. And as a result, I deny Ms. Murray's motion today to levy sanctions against Optimism."

Olivia wasn't surprised. The judge was also being very careful and deliberate in the scope of her rulings, following the easy and cautious way out. To any outsider, it would seem like she was taking a measured approach. At least Olivia hadn't felt any ill effects in the courtroom today.

"Now, I'd like to take up the issue of a trial date. I'd like to hear what each side has to say starting with the Plaintiff."

Grant stood up. "Given the magnitude of the issues involved and the time sensitive nature of this case, Optimism would ask that the court set the trial date for as soon as reasonably possible, with the court's schedule."

"And what is Astral Tech's position, Ms. Murray?"

"Astral Tech is also anxious to resolve these issues as expeditiously as possible."

"Very well. Trial will start a week from today. We're adjourned."

And just like that, the judge was walking out, leaving her a bit stunned. A week to prepare for trial? What a complete nightmare. But Nina Marie had also insisted that she wanted this thing to end sooner rather than later.

The silver lining was that the only issue remaining in the case was the theft allegation.

"What's the plan?" Nina Marie asked as she rose from her seat.

"The plan is that we're going to try this case. I need to figure out some logistics from my end regarding the law firm. But we'll need to start preparing for your testimony tomorrow. I'll need a lot of time with you, Nina Marie. You're the key witness for Astral Tech, especially since Clive is dead and the theft allegation is pointed in your direction."

"Don't you worry about me and my preparation. I will be ready. I'm willing to meet as long as it takes to prepare. You will have my full undivided attention."

"I'm going to need it. We're in an uphill battle here."

"I'll finish up some work and loose ends today, and I'll be all yours starting in the morning."

"Thank you."

"I'm going to get going. I need to swing by my house before I go in."

"I'll see you in the office later today."

Olivia gathered up her files and took a deep breath. She needed to get to somewhere that she could call Chet and brief him on the latest developments. He was going to flip about the trial being in a week.

Grant had already left the courtroom with Layton. Which was all well and good. Honestly, she didn't really feel like talking to him right now. Or anyone else for that matter.

But there was no sidestepping the phone call to Chet. She waited until she got into her car and made the call from the parking lot.

Dear Lord, I hope I don't lose my job over this. But she couldn't help the fact that her client was also pushing for an immediate trial. Regardless, she was in the client service industry, and when the client spoke, that was that.

She waited while Chet's secretary put her through.

"Chet Carter speaking," he said.

"It's Olivia. I've got news."

"I've read your emails about what happened on Friday with great interest. Sounds like you have quite a circus going on out there."

"I'm afraid it's only going to get worse."

"What happened?"

She closed her eyes and got ready to break the news. "Well, first off, we got a new judge. She'd conducted one of our prior hearings, and she is definitely biased for Optimism, but we can't prove it."

He sighed. "That's just part of litigation, Olivia. That's nothing that can't be handled. Don't forget that the jury has the ultimate say."

"About that, sir. The trial has been set for a week from today."

"What?" he yelled. "How is that even possible? That's preposterous."

"That's why I wanted to call you instead of emailing, because it's complicated."

"Uh oh. I don't like where this is heading, Olivia."

"Chet, the client was adamant that they wanted to agree to a quick trial date. There's a lot going on behind the scenes between these two companies, and both sides want to go to trial."

She was met by silence. This was it. This was where he was going to tell her to get on a plane home, pack her office, and be done with it.

"I know I've basically left you to fend for yourself on this case, Olivia, because you were up for it. Now you find yourself in a precarious situation, but it's a situation that only you know how to handle."

"What are you saying?"

"That you will see this thing through. You'll be first chair on Monday when this trial starts. I don't understand all the facts on the ground. I've been following all your updates, but you're right that this hasn't been a usual case. From the industry right on down to the players and the judges. Do the best you can. That's all I can ask of you."

Thank God he wasn't going to fire her. "I want you to have reasonable expectations. There's a good chance that they'll make the jury believe that Astral Tech stole the app."

"I realize that. That's why you can only do your best as a lawyer, and the rest is in the hands of the jury."

"What about support staff or additional attorney help?"

"I'll send you one paralegal and one junior associate. Given the client's tight fisted budget, I can't send out more team members than that. Originally, I was going to give them a bit of a price break so that I could try the case, but after following this whole thing, I think it's just better that you handle it."

"I'll do my best."

"Olivia, don't forget the objective. You've handled these wacky people much better than I probably would have. I didn't realize when we took them on as a client that we'd have so much additional baggage to deal with."

"Thank you. I'll keep you posted."

"Please do."

The call ended and she sat behind the wheel but still didn't start the car. Chet wanted to separate himself from this mess, and she really couldn't blame him. Yes, she wanted to be first chair at a trial—wanted to be the lead lawyer on the case arguing in front of the jury. But this was never the way she envisioned it. She did the only thing she felt she could do. She started driving and began to pray.

***

Stacey felt fabulous. She'd come into the office knowing that it was going to be a great day. After the party at Layton's, she was more sure than ever of her decision.

Her cell phone rang and she picked it up.

"Stacey, it's Sofia. I've been worried about you. I didn't see you in church, and you haven't answered any of my emails or texts."

Uh oh. She hadn't quite decided how the best way to play this was. "Sorry, I've just been busy with work and school."

"Work as in working at Optimism?" Sofia asked.

"Yes. It's totally fine, Sofia. What I thought happened to me didn't happen." It was easier to just claim everything was on the up and up. "I have no reason to give up a perfectly good internship at a major business because I was stressed out and delusional."

"It sounds to me like you're trying to convince yourself of things you know are not true. It's me you're dealing with, Stacey. I've known you, what? For ten years."

"I've grown up."

"Yes, you have, but I could see the fear in your eyes after what you experienced in your apartment. Now you're trying to put up a defense mechanism and pretend like it didn't happen, but after the fact you were trying to convince me that it did. You said you felt like it was real even when you didn't want it to be. Remember that?"

She sighed. "I have to get to work, Sofia. Is there anything else?"

"So that's it? You're just going to shut me out."

"Please don't worry about me. I'm doing great. Better than I have in a long time. My grades are solid, and I'm learning so much with this job. Just let me be."

"Do you plan on coming back to church?"

"I've really got to go. I'll talk to you later." Stacey didn't even wait for a response before she ended the call.

"Is everything okay?"

Stacey jumped at the sound of Morena's voice behind her. She turned around.

"Everything is fine."

"If you want to talk about it, you know I'm here."

"It was just someone from my old church. She doesn't want me working here."

"And how do you feel about that?"

"Like I want to do what I want to do."

"Good girl." Morena squeezed her shoulder. "You're a grown woman now. You need to start making your own decisions and thinking independently."

She nodded. "It feels good. I'm making the right decision. I'm confident of that."

Layton walked into the conference room. "Ladies, we're now set for trial a week from today."

"What?" Morena asked.

"Yes, it's great. We have a new judge and a great chance of winning this thing."

"Who is the judge?" Morena asked.

"Louise."

Morena only smiled in response. Stacey felt like she was obviously missing an important piece of the puzzle, but she didn't want to pry.

"Is there anything I can do to help get ready for trial?" Stacey asked.

"Actually, if you're up for it, I'm sure there is," Layton said. "Our lawyer, Grant Baxter, is in the other conference room. Let me introduce you to him. I imagine he would like to have some assistance."

"You take her to meet Grant, and I'll catch up with you afterward. We have a few items to discuss," Morena said.

"I'll meet you in your office in a few." Then Layton turned his attention back to Stacey. "Come with me."

Stacey followed Layton down the hall to the other large conference room. She walked into the room behind him and felt her eyes widen. Grant Baxter didn't look anything like what she would've expected. He was much younger—probably in his thirties—and was absolutely handsome with dark hair and bright blue eyes. But this was not the time for a schoolgirl crush. She needed to impress everyone that she worked with.

"Grant, this is our intern, Stacey Malone. She's currently in college and will work here after graduation. I thought you might be able to use her on any tasks you thought appropriate."

Grant reached out and gently shook her hand. "It's nice to meet you, Stacey."

"I'll do whatever you need me to. Even if it's just bringing you coffee or making copies."

"Thanks so much. I am running most of this case by myself, so I'm sure there will be plenty of things that have to get done to prepare for trial. So I'd welcome the help."

She smiled. "That's great. Thank you again, Layton." She turned to him. "This opportunity is amazing. I'm learning so many different things."

"You deserve it, Stacey. I'm going to run and meet with Morena now. You're in good hands with Grant."

Layton left the room, leaving her alone with the lawyer.

He smiled at her. "Are you really up for this? Because if you're not, then that's okay. It will be a lot of grunt work."

She nodded. "I'm ready. Just tell me what to do and where to start."

"Great. I've got a list of exhibits that we're planning to use at trial. Basically this is a list of documents. All the documents in the litigation, one hard copy each, are in those boxes that go all the way across the perimeter of the room. First thing is that we always make sure we keep that master set intact. But I'd like for you to pull this list of possible exhibits from the master set and make four copies of each of them. Can you handle that?"

"Most definitely."

"I'll be right here if you have any questions."

Grant had taken over the entire conference room table with lots of papers, and he also had his computer open.

She took the list of documents from him and started to work, pulling out documents from the master file and making copies. The industrial size copier in the conference room made the process pretty simple. But there were still a lot of documents to copy.

They worked in silence for a long time.

"Grant, can I ask you something?"

"Sure."

"Did you take this case because you're a New Age follower, or just because it was a good case?"

"I took the case on the merits. My own beliefs really didn't even come into the analysis at all."

"Really?"

"Yeah. I'd never been truly exposed to New Age theories anyway. So it's been a bit of a learning curve."

"I'm studying it. New Age I mean. It's so fascinating. If you're not into New Age, are you religious at all?"

Grant shifted some papers on the table. "Funny you ask that. Before I started this case, the answer would've definitely been no. But as of late, I've started to explore things a bit. I've started going to a church here."

"Oh, which one?"

"Windy Ridge Community Church. Have you heard of it?"

She nodded. "That's where I used to go."

"Why did you stop going?"

She took a breath.

"Sorry, if that's too personal of a question."

"Oh, no, not at all. I stopped going because I really feel like I found my niche with New Age. It seems to be where I'm supposed to be. At least for now."

"I feel the same way. But about Christianity."

"That's so strange."

"Isn't it?"

"I was raised in Windy Ridge Community Church. But I feel like I'm entering into a new phase of life. I'm ready for something new."

"I may be totally out of line here, so forgive me in advance. But I just have to say this."

"All right." Where in the world was he going with this?

"Just be careful, Stacey. I've been exposed to a lot of this stuff through this litigation, and it's much more real and dangerous than I ever could've imagined."

"I thought you were on our side? That you were our lawyer?"

He nodded. "In the lawsuit, yes, I am Optimism's lawyer, and I will do my best to protect the interests of the company. But there are things going on around here that go way beyond the lawsuit. I don't know if you have seen that yet or not. But I couldn't help but say something to you."

A shiver shot down her back. Because this man she had just met and barely knew had laid it all out on the table without even knowing it. "Thanks for giving me your opinion."

"Don't worry," he said. "I won't say anything else about it. We've got lots more work to do."

Stacey was left feeling a bit frazzled. Just when she thought she had it all figured out, Grant had to walk into her life and add to her confusion. How could this man who had just started going to church have that type of impact on her?

CHAPTER SIXTEEN

O livia had her game face on—today was the day. The trial was set to begin. The week of preparation had gone by quickly, but as she readied herself to step into the courtroom, she felt a sense of peace wash over her.

As difficult as this trial would be, she knew that the most trying battle was yet to come. What she needed to do now was face down the issues at this trial and meet it head on. She'd gotten a pep talk last night from Chet who assured her that he was happy with her performance under such unusual circumstances.

She met Nina Marie outside the courtroom doors. Nina Marie was going to serve as the company representative during trial so she would sit at the counsel's table. The one associate and paralegal that Chet sent to help Olivia would be in the chairs right behind the table.

As they walked into the courtroom, she almost ran head on into Grant who was walking with what she presumed was another lawyer from his firm by his side. He shook her hand, but they didn't exchange words. Layton was already seated as the Optimism representative at plaintiff's table. The other man she didn't know sat right behind them.

It took them about an hour to choose a jury, and then they were ready to go.

"Mr. Baxter," Judge Martinique said. "Let's begin with your opening statement."

"Thank you, Your Honor."

Olivia felt like she knew the case well enough to predict where Grant was going to go. Each side basically had the arguments that they had, and there wasn't much room left for additional creativity beyond that. But what each of them did bring to the table were their individual styles and modes of presentation.

"Ladies and gentlemen of the jury. I know I introduced myself to you during jury selection that we just finished, but I'll say again that my name is Grant Baxter and I represent the plaintiff in the litigation—Optimism. A company founded by the late Earl Ward twenty years ago, but that is still thriving today. Led by Layton Alito the CEO, the man you see seated at the table." He pointed toward Layton.

"You're going to hear a lot of allegations in this case. A lot of personal drama. A lot of distractions put forward to you by Astral Tech's lawyer. But at its core, this case is simply about theft. The evidence will show that Nina Marie Crane stole an application, what we would all call an app, that was created by Optimism CEO Layton Alito. Everything else will just be a sideshow to that simple fact that we will prove to you."

Grant kept going for about half an hour. She wasn't surprised that he didn't drone on forever. Studies showed that the jury could quickly lose patience with long opening arguments and Grant was no amateur.

When he took his seat, it was her turn. She looked up toward the judge.

"Ms. Murray, the floor is yours." Judge Martinique smiled.

Olivia couldn't believe the nerve of the judge putting on a smile. But Louise Martinique was a smart woman. She wasn't going to say or do anything that could come back to hurt her or her professional reputation as a judge. She'd do everything she could during trial to appear balanced. But Olivia had no doubt that the rulings would mostly go against her—or at least the rulings that really mattered.

Nina Marie gave her hand a quick squeeze under the table. Their relationship continued to amaze her. And she couldn't help but wonder that if she had more time, she could find out what damaged Nina Marie so badly to make her turn to darkness.

But for right now she had to focus on her opening statement.

"I'm Olivia Murray, and I want to thank you for your service on the jury." She made a point to make direct eye contact with the jurors. Her strength was in personally connecting with the jury. She didn't have as much pizazz or charisma as Grant. But she had heart.

"Mr. Baxter told you a lot today about the simplicity of this case, and he of course relied on his version of the facts. I'm not going to take a lot of your time in this statement because I believe the evidence presented will tell the story for you. Please hold Mr. Baxter to his opening statement. If this case is as open and shut as he would like you to believe, then you should be convinced when shown the evidence of exactly what occurred. I will submit to you that you will find the evidence woefully lacking to support a finding for Optimism on the claim of theft."

She took a deep breath. So far the jury was listening. She was about to drop the bomb. Her biggest and best argument. Whether they bought it or not was another issue entirely.

"This case isn't about theft. Ladies and gentleman, this is a case about a romantic relationship that went from hot and heavy to toxic in a short amount of time. Mr. Baxter, of course, didn't fill you in on these quote dramatic details because he knows that if you hear all the facts and not just part of them that you will come to a conclusion adverse to what he wants."

She walked toward the jury. "But the evidence will show that Nina Marie Crane, the current CEO of Astral Tech who was then the Chief Operating Officer, and Layton Alito the CEO of Optimism engaged in a romantic relationship. When Ms. Crane ended the romantic relationship with Mr. Alito, he was obviously distressed. The breakup was not amicable to say the least. And there was dramatic back and forth between the two of them.

But what there was not, ladies and gentleman, is any theft. Mr. Alito, spurned by his girlfriend, is not a man used to being rejected. A man of wealth and power and intelligence. Someone who didn't know how to handle being told no. The evidence will show that Mr. Alito took matters into his own hands. He wanted revenge. He wanted Ms. Crane to hurt as much as he was hurting. And the best way for that to happen was for him to go after the thing that mattered the absolute most to Ms. Crane. And that was the company she'd poured herself into for years, the company I'm here representing today—Astral Tech."

She paused to let her statements sink in. "The evidence will show absolutely no wrongdoing by any employees of Astral Tech including Ms. Crane. The evidence will show, however, emails documenting the tumultuous relationship between Ms. Crane and Mr. Alito. It will show Mr. Alito's temper. His utter surprise at being dumped by Ms. Crane. And then, ladies and gentlemen, it will show you the anger that filled his heart and his words as he tried to come to grips with the rejection. Is it pretty? Most certainly not. Do both parties bare some blame in how the relationship ended and the aftermath? Of course. But you will not be presented with a shred of evidence tying Ms. Crane to the alleged theft of the app." She wrapped up with a few closing thoughts and took her seat.

She felt good. The jurors had been with her the entire time, and she could see on their faces that they were at least starting to believe that this might be a lover's quarrel more than a business dispute. But she still had a long way to go.

Most of it would really come down to the two star witnesses. Their direct examination and cross examination. And ultimately who the jury believed. Unfortunately for her, she wasn't sure she believed her own client. How could she make sure the jury did? That's what had been keeping her up at night.

But Grant was representing the plaintiff, and he would put on his case first. Which meant he'd be putting Layton Alito on the stand after lunch.

"We'll recess an hour for lunch," Judge Martinique said. "I'll remind the jury of the same admonitions I gave before we started." She then went on to tell them about what they couldn't talk about.

The jury was dismissed and after they left the courtroom, Nina Marie leaned over to her. "That was brilliant, Olivia. We're going to win this thing."

"Don't get ahead of yourself, Nina Marie. We've got to get through this afternoon first."

***

Grant had spent the most time preparing for his direct examination of Layton. He'd almost put as much time into the cross examination of Nina Marie, but with cross he liked to adapt based on what the direct exam was.

But his direct exam with Layton should go smoothly. The operative word being should. He'd met with Layton for hours going over the testimony in painstaking detail, the way any good lawyer would do.

He was much more worried about Layton losing it on cross. If he did that, the case would be over. The jury would be much more likely to buy into Olivia's theory if Layton was a loose cannon.

Right now, Layton was a ball of confidence. Ready to attack his prey and more importantly to woo the jury. Layton had assured Grant that this was going to be a slam dunk.

The lunch break was over and it was time to put Layton on the stand. *Lord, help me.* That was all he could think.

"Mr. Baxter, please call your first witness."

"Thank you, Your Honor. Optimism would like to call Layton Alito to the stand."

Layton stood from the table and walked up to the witness box. He was sworn in, and then he looked at the jury.

Grant had to admit, on the outside Layton looked like he had nothing to hide. If only that were the truth. The good part was that Grant actually did believe that Nina Marie had stolen the technology. So now it was time to convey the story.

"Mr. Alito, I'd like to start by giving the jury some information about you. Please tell the jury a bit about your education and work background." Normally he wouldn't be able to lead his own witness or ask such open ended questions, but for background it was usually allowed.

"Sure. I graduated from University of Illinois with a degree in business. I then got my MBA after working for a few years and then I went to the PR industry."

"And when did you first start working at Optimism?"

"It's been about a decade ago. I became CEO of Optimism after the passing of the head of the company. I've been in that role ever since."

"And tell the jury a bit about what your company does."

"We offer a variety of New Age products to customers including technological applications, or apps, like the one in question here."

"And that's what I want to talk about today. Why did you make the allegation of theft against Astral Tech?"

"Because it's true."

"And how do you know it's true?"

"Because Ms. Crane had access to my computer and my servers while we were dating. I routinely caught her examining my files. I honestly didn't think she would stoop to the level of theft, but she did."

Olivia stood. "Move to strike the last comment he made."

"The jury should disregard the last comment made by Mr. Alito," Judge Martinique said.

But for Grant's purpose it didn't matter. Layton was sewing the seeds that Nina Marie was a deceitful and untrustworthy thief. And for the next thirty minutes, Grant walked Layton through his time with Nina Marie and the specifics of the theft.

Layton performed even better than expected. But as Grant sat down, the real test was about to come.

"Your witness, Ms. Murray," the judge said.

Grant sat in great anticipation as Olivia stood up from her seat and walked over toward the witness box. This was going to get interesting.

"Mr. Alito, isn't it true that you fabricated these allegations in the same way you fabricated evidence to implicate Ms. Crane?"

Whoa, going for the jugular. He jumped up. "Objection, prejudicial."

"Counsel, please approach the bench."

They walked up to the bench where the judge was frowning.

"Ms. Murray this is your only warning. I thought my prior ruling was clear. There should be no talk of this fabricated evidence."

"With all due respect, Your Honor, your prior ruling didn't specifically exclude the possibility that I could ask about this at trial. Just that you made no factual determination about who fabricated the evidence."

The judge narrowed her eyes at Olivia. "Well, Ms. Murray, I will make it clear now. You can't bring up this fabrication issue at all. Am I clear?"

"I just want the court record to reflect that the court has made this determination as it's something I will raise on appeal if need be." Olivia wasn't backing down.

"Duly noted. You may proceed."

"Given your ruling, Your Honor, I'd like to ask for a recess to determine the propriety of an interlocutory appeal on this issue right now."

"Fine. We will recess for the rest of the day. Be ready for whatever you plan to do first thing tomorrow."

"Your Honor, respectfully given the importance of this issue, I would like to ask the court for twenty four hours."

Judge Martinique sighed. "Very well. We'll reconvene first thing Wednesday morning. Mr. Alito, you may step down."

The judge dismissed the jury telling them they'd have Tuesday off and to return Wednesday.

Grant went back to his table where Layton stood. "We've got to talk."

"What happened up there?"

"This fabrication issue is going to come back and bite us in a big way. This judge has ruled that Olivia can't introduce anything related to the evidence fabrication issue. But Olivia is going to try an interlocutory appeal."

"And what exactly is that?"

"It's an appeal that can happen right now as opposed to waiting on the case to reach a verdict and then appeal. And if that remedy isn't available, if Optimism wins it will definitely be the basis of the appeal."

"So what are you saying?"

"I'm saying that we're in a tight spot because of what you and I both know you did. We could win here and eventually still lose."

"You'll stop talking to me like that."

Grant didn't even respond.

"I'm out of here," Layton said. He walked out and Grant didn't even bother to go after him. He was so over this all.

***

That night, Olivia sat in her conference room at Astral Tech typing away on her computer. It was getting late, but she wanted to have a solid draft that she could polish and add to on Tuesday. She had a team of lawyers back in the DC office doing supplemental research, and they were emailing her key cases for her brief supporting the interlocutory appeal.

She heard loud voices arguing with each other down the hall, and whatever was happening it sounded like they were not happy. She couldn't afford to be distracted right now.

She wanted to get up and yell at them to stop. But then she realized she didn't really want to get involved in whatever latest squabble was happening between Nina Marie and Matt. She'd witnessed the two of them in heated discussions lately at the Astral Tech office. She surmised that there was some type of power struggle going on between the two of them post Clive's death.

Trying to ignore the loud voices, she kept working on the brief until a sense of dread started to fill the air causing her fingers to freeze on the keyboard. Then the lights in the room began to flicker.

What's going on? she thought.

Her heartbeat sped up. Something was terribly wrong, and she was right in the middle of it.

Put on the full armor of God, she heard a voice say clearly. The sounds outside of the conference room got louder and louder. But they no longer sounded like human voices arguing. No, there was an awful shrieking. A loud moaning sound. She broke out into a sweat as fear gripped her entire body paralyzing her. She sat unmoving in the office chair listening closely to what was unfolding all around her.

She wasn't ready. Not yet. The battle wasn't supposed to be happening now. Not when there was so much to do to get ready. Was it really time to do battle? And why was it happening here at the Astral Tech office?

She was cornered. *Dear Lord, protect me now. I need You.*

Another piercing shriek filled the air. The room went completely black, enveloping all of her in a sea of darkness.

Was it better to stay in the conference room or try to get out of the office? Out of the building?

She didn't even know if escape was an option. It wasn't as if she was trying to get away from a human attacker. No, this was a spiritual battle.

Before she could make any decision, a strong force lifted her up out of the chair and threw her up against the wall, knocking the breath completely out of her.

This attack was unlike anything she'd ever experienced. Yes, the other spiritual assaults were painful, but as she lay on the floor crumpled into a ball, she wondered if the demons might try to kill her right there in the Astral Tech conference room. The sounds emanating from the forces of evil that attacked her were agonizing to hear and made her head pound.

She tried to shake off the shooting pain down her spine and stand up, but then another strong force knocked her hard flat on her back. She gasped for air.

This time she couldn't move as the demon held her down. She couldn't see a thing, but she felt the demonic presence as it kept her on the ground. A presence filled with hatred.

There was no way she could fight the demon off with her human strength and abilities. She was no match for their physical strength, and at this rate she would be dead soon. She needed the Lord.

"I rebuke you in the name of Jesus Christ," she said.

The demon writhed against her as she uttered the name of the Lord, but he didn't give up. All of her senses were on high alert.

Her skin burned as a string of foul curses came out of the demon's mouth. But she wasn't deterred in her quest. She was going to fight. She tried to open her mouth to speak, but she couldn't. It was if her lips had been sealed shut with glue. So instead she repeated the rebuke over and over again in her mind.

The demon's rough grip loosened. Not wasting a second, she broke away from him and ran in the direction of the door. She slammed her arm against the conference room table as she went, trying desperately to get out the door and make her way through the darkness, into the unknown of the hallway.

As she pushed open the door, thick smoke billowed throughout the hall. She choked as she breathed in the toxic air that filled her lungs and threatened her ability to take in any oxygen.

She dropped down low to the floor. Crawling on her hands and knees she headed toward the front door of the building. But she had a ways to go. She tried to move quickly, but it was as if something was pulling her back every time she made any progress moving forward.

Her nails scratched the floor, and a demon grabbed tightly onto her ankles with sharp nails tearing into her skin. She dug in refusing to let them take her back to the conference room. The demons weren't going to leave her alone until they reached their goal. And that goal was to kill her tonight.

But that's when she saw a clearing in the smoke and a faint light coming from Nina Marie's office. She took a deep breath that caused her to cough violently.

In front of the office stood Layton surrounded by forces of evil. She counted at least five hooded creatures that stood flanking him on each side. She saw them as clearly as she saw him. A chill shot through her body at the sight of literally seeing demons in physical form right in front of her.

She had two options. Make a run for the front door or stay and try to help Nina Marie.

Why in the world should she help someone who was evil? Someone who admittedly sought out the devil? A battle raged inside her as she weighed her options.

But succumbing to the forces of darkness wasn't her way. It wasn't right. She couldn't just let Layton and the demons kill Nina Marie. Could she?

Absolutely not. *Dear Lord, you wouldn't want me to stand by and watch her be killed by a human or a demonic force.* She knew deep in her gut what was right. Remembering the verse in the Bible that basically said that you shouldn't repay evil for evil but always seek to do good, she took a deep breath and crawled toward Nina Marie's door. She was going to try her best to save Nina Marie's life.

"Leave here," Olivia yelled.

That got the attention of Layton and the demons who all turned toward her.

She sucked in a breath and clenched her hands by her side. Her nails pushing into her flesh. She'd never actually seen a demon. These demons took a quasi human form except that their eyes were the color of fire blazing brightly. All five appeared masculine as they stood tall towering over Layton by quite a few inches. They were cloaked in black from head to toe, but their physical prowess was undeniable.

"You have no business in this fight. This is between Nina Marie and me," Layton said. He moved closer to the doorway.

She took a few quick steps and that's when she got the first look inside and saw Nina Marie writhing on the ground.

"Olivia, they'll kill you. You should leave," Nina Marie said. She looked battered as her hair was falling down out of the bun, and her face was streaked with bloody scratch marks.

"I'm not going to leave you here with them. It doesn't have to be this way, Nina Marie."

As she finished saying the words, she was tackled hard to the ground. Eyes filled with the pits of hell stared down at her.

She heard Nina Marie scream from the office.

"I told you. Get out of here. I rebuke you in the name of Jesus Christ," Olivia said. The demon rose up above her, and she got to her feet. Taking another step toward the office door, she felt searing heat.

"I have no problem destroying you, too," Layton said. "But Nina Marie is my first concern. Why would you try to aid one of the defenders of darkness anyway? Isn't that against your Christian values?"

She shook her head. "No, Layton. That's where you have it wrong." She steadied herself and took a deep breath. "The Lord will forgive and redeem those that turn away from the darkness and come to Him. It's not the Lord's way to condemn and kill. That's the way of Satan. Only your master acts like that."

"Stop it!" he roared.

His words were delivered with a punch that sent her stumbling backward, but she regained her footing.

As she took another step forward one of the demons outstretched his arm. While he wasn't physically touching her, she felt his powerful grip tighten on her neck.

"The demons will kill you, Olivia. This is your final way out. Your last chance," Layton said.

She refused to give in to evil. The Lord would protect her. She closed her eyes and started to pray. Asking God to give her strength. To provide an army of angels to come to her aid to combat the demons that stood in front of her.

As she continued to pray, she felt the demon's grip fall away from her. And then she saw Micah and another angel in front of her taking on the demons. While the demons were strong, the angels were stronger.

Flashes of light mixed with smoke and shrieks filled the air. And she was caught in the crossfire. Pain shot through her. Her side, her head, her legs.

But through it all, she kept praying. And she inched her way closer to Nina Marie who now lay on the ground seemingly unresponsive.

The fog of evil started to fade, and she knew the angels were gaining ground. Layton started to slink toward the front entrance showing his lack of true courage. He would leave the demons to fend for themselves.

She watched as he ran out the front door. The battle waged on between the angels and demons, but there was no doubt in Olivia's mind that the angels would prevail. Without Layton to lead them, slowly the demons began to disperse. Within minutes, the remaining demons were vanquished by God's angels.

She stood beside Micah and Ben. In awe to be in their presence and so thankful to the Lord for sending them to help her.

"I couldn't let them kill her," she told them. "Even if she's evil too. I just couldn't do it."

Micah reached out to her and touched her shoulder. "We understand. But know that there will come a time when she may not return the favor for you."

She nodded knowing that while she made the only decision she thought she could today, that it could have troubling implications for the future. "I wanted to believe that there's still a chance for her redemption."

"Only the Lord knows," the other angel said.

She breathed in a sigh of relief.

Before she could say anything else, they were gone. As quickly as they arrived, they disappeared. She knelt down beside Nina Marie and saw the blood coming from her temple. She prayed that she made the right decision in saving Nina Marie's life.

***

Grant drove quickly over to the Astral Tech office. He'd been trying to reach Olivia for the last hour. When she didn't respond, he decided to drive over to the office. He figured she had to be working, but he also couldn't shake the feeling that something was wrong.

As he pulled up in the parking lot, he immediately got an uneasy feeling. The inside of the building looked dark, but he saw that Olivia's car was still there in the parking lot along with another one.

He jumped out of the car, and his pulse quickened. Jogging to the front door, he tried the entrance and it was locked. But he could hear some commotion coming from the inside. Screams permeated the air, and he could also smell smoke. Was there a fire? He didn't see any physical signs of one. The entire situation seemed completely odd.

Pounding on the door, he waited but there was no answer. What should he do? Not hesitating for long he made the decision to break the glass. He ran back to his car to grab his jack and smashed the front door in sending glass fragments to the ground.

Ignoring the shards of glass, he quickly stepped through the broken door.

"Olivia!" He called out, over and over again with no answer. The entire office was pitch black. He smelled the remnants of smoke but couldn't see flames. While he knew his way around, it was still difficult in the dark. There were no screams or noises like what he thought he'd heard from the outside.

A flash of light so bright he had to shield his eyes burst through the room. And then the lights came on in the building. As his eyes adjusted, he ran toward where he knew Olivia worked. But he stopped short in front of Nina Marie's office.

There on the ground was Nina Marie with Olivia leaning over her.

"What in the world happened? Should I call an ambulance?" He rushed to Olivia's side.

"Yes," Olivia said. "I'm okay, but Nina hit her head. She's going to need medical attention."

He pulled out his phone and dialed 911. After talking to dispatch, he turned his attention back to Olivia.

"What happened here?"

"An attack," she said. "A direct attack. And I got caught in the battle."

"What do you mean an attack?"

"A demonic attack."

He felt his eyes widen. "Thank God you're all right."

"Yes, thank God." She nodded. "It was touch and go for a few minutes. But I'll tell you about all of that later." Olivia checked Nina Marie's pulse again. "She passed out a few minutes ago, but her pulse is still strong."

The sound of sirens were off in the distance. As he looked into Olivia's dark eyes, and saw the pain there, he knew then and there that the enemy was all too real.

CHAPTER SEVENTEEN

The last person Nina Marie had expected to call her was Layton. But he'd insisted that they had to talk in person. So against her better judgment, she went over to his house. She hoped he wasn't planning on trying to kill her—again. The surprise attack on her last night at the Astral Tech office had rattled her, but she didn't want to let him know that. She refused to let him see her fear. She touched her temple where the bandage still covered just one of her wounds. But the outward wounds didn't hurt as badly as her pride, which took a huge hit. She vowed that she wouldn't ever be caught off guard again.

She rang the doorbell, and he opened the door with a smile and kissed her on the cheek, sending her into a bit of a tailspin.

"Nina Marie, thank you for coming. Do come in and let me get you a drink."

She followed him into the living room where he poured her a glass a wine from his large bar in the corner. "Please have a seat."

"You have a lot of nerve after what you did to me last night." She sat down and took the glass of wine he offered, but she immediately gave it back to him. "You taste it."

He laughed loudly. "Do you think I'm trying to poison you?"

"At this point, nothing would surprise me, Layton."

He took a healthy gulp of the wine and handed it back to her. "See, perfectly fine."

"Why don't you cut out the niceties and tell me why I'm sitting in your living room right now only a day after you attempted to kill me in my office."

He nodded. "First, I need to apologize for that."

She crossed her arms. "You're going to need to do a lot better than that, Layton."

"I saw an opportunity and I took it. I acted hastily without thinking things through after what transpired in court. I let my emotions get the best of me."

"So you're sorry that you weren't successful in taking me out."

"Don't be so cynical. We're in a war here. I'm doing what I have to do which is why I called you here tonight to talk."

He was crazy if he thought she'd so easily forget what he did to her, but she did want to know what he had to say. "All right. I'm here, so talk."

"You and I have a mutual problem with regard to this lawsuit. I'm sure Olivia explained to you what she was trying to do with the evidence fabrication issue. But the way I see it, you're still going to lose this trial. Yes, you may prevail on appeal years down the road, after you spend all that time and money."

"What are you getting at?"

"The legalese are getting in the way of our true work, Nina Marie. This lawsuit is a damaging distraction to us both."

She couldn't help but smile and wonder why he'd had such a drastic change of heart. Maybe it had to do with the fact that she had the upper hand right now. "Layton, do I need to remind you, that you are the one who filed the lawsuit?"

"Yes, and I see the error of my ways now. We shouldn't be fighting against each other. The more we fight amongst ourselves, the stronger our enemies become. Again, I should apologize for yesterday. I saw an opportunity, and I tried to take it. But after giving it much thought I think I acted too hastily given the larger goals here."

"What are you suggesting?" She leaned forward on the couch.

"I'm suggesting that we put this lawsuit to bed. It's draining not only our money but also our focus. And the lawyers are driving me crazy. Somehow my lawyer thinks he's found God throughout this thing."

"Are you serious?"

"Yes, it's quite unfortunate."

"Maybe Olivia rubbed off on him."

"I don't trust him. He came into this as an open slate, and then he miraculously starts seeking out Jesus through the litigation? Something seems very off to me. He worries me."

"He isn't strong," Nina Marie said. She knew from her experience going after him.

"Not yet, but I feel he could be. Especially if Olivia remains in the picture."

"Interesting theory."

"And Grant and I are not exactly on the best of terms right now."

"That's what happens when you fabricate evidence and make your lawyer use it in his court filings."

"You're not blameless here either, dear. You stole the technology in the first place."

She wasn't going to admit that fact. "Let's just say for argument's sake, I agree with your assessment of where we're at with the litigation. What next?"

"We settle the lawsuit."

"What? Why would I give you any money? Especially after last night? I can't just forget about that and pretend like we're friends."

"Because it's better to pay me now than to give your lawyer money for the next five years as you fight this thing on appeal. Astral Tech writes me a check, and we agree as part of the settlement that you can still continue to sell the app. And while your ego is hurt because you were blindsided last night, you know if you think rationally that this is the best option."

"I could still win at trial."

He laughed. "I had the jury eating out of the palm of my hand. And you did steal the technology. They'll see that. This is a way to mitigate risks and make a business decision that benefits us both."

"And then what?"

"We start working together. We consolidate our power, and we rule this community like we were destined to. Like the evil one wants us to."

"Forgive me for my utter hesitation, Layton, but you've never wanted to share power with anyone. You're thirsty for power and want complete control, just like I do. Last night showed that."

"I agree, but I'm also a strategist. I believe that between the two of us we can really win the war. As much as it pains me to admit it, we need each other."

"You make some interesting points."

"And I'll be upfront with you. One of the things I'm concerned about is your lawyer. The sooner she's back on a plane to Washington, DC, the better."

"Really?"

"Don't tell me you haven't noticed her strength. We can't have her meddling in our affairs here. Trying to disrupt our work. Much to my surprise, she even stood up for you last night. She has a moral compass and that is dangerous if she decides she wants to get in on this fight."

"I know that you've attacked her, and she batted you away like a fly."

"Another reason to get her out of here."

"She won't like being told what to do, but she has a lot of potential."

He frowned. "Don't tell me you have it in your pretty head that you can turn her."

"Never say never."

"We can discuss all of those details later. For the immediate future, we need to decide if we're going to settle this case."

"A decision does need to be made."

"You know what to do here, Nina Marie. The evil one's goals are bigger than this lawsuit. I'll admit this suit had more to do with my personal animosity against you than anything else."

"And you're over that now?"

"I'm focusing on what really matters, and I think you want that too."

"Despite your best efforts at a sneak attack, you failed to take me out last night. Working with me wasn't your first choice."

"True. I can freely admit that. But it's where we are now. And even if we don't trust each other, we're much stronger united as one evil front than we are a house divided. This is an alliance of necessity."

"What will our members think of this unholy alliance between the two of us?"

"They will think whatever we tell them to think because we have the power and they don't."

Nina Marie needed a little time consider this proposal. She stood from her seat. "I'll give you a call later tonight with my answer."

"I understand." He stood up and grabbed her hands. "We can do this together, Nina Marie."

"I'll be in touch." She walked out of his house. She needed time to consult the evil one on this. Then she would decide how to proceed.

***

Grant's phone rang just after he jumped out the shower. He looked down and saw the screen. Why was Layton calling him this morning?

"Yes," he answered.

"Grant, it's Layton."

"What's going on?"

"You're fired."

"I'm what?"

"You're fired. We have decided to settle the case, and I won't need your services for the settlement agreement."

"Wait a minute. Back up."

"It's quite simple. I've come to an agreement with Astral Tech to settle. You're no longer required to be a part of this."

No way was he letting Layton off that easy. "I should refer you to the agreement you signed when you retained my firm to represent you. In that agreement, it clearly states that if you fire my firm without cause, we're entitled to all costs and the legal fees accrued."

"Do you really want to push me on this? I'm giving you an opportunity to walk away."

"And do I need to remind you that I tried to withdraw from the case and you blocked me from doing so? No way. Expect an invoice sent to you and if you don't pay it, I will bring suit against you for fees. I know you have the money."

"Send whatever you want. This is over."

The call ended and Grant stood in the middle of his bedroom totally perplexed. A flood of emotions washed over him as he took a seat on the edge of the bed.

Was this nightmare finally over? And what about Astral Tech? He had to call Olivia.

He called and waited for her to pick up.

"Hey," she said. "What is it?"

"Have you talked to your client?"

"No, but I'm scheduled to talk to her before court this morning."

He let out a breath. "I was just fired and apparently the case is settling."

"What? Are you sure?"

"Layton just called me, fired me, and went on to announce that the case was settling and that he didn't need my help on the settlement."

"Wow. That must be what Nina Marie wants to discuss with me, too. But I guess she has the decency to do it in person and not over the phone."

"You might not be getting the boot though. Layton and I were obviously no longer on good terms."

"I don't think I've fully processed this yet. I'm mentally still in trial mode."

"I have no idea what happened. But my guess is that Layton and Nina Marie must have kissed and made up after the fight they had Monday night."

"I can't believe she'd work with him after he tried to basically kill her."

"They're not acting rationally, Olivia."

"This is just the beginning," she said.

"Isn't it the end?"

"No. The real battle, Grant. It's about to start. Nina Marie and Layton working together to spread their evil throughout Windy Ridge. We have to be ready."

"Won't you leave to go back to DC once the settlement is agreed upon?"

"I need to figure out exactly what's happening. But I know one thing for sure. I can't leave here if I feel like I have unfinished business." She paused. "But I have to run so I can finish getting ready and meet with Nina Marie. I'll call you when I know more."

He still sat in shock. What was he going to do now? He wasn't bluffing with Layton. He was going to go into the office and send him an itemized bill ASAP. There was no way he was getting paid zero dollars for all he went through.

But more importantly than any of that was what Olivia had just said. What if there was a coming war in Windy Ridge? Would he be strong enough to do anything about it? And what would Olivia's role be?

He knew in his heart exactly what his next move should be. Hoping it wasn't too early, he dialed Pastor Dan's number.

"Hello," Dan answered.

"It's Grant. Sorry to call you this early."

"Oh, I've been awake for a long time. I'm a morning person. What's on your mind?"

"Can we meet?"

"Sure. When?"

"As soon as you're able."

"Aren't you in trial?"

"Not anymore. I'll explain when we're face to face."

"I can be at the church in fifteen minutes."

"Thanks, I'll meet you there."

Grant quickly got dressed and drove over to meet with Dan. When he arrived at the church, he saw that Dan was waiting for him outside the main entrance.

"Come on in," Dan unlocked the front door. "We're the first ones here."

"Again sorry about the timing, but I felt like it couldn't wait."

Dan led him down the hall to the office. "Have a seat and tell me what's on your mind. How are you doing after what you witnessed on Monday night?"

Olivia had filled Dan in on what had happened at the Astral Tech office. "It definitely impacted me, but if anything I feel more certain about how I want to proceed."

"So what's going on now?"

"Well, the short version of events is that Layton fired me this morning and is going to settle the case."

"I'm sorry, Grant."

Grant shook his head. "I'm actually relieved to be rid of him as a client, but I am going to go after him for my fees. But that's not why I'm here right now. Everything has really become clear for me."

"How so?"

"I'm ready to accept Christ. Become a Christian."

"You're sure that's what you want? Because God doesn't want us to make that decision lightly or out of fear. Especially after what you experienced the other night."

"I've never been more sure of anything in my life. I've taken the time. I know I still have a lot to learn, but I'm ready to take this important step. A step that I feel like I've been waiting my whole life to take."

Dan stood up and walked over beside where Grant sat, taking a seat too. Dan put his hand on Grant's shoulder. "Well then let's pray. I want you to repeat after me okay?"

"All right."

"And there isn't a specific formula to doing this. All that matters is the general substance of what I'm saying and that you truly want this."

"I do."

Grant repeated the prayer spoken by Pastor Dan, asking Jesus to come into his heart, making Jesus his Lord and Savior, asking for his sins to be forgiven.

It wasn't until the prayer was over that Grant realized his eyes were full of tears.

"It's okay, Grant. Let out your emotions."

"I'm not an emotional type of guy. But right now I'm feeling more than I've felt in a long time, if ever." He quickly wiped the tears away. "I finally feel like I have a purpose that's not just my job inside a courtroom."

"This is just the beginning. Accepting Jesus as your Lord and Savior is the most important step, but now you have the opportunity to learn and grow in your faith."

"About learning and growing. I'm a bit concerned about this alliance that seems to be forming between Layton and Nina Marie."

"Explain to me what you mean."

"After Layton fired me, he said that the was going to settle the case. My best guess is that he and Nina Marie are going to start working together."

"That's not good, but I can't say I'm surprised."

"I can't help but feel like it's not the end of my dealings with Layton. But that's where I'm a bit murky. How can I spiritually compare to these people who have been doing this for years."

"Because the God you believe in is much stronger than the devil."

He nodded. "Do you have any thoughts on what Layton and Nina Marie would plan to do?"

"They have a lot of different methods especially when you combine both groups, but their general goal is to recruit more members, to get people to leave the church. Either to come to their group or to just reject Christianity. And with the app, I suspect they will continue to target the young people in the community."

"I actually met a college student who was interning for Optimism. She said she used to go to church here."

"Stacey?" Dan asked.

"Yes. And unfortunately she seemed like she was committed to Optimism."

"Stacey is an interesting case. She walked away from her faith and got drawn into the New Age beliefs by Layton and others. But she had an experience that brought her back to the church. Hearing you say this makes me believe that she is back with Optimism now, though."

"What experience?"

"She believes she saw an angel and a demon in her apartment."

"Wow. Well after the events I saw transpire, I believe it. I didn't actually see angels or demons, but I could feel something happening."

"I've never seen an angel or a demon either. But we've talked before about the invisibility of spiritual warfare. So actually seeing a spiritual presence is not the norm. Sometimes they can appear to people through visions or dreams which is a bit different than what you or I would think of as actually seeing something. Regardless, though, I wouldn't get caught up in worrying about what you will and won't see. What matters is that you feel it and you prepare yourself for any battle that may ensue."

"And I do that through learning and using the Word of God?"

"Exactly. And seeking out the Lord in prayer. Building your faith day by day."

"I just worry that I don't have enough time to get ready."

"The Lord wouldn't have put you in this position if you couldn't handle it. And remember, you're not alone in this. You have me, the church, and Olivia."

"Thank you again. I'll get out of your hair. Sorry again for calling you so early."

"It's the best way I could've started my day."

Grant shook Dan's hand and walked out of the church, ready to start his new life.

***

Olivia met with Nina Marie at the coffee shop near the courthouse. Olivia wasn't going to tell Nina Marie anything about her discussion with Grant. She wanted to hear Nina Marie's version of events first.

"Thanks for coming early to meet me," Nina Marie said. She pushed her glasses up on her nose.

"What's going on?"

"Before I get into that, I wanted to thank you again for what you did for me Monday night."

She nodded. "It was the right thing to do."

"I'm glad you don't regret it. But now I need to explain something else to you and I wanted to do it in person."

"Okay. You're making me nervous, Nina Marie. What happened?"

"It's actually good news. I've decided to settle the lawsuit with Optimism."

"Why in the world would you do that right when we're ahead? I was planning on filing the interlocutory appeal this morning. Even if I don't get that, we'd most certainly have a good chance of getting an adverse verdict overturned on appeal."

Nina Marie nodded. "And I appreciate everything you've done, Olivia. You really have gone above and beyond working on this case. I've seen your tireless efforts. But as CEO I have to make a business decision. Especially with Clive's passing, I need to make sure I have the confidence of those working for me. This is the best business solution. Layton isn't asking for a large amount, and we can all walk away and get back to work. I hope you can understand where I'm coming from on this."

"So we're going into court today and telling the judge that the parties have agreed to a settlement?"

"Yes. And the best news for you is that you can be on a plane home by tonight. Isn't that great?" Nina Marie smiled.

Olivia wasn't so sure about any of this. But one thing she did know was that there was no way she'd be on a plane home tonight. "Aren't you going to need my help with the settlement agreement?"

"Layton and I will hammer out the terms. Any legal advice that I need from you can certainly be done over the phone or by email. I wouldn't want to keep you away from your home any longer."

"I'm just shocked that you would let Layton win." This was her only play to try and see if she could convince Nina Marie to continue with the trial.

But Nina Marie grinned. "Oh, Olivia. Layton will never beat me. I'm always looking at the long game. This is just a short term move that is in the best interest of the company."

"Surely you don't trust that man?"

Nina Marie laughed loudly. "Absolutely not, especially after he attacked me—and you for that matter. But I don't have to trust him for the purposes of this settlement. I just have to be able to put up with the annoyance and short term financial loss. I'm willing to live with that to be able to move forward with my work."

"If you've made your final decision, then that's what we'll tell the court."

"Yes, it's definitely my final decision."

"I'll work with Grant on any legal details."

"Actually, you won't."

"Why?"

"Layton and Grant had a bit of a falling out, and Layton let Grant go. It's not like he needs him any more."

"I'm sure Grant's not too thrilled about that."

"You can do better, Olivia."

"What do you mean?"

"I think Grant has taken a liking to you. Go back to Washington, DC and find a man who really deserves you. Grant is too weak for a strong woman like you."

Olivia couldn't believe that the conversation had shifted in this way. "If we're going to start giving each other unsolicited advice, then I have some for you too."

"I guess I deserve it after my comments."

"You should stay away from Layton. That man is toxic." Olivia reached out and touched Nina Marie's arm. "And you should see someone about whoever hurt you so badly in the past. I know you've sought solace in the darkness, but it's never too late to turn away from that."

Nina Marie's brown eyes narrowed. "You really think that I could ever be like you?"

"I think that you have some deep wounds that you haven't ever healed from. And I'm offering you a way out of that. To start over fresh and move on from this life you've set up for yourself. A way to start anew."

"I admire your tenacity, Olivia. And I'll be forever grateful for you trying to protect me against Layton. But in the same way that you feel so strongly about your faith, I feel about mine."

Olivia never wanted to give up on anyone. Even though she knew this woman probably worshiped the devil and practiced the dark arts. If there was even a one percent chance that Nina Marie would change her ways, then Olivia had to try. "I'm a fighter."

"That you are. But let me make one thing clear, Olivia. You will not be a fighter in this community. Go back to DC where you belong. I've grown fond of you, but if you stand in my way, I'll have no choice in the matter."

"Is that a threat?"

Nina Marie didn't respond.

"We need to go into court and let the judge know what's going on." Olivia stood up from the table.

They walked in silence toward the courthouse. When Olivia entered the courtroom, she saw Layton sitting at his table, but there was no sign of Grant. What a mess.

The judge entered the courtroom, and raised an eyebrow in confusion at Grant's absence.

"Your Honor, there's a matter we need to discuss before the jury is brought in," Olivia said.

"Yes, well, where is your opposing counsel?"

"Your Honor, I can answer that." Layton stood up.

"Please someone tell me what is going on," she said.

"I have terminated the attorney client relationship with Mr. Baxter. Also, both sides have come to a settlement on this matter."

The judge's eyes widened. Olivia thought it interesting that Judge Martinique wasn't in the know.

"Ms. Murray, what do you have to say on this?"

"I was informed this morning that a settlement had been reached between the two parties. That is why you are just hearing about the settlement, because I myself just found out before I came into the courtroom this morning."

"Has a settlement agreement been drafted up?" Judge Martinique asked.

"We're working on that, Your Honor," Layton said.

"Here's what we're going to do. I'm going to dismiss this jury. For all purposes, the trial is stayed pending the execution of the settlement agreement. If the settlement falls through, then we're back to square one. Does everyone understand?"

"Yes, Your Honor," Olivia and Layton said.

"Mr. Alito, I would advise you to retain new counsel for the purposes of negotiating and executing the settlement. Ms. Murray you will continue to represent Astral Tech for the purposes of the settlement?"

"Yes, Your Honor."

"Very well then. I'll dismiss the jury, and we can all be on our way."

***

Two weeks later on a Saturday morning Nina Marie and Layton sat in the Optimism conference room. The settlement agreement had been executed on Friday, so the lawsuit was finally over.

Nina Marie didn't like the continuous meetings on his turf, but right now she wasn't going to argue until it was about something that really mattered.

This alliance was something that the evil one wanted—at least for now. Nina Marie had sought him out and knew that she had to obey.

"So what is our objective here?" Nina Marie asked.

"First we decimate their congregation. The more people we can pull away for whatever reason and by whatever method we choose to employ the better. Just you watch, if things go as planned, the attendance will be down by around twenty five percent tomorrow. Also, if we have every member of our group convince just one person they know that attends Windy Ridge Community Church to miss Sunday morning service, we'll have a huge impact."

"And after that?" she asked.

"To close down that church once and for all."

"You do realize that Windy Ridge Community Church is just one church?" She could feel the sarcasm dripping from her voice.

But he didn't seem to be fazed. "Yes, it is only one church, but it's the most powerful church in this community. If we can take it out, then the rest of the churches will follow. Then once Windy Ridge is completely rid of churches, we can move onto the next city."

"Layton, I appreciate your enthusiasm, really I do. But in our spiritual efforts, just like in our businesses, we have to be realistic about what is achievable. Shutting down all the churches in this town is not feasible."

"I realize it's a lofty goal, and I'm not saying it's going to happen overnight. This is my life's work, Nina Marie. And I won't stop until the goal is reached." He reached out and grabbed her hands. "This is why we need to work together. If we're really going to change this community, then we'll need everyone on our side working together."

"That's going to be a challenge, but I've already had multiple meetings with my people. I'll tell you that they are skeptical of this all working out, but they are willing to try."

"We should have a joint meeting at my house. A party to celebrate our forming an alliance. Once we're all in the same space, I think our membership will enjoy getting to know each other better."

"I suppose if you and I can bury the past and move forward together then everyone else should be able to do the same." The thing was that Nina Marie hadn't exactly buried anything, but she was willing to play this game out to see if they could really achieve something great together. Layton was right that they had a better chance to reach their goals if they worked together.

"Then it's all agreed. I'll throw a fabulous party and we can start our work together." He paused. "There's one more thing I need to talk to you about. I'm excited to say that I've activated our secret weapon."

"And exactly what is that?" she asked. He was so cryptic.

"You're even going to be impressed with this one, Nina Marie."

"Well, why don't you enlighten me?" She sipped her hot tea and waited for him to explain himself.

"We have someone on the inside at Windy Ridge Community Church."

"What do you mean?"

"Someone who has been working with us for quite a while. Feeding us information on what's going on at the church. It's time we launch the first missile in this battle."

A loud knock sounded on the conference room door.

"Come on in," Layton said.

The door opened and in walked Beverly Jenkins. Nina Marie knew her as one of the members of the church leadership team. Confused as to what was going on, Nina Marie looked at Layton. "What is she doing here?" Nina Marie asked.

Layton grinned. "Nina Marie, meet Beverly Jenkins—our secret weapon."

***

Olivia and Grant sat at his dining room table having dinner Sunday night.

"Church attendance was way down today," Olivia said. "That absolutely can't be a coincidence."

"I mentioned it to Dan on the way out today, and he noticed. I think the leadership team was going to have a meeting tonight to discuss it."

She smiled. "At the rate you're going, you're going to want to be on that leadership team pretty soon."

He leaned toward her and took her hand in his own. "I have to thank you for all you've done for me, Olivia. You have undoubtedly changed my entire life."

"It wasn't me, Grant. It was God."

"But He used you, and you stuck with me even though I was completely unreceptive for quite a while. You didn't give up on me."

She squeezed his hand. "Giving up isn't in my vocabulary."

"What are you going to do now since the settlement is finalized?"

"Well, Nina Marie basically told me that if I didn't hop on a plane back to DC that she was going to come after me. She had wanted me to leave immediately but then acquiesced to me handling the details of the agreement from here. Now that the agreement is signed, she will expect me to go."

"It would be safer for you to return home."

"My work isn't done here, Grant. The battles that this community face lie ahead not behind. And the fact that Layton and Nina Marie are teaming up only makes them even more dangerous to all the believers in this town."

"It's still mindboggling to me that she'd want to work with someone who tried to kill her."

"I hear you, but she has a different mindset than we do."

"So what are you thinking of doing?"

"I'm going to ask for some time off. I more than deserve it after all the hours I've billed on this case. I know Chet will give it to me, especially since I have so much vacation time built up."

"You're going to stay here?"

She thought she heard hopefulness in his voice. "I would like to. If you're willing to rent your condo out to me."

He smiled. "Of course you can stay at the condo, but I'm not letting you pay rent."

"You're a good friend, Grant. I know you talk about how I've influenced you, but our friendship has helped me get through this incredibly difficult litigation and everything that has come along with it."

They sat hand in hand not saying a word. Olivia looked into Grant's blue eyes and felt a sense of belonging. She was thankful that they had found each other. Where this road would take them beyond that, she didn't know. But she knew she wasn't leaving Windy Ridge anytime soon.

***

"Phase one is complete," Micah said.

Ben nodded. "But the true battle hasn't yet begun. I'm filled with joy over Grant's acceptance of Christ. I was worried there for a while that he might not ever be willing to open up his heart and embrace faith."

"God is good, and He worked wonders for Grant. The plan of the Lord is still in place. Olivia and Grant are a very strong team. One that will only gain strength as their friendship continues to grow—as does their faith."

"But we have another alliance we have to worry about. Layton and Nina Marie are out to destroy this community."

"No doubt it will be a long and hard battle. But the church will rise up. There is no other option."

"Yes there is," a loud male voice said.

The two angels turned around to face the intruder.

"Othan," Ben said. "You have no place here"

"Be gone," Micah added.

Othan laughed. "This entire community will fall. You have no chance against the power of the evil one. Look at the two of you. Pathetic. Couldn't your God send anyone better? Someone worthy to fight against Satan's finest legion of demons?"

A searing pain shot through Micah as Othan wielded his dark powers. But Micah stood steadfast. "We aren't going to ask you to leave again," Micah said.

"Or what, you'll cast me out? That's only a temporary solution. The evil one's plan for this community is taking shape. And once the first shot is fired, you will be the one cast out. And your church be will destroyed. Burnt down to the ground by the flames of hell."

Othan disappeared leaving the two angels standing alone. Ben looked at Micah. "We must warn the others. It has begun..."

SNEAK PEEK OF FATAL ACCUSATION – WINDY RIDGE BOOK 2

Chapter One

Pastor Dan Light sat in his office at Windy Ridge Community Church and prayed. A chill shot through him, but it wasn't from the Windy Ridge winter night. No, it was from knowing that there was a battle on the horizon.

Ever since the settlement a couple of months ago in the lawsuit between the New Age companies that plagued Windy Ridge, he'd had an uneasy feeling that the groups known as Astral Tech and Optimism were planning a direct attack on the church. And on all the believers in the community.

Lord, help me prepare the people in this church for what is to come.

He was broken out of his prayer by the loud sound of heels clicking down the church corridor toward his office. He looked up at his doorway and smiled. Finally, some good news.

"Olivia, it's so good to see you." He stood up to greet her.

While Olivia Murray was small in stature, she was strong in her faith. The petite brunette attorney greeted him warmly with a hug.

"I'm glad to be here," Olivia said.

"How was your vacation?"

"It was great. I went back to DC and visited my best friend Lizzie. Along with dealing with some firm business." She took a seat on his couch. "And that's actually why I'm here. I have some news. Big news actually."

"What kind of news?"

"The managing partner at my firm wants me to help start up the Chicago office of Brown, Carter, and Reed. Grant has already told me I can continue to stay at his rental condo for free. Even though I'm going to still insist on paying him."

"That's great news," he said.

"So what have I missed while I was gone?" she asked.

"While there haven't been any direct attacks that I know of from Astral Tech or Optimism, I can see the results of their clandestine efforts. Church attendance is at its lowest point since I started preaching here."

"Oh no." Her dark brown eyes widened full with concern.

"Yes. And I also hate to report that Stacey Malone hasn't stepped foot back in the church at all. I fear that she may now be fully entrenched with Layton Alito and his people at Optimism."

She stood up and walked over to where he sat behind his desk. "I'm not going to walk away from here. You know that, right?"

"I do. But I also don't want you to underestimate how difficult this is going to be. We have to assume that Layton and Nina Marie have fully joined forces."

"As two powerful CEOs of lucrative companies, they have a lot of resources at their disposal. We knew that the lawsuit was just the beginning. I've been praying a lot about this, and even though it may seem like they have the upper hand, we're going to prevail. But we have to get organized and have a plan of our own. This isn't something that can be dealt with piecemeal."

He admired Olivia's staunch reliance on her faith. She was going to need it, as was he.

"Looks like I came to the office at the right time." Associate Pastor Chris Tanner walked through the door and made a beeline for Olivia.

"I didn't realize you were back," Chris said.

"Just got back from DC today. This was one of my first stops. I just told Dan the news so I'll also let you know that I've been asked to help start the Chicago office of BCR. I'll be here in the Chicago area indefinitely."

"That's great news, right?" Chris asked.

"I think so. I didn't want to leave Windy Ridge because I felt I had a lot of unfinished business to take care of. But I was concerned about how I could stay here given my job."

"The Lord really works in amazing ways, doesn't He?" Chris asked.

Olivia nodded. "I hear things are pretty tough right now."

"Yeah," Chris said. "Dan and I have been scratching our heads wondering how the forces of evil have been able to get to so many of our church members. We don't know their exact strategy, just that they're chiefly responsible for our shrinking numbers."

Olivia frowned. "We have to find a way to stop them."

"I agree," Dan said. "And I'm open to any suggestions you may have."

"There is one thing I'm going to do." Olivia paused and looked down.

"What?" Dan asked.

"I'm going to have a meeting with Nina Marie."

"Why?" Chris asked. "What good can come of that?"

"I've given it a lot of thought while I was away, and I still believe there is hope for her."

Dan thought that Olivia was being a bit naïve and overly optimistic about Nina Marie. "I understand that you don't want anyone to be led astray, Olivia. But Nina Marie is really far gone."

"I realize that, but I can't help but feel like I have to make an effort with her."

"You know she's not going to want to hear any of that," Chris said. "She made it her mission to destroy all the believers in this community."

"I hear your reservations. Both of you, I really do. But I'm not going to change my mind on this one. Please let me tackle this issue my way. At least for the time being."

"It's not that we don't want you to succeed. It's just that we're worried about your safety," Dan said. The last thing they needed was for something to happen to Olivia. She was the lead warrior in this battle. And regardless of what Olivia thought, Dan was entirely distrustful of Nina Marie.

"I'll be careful. I promise." She rose up from her seat. "I'm going to call it a day. It's been a long travel day, but I'll be in touch with any relevant information I can gather."

"Please do," Dan said. "And we're very glad that you're back here."

"Me too. Have a nice evening." She walked out of the office leaving him alone with Chris.

Chris patted Dan on the shoulder. "I know you're struggling right now. Not only because you see the decline in the church, but also because you just had to experience your first holiday season since losing Tina."

Dan felt his eyes get misty. Chris knew him all too well. The loss of his precious wife still weighed on him daily. He'd just experienced his first Christmas without her and it was devastating.

"You don't have to say anything," Chris said. "Just know that I'm here for you. Whatever you need. We'll get through all of this together as a church family."

"We're going to be tested," Dan said. He knew deep in his gut that it would probably be the biggest test of their lives.

"You're right, but we're not going to back down. We're going to fight this battle that the Lord wants us to fight. We're going to rid our community of these occult forces."

Dan only prayed that Chris was right.

***

Nina Marie Crane tried to keep her facial expression neutral as she sat across the table from Optimism CEO Layton Alito. Her sworn enemy had now become her ally. At least for a season.

She would never forget that Layton had tried to kill her—and failed. Only after his inability to remove her, did he want to join forces. But while she was definitely holding a grudge, she wasn't stupid. They shared common goals as far as the evil one was concerned. So for now, she was forced to work with Layton instead of against him. She was CEO of Astral Tech, and she had to think about what was best for the company.

They were currently sitting at a large oak table in his study. The room was expansive and immaculately decorated. As was the rest of his mansion.

"Thanks for meeting with me," Layton said. He looked as handsome as ever. His striking blue eyes making direct contact with hers. But she knew better than to be influenced by his good looks and smooth ways. Underneath that exterior was a lethal man with a totally depraved heart.

"What do you want to talk about?" she asked.

"Our source on the inside at Windy Ridge Community Church."

"Yes, yes. How is Beverly doing?"

"Very well."

"I still can't believe you managed to turn her," Nina Marie said. Beverly Jenkins was the financial administrator at Windy Ridge Community Church and a lifelong churchgoer.

"I can't take all the credit on this one. It helped that her and Louise started going to the same hair salon a few years ago. That changed everything. An unlikely friendship blossomed into something much more."

Nina Marie nodded knowing full well that having Judge Louise Martinique on the side of Optimism was a huge advantage to them. She wanted Louise to be on her side, not Layton's. But that would require a lot of work. "However it happened, it's a huge benefit to us now."

He smiled. "And the time has come, my dear. The plot has been put into motion."

"All right. So tell me about your plans."

"I can't tell you that part just yet."

She let out an exasperated sigh. "You're really starting to try me, Layton."

"Believe me. Once the news breaks, you'll understand. And you'll thank me for such a brilliant plan."

"But until then?"

"Hold tight and wait for the glorious news."

She took a sip of the merlot that Layton had provided her. He was always drinking wine. Really expensive wine, so she wasn't going to turn it down. Layton appreciated all the finer things in life. She wasn't quite as materialistic as him, but she fully recognized that she loved nice things too. Especially since she used to have nothing. Be nothing. Except a victim.

But that time in her life was over. She was in charge of her own destiny, and she'd never let a man control her again. And definitely not Layton Alito.

She'd placate him for now, but when the time was right, she'd destroy him. "Is there anything else we can actually discuss?" she asked.

"Enjoy the wine, Nina Marie. Why are you in such a rush?"

"Since when do we actually enjoy spending time together?"

He raised an eyebrow. "If I remember correctly, we used to enjoy it a lot."

"There's no way I'm ever getting back in bed with you." If he thought that was a possibility, she was going to shut that down right now.

He waved his hand. "Don't be so tightly wound. Relax. I do have one more thing to discuss."

"And that is?"

"I heard an interesting rumor this morning."

"Yes?"

"That the law firm of BCR is opening a Chicago office."

"That's interesting. But why do you care what our former law firm does in Chicago."

He leaned in closer to her. "Because I heard that your favorite lawyer is going to move here to start the office."

"What?" Her hand shook and red wine splashed on the oak table.

"Ah, so I see that this does bother you."

"It should bother you a lot more. I don't have to remind you how strong Olivia Murray is or what a threat she could be to our enterprise." Nina Marie still stayed up at night remembering how Olivia had chosen to save her life. She still hadn't fully come to grips with someone acting as selflessly as Olivia did. But even though she was grateful, she couldn't have Olivia spoiling everything they were working toward.

"You should have a chat with her. Feel her out."

"How did you even find out about this?"

"Once again, Louise came through. She knows everything that goes on in the legal community. And the opening of a BCR office in Chicago is a big news item for law firms around here."

"Leave Olivia to me. I can take care of her."

Layton reached over and gripped her hand. Hard. "Make no mistake. If you don't deal with her appropriately, then I will."

"Understood." She pulled away from his grip. "And don't put your hands on me." She'd had enough of this infuriating man. Throwing back the rest of her wine, she stood up. "I can see myself out. When you're ready to actually tell me the plan with

Beverly, let me know. Until then, I think we don't have anything else to discuss."

***

Olivia walked into Grant Baxter's law firm the next day to take him to lunch. She had to admit that she had missed seeing him while she took her time off. She had never expected that her former opposing counsel would become such a good friend and a source of strength in this crazy battle.

She had one more day before she started work at the Chicago office of BCR. She walked up to the front desk and smiled at the receptionist.

"Grant's expecting you, Olivia. You can walk on back."

"Thank you." She strode down the long hallway passing Ryan Wilde's office along the way. Grant had the last office.

When Grant saw her walk in, he smiled widely and his blue eyes sparkled. His thick dark hair looked as if it had been freshly cut.

"It's great to see you." He rose from his chair and hugged her tightly.

"It's good to see you, too. It's nice to be back in Windy Ridge even though I did enjoy my time in DC."

"How's Lizzie?"

"Great. She's thinking about transitioning to a smaller litigation boutique to get more courtroom experience. It's a big decision for her."

"I can understand that."

Grant had left a big law firm to start his own, and Olivia knew how much stress that had put on him. Olivia had misjudged him when they'd first met. Assuming he was just in it for the money, but there was a lot more at stake for him that that. She understood that now.

"You ready to go to lunch?" she asked.

"Yes, I'm starving."

They exited his building and walked down the street to Grant's favorite pizza place near his office.

Once they got settled in a booth and placed their orders— hers a slice of cheese and his two slices of supreme, she looked up at him. "Tell me what I've missed in Windy Ridge."

"I didn't want to bother you while you were away, but I think something is going on with Pastor Dan."

She thought Dan had looked tired yesterday, but she had been tired too so she didn't think much of it. "How so?"

"He seems really depressed. I know the holidays had to be rough on him, but I can't help but think there's something else deeper going on."

"Did you ask him?"

"Every time I ask how he's doing, he claims he's doing fine."

"Maybe it's just a cumulative effect. He's been through so much. First the death of his wife, and now this spiritual battle in his own backyard. He's taking it all very personally—especially the decline in church attendance."

"Whatever it is, I hope he can snap out of it. The church needs him. The community needs him."

She reached over and squeezed Grant's hand. "It's going to be okay. Pastor Dan shouldn't have to bear the burden for all of us. We'll get through this together."

"I've missed your optimism."

She laughed. "Please don't use that word."

The pizza arrived and they ate in silence for a few minutes.

"How are you doing right now, Grant?" she asked.

"I've still got so much to learn and a lot of questions. But I haven't wanted to burden Dan with them so I've been talking a lot more to Chris."

"Your new found faith is already strong. It's perfectly normal to have questions and want to talk things through. I'm glad I'm back now."

"I'm glad you're back, too. I really missed you, Olivia."

Her heart constricted at his kind words. "We've got a long fight ahead of us. But there's no one else I'd rather have by my side."

"Let's hope this is a new year filled with many good things to come."

She hoped that was the case, but she also knew that a storm was just around the corner.

***

As Othan exacted the punishment that was required, his fellow demon Kobal groaned in pain. They stood outside the L in Chicago as people bustled back and forth to get on and off the crowded train during the evening rush hour.

"You failed again," Othan said. "Your charges have gone back to their Christian ways. What do you have to say about that?"

The less powerful demon stared up at him. Othan enjoyed making him squirm. Kobal had great potential, but he needed more focus.

"I'm sorry, Othan," Kobal said. "I did everything I could. But the pastor was able to intervene. I wasn't able to convince them that the way of darkness was for the best. Even with their greedy and lustful ways."

"Enough excuses." It was time to see what Kobal was really capable of.

"I'll do whatever I can to make it up to you and to the evil one." Kobal stood proudly. His demonic form wasn't what most people would expect for a demon. No, Kobal presented himself in human form just like Othan. Yes, they could transform if necessary, but their ability to blend into the population gave them an edge.

"I'm glad you feel that way." Othan patted Kobal on the shoulder. "Walk with me."

They walked down the subway platform as the snow started to fall more steadily. Othan adjusted his winter coat a little tighter. Not because he actually was impacted by the cold, but mainly out of habit.

"I'm anxious to start a new assignment," Kobal said. He looked directly at Othan with his blue eyes sparkling with excitement.

"You've no doubt heard about our work in Windy Ridge."

Kobal's eyes widened. "Yes, it's the hottest topic in our community right now."

"You're going to be working with me on various issues related to Windy Ridge Community Church."

Kobal gasped. "I won't let you down. This is a huge opportunity."

Othan couldn't help but smile. "If you fail, then I will destroy you. Do you understand?"

Kobal nodded but straightened his shoulders. He was an arrogant demon who often acted too hastily without thinking of the consequences. He reminded Othan of himself years ago. But to be successful, Othan would need someone like Kobal who could blend in with the humans.

"What do I need to do?" Kobal asked.

"First, I'm going to have you shadow Pastor Dan. There are going to be some events happening soon, and I'm going to need you to turn the screws where he is concerned. I've already had Zebar tailing him. But I need someone with more power and who can inflict more pain."

"I can do this."

"I know. Kobal, this is going to be one of our greatest battles. With victory in Windy Ridge, there will be no stopping us. The evil one will give us everything we ever wanted. Failure is not possible."

Kobal brushed the snow off his blue wool cap. "I'm ready to go to work."

"Perfect. Keep me updated." The plan was a great one. And once Othan helped the evil one succeed, then he would be handsomely rewarded.

EXCERPT FROM EXPERT WITNESS

Chapter One

"All rise." The bailiff's deep voice echoed through the crowded Atlanta courtroom.

Sydney Berry took a deep breath and stepped down from the witness stand. Unfortunately, her expert testimony as a forensic artist in the murder trial of businessman Kevin Diaz wasn't over. She'd have to come back tomorrow and testify about her sessions with the eyewitness and the drawing she'd created of the suspect. The goal—to get the sketch of the suspect introduced into evidence. It would bolster the eyewitness testimony to have the contemporaneous drawing in front of the jury.

If the defense attorney was able to tear apart her testimony, the prosecution's case would be severely weakened. And a guilty man likely would walk free. She refused to let that happen.

She walked out of the courtroom doors, and then the other bailiff standing outside nodded to her, indicating she was on her own. *Dear God, please give me the strength to get through this. Let my testimony help the jury so that justice may be done for the murder of an innocent woman.*

"Ms. Berry!" A male voice rang out down the courthouse hallway.

The last thing she wanted to do right now was deal with the press. She'd refused every media inquiry thus far, and she would do the same again today. Because of Kevin Diaz's position in the community, the local Atlanta media were having a field day covering the trial.

"No comment." She turned around and came face to face with a tall man in a dark suit and a navy checkered tie. No, he didn't look like the press. He had to be a Fed. His dark brown hair was cut short, and his eyes were a striking deep green.

"I'm not a reporter," he said. "Please let me escort you to your vehicle, and I'll explain."

She took a step, and he followed her.

She turned to him. "Who are you?"

He looked her in the eyes. "I'm US Marshal Max Preston."

Close. She had figured him for FBI. Having dealt with the FBI quite a bit in her line of work, she knew its style, and he fit it perfectly down to the gun she caught a glimpse of on his right hip. Though she wasn't accustomed to consulting for the US Marshals, they were obviously built from the same mold.

"As you can tell, I'm a bit preoccupied right now with this trial." She reached into her pocket for her business card. "Here's my card. Contact me and we can set up a consultation. But it will probably be a few weeks before I can fit it into my schedule." When he refused the card, she pocketed it and pushed open the courthouse door. The summer heat of Atlanta hit her, and she already felt her hair starting to frizz.

"I know this is bad timing, but I need five minutes," he said, following her outside.

The persistent marshal wasn't taking no for an answer. They walked down the courthouse steps on to the sidewalk.

"Really, sir, this isn't a good time."

He touched her arm. "It's important, Ms. Berry. I wouldn't come to you like this otherwise, but I really need to talk to you. Now."

Then she heard car wheels screeching loudly. Looking toward the street, she saw a dark SUV barreling down the road in their direction at top speed. Instinctively, she took a step back.

The tinted window rolled down, and the sound of gunshots exploded through the air. Before she could duck, she found herself hitting the sidewalk hard and tasted the faint taste of blood in her mouth.

Screams and mass chaos erupted around her. As she looked up trying to determine what had happened, she realized that the US marshal with the bright green eyes was on top of her, shielding her body with his own. He had knocked her down. Probably saving her life.

"That's what I wanted to talk to you about," he said quietly in her ear. "Are you okay?" He lifted his weight off her and his eyes scanned her from head to toe, as if looking for signs of injury.

"I'm fine." She paused, trying to catch her breath. "Wait a minute. You think those bullets were meant for me?"

He gently pulled her up off the ground and wrapped one arm around her shoulder to steady her. "Unfortunately, I do. I need to get you to a secure location. Now."

As police officers swarmed around them, he flashed his marshal's badge and was able to get through the crowd. He pulled one of the officers aside. "Neil, we need to talk."

"What happened here?" the officer asked him.

"Drive-by shooting. Approximately five shots fired. Two men, driver and passenger."

"Did you get a visual on either?"

"Negative, but they were in a black Chevy SUV—model year late nineties. I'm assuming it was stolen, and they're probably dumping the vehicle as we speak."

"You're probably right about that."

"Look, Neil, call me if you need anything else, but right now I need to get this witness out of here. When it's safe, we can provide official statements. Please keep me in the loop. You have my info."

The officer nodded at Max and then looked at her closely. Recognition spread across his face. He must have been following the Diaz trial. "Of course. Whatever you need, Max."

Max took her arm and led her down the street away from the courthouse. "I should try to explain why I came here today. I think you're in more danger than you could know."

"With that lead in, I guess you already know me pretty well."

"Yes, I do, Ms. Berry."

"Please, call me Sydney. After you saved my life I feel like the formalities are a bit much. Can I call you Max?"

"Of course."

"So what's going on exactly?"

He gently touched her back and guided her to his car, which he'd parked in the lot down the block from the courthouse. He opened the door, and she got into the nondescript gray sedan. Only then did he start to explain.

"I used to work in the gang unit at the FBI." He paused. "But I came here today to warn you that there was chatter amongst the gang networks about you. Have you ever heard of the East River gang?"

"Yeah, they're pretty notorious." She wasn't ready to provide her specific knowledge of the East River gang to this man she just met. Even if he had saved her life, she thought it better to proceed with caution. That was the way she lived now.

"Well, I put two and two together and I think the East River gang has decided to go after you because of your testimony here in the case against Kevin Diaz."

"Kevin Diaz is a businessman with multiple thriving companies. What connection could he possibly have to the East River gang?" She kept her voice steady even as her mind started to play out the implications of this new piece of information.

"Kevin's cousin is Lucas Jones who just happens to also be one of the power players in East River."

She looked over at him. "Wow. I had no idea they were related." She paused. "And now you think they're coming after me because of the family connection?"

"I'll be honest with you. I'm one of the only ones who believe that Lucas Jones would take action for his estranged cousin. Most of my former FBI colleagues believe that the two of them aren't on speaking terms. But I do and that's why I'm here. I had a feeling that East River would retaliate against you and today's events only confirm my hunch."

"Are you sure?"

He kept his eyes on the road. "I felt pretty strongly about it before, but you were almost gunned down in broad daylight outside the courthouse. So, yes, it's a threat I take seriously. The US Marshals' office is taking it seriously."

"What does all of this mean?"

"It means that for the time being you'll be in my protective custody. It was one thing when you were just testifying in a murder trial against Kevin Diaz. But circumstances have changed. If you're a target of the East River gang because of your testimony that impacts everything. First and foremost your personal safety. When you agreed to testify as an expert witness for the state, it wasn't under these circumstances."

She took a second and looked out the window as they drove. "Is all this really necessary?"

"Most people are thankful for the protection, Ms. Berry."

I can take care of myself, she thought. "It's Sydney, remember? And it's not that I'm not thankful. It's just that I'm having a hard time processing all of this. I'm not exactly used to being shot at when testifying in a major trial. Not to mention being told that I'm going to have my every move shadowed by someone I just met. I just need a few minutes to think it all through."

He nodded. "If you decide to continue to testify tomorrow, I'll make sure you are able to safely arrive and finish your testimony. Then we'll determine the next steps after that."

"What do you mean *if*? Why wouldn't I testify? I already committed to it."

"That was before you knew about the danger to your life. The prosecutor will have to talk to you about the risks involved. And then we'll need to lay low until there's a proper threat assessment conducted on the risk to your life from the East River gang."

She couldn't believe what she was hearing. "Wait. Are you talking about putting me into the witness protection program?"

"That would be premature at this juncture."

"But you're not ruling it out?"

"I never rule out any course of action. Doing so is the easiest way to get you or someone else killed. But the lead prosecutor and state's attorney are going to be fully briefed on the current security issues, and they may seek that route for you. Especially after what just happened."

"Unbelievable." She lived a solitary life so she didn't have to worry about a family, but this marshal was throwing her a curve. Granted, he was just doing his job, but that didn't mean she felt comfortable with him taking over. She was a private person. She'd only trusted a man once before, and she shuddered thinking about him.

"I know this is difficult for you. If it makes you feel any better, I'll do everything I can to keep you safe and try and give you as much space as is reasonable."

"I guess I understand. But how could the state not have known about this connection to the East River gang?"

"Since there isn't any proven contact or links between the two cousins, I don't think the state believed this was a relevant issue. Lucas thought Kevin sold out by working in corporate America. Or at least that's the story that's on the streets."

"But you're skeptical?'

"Yeah. I'm not doubting that there's friction between the two of them, but I don't buy for a minute that Kevin Diaz is completely on the up and up. The FBI is investigating his operations trying to find any other ties to East River or organized crime. However, it's not their top priority. Like I said, I was the one driving that charge, and now that I'm gone it's less of a focus. Regardless, in my opinion East River made clear today that they don't want you to testify."

"But I've already started my testimony."

"And they don't want you to finish it," he shot back. "You've only gotten through the preliminary questions. Nothing you've said so far will hurt Diaz. It's the rest of your testimony that would be problematic for him. So for tonight we have to be on lockdown. I'm taking you to a safe house in the area."

"I'll need something to wear for court tomorrow."

"Don't worry. All of that will be taken care of. We have a fully stocked safe house, and if need be we can send out for any additional necessities."

She leaned her head back against the seat and closed her eyes for a second trying to steady her ever escalating nerves. She liked to be in control, and right now things were spiraling quickly into a place she didn't like to be. *Lord, I need you now.*

"Are you all right?" he asked.

"Yes. How much farther until we reach our destination?"

"It's just outside the city, so only a few more minutes."

"Sorry to sound impatient."

He glanced over at her. "You were just shot at. You have every right to feel a mix of emotions. I'm actually quite impressed at how you've held yourself together."

She wanted to change the subject and take the focus off of her. "Are you from around here?" she asked.

"I'm from Chicago, but I've lived all over working for the FBI. For the past few years I worked out of the Atlanta field office. And now as a marshal, I've been assigned to the Northern District of Georgia."

"I like living in Atlanta," she said.

The car suddenly swerved, stopping her from continuing her thought. What was going on?

"Hold on," he said loudly.

She gripped onto the console.

Then he slammed on the brakes.

***

Max's day was going from bad to worse. If he hadn't gotten to the courthouse when he had, his witness might have been killed—gunned down in broad daylight. And now a man stood waving his arms right in front of his car in the middle of the road.

Max had to swerve to keep from hitting him. But it was close. And now his senses were screaming that something was terribly off. They were winding through the suburbs on the way to the safe house. What was this man doing?

He thought of Sydney. How much more could she handle today? She certainly hadn't signed up for being a target of the East River gang. His years in the FBI gang unit had shown him just how ruthless a group like East River could be.

"Are you going to get out and see what he needs?" she asked.

They sat in the car, not moving, as the man approached. Max estimated him to be in his forties, approximately six foot tall and two hundred pounds. He definitely didn't look like a damsel in distress.

"What's wrong?" she asked Max.

"I don't like this."

"He probably needs help." She reached over and grabbed his arm. "We can't just ignore him."

"Stay in the car, okay?"

Before she could answer, he checked his sidearm and then opened the door.

And that's when the man lunged forward. The attacker was fast, but Max was faster.

Sydney screamed, but Max stayed focused on the threat in front of him. But when a gunshot went off, he instinctively turned to look. And there was Sydney wrestling another man with a gun.

He didn't have time to do a thorough analysis of the situation, so he quickly launched into action. When his attacker landed a blow that connected hard with his jaw, pain shot through his head. But it wasn't enough to lay him out. There was no way was he going to lose his first official witness as a US Marshal. With a swift uppercut he made contact with the attacker's face. Calling on his martial arts training, he followed with a precise kick to the ribs. His assailant landed on the ground with a resounding thud.

He drew his gun and turned, ready to take the shot to save Sydney's life. But somehow she had gotten the other guy on his knees and the man's gun was now in her hand. How in the world had she managed that? "Keep that gun on him, Sydney."

"You don't have to worry about that," she said.

He pulled out his handcuffs and secured the original assailant. Then he walked over to her. The other man was on his knees with his hands in the air. He pulled out a second pair of cuffs from his jacket and put them on the perpetrator.

He would need to call this in ASAP, but he also needed to get Sydney to safety. What if others were coming? These guys could have been waiting for them. Which meant additional threats could be in the area.

He pulled out his cell and put in a call. Backup should only be a few minutes away. That would give him a moment with the suspects. He read them their rights since he didn't want to get caught in a legal snafu, and then he looked at the first man.

"Who sent you?"

"I'm not talkin." The man's blue eyes weren't filled with fear but determination. Clearly he was a hired gun.

Max walked over to where Sydney stood beside the other man. Her auburn hair had come loose from her ponytail. "You sure you're okay?" She looked shaken as she gripped her hands together, but after a moment answered him calmly.

"Yes."

He turned his attention to the man. "You got anything to say?"

The guy grunted, and Max took that as a no. No surprises there.

As they held the men at gunpoint he leaned in to her. "Where in the world did you learn to incapacitate an attacker like that?" He guessed her to be only about five feet four, but she was a powerhouse.

Her brown eyes were wide as she looked up at him. "Self-defense classes."

"That looked like a whole lot more than self-defense class."

She shifted her weight from one foot to the other. "I'd rather not talk about it."

He was intrigued. Sydney Berry had secrets. And if he was going to be able to keep her safe, he probably needed to find them out. But at the moment he was just glad that her first secret actually worked to their advantage.

He was kicking himself for taking his eyes off of her earlier. She was his first and only priority. Granted, she wasn't officially in the Witness Security Program, known commonly as witness protection, but he had been tasked to keep her safe until everything could be sorted out.

Sirens sounded in the distance. He looked at her. "Why don't you get in the car? I'll handle this, and then we can be on our way."

She frowned but then got into the sedan.

A moment later the local police arrived, and Max filled them in on the specifics. He'd also looped in his FBI contact. Then he made the call he was dreading. Reporting this incident to his boss, Deputy Elena Sanchez, was hardly the way to make a good first impression, but he had no choice.

Then finally he was ready to hit the road with Sydney. But not to the original safe house. That was too risky now.

He wouldn't feel even an ounce better until Sydney had safely completed her testimony in the morning. And even then the threat of the East River gang still loomed large.

Once they'd been driving for a few minutes, he decided to break the silence. "Want to talk about what happened back there?"

"You think those men were connected to East River or someone else associated with Diaz?"

He decided it best to be open and honest with her about the threat. "I think East River has put a hit out on you."

"I had a feeling you were going to say that," she said.

He saw her look out the window and take note of her surroundings. "I know it seems like I'm driving in the other direction now, but given what just happened we're going to an alternative safe house."

"But we're not staying there long?"

"No. After you testify we'll go to another location. This is just for tonight. We have a list of safe house options already planned for you."

"I guess I don't get much of a say in this, huh?"

"You always have a say, but you should know that I have your best interests in mind. Also, I'm sorry about what happened back there, however, I'm thankful that you were able to defend yourself."

"Me too," she said quietly.

He looked over at her. As she stared out the window he could see the tension tightening her features. He tried a different topic of conversation. "How long have you been a sketch artist?"

She turned to look at him, and her shoulders immediately seemed to relax. "I've been drawing forever, but I started taking it seriously during college. I didn't finish school and instead took art classes with my tuition money. Then I started with small jobs and it grew from there. Referrals are very important in my business. But I do more than just draw faces. That's what you think of when you think of a sketch artist. I'm a forensic artist. I can do a lot more, like crime scene re-enactments and stuff like that."

"I imagine the work comes and goes." He wanted to engage in conversation to try to calm his own building nerves, as well.

"Yes. I've been very busy as of late, but those first few years were tough. I took other odd jobs to make ends meet. I worked at a library for a bit and as a server at a restaurant. All to pursue my real dream." She shrugged. "With all the high-tech advancements, the field is changing a lot, it's really exciting. Computers can do a lot, but there's still something to be said about a human hand."

"I'm a big fan of using technology in investigations. I had an experience with a traditional sketch artist in the past who wasn't on point." That was an understatement, but he didn't think it was the best time to go into his misgivings about sketch artists right now.

"Don't get me wrong. The technology for doing things like facial reconstructions or accident simulations is absolutely amazing," she replied. "But I still trust my abilities to use pencil and paper and sketch based on the eyewitness interview for the purposes of identification."

He didn't reply because it only would have led to an argument that he didn't think she would want to have right now.

"You said you were at the FBI before. How long have you been a marshal?"

He didn't really want to give an exact answer. "Not very long." He could feel her gaze on him as he drove.

"Hey, don't tell me I'm your first witness."

He smiled. "Okay, I won't tell you that."

"Wow." She blew out a breath. "I *am* your first witness."

"That's true, but I'd been with the FBI for a decade. It's not like I'm new to law enforcement, so I'm not a true rookie."

"I can imagine that working as an FBI agent in the gang unit is a lot different than guarding a witness, though."

"Don't give it another thought. You're safe now, and you'll stay that way."

"No offense, but we just met. You're asking me to put a lot of faith in you."

"I know. But that's the way it has to be. No one else on our team has the same knowledge of the threats to you like I do. I'm thankful that I got assigned to your case and was able to connect the dots, or this afternoon might have ended very differently." He paused as he pointed to a house up ahead. "We're here on the right."

"This looks like a regular neighborhood."

"That's exactly the point. We're trying to blend."

He'd actually never been to this safe house before during his training, but he was getting the idea that they were all generally the same. This was a two-story house, painted a pale blue on a nice size lot.

He pulled the sedan all the way into the driveway and stopped the car.

"Can I get out?" she asked.

"Yes, but first let me just do a quick security check. You stay here and keep the doors locked."

Before she could answer he had jogged up to the front door and opened it. He quickly surveyed the house, conducting a security sweep. Satisfied it was all clear he went back outside to get Sydney. Her expression appeared unreadable as she sat in the passenger's seat. He really wanted to know what was going in that head of hers.

He opened the car door for her, and she stepped out bedside him. She was a pretty woman, no doubt, with a simple and natural beauty about her. But she gave off a very strong vibe. One that said loudly, "Back off."

"This way," he said. He took her arm and escorted her to the front door, even though he got the feeling she didn't appreciate him invading her personal space. "Another marshal will be over in a bit with dinner and everything you'll need for tonight and tomorrow."

"You aren't leaving, are you?" she asked as she made direct eye contact.

"No. I just didn't want you to think we were going to be totally shut off from the outside world without the things you would need."

"What I really need is to be at my own home."

"I understand. Let's get through your testimony in the morning, and then we can re-evaluate."

"I'll hold you to that."

He walked over to where she stood in the living room. "I promise. And I won't make you promises I can't keep. I hate it when people do that to me and—"

A loud crash rocked the room as glass flew against his body. His face burned and he felt blood trickling down his cheek. Smoke surrounded him. He dove toward Sydney, hoping it wouldn't be too late.

***

EXCERPT FROM OUT OF HIDING

Chapter One

Sadie felt the bullet whiz by her head as she crouched down in the wet dirt. Darkness surrounded her, but she wasn't alone. Her gut screamed loudly that something was terribly wrong. And she always trusted her gut. She had company, and if that bullet was any indication, they meant business. The sound of the crackling leaves told her someone was moving quickly in her direction.

Dressed in all black, she lay flat on the ground in the dark woods. No one was going to see her. That bullet wasn't meant for her but was intended for someone else. Who? She didn't want to stick around long enough to find out. She prayed that Megan wasn't out here in the woods tonight—alone, scared, and with bullets flying. It was no place for a sixteen-year-old girl.

She checked her gun and kept her position low against the damp, muddy ground. Her night vision goggles were a blessing. It was then she saw what she dreaded the most. The letters FBI on a dark-colored flak jacket as an agent trounced his way through the woods. Why the FBI was involved in whatever was happening in these woods she didn't know, but she didn't like it. They were invading her turf.

Sadie had her first solid lead on the Vladimir network in El Paso, and she didn't want to give up the opportunity. She'd been on stakeouts for weeks, desperately trying to determine if Igor—the man who had taken everything from her—was in El Paso. Her intel had been that something related to the Vladimir crew was going down in the woods tonight. She had hoped that whatever it was wasn't going to involve Megan—the missing girl she was looking for. Sadie knew that Vladimir's crew was responsible for her disappearance. That's why she'd sought out the job just days ago.

Technically, she was still in the Witness Security Program commonly known as Witness Protection, although they didn't consider her to be in immediate danger anymore. She'd followed all their rules over the years. Her new life, her new name, everything. Done by the book. Not a single deviation from the protocol given to her by the U.S. Marshals. There was no way she'd let them know what she planned to do now that she had confirmation Igor sought to set up shop in her own backyard. It was only a matter of time before Witness Protection realized Igor's activities had expanded down to El Paso, and then they'd want her to move. She needed to act fast if she had any chance of taking out Igor's network.

She slowly stood up using a large tree as a shield. Thankfully, she was small of stature. By the time she'd registered the crunch of a stick right behind her it was too late. A large hand grabbed her shoulder with another muffling her scream.

"FBI, don't move," the deep voice said directly into her ear.

Didn't matter who he was, when a man put his hands on her, he was going to pay. She'd trained for moments like these. She slammed her foot down on his, and he groaned. But he didn't loosen his grip. Was this guy made of iron?

Trying another approach, she went limp in his arms, shocking him into loosening his grip, giving her a moment to slide away. She'd only taken two steps when he tackled her, knocking her to the ground. She could barely breathe. She squirmed against him, but she was no match for his size and strength. He had to have been at least a foot taller and a hundred pounds heavier. For a moment, fear seized her. She said a prayer asking God to keep her safe and then fought back.

"Stop struggling," he said quietly, his voice steady. "I promise I'm not going to hurt you."

She didn't believe him. She knew better than to trust the Feds. Trust them, and she could end up dead like her parents. He adjusted his grip just enough for her to knee him in the stomach. Big mistake on her part. Now he seemed raving mad.

"I'm trying to save your life here. You have no idea what you've gotten yourself into. You should not be here in these woods right now."

The thing was, she actually wasn't a stranger to life-and-death situations. So this one didn't faze her too much. "I already dodged one bullet and was doing just fine on my own."

"You'll have time later to explain how you ended up in the middle of an active FBI investigation packing heat and wearing night vision goggles. For now, let me get you out of here safe and sound."

She shuddered. Those promises had been made to her before. And they'd been broken—every single one of them.

"I'm not going anywhere with you," she hissed. She struggled against his secure grip.

"Yes, you are, ma'am. Listen to me." He paused, his breathing ragged. "Things are only going to get worse. You might not be as fortunate the next time a bullet gets fired. And I don't want to have your death on my conscience. I have enough guilt to last a lifetime. So when I say three, we move for that next tree. You hear me?"

Realizing her current options were limited, she relented. He was right. Her best move for now was to retreat. She'd taken a taxi tonight and made her way to the woods on foot. It wasn't as if she had her own ride out of danger. She'd have time to get away from him once they got to safety. "Okay."

"One, two, three, go go go!" he said in a low voice. They sprinted from their current position to the next tree and squatted down. That's when she heard another round of gunfire. Automatic weapons this time. Her heartbeat quickened, but now was not the time to panic. She'd been in worse situations without the valuable experience that she now carried with her after years of being a private investigator.

"What next?" she whispered, trying to catch her breath.

"Make a run for that far tree. My Jeep is beyond it. I'm hoping that will work."

"And if not?"

"I'll think of plan B."

He sounded so sure of himself. Typical for FBI types. She wasn't going to count on him to get her out of here safely. She'd survey her options once they made it to the next tree before she jumped in the Jeep of a total stranger—even if he was in the FBI. Hadn't she already learned that tough lesson?

"Now," he barked.

She ran ahead of him using her small size and speed to her advantage, making it to the tree first. Though he wasn't far behind. She saw the dark Jeep parked behind a cluster of trees providing them with additional cover.

"Let's go for it," he said.

Making a split second decision that she prayed she wouldn't regret, she slid into the passenger side and ducked down low. Before she could even steady herself, the FBI guy had turned the ignition and floored it. The bumpy ride had her on high alert as he navigated the vehicle over the rough terrain.

She stayed down not knowing if they were safe from the gunfire and started plotting her escape. No way was she being taken in by the FBI to "explain herself."

They drove a few minutes in silence as the Jeep weaved through the wooded area and onto the country road that would eventually lead back into town. Then he spoke after checking his mirrors. "We're in the clear."

She eased up into her seat and looked around at her surroundings, including the man driving. She wasn't wrong in her initial assessment. This guy was tall and bulky. She already knew from the encounter in the woods that he was strong. His brown hair was cut short. She couldn't see his eyes since they were focused on what lay ahead. She told herself to remember that he was one of them.

He glanced over at her. "You want to tell me now what you were doing out in the woods?"

"My job," she snapped. Who knows what he thought she was doing, but her answer was completely truthful.

"And what job is that?"

She sighed, already not enjoying this line of questioning. "I'm a private investigator."

"You're not plugged into our FBI investigation, though. I would've known it."

"I have no idea what investigation you're working on." She let out a deep breath and figured she needed to provide an explanation. Maybe it would help her get away from him sooner. "I was in the woods searching for a missing girl. You may have even seen a local news story about her. Her mother recently hired me. I've been looking everywhere. I didn't see or hear anything until I felt the first bullet whiz by my ear." She was telling the truth. She had to make sure Megan wasn't in those woods tonight. It appeared that her leads had been correct. Something was going on with the Vladimir crew. And the FBI was involved. She said another silent prayer for Megan.

"Wow," he said. "You were in the wrong place at the wrong time, Ms. P.I. lady. I'm going to need to bring you in, though. Gotta take your statement. Make it official." His southern drawl was unmistakable.

"I don't think that's a good idea."

"I promise it'll be quick. You are carrying a weapon. I assume you have a permit for that and all."

No way she'd allow him to take her in, but she didn't have to tell him that. Her past struggles with the FBI were her own. Better to have the element of surprise.

"Uh, oh," he said. He jerked the wheel hard to the right sending her into his right arm. "We've got company. Hold on."

"I thought you said we were good."

"They came out of nowhere."

She turned around and saw a large dark SUV that was gaining on them. But FBI guy had some moves and was taking the curves on the dark country road with finesse as he drove toward the more populated area of town.

"Who are these people?" she asked as she clenched her fists. Were they connected to Vladimir?

"The less you know the better."

"Why don't you let me take a shot? I could probably blow out their tire."

"You're that good of a shot?" he asked with disbelief dripping from his deep voice.

"You better believe it," she said without hesitation.

He paused for a second and glanced over at her. "If you think you can, then go for it."

She was going to show this FBI guy that she was no slouch. In fact, she could probably outshoot him. All the time she'd spent at the range over the past few years had paid off. She turned around and was glad they were in a Jeep. Granted it didn't provide them with much, if any, protection, but it also meant she'd have an easier time getting off an unobstructed shot.

Steadying herself she took a deep breath, aimed, and pulled the trigger. It only took one shot, and the right front tire of the car chasing them was done for. The pursuit ended abruptly as they began to skid, the car circling in on the blown tire. "Got 'em."

"Well, Ms. P.I. lady, I'm impressed."

"You should be." Then she turned the gun toward him.

"Whoa." He lifted up his right hand at her while keeping his left on the wheel. "Just put that thing away."

Her hand was steady. "I have no reason to use this on you. But I'm not being taken in for questioning. I didn't do anything wrong."

"I never accused you of anything," he said with a raised voice. She watched as his hands tightened on the wheel.

"Take me downtown. Let me out and drive away. It's that simple."

"You're crazy, ma'am."

"No. But I'm the one with the gun right now, so I hope you don't try anything crazy."

"You're hiding something."

"It's none of your concern. Just act like you never saw me tonight."

"You know that's not possible. I'll have to write up this whole thing."

"Be creative," she countered. "Now let's get downtown. And don't try anything because I'd really hate to shoot you."

He let out a deep breath but started driving toward town as she directed. Good, she thought. She doubted that he'd let her go indefinitely. But she needed to get away and deal with this problem on her own terms. That meant not being taken in for questioning by the FBI tonight. She needed time.

When they reached the more crowded streets of downtown El Paso, she was ready to get away from him. "Slow down. Let me out. And keep on driving. Do you hear me?"

"Yes," he said in an even voice.

"Good."

He did as she asked and slowed down. She never took the gun off of him as she opened the door slowly. With the light from the streets flooding in, she could see his eyes were light blue. And questioning. "Just pretend I was never here. For your own good and mine too, okay?"

She couldn't shake the thought that she'd seen him before. She backed out of the Jeep, and he didn't say anything in response. She slammed the door shut, and he pulled away. She didn't waste any time weaving her way through the Saturday night crowd.

She was safe for now, but she had no doubt. The FBI guy would find her, and when he did, she'd be in a ton of trouble.

***

ABOUT RACHEL DYLAN

Rachel Dylan writes Christian fiction including inspirational romantic suspense for Love Inspired Suspense and the Windy Ridge Legal Thriller series. Rachel has practiced law for almost a decade and enjoys weaving together legal and suspenseful stories. She lives in Michigan with her husband and five furkids--two dogs and three cats. Rachel loves to connect with readers.

Connect with Rachel Dylan:

www.racheldylan.com
@dylan_rachel
www.facebook.com/RachelDylanAuthor